MW01236303

Cold Blooded Book IV

(The Nick McCarty Assassin Series)

Bloody Shadows

by

Bernard Lee DeLeo

*****

PUBLISHED BY:

Bernard Lee DeLeo and RJ Parker Publishing Inc.

ISBN-13: 978-1512144604

ISBN-10: 1512144606

Cold Blooded Book IV: The Nick McCarty Assassin Series

Bloody Shadows

Cover Illustration by: Colin Matthew Dougherty

*****

Printed in the United States of America

5.15.15

DEDICATION

As it will be with every novel I write from now until my own End of Days, I dedicate this novel to my deceased angel, wife, and best friend: *Joyce Lynn Whitney DeLeo. (d. October 14, 2014)*

Chapter One

Geezer

Dan Lewis walked along the coastal trail from Lover's Point in the darkness with some trepidation. "We're nuts to be used like this for bait, Deke. I'm too old to take a spill into the rocks. Any old person supposedly being mugged down here on this stupid trail in the dark deserves what they get."

Deke snorted as if agreeing when hearing his name mentioned. He ambled along happily, sniffing everything in sight. This was the third weekend night out on an after dark excursion for Deke with his new walking chaperone.

"You do know we can hear your every word Geezer, right?" Nick's voice, along with his partners', Gus and John, revealed their amusement at Dan's take on the night walks, as bait.

"I was counting on it, Muerto. I can't believe you accepted Sergeant Dickerson's suggestion to try and catch this guy who calls himself 'The Night Stalker'. Just because Pacific Grove gets a little bad notoriety doesn't mean an intervention is needed from the infamous El Muerto, Payaso, and El Kabong."

"There's a beautiful full moon tonight, as soon as the usual fog cover lifts fully. The temperature's in the sixties. You have Rin Tin Deke at your side – otherwise known as Fang the Ferocious. What more could you ask for?"

"It is pretty out here," Dan admitted. "I can't believe that many old dunces come out here to walk in the dark at this hour. One slip, and it's a one way ticket to hip and knee hell, or worse. Carol and I walked in daylight on pavement. No way would I have let her chance those knees of hers on this goofy path."

At the mention of Dan's recently deceased wife, there were no more comments. "Sorry, guys. Every damn thing in the world reminds me of her, even when I'm doing stupid shit like this. How much further do you want me and Deke to go, Muerto?"

"Are you good to Otter's Point. That's where the path starts getting more tricky. No one's been mugged and robbed that far along," Nick answered.

Dan made clucking noises of disdain. "Why don't I walk to LA as long as I'm at it? Oh hell... who am I kidding... anything with a little bite to it is great these days. Deke's helping out anyway. He loves smelling every plant, and watching the squirrels or chipmunks or whatever those ground rats are scurrying around at our approach. His pausing at every episode of ground rat interaction gives me a still moment. The waves are sure smashing the shore tonight, but the wind isn't really all that bad."

"We'll pull up stakes if the ground fog covers too much," Nick said. "I really don't want you taking a nosedive on the path. Payaso and El Kabong are shadowing you at intersecting streets down to the ocean with the car. I'm within striking range near the houses, parallel to your movements. Kabong will join me shortly. This is the usual time and conditions when 'The Night Stalker' and his crew strike."

Dan glanced around. "Damn, Nick. I don't see you anywhere."

"That's the point, Geezer. If you could spot me, so could they. You have three suspects approaching from the opposite direction as we speak. Payaso, you lazy ass rogue, start looking for a getaway car. They must be close by between here and you."

Dan smiled for the first time all evening since his walk as bait began. I might be with you sooner than I imagined, honey, he thought. Please... God in heaven... let it be so. Dan walked on, whistling Carol's favorite song, 'House of the Rising Sun'. As the three hooded figures approached, Deke began a low snarling growl.

5

"Don't you ruin this for me, Deke. When I say run, you run."

Deke snorted in answer, having heard his name, and sensing no bad vibes emanating from his companion. He hunched into a slowly developing attack form.

"Hey... O.G., what time is it." The lead man slowed, with his crew coming to a stop behind him. "Nice night out, huh pops?"

Dan chuckled, taking his time while looking at his illuminated dial in the dark. "Sorry, kid, it takes a moment to focus at my age."

The leader stalked toward Dan - his dark shape probably terrifying at night on a path near the ocean meant to be only walked in the daylight, devoid of any other human being. "Who you callin' kid, you old shithead?!"

"Well... I'm callin' you kid, kid. Compared to my age, you'd probably be wearin' diapers to prevent accidents of youth."

The click of a knife blade jolting into place accompanied the leader's next words. "No time to answer all that O.G. Keep yo' dog in check so he don't get hurt, and give us your wallet, money, watch, and every other damn thing on your old ass."

Dan smiled. He bent down, and stroked Deke's head. "Stay! Don't move, Deke!"

Deke whined momentarily, but laid down with his head on his paws. Dan turned around to face the pack. "There you go. Deke won't hurt you. As to my giving you everything on my person, that's not happening."

The leader snorted amusement, dancing around a bit with his two companions enjoying the show. He stopped suddenly, sweeping the blade of the knife an inch away from Dan's neck. Dan didn't even flinch. "You think you bad, huh O.G.?"

6

"Nope," Dan replied. "I just don't give a shit, kid. My wife and best friend for decades passed away and left me behind. It's too bad you didn't work your knife instead of your mouth. Unfortunately for you, my friend cares more than I do about me for some reason."

"Who you talkin' about, old man?"

"That would be me." Nick streaked around the leader's two companions, and buried the seven inch blade of his knife up through the leader's chin into his brain. He pulled it free, and slashed the throat of the man nearest the leader. The third man turned to run, but stopped short as another blade pierced his heart in a jolt of thrust from yet another knife. "Nice timing, John. I hardly heard you at all, El Kabong."

"Thank you, Nick." El Kabong wiped the blade of his knife on the twitching body's jacket. "It's chilly tonight. I've got spatter on me, and so do you, Muerto. We'll have to hope Gus remembered to pack extra jackets. That punk even got blood on your mask."

Nick pulled off his mask. Even though there was only moonlight, Nick saw the splatter on his new black Muerto mask. "Damn it! I just received this yesterday."

"Uh… Nick… I thought this was supposed to be a turnover of bad guys to the police," Dan said.

Nick put his arm around Dan's shoulders leading him in the opposite direction a few steps. "I may have neglected to mention this Dan - when I was building this op as a great endeavor for the weak of body and head. El Muerto doesn't like courts, jurors, and especially lawyers. Sure, if these three would have dropped their weapons, knelt on the ground, and clasped their hands behind their heads - while begging for mercy those other poor old couples didn't get, that they mugged on their two month long rampage, maybe they would have seen another day."

7

"Not to show disrespect, El Muerto, but you didn't allow them even a few second's time to surrender before you and El Kabong stabbed the shit out of them," Dan replied, kneeling next to Deke, aware of the dog's aversion to the smell of blood, especially on bodies he had nothing to do with.

Nick wiped his blade, while looking over Deke. "So… what's your point?"

"Officer Dickerson will be displeased when it was only a couple of days ago he asked you to put your keen writer's mind to work helping him find the muggers terrorizing our small community. I think he had it in mind to arrest and bring them to trial."

"Instead, my buddy Neil will find these three hoodlums, complete with weapons. Let's get some facials so we can send them into our other interested party, Kabong. I'll do the DNA swabs. You do the facials."

"Yes, Muerto." John used his iPhone to take the pictures and a short video while Nick gathered DNA swabs to put with the pictures in order.

"You getting all this, Payaso, my silent partner?"

"Yes, Muerto, I'm keeping my mouth shut while you and Kabong go on another bloody rampage. I'm awaiting orders for pickup. If it weren't for Fang and Geezer, I'd leave you bad boys to walk home. When we planned this, we were to alert the police before those three ever reached Geezer, while we covered him in case the cops were slow."

"I wanted Kabong to practice his woodcraft. Besides, I read what they did to that old man and his wife a few days before Neil called me in for a consult. They beat the two senseless. The old man died in the hospital. I didn't feel like paying a hundred and fifty grand each per year while they incarcerated these three. Okay,

8

I'm done Payaso. Drive by when we get to the other side of the street."

"Wipe your feet before you get in the car, and strip anything with splatter off before you get in the car."

"Yes, Dear. Anything you say, Dear," Nick joked as he led the way to the street. The ground fog had increased significantly, which worked to make the three men and Deke nearly invisible until they reached the other side of the highway in the lights from Gus's new Ford Edge. "Strip down Kabong or Payaso will nag the shit out of us all the way home."

John smiled, keeping silent, while listening to his friends argue back and forth. He could not remember a time in the last month he had been with them when they weren't arguing. Once inside the SUV with Dan in the front next to Gus, and Deke in the back with him and Nick, John made sure to bundle his jacket, knife, and black Nitrile gloves together in his lap as did Nick.

"We did much good tonight," John said. "Everyone will be happy. It won't take them long to figure out those three were the muggers terrorizing people along the ocean front. How will you handle Neil, and when do you think the getaway driver will check on his buddies?"

"I'll go see him first thing in the morning," Nick replied. "I'll bring along the research I did on those assholes' last six muggings. They always took place when there was loud wave action, ground fog, and between nine and ten at night. This was their first time during a full moon though. As to the getaway driver, did you spot him, Gus?"

"I have his license plate number. He's in an old beat up silver Buick, hoodie in place. Want to round him up later? Once we find out who his partners were, we'll be able to locate him. He'll never find them in this fog. When he doesn't hear from them, he'll drive along here a few times and then leave eventually. We could follow him if you want."

"If Dan's okay with a bit more time spent with Muerto, Payaso, and Kabong, I'd like to hang around to get on his trail now rather than later," Nick replied, jostling Dan's shoulder. "How about it, Geezer?"

"You three are the most entertaining diversion I could possibly hope for. Deke is also a great companion on a walk. Truthfully, I'd do anything to stay with you guys. The nights are the worst. These past nights as bait with Deke beside me have allowed some uninterrupted sleep for the first time in a long while. I'd like to stay, if I'm not messing with the 'Unholy Trio's' killer Karma."

"Killer Karma, huh?" Nick absorbed the raucous agreement to Dan's assessment from his fellow 'Unholy Trio' members with amusement. "Good enough, Gus, we await our getaway driver's arrival. While we're not mincing words, Dan, I get the distinct impression you were inviting a knife to the throat. What's that all about? I wouldn't be stupid enough to assume to know Carol's feelings on the matter, but I doubt she'd be very happy with a 'suicide by thug' plan. The 'Unholy Trio' could use you to stick around. It pays a very uplifting amount of money for you and your kids too."

Dan shrugged. "My kids are fine since you ended my last problem with the loan sharks, which by the way was the dumbest thing I ever did. That kind of stupidity will not be repeated. I get moments like tonight with that shithead threatening me, where I may shoot my mouth off, because I really don't care. If you have a problem with that, Hemingway, kick loose of me. I'll understand."

"Nope," Nick replied. "That won't happen, Dan. I'm not much on this touchy feely stuff, but perhaps you should focus on the good when you end a threat like tonight. Carol would have walked with you at your side to nail these guys. I'm actually sorry

I didn't think about asking you both, but I assumed in error you two would probably outlive me and my professional choice of careers."

"I assumed in error I would go long before Carol, but what passes for life without her can only be endured with certain ground rules. One of them since joining with your little group is that I ain't taking shit from anyone, and especially not from a murderous young bastard like 'The Night Stalker' guy tonight. I'll take my shots when I can if they don't endanger you guys, but I will take them no matter what."

"That's fair enough, Geezer," Nick said, with endorsements from his 'Unholy Trio' partners. "Speaking for us unholy guys, we'd like for you to stick around. We all know that bullshit about time healing all wounds is just that: a load of crap. Gus, John, and I would like to give you something else to help you through the trail of tears with something extra tucked in for your kids in the way of a monetary supplement. You'll earn it... like tonight, and we'll allow certain smartass slaps in the face of death as you did on this final resting of 'The Night Stalker'."

Dan nodded. "Good, because you can kiss my ass otherwise."

During the enjoyment of that particular gem, Gus pointed toward the front. "Here he comes. I'm guessing, but his headlights look like the ones I saw when I spotted him. We'll know shortly, because he'll be slowing down looking for his pals."

"Yep," Gus reiterated, "that's the one. He'll be floating back this way in search of what cannot be: a meeting with dead men."

The suspected vehicle returned, slowing and searching.

"He's sayin' 'where are my thugs'? Speak to me... speak to me," Gus joked.

"Well he'll have to get one of those folks that speak to dead people for that," Dan answered with a straight face. "I'll do it, but it'll cost him – 'yo, player... I'm dead, dimwit... move into the light, or whatever you see... probably shadows, darkness, and your spine being ripped out of your asshole."

The four companions enjoyed that word picture together as they watched the driver's vehicle do another lap. The driver stopped near where his companions met their doom

"I think he must have triangulated their cell-phones through a third entity," Nick said. "Let's see if he wants to find his buddies or not."

Near where the bodies were left, the driver parked the vehicle. He exited with extreme deliberation, his head moving to search for anything out of place. When he didn't see any movement, he tried calling one of them on his cell-phone.

"Oh gee, I believe that ship has passed," Nick said, listening to the confiscated cell-phone doing a Rap version of something remotely familiar in the back of Gus's Ford, but unrecognizable. "Okay, cross musically inclined off the list of skills. "We wanted a live one. Geezer! Go collect that puppy."

Dan grinned appreciatively, knowing Nick was testing him. "Ten-four, Hemingway, but I get to do it, and you other butt nuggets stay in the car, no matter what."

"Agreed. You have your stun gun." Nick waved off his two Unholy Trio partners while Dan stared out the window. "Take Deke so you have a reason for walking the asshole won't suspect."

"Thanks," Dan said, exiting the Ford, and leashing Deke.

"Are you sure about this, Nick," John asked.

"Hell no," Nick admitted, easing out of the Ford through the same door he had allowed Deke to exit. "Stay here until the last second. Don't ask me when that'll be, because I don't know. We need to let Dan work some of this shit out on his own. I'll go help him when needed. Stay focused. It's early by the crow flies, and I see a beer and a shot on my horizon."

"Acknowledged," Gus said with a sigh. "Save him if you can, Nick."

"If I can," Nick replied before easing the door shut.

* * *

"Well hello," Dan called out with a wave of his hand. "It's nice to see another walker out here on a night like this."

The man glanced down at Deke with a wave off. "I ain't no damn dog walker."

"Say… you wouldn't be looking for those three guys who tried to mug me a little while ago, are you?"

"Oh boy," Nick mumbled loud enough for his cohorts Payaso and Kabong to hear along with the 'Geezer'. "Plan B guys, steady as she goes."

* * *

"What's plan B, Gus," John asked as Gus started his Ford.

"Drive the hell into position fast, and get a gun in your hand as you arrive," Gus replied through gritted teeth.

"On it," John said, fumbling around in his equipment bag.

* * *

"What the hell are you sayin' old man?" The driver edged nearer to Dan, his fists clenched. "Are you sayin' you know where my friends are?"

"Sure do, kid. They're lyin' dead over there not more than twenty yards away." Dan pointed in the exact direction where the bodies lay, having made a point of remembering by way of the vegetation, and rocks along the path. "I can show you if you'd like."

The driver stared at Dan as if he were a new arrival on planet earth. "Did you kill them?"

"Sort of," Dan admitted. "I was bait for your punk friends to mug. Unfortunately for them, I brought along a couple friends of my own. They made sure your buddies would never hurt another soul."

"Maybe I cut your heart out right here, old man." The driver clicked a switchblade into place, jutting the blade threateningly toward Dan.

Dan eased slowly down to calm Deke. "Stay Deke. Don't move."

After standing straight again, Dan gestured at the guy in the dark with the knife. All fear of death was a thing of the past. "I was discharged from the Marines back in 1969, kid. I've been on borrowed time ever since. You know what they say though, there's no such thing as an ex-Marine. Maybe I'll take that knife away from you and shove it up your ass."

The driver laughed, pocketed the knife, and began drawing a 9mm Glock from his waistband holster. "I believe you."

Before he cleared it from its holster, he was dead, Nick's knife jammed to the hilt under the driver's chin. He pulled it free of the twitching body as the man dropped to the roadside. "C'mon, Geezer."

"You should have let me handle it, Muerto," Dan replied as Gus skidded his Ford to a halt near him while Nick took a quick picture, and fingerprint impression."

"You can't always get what you want... you can't always get what you want," Nick sung the old lines from the Rolling Stones song perfectly as he stuffed the driver back into his car.

"I guess we won't have much to worry about besides your singing," Dan observed. "This fog will make it impossible to see this guy's car until someone gets within a few feet of it."

Gus motioned impatiently. "Will you two get in the damn Ford? I've had enough playing cops and robbers tonight. Let's go sip a couple on Muerto's balcony and call it a night."

"Yes," John agreed, sticking his head out the rear window. "I am starving to death too. Playing cops and robbers gave me an appetite."

A moment later, Gus drove slowly toward Nick's house. The fog made it impossible to see more than a few feet past the headlight beams. The fog lamps made the driving slightly less dangerous, but it was a treacherous drive. Gus breathed a sigh of relief when he parked his new Ford.

"Man, I think I'll walk home if this fog doesn't lift," Gus said. "You won't be able to go home either, John. The driving would be brutal to the Carmel Valley house."

"John can sleep over at my place if the fog doesn't lift," Dan offered.

"You cannot trust me, infidel. Are you not worried I will slit your throat in the night like an Isis coward?"

Dan chuckled while roughing Deke's head. "I'll take my chances, throat-slitter. Wake up, Deke, we're home. I think Deke wants a beer."

At the mention of the word beer, Deke began bouncing around in the back until Nick opened the door. Deke streaked for Nick's porch. Nick shook his head as he eased out of the Ford with his equipment bag. "You'll have to wait until we get to the porch, goofy. John reminded me I promised I'd look into that supposed Isis training camp Paul mentioned yesterday. He says they have satellite footage of gunfire, and even explosions."

"How is your friend, Mr. Gilbrech," Dan asked as they neared Nick's door. "It's been a while since he contacted you. That Isis bunch killing at will overseas makes for bad press here. Who in hell would let any of them into the country to start training camps."

"They need jobs," John replied, which garnered much amusement from his companions. "Perhaps they are training in these camps to be short order cooks."

"I'm glad Paul didn't mention my going over in the sand," Nick said, disabling his alarm system, and using his retina scanner he had installed for Rachel and Jean's protection. "Gus can tell you. Our last jaunt over in looney land turned sour after I finished the job. We were lucky to get home, and we unknowingly brought along a couple of problems I had to sort out close to home."

"It was bad," Gus agreed. "Nick handled Nazari, but our CIA contact tried to have us killed. It piggy-backed with us home. I wouldn't mind taking a look at this suspected training camp. Where the hell is it, Nick?"

"I have to establish an alibi for my meeting with Neil tomorrow. Rachel and I fixed everything up on the balcony, so let's take the conversation there."

Rachel met them inside the door, very far along in her pregnancy, and showing it. "Hi guys. Jean and I were on the balcony watching the fog show. How many did you kill tonight, Muerto?"

"I have no idea what you're talking about, Dear," Nick replied, as his companions hid amusement in varying degrees. "We

16

would love to join you on the balcony. I'm surprised you're allowing Dagger to stay up tonight. Although it's Saturday night, I figured your 10 pm curfew was still in effect."

Rachel shrugged. "She rolled me again as usual. Without you around, Jean either blackmails me into submission, or promises something extraordinary in exchange."

"Don't leave us hangin'," Gus said, as they followed Rachel upstairs with Deke already causing a commotion with the aforementioned Dagger on the balcony. "Which was it?"

"Blackmail."

"Details," John said, exchanging amused glances with Gus.

"Never you mind, John. What goes on in the Muerto household stays locked forever inside the minds of its inhabitants. By the way, Tina joined us, Gus. She walked over, claiming she needed to get some air, and keep the size of her ass in check… her words."

Gus coughed to cover his snorting enjoyment of his wife's words. "I have no comment on your quote from my lovely wife that would not lead to either my evisceration or emasculation."

"Noted," Rachel said. "I am glad to see you all back here safe and sound, especially your new recruit: Dan. Bait again, I'll wager."

"No comment," Dan said. "I wish you were as observant of items at the Café Monte when my coffee cup is empty."

Rachel gasped outside the door of the balcony. "Dan!"

"I call 'em like I see 'em, my friend."

Rachel smiled. "Do you know why it's unsafe to belittle servers of your food at a restaurant, Dan?"

"Uh oh." Dan shrugged. "I need to walk more anyway. It's Holly's Lighthouse Café from now on for the 'Geezer'."

"Fine... you can keep coming to the Monte, Daniel," Rachel stated. "Without retribution."

"Can I bring my own coffee?"

Dan's final thrust hit home, and Rachel enjoyed the barb along with the rest of the crew. Jean watched the group with excitement. She knew every time her stepdad went out with the three companions with him, bad people died. Jean harbored thoughts of being just like him, and she weighed the input everyday as to the shortest route to get there. She knew bypassing her Mom would be a written in stone fact. Since learning how to throw daggers, Jean practiced daily with Nick at her side. Nick had helped her find a knife to learn how to throw with deadly accuracy. It was perfectly balanced with a seven inch blade, Nick bought for her at a gun show after handling the knife with the expertise of a without peer assassin's touch.

"Can I stay while you guys talk," Jean asked.

"I'd rather you didn't, Dagger, but I'll leave the decision to your Mom. I stopped pretending or ignoring the interest you have in what I do. You've seen so much I can't hide what I am or what I do without endangering all of us, so look to your Mom. She calls the shots as to your involvement as a kid. She already knows you remind me too much of me when I was a kid. I can only hope to turn you from the dark side."

Jean's face turned feral, all aspects of a pre-teen kid disappearing. "You saved me when I was duct taped in a van, heading for death, Dad! Mom can't erase that. I'm happy you haven't tried to erase it. No one's taking me anywhere after what you've taught me. You never have to pretend for me... ever!"

"Oh shit!" Rachel hugged Jean to her without any pretense. "You are something else, baby. I'm to blame for everything because of what I tried to ignorantly do with your real Dad. I'm an idiot after all we've gone through to make the assumption you're an ignorant kid needing something beyond my grasp to provide. I'm proud of you. The way you handle those knives is scary good."

"It's okay, Mom. Everyone here knows we're the 'Addam's Family'. Don't worry about it so much. Tina even refers to Dad as 'Gomez'. When my baby brother, Quinn arrives, I'll take him under my wing. He'll be a premier killer in no time."

"Oh...my...God," Rachel mumbled, her face tilted to observe the universe with a ceiling barring the look of humble thoughts, praying for an absolution not forthcoming.

"Calm down, love," Nick soothed. "It's not a bad thing that Dagger can protect herself. She can throw the target type knives as well as anyone I've ever seen, including the people who have won fame with them. Yes, I have taught her how to throw the knife she has to carry for protection, and she does so with deadly accuracy. Such is life in our world. If you have to blame anyone, blame me... as always."

Rachel gripped her mate in a gasping acknowledgement of facts in reality. "Jean and I are only alive because of you! I'm sorry each new instance of my preteen daughter's deadliness upsets my Mommy hormones."

Rachel released Nick, and embraced her daughter. "And you, Daughter of Darkness, I see what wells within you. I'm proud of you. You don't run, hide, or fall on your face crying. You know right from wrong, and you're the strongest willed kid I could ever know. You're a Nick clone for sure, carrying someone else's DNA. I know if there's a way to stay alive in a bad situation, you'll find it. Thank God that's true."

Jean pushed Rachel aside. "So... can I go on Dad's next mission?"

Rachel went for the throat immediately with both hands to much amusement. She shook Jean's head as if really throttling her. "You... are... so... grounded."

"You can't ground me. I haven't done anything," Jean replied in a vibrating gargle.

"Actually, everyone will be going on this next mission." Nick hugged both females in his life. "I'm calling Cassie, and see about a book signing gig in Olympia, Washington. If you ladies can start talking about specifics while I contact my agent, I'd be grateful. It would be nice if you three maybe scrambled together some food in the kitchen, it would be much appreciated."

"C'mon, Rachel," Tina said, heading for the door, after kissing Gus. "Let's do Gomez's bidding while picking out a movie. I've had enough of the fog scene anyway. These three will be boring the hell out of us with 'Addams Family' business anyway if we stay here."

Chapter Two

Mission: Isis

Rachel followed with only a brief headlock on Jean to get her headed in the right direction. Deke stayed near his bowl, savoring the beer Nick had poured for him. Nick served his companions with what they wished from the new bar and refrigerator on the balcony now. He held up his own shot glass to be toasted, which the others met with theirs.

"I'll do this in sequence, the first being Sergeant Dickerson. The explanation of how he should proceed will keep him busy until our morning meeting. I'll call Paul afterwards to apprise him of our local issues, along with plotting to take a look at his Isis training center near Olympia. Lastly, I'll call my agent. She should be ecstatic about my moving forth so soon on another book signing. If any of you have any objections, spit them out, including you 'Geezer'. I have a great role to play for you as bait again."

"Let me guess, a misdirected old putz, wandering around where he ain't supposed to be, near the suspected Isis compound. How am I doin'?"

"Gee, you're really good at this, Dan," Nick said. "I better get busy before it gets any later. I'll probably catch hell from Cassie, so I'll touch base with her tomorrow."

Nearly forty-five minutes later, Nick finished his calls. Jean delivered a tray of appetizers during his call to Nick's CIA boss, before waving goodnight quietly. "Paul was all excited, thinking my suppositions sounded real good. He even told me not to bother coming over until he checked a few things. When the fog clears in the morning, I wonder what our friends in Blue will think."

"I believe Neil thinks you're a little nuts anyway," Gus said. "I wish there were a way to let him in on what we do, but it's not like Pacific Grove is little Chicago. Those mugger assholes were the first worrisome case they've had in quite a while. Even Neil mentioned that. An ongoing story of tourists getting mugged in a place where tourism is king makes for a long day at the police department."

"What did Paul say about the pictures? Any hits yet?"

"Yep. He confirmed they were from a gang in San Jose with criminal records dating back to practically the moment they started walking, John. Naturally, he's uneasy about us risking our necks locally, but he knows the deal. If we can help our guys in Blue with their hands tied behind their backs, we will. This is home. It's not like we're working in some gray area. We caught the bastards red handed. Making sure we didn't have to pay for their incarceration is a bonus. Our boss loved my book signing cover plan in Olympia to check out the Isis compound."

"I bet you didn't tell him you planned to engage El Muerto, Payaso, and El Kabong to sort out the Isis problem," Dan said.

"I didn't have to. Paul immediately told me if I decided to do anything about the compound I was to exclude our heroic trio from making any movies. Heh… heh."

"He's right, Muerto," Gus said. "Olympia isn't far enough away from the Isis compound to make cartoon movies when you're less than an hour away doing book signings."

"Yeah, well too bad. If I'm less notable, the media would call it a 'Crusader' massacre of a simple Islamic village, or some such crap. We get the goods on these Isis freaks, and we can make a statement about the dangers in creating 'No-Go for non-Muslim zones' here in America. At the rate they're allowing these zones in Europe for importing weapons, and training for jihad, they'll have it all under Sharia Law in a few years."

"Nick is right," John said. "This must be a bloody statement. The movies we've done have made a difference. We are under a Death Fatwa already, because of our YouTube videos. We have hurt them. With a brutal reminder we are not done at this Isis compound, the statement will be made all over in Islamic circles. I hope you have a plan for me, Muerto. I can infiltrate these goons easily."

"I didn't know if you would want to risk it so soon," Nick replied, leaning forward. "It could mean locating vital evidence for our statement. It would give Paul a blueprint for what Isis has planned in the media run underground here, where they ignore the Islamist threat no matter what they do. I want you to sleep on it. I'll have to work out details starting tomorrow morning. We can all meet down at Carol's beach. I'll bring the coffee, but anyone wanting sugar packets or creamer, bring your own. I'm tired of you guys whinin' about extras."

"You always seem to remember the whiskey," Dan mentioned.

"That's for special occasions. Tomorrow morning ain't one of them. Even with my working out every day, as always, Rachel has been making snide remarks about my small daily celebrations – 'what if my water breaks', 'what if Jean breaks something at school', 'what if stars fall out of the sky', 'what if I awaken while you're downing shots at the beach with indigestion', 'what if I stub my toe'."

By Nick's ending lines, as he paused between each one, his friends were causing so much amused racket, Rachel made an appearance. Silence followed abruptly. She read the room correctly. "So... the meeting's over, and I'm being held up for ridicule, huh?"

"I was just explaining why I'm cutting back on my Irish coffees during our morning meetings. They thought my reasoning was very funny, Dear."

"I'll bet they did."

"Don't take that attitude, Mrs." Gus shunned her, hand to the side of his face while turning away. "I tricked a few of your gems out of Tina while we male targets of opportunity were out of range. You don't even want to start comparing our small dalliances with the everyday crap you pull. Perhaps now would be the time to air out some of your lunch dates with Tina."

"That traitor! How... crap!" Rachel shut up immediately as she recognized she had been lured into a trap, which was immediately enjoyed by Gus's viewers. They knew instantly Tina had never said a word, and it was all a supposition by Gus, weighing facts in evidence. "That's just mean, Gus."

Gus stood to wrap an arm around the penitent Rachel. "When you make one sided stabs at my brother, Nick, who has saved my black ass more times than I can count, I am duty bound to enter into a defensive mode, where I have figured out many things you and Tina have done since banding together as the 'Sisterhood of the Nagging Pants'."

Rachel tried an outrage ploy, and abandoned it while eyeing the amused faces around her. She giggled. "Okay... okay, maybe I've played the do as I say not as I've done card a few times."

"Admitting you have a problem is the first-"

"Don't even go there, John! How can you, a Muslim, speak to me about liquor intake? You're not even allowed to have the fermentation of grapes or wheat pass your lips. You drink with these guys all the time, you sinner!"

"You stole that line from 'The Thirteenth Warrior'! Besides, Islam is a religion much like the Christian and Jewish religions, and every other religion on earth. We are hypocrites – the only difference being, we pretend to be Godly while massacring innocent people for doing the same thing. I work to cleanse the many sins I am guilty of from my past. To do so, I must also

24

commune with the Jack Daniels. What other lines do you know from a movie you profess to hate vehemently, Ms. Hypocrite?"

Rachel smiled and gripped John's arm. "It's a small thing, little brother."

John sat down dejectedly, hands over his face. "I have been out quoted by an unbeliever, using my favorite line from my favorite movie. This humiliation will not go unanswered!"

Rachel poured him another Jack Daniels. "We Christians are good sports. Think of all the times Christians walked into Roman arenas as happy meals. Seek the council of your friend Jack here. Are you goofy enough to agree to another undercover assignment, John?"

John shrugged, sipping his Jack Daniels with pleasure. "I am very good at it. I believe it is time for that wayward soul, Ebi Zarin to make an appearance. These Isis jackals I have seen on the news butchering everyone will meet the El Kabong. I will lead them to their promised land. Unfortunately for them, it will be El Muerto and Payaso waiting for them instead of Allah."

"I think it's the Jack talkin', Muerto," Rachel said, patting John on the shoulder.

"I don't think so." Nick peered into John's eyes with a smile. "He's fine. Besides, he can take all night to decide."

"What's this about anyway?"

"I have to get in touch with Cassie about arranging the book signing in Olympia, Washington, like I mentioned. There's a suspected Isis compound near there. Paul would like us to check it out. Would you, Tina, Jean, and Deke like to accompany us?"

"I've never been in that part of the country. I'll talk it over with my bestie now that it's a definite future endeavor, and see how she feels about it. I know Jean will want to go. Deke goes where the beer is. When you say check on an Isis compound, you don't really mean check on it."

"Paul said to check it out," Nick countered. "He's the boss now. You know me and orders."

"I do indeed. I can't think of one you ever obeyed," Rachel fired the parting shot as she walked through the doorway.

"That's unfair," Nick called out as Rachel left to the amusement of Payaso and Kabong.

"Actually, I'm trying to remember an order you ever obeyed myself," Gus said. "The only relationship with Paul as the boss is you accepting a job if you actually want to do it anyway. Then, instead of completing the job as directed, you dress in a comic book character costume, kill everyone, and take movies. How am I doing, John?"

"Do not seek my support in this disrespect of El Muerto, Infidel," John replied, shunning Gus. "Mr. Gilbrech outlines a mission in vague terms, allowing Muerto to fine tune it into a result acceptable to everyone."

"Thanks, John."

Gus chuckled. "John's only saying that because he starred in the last movie as El Kabong, you suck-up."

"Yes… and what is your point? You are jealous, Payaso. There are already over two million hits on my El Kabong clip. I am more famous than a cat video."

Dan listened contentedly to the familiar bantering. When they paused, he stood. "I'm going to walk home gentlemen. I'll have my cell on if you need me for anything before tomorrow morning. We're still on for tomorrow morning at the beach, right?"

"Yep. Is it too early for you?"

"Nope. I don't sleep much anymore, except in snatches. I had a good workout today, so maybe I'll be able to string a few hours together. Thanks for the invite to Washington, Nick."

"I'll walk you out," Nick said. On the way, Nick addressed a growing concern. "Tonight was a little weird because of who we were hunting. I don't want you going to Washington with us to commit suicide. I didn't like the way you took on the driver, Dan."

"Would it be so bad to go out with my boots on, Nick?"

"Not at all," Nick replied, pausing to look Dan in the eyes. "I don't want you doing it with us, my friend. You going out in style might be very appealing to you; but with us, it could endanger our mission, or get one of us comic book characters killed. That's not to mention the repercussions put on your kids, and the way we would have to handle your death in the field. I can use you on this, but only as an asset, and not an expendable one. I want your word on it. In return, I won't ever say anything stupid like time heals all."

Nick watched Dan smile before thinking it through, considering options, including lying. Dan's mouth tightened. He nodded, and held out his hand. Nick shook it.

"You have my word," Dan said. "No suicide during comic book capers. That doesn't mean I'll let one of you youngsters take a bullet for me. If you want that guarantee, you can go fuck yourself, Muerto."

"Understood. You're in. I'll see you tomorrow."

"You will indeed, Nick. Sorry about tonight."

"Don't worry about it. We needed to clear the air, so we're on the same page."

Nick hit the security remote pause as he watched Dan trudge down the stairs. He detoured to the entertainment room to wave goodbye before leaving. Nick reset the security system after Dan closed the door, pondering his own future, and thinking he would have tried the same thing Dan did. He couldn't endanger Gus and John, or his own family's wellbeing. Nick had no intention of risking everything on Paul being able to keep his pet assassin out of prison. Nick returned to his friends.

"You gave Dan the lecture, huh?" Gus handed him a refilled shot of Jack. "I saw it in your eyes after the driver adjustment that you'd have to talk with him about it."

"He's lost without Carol, and nothing the three of us can do will make it any better. I can use him, and fill time on pursuits doing good work. He understands that, and I know he's thankful for the money. I had to make sure he knew not to try the suicide on our op anymore. Another second with the driver, and Dan would have been with Carol. I don't blame him for it, but he can't do that with us."

"I liked the role you have for him in this op," Gus said. "If John can get inside, Dan wandering around as if lost, might install two guys on the inside of the compound. One of them may be able to find out where they might have others detained."

"Gus is right," John said. "We have no idea yet how this compound works, or if they have families held hostage there or not. If I can gain access, then finding out if others are being held would be much less difficult if Dan can infiltrate as well. I wish we could do more for Dan, my friends."

"That's not in our purview, John. We do what we can, but no matter what anyone says about the deathbed, we die alone. Dan held onto Carol to the last second, but in the end, callous as it may sound, I doubt she knew he was there. He's dealing with it. Dan understands now, but I had to make it clear. I'm not taking casualties because Dan decides to use our mission as a way to eat a bullet, but not from his hand. Again," Nick said, holding his shot glass up, "here's to Carol and her live mate, Dan. May God have mercy on our dark endeavors, and prevent them from eventually contaminating our old friend."

The three men toasted, each with his own thoughts to Dan's part, and the road ahead. Each knew it would not be for the faint of heart. They shared the toast understanding each made a pledge to the other, that they would not allow anything to turn such a commitment into a death pact. Nick drained his, and refilled.

"I knew Dan and Carol a very long time. I hate even the word soul-mate. No one knows what the hell that touchy feely tag means. Those two were bonded beyond clichéd crap like soul-mate. I'd rather Dan didn't die while earning his commission with us. I also don't want any of us and his kids saddled with the results of an errant decision on his part. I needed to make it clear I'm allowing Dan in on our gigs no matter what he does. If either of you have a problem with that, now would be the time to voice it."

"I'll ride with my friend Dan to the end of the string," John said immediately.

"Ditto!" Gus acknowledged immediately. "We'll keep an eye on him, Muerto. If he slants off the reservation, Kabong and I will conference you on it. In the long run as Rachel quoted earlier from 'The Thirteenth Warrior', it's a small thing, brother."

I'm glad to be in the company of warriors after so many years by himself, Nick thought as he grinned and refilled his glass. "If it happens, we will make the Geezer's passing memorable."

"Hell… yeah… we will," Gus added. "After that last trip to the sand with you, I don't even know what fear is anymore. Once your life passes before your eyes more than a few times, you start thinking I've seen this movie. Change the damn channel."

That statement amused Gus's audience of two completely for a moment.

"Let's get down to business. All kidding aside, I see you want to do the infiltration ploy, John. Do you have a plan for getting close so that you can infiltrate this group?"

"Of course," John countered. "I have to establish myself at a Masjid immediately in an area between your signing and the compound. They will be recruiting there. It is not a coincidence when the FBI dolts look into the people caught setting off bombs, they are always frequenters of a Masjid. Even if the Imam running the Masjid is unknowing of these defilers of holy places. Isis and their ilk understand the reticence of law enforcement to investigate Masjids; because the politicians will hang them out to dry, trying to be politically correct with a deadly enemy. It is insane, but I will find a Masjid in the area where I can be certain I will cross paths with the Isis acolytes."

"How?"

John grinned at Gus. "I will hack into everything until I find a membership role with a number of participants from the suspected area where the Isis compound is located. They will have P.O. boxes instead of addresses."

"You, my friend, are a very fine addition to our team," Nick complimented John. "That is a great start to your infiltration endeavor. We'll have to get you into a residence nearby where you locate some suspected recruiting depots."

"Yes," John replied. "I will be freshly moved in, and looking for work. It will be as you call it 'a cinch'."

Gus held his glass for toasting purposes. "Here's to John. You have rhino balls to infiltrate those throat slitting assholes."

"No," John replied, gripping Gus's wrist, negating the toast. "I am a man with a second chance. I have the deadliest backup I can imagine. I'll get in. It will be my fault if I do not get out.

Kabong, with the help of his deadly friends, Muerto and Payaso, shall triumph."

The three men toasted solemnly on that note.

* * *

Nick typed with passion, threading in new scenes of violence and destruction for his character Diego. Having already sent Diego's latest adventure, 'Assassin's Folly', to his agent Cassie, Nick could start his frenzied new adventure with the whispers of his last novel fresh in his mind. He had allowed more emotion into his character than ever before in 'Folly'. Nick plotted to tie his new novel into the Isis compound adventure in Washington. He grinned appreciatively, anticipating the day when it would be released; because most of what transpired if his hit on the compound was successful, would be true. It was a small gamble he had taken in past Diego novels, involving real life events.

Knowing how much Dan's deceased wife Carol loved every small scene casting Diego into a usually ill-fated affair, Nick made Diego's next venture in the company of a woman forced on him by happenstance. Diego had to earn her trust in order to find where his prey were hiding without revealing his true identity. In doing so, Diego began to lose his way, caring for the woman more in each scene. Nick's fingers worked the keyboard with an intensity lacking somewhat in his writing lately. When Deke moved at his feet, he knew he was not alone. He saw the time on his laptop only slightly after 6 am.

"Someone's an early bird this morning, as usual. Only Deke bumping your leg alerted you to my stealthy approach, Muerto." Rachel threaded her arms around him from behind, reading from the screen over his shoulder. "Oh Diego, you cad. He's leading that poor woman, Fatima, into his dangerous cat and mouse killer game. She'll fall desperately in love with him, revealing at his insistence every secret in her life."

"Hey! What the hell?" Nick reached around to grip the backs of his wife's bare legs, his fingers gliding in satin smooth touch along her skin. "I'm writing this story, and none of what you said is happening... well... maybe a little, but it's not what you think. Diego's falling for her. I'll make Fatima into a Black Widow, a woman with a voracious appetite for feasting on trusting men, caught in her web of deceit. Diego won't have a prayer."

Rachel moaned, hugging Nick tighter as his hands continued their soothing journeys. "I don't... believe you. He'll put a bullet in her head soon."

"He will not. Did Quinn, the unborn alarm clock drive you from your bed, Dear?"

"Of course. He's becoming as loveable and annoying as you are. I have a feeling I'm going to be a couple weeks early. Jean was a week early."

"Wow, that's going to cut it close." Nick spun off the chair, reversing the hold on Rachel, his hands opening her robe to begin their work at the front, again with feathery strokes. "I'm not sure when we'll be leaving for Washington. I have to call Cassie. When we go to your next Lamaze class on Tuesday, we need to ask the instructor what she thinks."

"She doesn't know shit! Lisa's had one baby, and the woman acts like she's been popping out babies alone in a cornfield every year. I've had a baby. We're only going to the stupid class so we can get synched together on the breathing, and what you'll need to do when I'm goofy with pain. I'll make it through the trip to Washington. Now come to bed, and help me relax after mentioning the Earth Mother Lisa."

"Okay," Nick agreed, following Rachel toward the stairs with Deke on his heel, "but it's never a bad idea to seek the advice of experts. Just sayin'."

Nick prevented a spinning, gasping attack of outrage, holding onto his incensed Rachel in a tight, but supportive hug. "I didn't know I could ring your bell so easily with just the mention of the Earth Mother. The all-knowing, all-caring brood mother of the earth's 'Clan of the Cave Bear'.

Rachel relaxed in his arms with a giggle at his reverent chant of their Lamaze instructor. "Maybe I am being too rough on the arrogant, condescending little-"

"Woe there, my lady." Nick prodded her onward in their bedroom journey. "You're working yourself into a state even I, the proficient and caring, long suffering Nick can't relax you from."

"We'll see."

* * *

"Nick's late," Gus announced unnecessarily for the consumption of his two bundled friends, John and Dan. "Nick's never late. Plus, he volunteered to bring the coffee."

John pulled a flask out of his jacket. "Take a hit of this, Payaso. It will make you less grumpy."

"I love you, man." Gus took a swallow, his eyes watering. "Oh my. I feel better already."

John accepted his flask from Gus, taking his own pull of it before offering it to Dan.

"I'm fasting for a few days, John. Thanks anyway. Here he comes now." Dan gestured at the steep road leading down to what was now known as Carol's beach. "He brought the family with him. Nick's become quite the family man."

"Yeah, he's a saint," Gus replied, making gagging noises. "Give me another hit, John. Dan's fawning over Nick has left a rotten taste in my mouth."

"They sell that stuff called Listerine for that ailment," Dan fired back. "It wouldn't hurt you to get acquainted with your toothbrush again either, Payaso."

The three of them were enjoying Dan's dig as Nick supported Rachel across the empty coastal road with Jean holding Deke on leash while waving at the three men. They joined together in the usual morning greeting and banter. Nick held up a huge thermos, he extracted from his backpack, while Deke and Jean skittered down along the actively high waves of an unfriendly beach morning day.

"I have the elixir of great things in this jug, my friends, along with carting down beach chairs, because I knew none of you lazy bastards would bring your own seat. My assistant, the lovely Rachel, has deigned to provide ceramic cups for this wonderful encounter. While we enjoy this rather bleak, wind driven morning, I will contact my agent, Cassie. We listened to the news all morning... I mean most of the morning. They haven't found the thug deposits yet. Have any of you heard anything different?"

"Not I, El Muerto," John declared. In lower voice he said, 'I did watch the news."

"Same here," Gus added. "It's unfortunate some Sunday morning stroller will have their morning ruined."

"When I didn't hear it on the news, I drove into Monterrey and called it in from one of the only payphones in the Western Hemisphere," Nick said. "A payphone that does not have one of those damn security cams around it. We may as well be living inside a bubble."

"This from the serial killer supreme," Gus said. "You're peeved because you can't be El Muerto everywhere you want. Even good deeds have to be carefully chosen in this day and age."

"Let's go sit, and pour the coffee. I smelled the booze wafting out of you and Abdul the Terrible already, Payaso. C'mon. I have to call Cassie."

The men moved to a great spot on the beach where the scavenger birds flew in to check them out, and peck each other for position in gaining handouts. John, who could never get enough of the birds' antics brought a stale loaf of bread with him. Gus made him sit twenty feet away from them, because the birds would literally engulf him. John laughed uproariously at the assorted scavengers, talking to them, and scolding them by names he made up as he went along. He could hold a bit of bread in his fingers, and three birds would flutter like huge hummingbirds near his hand. When he tossed the piece, it would be caught in the air.

"I think we need to get John looked at," Gus said. "Kabong is nuts for those birds."

"He's damn entertaining though," Dan replied. "I think the goofy birds recognize him now. I only believe he's in denial about them being flying rats. Good coffee this morning, Nick."

"That's because Rachel brought the fine china down to serve it in. There is a difference." Nick fingered Cassie's private number. She answered on the second ring.

"Nick! Oh my God, I love 'Assassin's Folly'. Linda called me. She's sending you a galley with very few changes. They want to publish it in the next couple weeks. They need a hit, so they've cranked up the marketing barrage already with hints in all the major outlets. Linda doesn't want anything delaying the release. She thinks springing it out in the public by surprise will make a real splash, instead of the usual months of teasing crap. Best of all, not one word about plot changes."

"That's great, Cass. Listen, what kind of contacts do you have in a place like Olympia, Washington? I know they have a big Barnes and Noble bookstore there. I have another bit of personal business in the same area, and I thought doing a book signing would be great since 'Assassin's Folly' is coming out."

"Holy shit, Batman! Let me call Linda. Maybe she could do a rush printing of a couple thousand books, and we could do a real extravaganza there with the first raw print run. I'll call you right back!"

"I…" Nick began, but realized his agent had hung up on him. "I know it's wrong, but load me up with one, Gus."

Gus and John, who had returned from his birdman duties, grinned at each other, and then shrugged in unison. Dan laughed.

"I think you're a little late to the feed, Muerto," Dan explained. "I believe Heckle and Jeckle imbibed your share of whatever might have originally been saved for you."

"Just as well." Nick watched Rachel trailing Jean and Deke near the shoreline. He sipped his un-Irish coffee wondering not for the first time how long his string of blessings would last. Being a cynical psychopathic killer, Nick believed it would end soon. Glancing at his friends, he hoped it would be just him. He took a deep breath, letting it out slowly, deciding it was never a good thing to develop a conscience.

"Muerto… you have visitors." Gus nudged Nick out of his reverie.

Nick glanced toward the small line of beach parking places in the dirt. US Marshals Tim Reinhold and Grace Stanwick plodded gingerly down into the beach sand toward them. Not so long ago, they handled Rachel, Jean, and Deke in the witness protection program. During the cross-country journey in which Nick freed his chosen family from needing witness protection, Grace and Tim became aware Nick was one of the deadliest assassins in the world. Since then, with Nick's rogue assassin days behind him, he had consulted on some deadly cases, helping them rise in the Marshal's Service. Thanks to his intervention on Tim and Grace's behalf in the cases leading all the way to the Attorney General's Office, official ties with the Marshal's service, FBI, as well as the NSA and CIA were now part of his life. Nick also the had full backing of the new CIA Director, Paul Gilbrech, because of his willingness to be a secret enforcement arm on United States soil. Nick smiled, cursing himself inwardly for the jinx he instigated to bring the Marshals for a visit.

"Well, well, well! Look Tim, we have them all together, including their old fossil recruit," Grace declared, arms folded over chest, complete with shaking head. "Do we have enough sets of cuffs for all of them?"

"Who ordered the set of government stooges for breakfast," Nick asked, glancing at his friends. "It wasn't you, was it, fossil?"

"No way," Dan answered. "Damn, Timmy, I would have figured you'd have shot this foul mouthed dowager by now in self-defense before she spews something that will get you killed. Didn't you say Grace Slick's getting a cameo in the new book as an old whore with gout, Hemingway?"

"It's my next scene," Nick replied to much amusement at Dan's retort.

"Dowager? Really?" Grace smacked her partner in the back of the head. "That's enough enjoyment out of you, Reinhold. Can we talk to you in private, Nick? Paul let us in on a particular plan being formulated in the great Northwest, because we requested your help through him a couple weeks back. You can fill in your social circle if it interests you."

"Damn, Paul piggybacked a Marshal's gig on you, Nick," Gus said. "At least he's allowing right of first refusal."

Nick handed Dan his coffee cup. He imitated 'The Terminator'. "I'll be back." While following the two Marshals to their vehicle, Nick smiled, noting something beyond the scope of less enlightened observers. He entered the rear of their all black SUV. Tim slipped into the driver's seat, while Grace sat crosswise to glare with a grin at Nick after shutting the door.

"You two are finally sleeping together." Nick watched the startled look springboard across Grace's features with amusement. She started to stammer out denials, but Nick waved her off. "Too late, Grace Slick, what the hell do I care? Spit out what my boss allowed you to add to my journey north. Yes, I know you and Tim have jurisdiction over the entire west coast sector. Is someone breathing down your necks over at the DOJ?"

"How... oh, the hell with it. Yes, we've been working a damn serial killer case in the Seattle area in conjunction with the FBI's special branch, led by a woman named Kaitlin Anderson. She thinks she's the second coming of a real life 'Criminal Minds' TV show character. There's a guy in Seattle, maiming young prostitutes as if he were 'Jack the Ripper'. He's the TV show wannabe's worst nightmare: random slayings, random time intervals, random ages, random appearances, and random races – nine victims so far, not counting the three pimps they can't connect for sure."

"I read about him. 'The Seattle Ripper', the press calls the killer. On the positive side, I heard prostitution is down," Nick commented with the express purpose of getting a rise out of Grace. He was not disappointed.

"That is fucked up, you psychopathic-"

"Grace!" Tim shook his head at his partner. "Nick's messing with your head. Stay on point."

"Heh... heh. Okay, so we have a slicer and dicer carving the prostitute population, while an FBI special branch bimbo condescendingly blames you and Tim because she's locked into a serial killer motif in one of her text books."

Tim glanced back. "Exactly. Grace can't get her to consider any other approach, but the FBI formula zombies are attacking us, claiming we're shackling their investigation with incompetence. We've only been allowed in support, and belittled every step of the way. The son-of-a-bitch hacked a fourteen year old runaway into pieces a couple days ago after a two week layoff."

"The AG called us on a conference call," Grace admitted. "This has gone nationwide, Nick. In another few weeks, this bastard will be doing interviews with CNN about policing agency complete helplessness. The AG asked for you. He says name your price. If you can bring the asshole in alive as if it were a law enforcement task force effort, he'll double your asking price. Bottom line is he wants this killer stopped, by any means necessary."

Nick shrugged, because he had something in mind for this serial killer, and it had nothing to do with giving out credit to law enforcement. He stayed silent as Grace's mouth went to full torque. Her fists clenched in absolute rage as what Nick wanted blasted into her head. Tim grabbed her hand.

"Don't Grace. Paul said Nick would insist on it. At least he trusted us with the truth. We want to stop this perverted psychopath. We can't be choosy about the method."

"Damn it, Nick! Couldn't we do this by the book with your insights? You could even get official credit with Nick McCarty, bestselling New York Times author, consults with the FBI and the US Marshal's Service to bring a murdering psychopath to justice."

"Heh…heh."

"Get the hell out of our vehicle!" Grace turned to sit rigidly in her seat. "I'll need a few moments before Tim and I say hello to Rachel and Jean. I have to erase your presence from my memory banks. Mr. Gilbrech warned us you'd pull this crap! There is no way in hell we're letting you play out your comic book fantasies on this operation, so get your fucking El Muerto ass out of my backseat!"

"Nice seeing you two." Nick exited the vehicle, barely containing his laughter, knowing Paul had shared his El Muerto identity with the marshals. He had reached down deep for his inner uncaring psychopath, and felt relieved when his cold blooded killer surfaced. "Have a nice day, kids."

Nick returned to his chair with a look of satisfaction that elicited worried looks from his partner, Gus.

"Uh oh. What did you do Muerto?"

"I think I separated us from a cluster fuck of biblical proportions, Payaso."

"Oh." Gus settled into his beach chair. "It's good you've grown a set, and learned how to say no. I'm sure Rachel and Jean will be thankful. I know I am."

"I am confused."

"And I, John." Dan leaned forward in his small beach chair, pausing as he saw Tim and Grace walk down to the shoreline before meeting with Rachel and Jean in a happy reunion. "Care to share, Muerto?"

Nick explained the parameters, complete with comical insights about Tim and Grace sharing not only a vehicle, but also a bed. He outlined the Marshals' problem then in detail. "I like this for our secret identities."

"He butchered a fourteen year old girl, Muerto. Is that some kind of comic book collateral damage?"

The Terminator surfaced in spite of the silence, the ocean, and his beloved adopted family nearby. "Listen to me carefully, Dan. I'm not a robot someone launches like a weather probe. I do things within a multitude of unknown circumstances. I pick and choose the way and the how I do it. Don't confuse me with a social worker or a government incompetent, who can spout all the politically correct jargon, but get nothing done. Mark what I say now. Timmy, and Grace Slick will take what I said back to the Attorney General. That's when we find out how desperate they are to get this 'Ripper'. If they decide they want this prick at all cost, I'll gladly go collect him... as El Muerto. Payaso and Kabong follow my lead. Maybe this would be a good time for you to shed us as a business entity, Dan. We'll all be friends no matter what you decide. I will cover anything to do with your living costs as separation pay. Hell... the unholy trio will pick up the morning bar tab, right guys?"

John reached out to grasp Dan's hand. "I am always your friend. I admit I have done violence on a number of levels, and in a number of circumstances. With Nick, I know I am on the right side of what I believe. We can still be friends, Geezer."

"I don't do touchy-feely, Dan," Gus said. "I respect any decision you make. Because of circumstances beyond even your combat and real life experiences, Nick is my brother. I trust him beyond any outside source. That will never change. This is a good point for you. Now's the time to bail. No matter what though, we don't kill our own. You can walk away clean."

"Amen to that," Nick said. "We're your friends forever. I can envision how you feel. In a case with a child killing asshole attached, there is a temptation to spread the cape, and goose Superman in the ass. Unfortunately, we have our own kryptonite to deal with. I believe Tim and Grace to be fine upstanding, and trustworthy human beings. The people they work for and control this country... not so much. If lies were nickels, I would have been smashed flatter than the Road Runner under a cartoon boulder. Here they come, family... and the government ding dongs. Think about it, Dan. There's no hurry."

Nick stood as Deke reached him, exuberant and sandy from tail to snout. "Oh hell, Deke. I'm going to spend the rest of Sunday morning separating you from the beach."

"We'll be talkin' at you, Nick," Grace said on the way by.

Tim shook hands with Nick. "Good to see you, Nick. We need you on this, but I believe you're right for holding out. Even Grace and I don't know what the hell the FBI's end game is on this. If they could have thrown us under the bus already, we'd be wearing tire tread marks from one end to the other."

"Watch your six, Timmy. It ain't over yet."

"Understood."

Jean and Rachel joined Nick then, both wearing the suspicious masks of past occurrences. "Okay, what have you done, Muerto?"

"Nothing, Dear. In this case of the Grace and Timmy show, it's what I refused to do. All will become clearer. It's a process."

"Grace was really pissed, Dad."

"Sometimes we have expectations that can't be met, Dagger. Grace found herself wishing for candy and the Easter Bunny, but instead her Easter basket was filled with Brussel sprouts and canned spinach. You look tired Hon. Why don't you sit down in my chair, and I'll jog to the house with Deke, spray the bugger off, and come back with the car?"

Rachel grasped Nick's hand, leaning in to kiss him. "Thanks for being a mind reader. I don't know how you pluck those wishes out of my head, but I do appreciate it. Can you sprint uphill too? I have to pee."

"On it. Come Deke, I'll race you to the house. Maybe you can shake off half the sand on the way."

* * *

Nicks iPhone dinged. He saw it was Cassie finally calling back. Gus, John, Dan, and Deke at his feet decided to stay with him in their favorite hangout on the deck. Nick wrote, while his three companions plotted out the areas in Washington, they would be either baiting serial killers or infiltrating a terrorist compound. The three worked from new laptops, networked together. The only sound in the last couple hours had been Dan cursing his less nimble computer savvy. Nick answered.

"Hey, Cass. Tough time getting a gig in Olympia?"

"I need two weeks, Nick. Please! Our publishing friend, Linda will move heaven and earth to get a print run to the bookstore in that time frame. She's already launched it. The only thing she requests is a signing in Seattle, and possibly a few signings at small shops in each area. She wants to do a print run of five thousand. Linda told me they'll work a deal with the printer so these will be numbered copies of a much larger first edition printing."

"That's nice marketing, Cass. Sure, two weeks will be fine. If I have to leave earlier than that, I'll hang around for whatever you can arrange. Gus will be with me, so we should be able to sell a bunch of 'Caribbean Contract' too."

"Don't worry about that. I've already talked to the store in Olympia. He's ordering in more of your complete line of novels. We're doing a consignment deal with 'Assassin's Folly' because of the numbers. How's the new novel coming? Did you title it yet?"

"I'm considering 'Dark Interlude', and yeah, it's coming along great. My assassin Diego opens himself up to a relationship with one of his marks, a woman named Fatima."

"I'm hooked already! Send me the first twenty thousand when you get there."

"I passed that yesterday. I'll e-mail it later today in Kindle form."

"What's gotten into you? You're writing at a Nora Roberts' pace."

Nick enjoyed that comparison for a moment. "No, I'm not even close to 'La Nora', but I am having more fun lately with the writing. Are you making the trip out this time?"

"Are you kidding? I wouldn't miss it. We'll hit all the sites. I hope you're bringing Rachel and Jean along with Gus."

"Yep, and Deke the dog. Rachel thinks she's going to be early delivering Quinn, so this trip may be more exciting than it should be."

"I'll warn the pediatric wing around every major signing," Cassie said. "This signing excursion will absolutely put you into the upper stratosphere, Nick. I'll have to convince you on a really big stay in the heartland next."

Nick smiled, thinking about the Detroit area, where the Middle Eastern population had skyrocketed. "The heartland is a neglected area, Cass. We'll talk about it."

On a side note, you really took that 'Big Texas Son' book killer off the radar. He hasn't checked in with a book killing in quite a while. I never thought it was a good idea to engage those bastards on a personal basis, but you proved me wrong."

The fact he had done much more to the 'Book Killer' Big Texas Son than reply to his book killing reviews brought another smile of satisfaction to a real killer's mouth. "Yeah, we have to confront them, Cass. I think authors who hide away, or worse, get devastated by these people with hidden agendas is the wrong formula. If we can keep a sense of humor, and remember that most of these 'Book Killers' haven't even read what they're killing in the Amazon marketplace, the key is common sense confrontation.

For instance, why do a one star hit piece on the latest novel in a long selling series, but offer no specifics, or even hint the 'killer' had even read the 'Look Inside' feature on Amazon. I promise never to lose my sense of humor when confronting them, but I will have my say."

"There's no question you've handled legitimate criticism very well, especially repeated hits on your first novel. Reminding the detractors that everything they were turned off about in the first novel was illustrated in the preview feature, even helped with the first novel in your series. It's always been policy not to confront readers."

"I agree with the policy if an author can't confront with anything but whiney crap, or 'how dare you question my writing' episodes. Anyway, let's get this new signing endeavor in the works in any time frame you can manage. I'll await your confirmation from Linda."

"On it, Nick. See you in Olympia for sure."

"You sure will… bye Cass."

"That sounded interesting, partner," Gus remarked. "Your agent's unknowingly covering our terrorist play, huh?"

"She even threw in an added stop in Seattle," Nick replied. "It's Karma, brother. I believe the serial killer's luck has hit the deadline Karma train track leading only one place. He will board, unaware he's traveling with the Unholy Trio, accompanied by possibly OG, the herald of doom."

"I like just 'Geezer' better," Dan said. "The only thing I am is a herald of my own doom playing around with you bunch. I'm in all the way for this by the way."

"We can use you, OG," Nick replied. "I'm glad you're coming along. I can't say you're the conscience for our group, because the 'Unholy Trio' doesn't have much of a conscience

45

anyway. Your input is welcome though no matter what. Neil hasn't called. I'm wondering if his imagination is running away with him about our antics in ending the mugging gang. I hope he doesn't start making life miserable around our Pacific Grove base. I wish there were some way to adopt him into the fold, but it's just too damn risky."

"Did you hear that, John," Gus asked. "El Muerto is finally worrying a bit about the local police force putting two and two together in spite of his crappy e-mailed conclusions as the Pacific Grove police force 'Castle'."

"Yes, I am impressed by his reticence to put us all behind bars."

Nick began a smartass retort, only to be interrupted by yet another call, this one from his boss in name only, CIA Director Paul Gilbrech. "Paul, old buddy, how's it hangin'?"

"It's a go, Nick," Paul stated with no preamble. "The powers that be want the serial killer terrorizing Seattle and the Isis compound near Olympia. You have a get out of jail free card no matter what you do to end either threat. I'm putting it into writing to you with my signature."

Nick stayed silent for a moment, absorbing what such a guarantee would entail. "Damn, Paul, you've bludgeoned any response I have into sand. How exactly does such a thing happen in your reality, pal?"

"More and more big name people are seated at the table since all these Isis executions with public outrage have surfaced in the media. I want it all stopped, Nick. Do it with your comic book identities, or anything else you envision. I'm writing off on it. Screw these whack jobs, and their politically correct nonsense! I know one thing: if I back you, at least I know whatever the hell you do will be for America."

"You have chosen wisely," Nick replied. "We are on it right now as we speak. Your attitude is a game changer, my friend. I will do everything in my power to make sure it comes out in our favor."

"I know you will. Talk to you soon... I hope."

Nick heard the disconnect with a grin. "Well... alright then. That call was a little over the top from what I'm used to. We have cover never before experienced. God only knows how real it is, but Paul's signing on personally. About the only thing that guarantees though is we get to sit in the interrogation room with the CIA Director."

"Meaning we don't know how many people Paul read in on this mission, right?"

"That about covers it, Gus. Whatever we do, we'll be looking to get screwed like always. If we're really getting blown angel kisses then whoopee. I want to hear from our US Marshal contingent. They don't lie, because they know I can smell it on them. Cassie told me two weeks before this that my publisher can have an emergency first numbered edition of 'Assassin's Folly' delivered on site for a signing. If things keep progressing in our favor, we'll go North early, and recon our hunting grounds.

"I heard you mention the name of the new novel might be 'Dark Interlude'," Dan said. "I think a better title might be 'Dolt's Delight' or 'Washout in Washington' or-"

"That's enough out of you fossil."

Chapter Three

Home Adjustments

Nick walked his crew to the door after they said goodbye to Rachel and Jean. "I'll call you guys with an update the moment Neil calls me with his horrible discovery of dead thugs. That was a good session with mapping moves on paper. We'll be ready when I get the word from Cassie. This may be really good, timing wise. I'm thinking maybe we can take care of the Seattle Slasher, or whatever the idiots in the media are calling him."

"Ripper," Dan put in. "How exactly do you plan on finding out the identity of the new 'Ripper'? I've been confused with your information gathering technique."

"The police proceed according to their computer models furnished by the FBI, who now has an omniscient presence on site, with an agent in charge more worried about making the criminal square pieces fit into her round holes. The Feds are not incompetent catching bad guys if they're actually connected to their victims. When they get a killer murdering people on a random basis, these task forces lose all sight of reality. I don't blame them in a way. I never came close to being caught. Granted, I was a professional assassin, but it's even more difficult to take down a random killer. In most cases there are no people with any kind of connection or reason for the victim to die."

"Those are all great excuses for the locals and FBI to miss catching the killer. I'm interested in how you'll do it."

"Come along, and I'll show you OG. Right now, I have more writing to do. Diego romance stirs my creative instincts."

"I can't wait to hear what your pet Marshals say when they get the word you have Carte Blanche to handle the 'Ripper'."

"They're used to it, Gus. Go home. I have one hour to write before my agreed upon Dagger throwing knives lesson starts. I'll be in touch."

Nick gave them a final wave and shut the door, looking down at the ever present Deke at his feet. "See, this is what causes writer's block, Deke. When we literary artists are constantly interrupted, it leads to multiple excuses as to why we can't write. The dreaded 'Block' could start at any time with what I've gone through these past days."

Deke snorted on cue, shaking his head, before staring into Nick's face once again.

"Yeah, you're right. I'm full of shit. Let's go get Diego on the path of love before Dagger tears into any more targets."

Deke fell in behind Nick with wagging tail.

* * *

Jean threw with force while on the move, hitting the target.

"Nice hit! You're getting the move to either side very well," Nick complimented his pupil. "You're taking the extra split second now to hone into your target. I love your progress. Ask your Mom. She's really doing better than anyone I can think of at her age, not that I have much experience in underage knife throwing competitions."

"Yeah," Rachel agreed with rolling eyes. "She's deadly. I wish I could get more behind this exercise; but with no other positive outcome than killing things, I find it on the same basis as violent video games."

"Except that if someone were to try and take Jean off the street by surprise, I believe you'd think differently about her reactions," Nick said. "Throwing knives hones concentration. That is an excellent life lesson. Throw your knife, kid."

In a split second, Jean drew her Italian Stiletto and hit the target dead center. She smiled at her Mom. "I'm deadly, Mom. No one will ever blindside me into the back of a van on my way to be maimed and tortured… ever again."

Rachel sighed, walking over to hug her deadly daughter. "I'm with you, but discipline means more than killing people."

"Dad has that covered too. He's teaching me combat knife strategy."

"Oh goody," Rachel said, eyeballing the suddenly uneasy Nick.

"Gee… thanks for throwing me under the bus, kid. Maybe you can get your teacher at school to instruct you on combat skills from now on."

"Don't worry, Dad," Jean replied with confidence, while collecting all thrown knives. "If the Momster tries to limit our lessons, I'll blackmail her into submission."

"Momster?! You're toast!"

Nick barely scooped the 'Momster' into his arms in time before she reached her intended target. "Easy, babe, Jean's eating your lunch. She'll be skilled in all the self-defense I can teach her. She has good moral fiber, and she won't kill anyone not deserving of it. I'm sorry, but that is what you married. I've tried not to allow my more psychopathic leanings infect us, but they can't be simply ignored. I see all things in black and white, with very little gray."

Rachel's body relaxed into defeat once again. She covered Nick's hands gripped around her. "Although I acknowledge I cannot keep my sanity when baited by this offspring of the devil, I do once again recognize your point, Muerto."

Nick patted her shoulder as Jean giggled. "It was the 'Momster' tag. Take comfort in the fact you will have your revenge with my backing at Dagger's most vulnerable moment."

Rachel brightened instantly, pointing at her now uneasy daughter. "Oh yeah, baby! This disrespect shall not go unanswered. Thanks Muerto. We'll work out our signals later."

"No fair! Dad... what kind of crap is this? You're siding with her? I'm funny, tolerant of what you are, and your protégé. You can't just throw me under the bus like this."

Nick walked over to put hands on Jean's outraged shoulders. "There are more lessons in life than throwing knives, kid. Someday, if you're lucky, you'll find someone who means more to you than anything else in the world. It's a partnership beyond kids, jobs, and life itself. You and Deke are beyond everything else in my world except for one: the Momster."

Jean hugged Nick. "Yeah... I know. You do realize Mom and me will be at each other's throats for the rest of our lives with you as some helpless referee, right?"

Nick hugged her back. "I'm a writer with imagination. Believe me. I've seen the future, and I'm not running away, kid."

"Good!" Jean pushed away. "I bet I'm throwing well enough to take you, old man. Want to have a go at the knife wielding Dagger?"

"Sure. Shall I use my left or right hand?"

Jean's jaw dropped open as Rachel enjoyed her daughter's shock therapy. "You're right handed! What do you mean left or right?"

Nick plucked a throwing knife off the table with his left hand, while keeping his eyes on Jean, and whirled with force, sending the blade into the target center, buried to the hilt. "I mean right... or left, little one."

Jean stared at the knife hilt in disbelief, glanced at Nick, and turned away with arms over chest. "I hate you!"

Her statement led to hilarity, with Jean unable to resist joining. Even Deke, sensing something like a treat bounded around his three human mates. They heard the motion sensor alarm begin pinging first, followed by the doorbell ringing. Nick peered into the monitor inside the door leading to their backyard, and sighed.

"Rats, it's the cops. I'm taking you two out to dinner. Pick a place with steak so I can bring back multiple bone treats for my four legged brother, the Dekester."

"By your command, Muerto," Rachel said, putting an arm around Jean. "Stay out of jail."

"Will do. I'll bring Neil in if he's not here to arrest me." Nick listened to the pleasant tittering of laughter at his caveat as he answered the door with a smile of one who enjoys what is within his grasp. "Neil! How the heck are you? C'mon in. I guess you received my thoughts on the muggers, huh?"

Sergeant Neil Dickerson nodded in acknowledgement, a chill running down his spine he could not explain, or cared to. He shook hands with Nick McCarty, he knew to be a bestselling novelist with a book at that moment in the number one slot on the New York Times Bestseller list. The incongruity of what he knew and what he suspected made his hands sweat. Nick noticed, as he drew the Pacific Grove policeman inside the doorway.

"You don't look so good, my friend," Nick said, releasing Neil's hand. "Would you like a shot of nerve tranquilizer? That is... of course, if you're off duty."

"I am off duty, Nick. Ah... sure, I'd like a shot. How about a double on the rocks?"

Nick grinned. "My man! Come with me, my friend."

Neil followed Nick into the kitchen, where Nick prepared two small glasses with ice and a double shot of Bushmills in each one. "I'm taking the girls out to dinner tonight, so I'll have a taste with you. Did something go wrong?

"Not really, Nick. Some joggers found the bodies of three dead guys along a path near Lover's Point, and another in his vehicle on the street nearly opposite of where they were found." Neil sipped his beverage. "I have a feeling the mugger problem is over. You were right on all counts with the supposition you sent me. I'm not so sure as to how these guys ended up dead though."

"Good Karma?" Nick sipped his whiskey, watching Sergeant Dickerson closely.

Dickerson grinned. "Maybe. We don't have any leads or suspects in the deaths of these muggers, and from where they were killed, I doubt I'll get any either. Correct me if I'm wrong, but it may not be a good idea to involve our 'Castle' of Pacific Grove in any more cases. I know you have credentials with the FBI, US Marshal's Service, as well as the CIA, Nick. Do you have a license to kill too?"

Nick laughed. "Nope. I don't have a license to kill. Do you know for sure the dead guys are the muggers you've been after?"

"Yep. We contacted prior surviving victims. The dead guys were identified right away as the ones. I bet they never figured they'd need masks, because the idiots thought they had a sweet gig going in the dark and fog. We're looking into revenge killings, but no one knew who they were until today. You can imagine how tough it is to get someone to talk to us on a Sunday. They seemed to enjoy the news though. I wanted to come by in person to update you on this. I'm not going to pretend with you, Nick. I think you trapped and killed those guys. They deserved it, but I could go to prison as an accessory to murder if you were ever implicated. I'll make certain that does not happen in this case, but I think maybe our 'Castle' TV show joke is over."

"Wow. That's a lot to absorb, Neil. I'm sorry you feel you're leading me to murderous ends. If you do believe what you're saying though, I won't be offended if I'm not called on as your 'Castle' type writer contact. We can still be friends though, right?"

Neil gulped down the rest of his drink while standing. "We will still be friends. It would be idiotic to admit to any of what I've said, but I'd like to think I could still call on you if my back's against the wall."

Nick stood with him, with Deke nosing around both men. "I'd be happy to help in anything you would like my input on, my friend. I don't think depending on me for the murderous role you think I'm playing out is an option or reality, but I am good at profiling."

"Yeah… you are." Neil held out his hand and Nick grasped it. "See you later, Castle. Have a great dinner with your family. I guess Rachel's really close by now, huh?"

"She is indeed, and thinking she will be early. We'll be going to Washington for a couple of book signings. I'll let you know the dates. I'd appreciate it if you could have a squad car swing around for a check once in a while."

"Count on it."

While watching Neil walk to his car, Nick put Gus, John, and Dan on a network call. "Neil's been by. He has a wild theory about the criminals he asked me to look into. Apparently, he believes their deaths were due to me, a lowly author of fiction books. It ends there though. No need to say anything else about such an outlandish fable. I'm taking Rachel and Jean out to dinner. Would you guys like to meet at the beach tomorrow morning?"

"I'm in," Dan said.

"I'll bring the coffee this time," Gus said.

"I will again bring the magic elixir if you would like a taste," John added.

"See you guys on the beach then." Nick disconnected. When he turned, Rachel and Jean were behind him, dressed to go out to dinner.

"I'm famished," Rachel stated, rubbing her rather extended stomach. "And so is Quinn."

"What she said," Jean added, "but with gasps of that's just disgusting."

Nick again interceded on a Rachel beat-down of Jean. "You two need to work this confrontation stuff down to small disagreements without this unseemly mother/daughter blend of insanity. Otherwise, I go straight for the throat of the youngest."

"Uh oh," Jean said, waving her hand in abdication. "Just testing the boundaries. Fail!"

"You two will drive me insane!" Rachel clenched fists at her sides.

"It should count on my part that I am not doing so consciously, Babe," Nick said.

Jean's giggle and silence illustrated her instinctive knowledge about the unstated parameters. Nick gestured at the perpetrator of parental agony. "Keep it up, Dagger, and the only weapon or electronic gear device in your hand will have to arrive by way of imagination."

"No fair! I always get screwed because I'm the smartest. You and the Momster should learn to build better barricades between you and the rest of us unfortunate inmates on the good ship 'crazy planet'. Some of us didn't ask to be shipwrecked here with you two weirdoes."

Sensing she may have gone one step beyond in her defense tactic, Jean immediately recanted her last statement. "Uh... no offense of course. I was simply pointing out the plight of us less fortunate travelers, doomed to share space on the same vessel not of our making."

"Wow," Nick said, grabbing Jean's ear as she danced on her tiptoes in distress. "That was a neat, well-spoken cry for help, don't you think, mistress of the 'crazy planet'?"

"Let her go, Muerto. In another few moments, you'll be ditching us, and heating a can of soup. I think I'll be less annoyed when sitting in a nice restaurant such as the Old Fisherman's Grotto in Monterey. It'll be just the three of us for a change."

"Sounds good. That place is a crack up. They have that sign that says 'No Strollers, No High Chairs, No Booster Seats'."

"We better go there now while Quinn's still baking," Rachel said. "Once he's out of the oven, we'll have to wait years to get in there."

"First off," Jean said, her face crinkling into distasteful disapproval, "yuck! How dare you speak of my unborn brother as a bun in the oven! We should never go to a place where they discriminate against kids."

"That makes it unanimous," Rachel replied, yanking Jean toward the door, "the 'Grotto' it is. Besides, it's a clear night with no ocean fog. It'll be beautiful on the Wharf."

"I protest this," Jean called out as she was dragged through the door.

"You'll get over it," Nick replied, setting their security system. "They have great desserts there too. I'll get you something special."

"No way do you get the dessert tray anywhere near the Momster." Jean ran for the car.

* * *

"That was so good. Jean won't have to browbeat me into staying away from the dessert tray tonight. I'm stuffed."

"You did very well, Hon," Nick complimented her. "You ate small sized portions, and drank plenty of ice water with lemon."

Jean made gagging noises. "Quit sucking up, Dad."

"You're really cruisin' tonight, Dagger. What the heck's gotten into you today," Nick asked. "You've been trying out every sarcastic remark you can think of on your Mom. Is something going on I don't know about?"

"She won't let me go to the school dance."

"You're only nine years old for God's sake," Rachel said.

"I didn't even know they had dances for kids under thirteen," Nick replied. "Man... I'm old. When does this dance take place and what time do they have something like that?"

"It's next Friday right after school," Jean answered, Nick's questions giving her hope, because Rachel's mouth was tightening. "My whole class is going. There will only be kids there from nine years old to twelve. It will be in the gym. It's not like we'll be getting motel rooms afterward."

"Jean!"

Nick turned away, his face betraying the humor threatening to break free. He faced the music finally as Jean was giggling, accompanied by glaring laser beams of anger from Rachel's eyes. "Look, would it help if I volunteered to chaperone this event. They do have chaperones, right? I could make sure there's nothing dangerous going on – no slow dancing gropes, no exchanging room keys, no sneaking behind the bleachers."

"I thought we agreed we were not giving in to this nine year old terrorist," Rachel said. "Where's my backup?"

"Woe there. I didn't know this was decided. This is the first I've heard of it, so naturally, I thought we were discussing the event. If you say no, I'm backing your call on it."

Nick could tell Rachel was having second thoughts.

"I may have jumped the gun in not talking to you about it," Rachel admitted. "I figured you'd think it was cute, and no big deal. I'm having trouble thinking of nine year old girls at dances. My Mom used to say they had square dances, and promenades with kids in the younger grades when she went to school. Nowadays, all I can picture is wild assed bands, drugs, and child predators."

"I can't disagree with your perception," Nick replied. "Although the music may be loud, and a lot different than a square dance or promenade, it'll probably be the girls dancing with each other. The boys will all be lined along the wall, watching. That's where I spent my first dance, huddled against a wall with other boys too afraid to ask a girl to dance."

"You did?" Jean, instantly interested in this new Nick story, forgot all about the dance. "I bet you were cute. Why didn't you ask a girl to dance? Didn't you like any of them?"

Nick shrugged. "I was thirteen, living in a Foster Home with a bunch of other kids. I couldn't dance, and I didn't want to learn with what I figured would be all my class laughing at me. I wasn't alone. I had plenty of company on the wall. Yes, I had crushes on a couple of the girls. If one of them would have said hi, I would probably have fainted."

"You were a wallflower. That is so cool. I bet you got really popular later in school. You probably had all kinds of girls hanging around you."

"We didn't have girls where they sent me. Shortly after those early dance times, I hurt some boys real bad. When I did my time, I quit school after I reached sixteen before I did something that landed me in prison for the rest of my life. I joined the Army. They liked me. After finding out I was good with languages, I did receive a lot of schooling. You two already know I eventually made it into Delta Force, but alas, no childhood sweethearts. That's the scoop on my high school love life. The picture of a sandy haired freckle faced Rachel reminded me so much of a girl I knew in high school, I went to meet your Mom, and then I drove East to take care of the guy who wanted her dead."

Nick's telling of his earlier days in such bleak terms caught both Rachel and Jean by surprise. "Hey... it happened long ago, and now I'm here with you two, living the dream."

Rachel turned to Jean. She clutched Jean's hand in hers. "As long as Nick chaperones, you can go to the dance. After that story, I'd probably let you hitch hike to Cleveland."

That statement earned some laughs, and a hug from Jean. "Thanks, Mom. I feel like finding something special on the dessert tray now."

Nick motioned for their waitress to inquire about dessert. She left Jean with a dessert menu with more choices, promising to return in a few moments. Jean settled on cherry cheesecake. With it in front of her, Jean ate tiny bites, rolling her eyes, and making over the top noises of enjoyment until she broke Rachel.

"Curse you, Daughter of Darkness!" Rachel signaled the waitress for a serving of the cherry cheesecake too.

Two men in suits, Nick saw enter the restaurant, caught sight of him. They spoke together, and then walked toward Nick's table. Always positioning himself to see the entrance to any place he frequented, Nick knew his quirky precautions amused Rachel and Jean. Nick leaned back in his chair while smiling at Rachel's irritation ordering the cheesecake. He also shifted a hand to his .45 Colt under the back of his light jacket.

"We have company, girls. No matter what, do not leave this restaurant until I find out what's going on. If I leave with these guys, you and Jean head for home."

"Understood," Rachel acknowledged.

The waitress brought Rachel's cheesecake as Nick's visitors arrived, the short haired, beefy blond one in a black suit leading. His partner looked to be a few inches over six feet tall, and a couple inches taller than the blonde. The taller one's lean featured face, and nearly black hair trimmed to an even stubble, made the smile he was gracing Nick with a menacing sight.

"Mr. McCarty," the blonde one began, "I am Mr. Smith, and this is my associate, Mr. Jones. My employer would like to speak with you. He has a limousine waiting in the parking lot. We would like you all to come with us, I will of course pay your tab."

"My wife just now ordered cheesecake, and my little girl, isn't finished with hers. I think we'll stay. Have your employer call me. I'm sure if he found where I was dining tonight, he can find my phone number."

Mr. Smith smiled, leaning forward with his hands on the table. "I'm afraid we'll have to insist, Mr. McCarty."

It was then the barrel of Nick's .45 Colt barrel end peeked out from under the napkin Nick held over it loosely. "I don't think so, Mr. Smith. I'm going to stand, and you two will walk out of the restaurant in front of me. Walk with your hands holding the bottoms of your suitcoats at your sides. If you let go of the suitcoat with either hand for any reason, I will blow the backs of both your heads off. In case you don't know your weapons, this is a .45 Colt loaded with hollow points. Do you understand what I just said, Smith and Jones. I'll need an actual affirmative answer now or I commit murder right here in this lovely restaurant."

Mr. Smith looked into the Terminator's eyes without any doubt he would be the first to die. He straightened slowly, his hands gripping the bottom of his suitcoat. "I understand."

"What is wrong with you, Carl? He cannot get us both, even if this was not a bluff," Mr. Jones said, beginning to inch his hand toward the inside of his coat. His hand froze when Rachel laughed. She had shifted nearer to Jean, giving Nick more room.

"Nick won't warn you again, but I'll do you a favor. I will," Rachel said. "He will put a bullet in your brain before you can get your fingers inside the suitcoat. I'll get our daughter out of the way, because there will be blood, but it won't be ours. Sorry, Mr. Smith, but when Mr. Jones reaches, you'll get a new hole too."

Nick grinned, but never took his eyes away from Smith and Jones. He planned on killing them. He preferred it didn't happen in the restaurant, but he would not hesitate for a split second. Both men would die faster than they considered humanly possible. Nick knew one thing for sure, Rachel and Jean would be just fine. Jones gripped the bottom of his suitcoat, his mouth tightening into a slash of promised retribution.

Nick stood slowly. "Lead the way, gentlemen. Let's go meet your employer. I'm sure he can explain all this to me. See you in a little while, girls. Only one piece of cheesecake, Dear."

"Brat!" Rachel called after him as he followed Smith and Jones.

Outside the restaurant, Nick followed the men through the crowded Fisherman's Wharf walkway with absolute concentration. When they reached the outskirts of the parking area, Nick halted the men. He looked around at the thinning numbers of people. "Hand me your weapons. Do it oh so very slowly. One twitch I don't like, you both die. You first, Mr. Jones. That's it... you don't need two hands. Stretch it out to me, big boy."

Nick took the Glock 9mm from Jones, quickly sticking it inside his belt. "You're next, Smith. A Taurus, huh? Nice. Okay, guys, one last thing, did one of you drive the limo, or does your boss have a driver?"

"I drove," Jones answered. "You had better pray to God our boss loves you, or I will make you pray for death along with your girls."

"Oh good, a mook who likes to threaten. Don't worry, Mr. Jones. I will be very loveable for your boss. You'll see."

Jones smiled. "I hope he hates your guts."

"Anyway, when we get to the limo, you go ahead and get in the driver's seat, Mr. Jones. Keep your hands on the wheel, and I'll have you drive us a little ways down Del Monte Avenue. I know a short turnoff there where we won't be interrupted or overheard. The damn FBI has ears on me half the time. They have those gizmos they can listen right through a parked car with."

They resumed the walk to the waiting limousine, but Smith glanced back. "Why is the FBI listening in on your conversations?"

"You probably know already, Mr. Smith. I kill people for a living."

"But... you write novels."

"It's a cover. I figured maybe your boss needed a job done." Nick kept fishing for background. "I have to keep my cover alive, or my base here won't be safe. You two really don't know what I do in reality?"

"We know you were in Delta Force," Smith answered. "I saw in your face you would have killed us both in the restaurant. We didn't know you were a professional. Our employer didn't say anything about it.

"That wasn't very considerate." Nick kept following the men to a limousine parked at the outer edge of the parking lot, nearest the walkway. "Go ahead and get behind the wheel, Mr. Jones, but remember to grip the steering wheel after you get in. I'll enter carefully in the back with Mr. Smith. Let me get the door, Carl, and then you slide in first. I'll follow."

Carl nodded his assent, Nick opened the limousine door after Jones entered the driver's side, and gripped the steering wheel. Nick saw a glimpse of a smiling paunchy man with dark, well-groomed hair in an immaculate light gray suit. Nick could tell within seconds this guy knew who he was and what he did. Nick entered the vehicle with his Colt pointed at the boss's head.

"Hello, Mr. McCarty. There's no need for you to point a gun at me. I'm here to make you a very rich man."

"Gee… that sounds wonderful. Head down Del Monte Avenue as we discussed, Mr. Jones. I'll tell you when to turn right."

Jones looked back at the man smiling at Nick. "Boss?"

"Do as he says. I wish you would have accepted my invitation for your whole family. I only meant to take you to my estate in Carmel Valley. I came down from San Francisco to meet with you, and discuss a highly lucrative business proposition."

"As I explained to Carl, the FBI has been bugging my house, and following me around. We're going to a spot only a mile down the way, where I know they won't be able to stop. It would be best not to speak until we get there."

"I like your thinking. May I call you, Nick?"

"Sure." Nick watched Jones pay the parking fee. He turned the limousine onto Del Monte Avenue. Nearly three quarters of a mile down the way, Nick knew they were close. "Next one on the right, Mr. Jones. There it is."

Jones turned right into the turnoff. It led to a park that was closed. The streets running adjacent to the stop sign were empty and dark.

"Perfect. We can talk here. Go ahead and shut it down, Mr. Jones," Nick told him.

Jones shut off the engine. Nick shot Smith in the head, and then Jones through the head twice, the second shot after his head pitched between the steering wheel and window. Nick then shot Smith again in the head, while watching his host go into cringing shock, his hands trying to work the door handle.

Nick turned the .45 Colt in his host's direction again. "Put your hands on your knees. That's it. Now, tell me who the hell you are and why I should care."

"There...there wasn't any reason for this. I...I merely wanted to hire you."

"Skip the lectures. What's your name? You know mine, and where you could find me and my family at dinner, so I'm guessing you had someone watching my house. Since I didn't notice, it means they were doing it from somewhere nearby with a remote viewing. I always notice, because I check anyone strange milling around, or any vehicle that I've never seen. Did you put a cam somewhere across from my house?"

"Yes, but it was only because I do know what you do besides that writing career. My name is Milton Formsby. I had ties to Tanus Import/Export through Jason Bidwell, and through Max Stoddard at Fletcher Exports. I found out through great expense who killed Hayden Tanus, Jason, and Max. Those were the most incredible hits I had ever heard of. You and I have done business before. I put out the hit on Paulo Cortesa."

"That was you, huh? Then you're really playing this the wrong way. I have an Internet drop you're familiar with. Anything done in the way of a sanction is done anonymously through the drop. If I handled Cortesa for you, then what the hell did you front me in my own backyard for?"

"I…I have a special job for you. I need a very well placed man taken out in the CIA. He's starting a task force to shut down my overseas interests in collusion with the DOJ and IRS. My sources tell me if he died, we have a man in place who will get appointed easily. The task force, and court cases will be dropped."

"Again, why come here in person? Secondly, who did you share my whereabouts with after you found me? That's a deal breaker." This is getting more interesting by the second, Nick thought, but this is major bad if everyone and his brother knows who I am and what I do.

Formsby shook his head vehemently. "No one knows… no one. I need a killer like you on staff. Someone without hesitation or conscience. You would be rich beyond your wildest dreams. Anything you want would be yours."

"I already have more money than I know what to do with, Milty. After what I did to Hayden, Jase, and old Max to protect those two girls you sent your cheap thugs to collect, I'm shocked at your thought processes." Nick looked around comically. "I'm being punked. Where's the hidden cameras?"

Formsby wiped his face on his sleeve. "It was stupid for me to have you approached like that. I need Paul Gilbrech killed in such a way as to not cause an incident. I will pay you twenty-five million dollars for the sanction of that asshole."

"Paul Gilbrech... the new CIA Director?" Nick began chuckling, not because of the reason Formsby figured, but because he could picture Gilbrech's face when he told him later. "You are nuts, Milty. He must be close to really frying your nuts for you to try and hire a sanction on the sitting CIA Director. Where the hell did you ever get the idea someone could simply pop into the CIA Director's chair just because the old one dies. It's a political gig, and Congress has some say in it."

Formsby leaned toward Nick excitedly. "The fix is in. I have a very highly placed contact inside the CIA. He guarantees the replacement will be a sympathetic guy I can do business with."

Nick smirked, rolling his eyes, to continue playing Formsby. *I need proof about some guy that's so in the know at CIA.* "Baloney, Milty. What is he some 9th level clerk?"

"Way above that, Nick. He's Lee Collister, The National Security Advisor. He has the President's ear on security measures and appointments as you probably know."

Nick kept fishing. "Why not wait until Gilbrech gets the boot? Let your man Lee undermine him behind his back. Your legal teams can keep the government forces tied in red tape for a decade."

"That bastard Gilbrech wants me labeled a terrorist, subject to exposure, and instant seizure of my holdings. If he follows through on this task force overseas, I'll lose everything. I can run, and stay in hiding for the rest of my life. I'll still have plenty of assets to survive very well, but I am building a dynasty! You sanctioned Bidwell and Stoddard on their own boat, making it look like a leaking gas line or something – sheer genius. I know you could take out Gilbrech."

"You've touched me, Milty. I don't want you to spend the rest of your life on the run either." Nick shot Formsby between the eyes. He had a few moments to spare so he waited until his last victim convulsed for the final moment on the brink of eternity instead of shooting him again. Nick looked around the inside of the limousine with disgust. He smiled while getting out his cell-phone – I get messier every year, Nick thought with a sigh.

"Nick?"

"Yep, it's me, your goofy husband. Did you happen to answer with our special phone?"

"Of course, goofy. I realize when you get called away during a meal, I will have to raise the threat level to DEFCON 1. We just now came through the door, but I have the phone and jammer on. It's green."

"Outstanding. You're the best. Can you drive out to my Carmel Valley place where I have John staying later on when I call? I could ask him to give me a ride, but I'd rather be riding around with you for a host of reasons."

"One of them being security cameras caught you on cam everywhere between the restaurant and parking lot, huh wise guy?"

"It's not very nice of you to pull the smartass card on me tonight. I did buy you a lovely dinner at a great place. I didn't request a stopover by Smith and Jones."

"I'm sure they deserved to be shot for picking those two names alone. Call whenever you're ready. The meal and the story, coupled with your solving the dance dilemma means you're golden with me and Jean. Will this be a tough one to alibi in the clear on?"

"I don't think so. After I make arrangements with John and Jerry, I'll be waking our CIA Director friend Paul. He's going to love me. I have to go. Unfortunately, I have some electronic gizmos to collect for my CIA buddy, so I have to get busy. We live in the age of GPS bullshit trackers everywhere, so I'll have to deliver the limo to Jerry hopefully tonight if he can meet me. I'll be callin' soon for you to either meet me in Carmel Valley or better yet, at Jerry's."

"You love all that electronic garbage. Don't pretend, you closet geek. Bye for now." Rachel disconnected with a laugh.

Closet geek, huh? Nick thought, looking at the phone. I think it will be time for a pre-natal exam when I get home.

* * *

Jean waited anxiously for Rachel to get off the phone. She relaxed slightly when Rachel laughed while disconnecting. "Is Dad okay?"

"Other than being the most cold blooded killer on earth, he's fine. He wants us to pick him up at John's when he gets done with cleanup."

"It's like you said though when we left the restaurant, Mom. They'll have him on surveillance all the way to the limo with those guys. The Wharf has cams everywhere."

"Jean. One thing we know about Nick: there won't be any live witnesses. We can only guess at what he has in mind now. I'm not that fond of thinking like Nick."

"I am," Jean said. "He'll have two or three plans acting out in his head, depending on his time intervals between interactions with the rest of us humans."

"I didn't ask, so it's possible Nick has them in custody for his CIA buddy, Paul. He did mention Paul would be interested."

"But did he mention his friend, Jerry." Jean giggled at Rachel's startled look. "I can tell on your face he did. That limo will be on the way to reconstructive auto body surgery."

Rachel sighed, while kneeling down to pet the ever attentive Deke. "Wow, and Nick thinks I'm a smartass. Just treats tonight, Deke. We're at DEFCON 1, so no street walks. You can ride with us to collect the Terminator later."

"That was a neat story Dad told us at dinner. We need to force him into telling all."

"I'm certain I don't want to hear 'all'. I'll let you annoy him with questions about his past. I think I'll stay with the term blissfully ignorant."

"Until bad guys show up at our dinner table to take us for a ride," Jean replied.

"Yeah… until then."

* * *

John answered on the first ring. "Uh oh, did your car break down somewhere?"

"Nope," Nick went on with their vague discussion. "I know it's late, but our freezer broke. I was wondering if I could put our meat in your freezer until I fix things."

"Of course. Luckily, I have plenty of room in the freezer."

"Thanks, John. I'll be over shortly."

"I'll get the freezer bags ready."

Nick's next call while he dissected the tablets and phones was to Paul Gilbrech.

"Oh boy… Nick McCarty. How are you, Muerto?"

69

"Is your line secure?"

"Did you just insult me? There's nothing I can do about it, but did you just insult me."

Nick grinned. "I'm covering all the bases tonight."

"Sorry. How can I help?"

"A guy named Milton Formsby hired me tonight to kill you."

Silence. Nick could hear the ocean nearby. "Did I say hired? Sorry, Paul, I meant tried to hire me. I figured since you were in such a playful mood, I'd trade a few with you."

"Not funny, Muerto. I remember Frank, the guy who decided to use his position in the NSA to take you out. He thought he was untouchable until they found him on the roadside at room temperature. I may do a number of things in this job, but ordering your sanction ain't one of them. Thank you for not taking the job."

"I thought you'd get a chuckle from that play on words, Paul. My bad. It was a shocker to have a guy actually try and hire a hit on the sitting CIA Director. From the way he tried to sell me on the job, I know you must be doing good things. This clown had paid his way to my home base, gathering information that must have cost him a fortune. He found out who I was in the old days under Frank, and sent two pros into the restaurant I was eating in with Rachel and Jean to collect all of us."

"Good Lord. How many dead?"

"The two henchmen and Milty. I'll send you the pictures after we talk. The memory cards from their phones and tablets will have to ship to you tomorrow morning. I managed to take it outside to a private spot, but at least I found out he hadn't shared my info. Even his two daisies he sent in to get me didn't know

70

anything other than my writer identity, and that I had been in Delta. This could work out real well for you, but I'll need a bit of cover."

"You got it, Nick. What do you have in mind?"

"I heard from Formsby you were starting a task force overseas to bring him down, including partnering with the DOJ and the IRS to take the lead here in the states. I'm going to make everyone here disappear. That will leave you with an open field to get warrants, and bring his empire down without interference. Whatever you had on him was pure gold, because Milty knew you had him. The rat in your government minion circles who thought taking you out would end the hunt for Milty's head is Lee Collister."

"Holy shit! The National Security Advisor? Your advice is solid. I'll raid everything tomorrow morning. I already have the warrants, and people in place to hit everything he owns overseas, and in the States, including his Carmel Valley estate near you. I held off, because we heard he was planning to battle us in the courts forever until he had his cleaners fix things. I have a guy at the Department of Justice I trust implicitly. He's already told me you're pretty popular with the Attorney General. Are you moonlighting on a steady basis now?"

Nick made snorting noises. "Good one, Paul. Anyway, here's the deal I need. I'll be on security cam footage all the way from the restaurant to the limo Milty awaited my arrival in. Once you bang down Milty's empire, the dragnet searching for him might run across my back trail. Since you now know Milty will be impossible to find, I'll need you to steer the investigation somewhere else after they raid his places."

"Done deal," Gilbrech replied. "I'll find out what I can on Collister, but he wasn't even on my radar. I've met him a bunch of times, both socially and professionally. Formsby sold anything to anybody overseas, including regimes, and terrorist enclaves in places we're at war in. That made him a traitor, and a murderer.

71

The National Security Advisor taking money from a bastard like Formsby can't be allowed to stay in a position like Collister has. If I can't get him legally, would you take the sanction, Nick?"

"Since that lowlife Milty possibly whispered in Collister's ear about me, I'd certainly consider it. I'm not going to commit suicide killing him, but I'll await any information you can gather. You're taking a big chance going after the National Security Advisor legally. You'll need eyes in the back of your head for that kind of caper, my friend. Stay in touch. I have to get going – miles to go before I sleep."

"I'll bet. Thanks for all this, Muerto, especially not taking me as a sanction. How much did the prick offer?"

"Twenty-five million, buddy."

"Lord have mercy! I would have killed myself for twenty-five mill!"

Nick was still enjoying Gilbrech's line after disconnecting minutes later, traveling to his Carmel Valley place where John stayed. That Paul had used Gus's favorite exclamation of surprise at anything of a Muerto nature continued to entertain him on his way. He drove very carefully with three dead bodies sharing the vehicle with him. There was blood of course everywhere. John had the attached garage open with the light on. Nick drove in, and John closed the electronically controlled door. John had the three body-bags waiting along with a gurney near the door. Nick motioned him back.

"I'm covered in blood, John. Hand me a wet towel, and a plastic garbage bag."

"There is what is called an 'understatement'."

"Great… another smartass," Nick mumbled. John returned with the towel and garbage bag. Nick wiped off his hands, put his personal things off to the side, and his outer clothing into the garbage bag. "I just bought that jacket too… damn it."

Nick slipped his shoes back on. He then loaded the body-bags himself, before lining them in front of the door entrance to the house. After wiping down the bags, he again wiped himself off, and his shoe bottoms. "Okay, John, let's load them. We should never have taken so long emptying the freezer out. Gus kept making excuses about his boat. No more procrastinating for the ancient mariner."

John grabbed one end of the first bag. "Yes. One week later, and we would have had no freezer room. Despicable! This cannot be tolerated. The Bloody Muerto nearly left without a space for the victims of his killing sprees. Inexcusable!"

"Very funny, John. We need to speed things along. We'll have to load these suckers on the cart to take them out to the freezer. One day soon I'll show you the workings in the rest of my subbasement under the trees. I have to wipe the inside of the limo down a bit before I drive it to Jerry's place."

"Does Jerry know about this?"

"Not yet."

"Can I listen to that conversation?"

"No."

* * *

"Hey Nick," Jerry answered sleepily. "It's eleven on a Sunday night. Some of us blue collar guys go to bed early when they have to work. What's up?

"I have a beautiful limousine which will have to be completely revamped electronically, and interior cleaning. I wiped up most of the unfortunate mess, but it will need detailed, carpets and all. No broken glass."

"Hollow points, huh? We'll have to scrub it electronically though, which will be a bit tougher than the dry cleaning bill. Who do I call after it's finished?"

"No one. It's yours, and it comes with twenty-five large for taking it on short notice."

"Good God, man… why are we talking on the phone. I'll have the door open for you to roll in with my new car in half an hour."

"Perfect." Nick disconnected, and finished dressing with clothes he kept in his other property's closet. "Man, that shower felt good. I told you Jerry wouldn't mind. I thought I'd have to go home with Rachel, and chance taking the limo over to Jerry in the morning. Instead, Jerry's hopping right out of bed to open for me. How about that?"

John handed him a small bag with the twenty-five thousand from Nick's safe. "I'm sure the money had nothing to do with it."

"A small part perhaps."

"Shall I call your lovely wife, and tell her to pick you up at Jerry's in a half hour?"

"Yep." Nick entered the limo, making sure the seat cover stayed in place. John opened the door. "See you tomorrow at the beach, John. We'll need to talk again, but after Gus and I walk Jean to school with Deke. We must have everything natural for a couple days because of our freezer deposits."

"I cannot wait, Muerto."

Chapter Four

Alterations

Jerry opened his end bay door as Nick drove into his parking area. Nick continued into the open repair bay. Jerry closed the door, and waited for Nick to exit. The two men shook hands. Nick gave him the bag. "How do you like my ride?"

Jerry walked around it slowly, contemplating it from every angle. He opened every door to peek in with mini-flashlight in hand. "It's gorgeous. I'm glad you load your own hollow points. At this range with the cannon you pack, I would have had to part this puppy out piece by piece. This can be sanitized perfectly. "I'll rework the electronics and tracking tonight before I go home. Damn... this is nice, Nick. I wouldn't have needed the money to take this beauty."

"A deal's a deal, and I know this sucker won't show on anyone's radar ever again. The girls will be by for me in a few moments, so I'll wait outside while you get started. Enjoy, my friend, and thank you."

"Anytime, Nick. Should I ask if they were all bad?"

"How should I know?" Nick waited for Jerry to quit enjoying his answer before going on. "They interrupted my dinner on the Wharf. They were up to no good."

"Well, brother, they won't do that again. Say hello to the girls for me."

"Will do, Jer. Goodnight." Nick walked out Jerry's small door exit in time to see Rachel drive into the parking lot. He jogged to the rear door as he saw Jean in the front next to her Mom, and Deke the dog with his head poking out the rear passenger side window. Nick shoved in next to Deke, taking his happy canine friend immediately over his lap. "You could at least let me get belted in, Deke. Hi girls. You should have slept in the safe-room, kid. Tomorrow's school."

"I know," Jean answered with a sigh. "I wanted to see you. That was scary tonight. They knew where to find us. That hasn't happened since we were on the run."

"I have the CIA Director on the case, so we'll do what we can on our end. It may be no one will be looking around for at least a few days. The people who may look after that will run into a wall. The bad guy head was in the limo, so his employees may assume he's gone into hiding, because he was in legal trouble. I can't answer for secretaries, assistants, or computer logs of appointments. I would think he'd keep his meeting with me mostly secret. Paul's taking care of the video log of my escorting Smith and Jones to the limo. There's one suspicious guy way up the food chain I have to wait on."

"It's laughable you're the one man sanction wing of the CIA," Rachel commented.

"Did you just insult me?" Nick used Gilbrech's earlier line.

Jean giggled.

"You're like the CIA's 'Dirty Harry', the detective in San Francisco, Clint Eastwood played long ago in the movies. Every dirty job gets funneled to you through your buddy, Paul."

"He had nothing to do with this, except the limo guy wanted to hire me to kill him."

"No way! He wanted you to blitz the CIA Director of the United States? Good Lord."

"That's not all, Rach. He was going to pay me twenty-five million to do it."

Rachel held silence for a moment. "Are you sure you're really all that friendly with Mr. Gilbrech?"

"You're getting to be quite the comedian, Mrs. McCarty. Paul claimed he would have killed himself for twenty-five mill."

The three of them enjoyed the dark humor for a moment.

"We shouldn't be talking like this in front of the Daughter of Darkness."

"I already gave Jean my word I wouldn't hide anything from her having to do with her safety. This has to do with all of us. It could be a real good time to go on tour in Washington though. I'll mention it to Ms. Kader tomorrow morning if Gus walks along and holds Deke. I'll help Jean get ahead of her assignments. She didn't miss a beat on the trip back East."

Nick saw they were drawing near their home. "Take a tour around the block. I want to check out the parked vehicles."

"On it, Muerto." Rachel steered past the house and up the steep block to the top and back down with Jean mimicking Nick's focus on vehicles. When they completed the block inspection Rachel drove into their garage after Nick opened the garage door by remote. "Was it clear?"

"I believe so. Let's close the garage door. I'll go in the house first. We can't be too careful. I know I could let Deke check first, but he's my beer buddy. I don't want him taking the first hit." Nick left the vehicle while checking the clip from his Colt. He ordered Deke to wait as he went in to check the house after disabling the alarm.

"Hey," Rachel called out. "I don't want you to take the first hit either, Muerto."

Jean made a snorting noise. "That'll be the day."

Nick returned moments later. "All is clear on the home front." Nick kissed Jean on the top of her head. "Right this way little missy to your bedroom. I will be awakening you early. Thanks for coming with your Mom tonight. It gave me that much more cover."

Jean threw her arm around the lower part of her face while going into a crouch. "The dangerous Dagger, Daughter of Darkness, saves the famous El Muerto."

"We're doomed," Rachel declared to the ceiling while putting the dangerous Dagger in a headlock on the way to the stairs.

"I don't know about you, Deke, but I could go for a couple of beers on the deck. Care to join me?"

At the word beer, Deke launched onto his hind legs hopping in tandem with Nick to the stairs. "I think you have a drinking problem, Fang. I may have to stage an intervention; but for tonight, we'll let it pass. Now, get back on all fours before you break something."

* * *

Nick escorted Jean with Deke on leash, past Gus holding the screen door for them.

"Did you hear what happened, Uncle Gus?"

"No. I couldn't drag the details from closed mouth Uncle John. I knew something happened from the fact he couldn't shut his mouth during our phone conversation. All he could say was 'you must go to the beach this morning, Payaso' over and over. We can't leave your Dad alone for ten minutes without missing an adventure. Are you ready for school, or did you ignore your studies all weekend?"

78

Jean rolled her eyes while taking Deke's leash. She adjusted her school pack. "Big chance of that. I had to work like a slave under El Muerto, with his minion, the Momster handling his light work."

"Keep talking, Dagger, and tonight you'll have a little writing exercise to perform called 'I will write it is wrong to disrespect my parents five hundred times'. You'll love that one. It's really fun. Is there any other verbal treasure you'd like to share with Uncle Gus?"

"The Daughter of Darkness has point." Jean lowered her head, and scampered with Deke down the walk.

"I see Jean is still working on her parental one liners."

"She has the adrenaline rush from last night running through her. I'm glad she slept as much as she did." Nick quickly went over the details, hitting all the high points in a matter of minutes while he and Gus trailed Jean and Deke.

"I'll say one thing for you, Muerto: when your life goes into the toilet, fifty hands reach for the flush handle."

"What? Leave it to you, Payaso – always looking at the negatives. I encounter the good fortune to uncover and end a plot to assassinate the United States CIA Director, who also happens to be a friend of ours, and you act like I walked into a wood chipper. I expect more from my sidekick, the deadly dangerous Payaso."

"Turn that record over, Muerto. You have a billionaire murderer pay his way to your family's front door, and you think the roses are in bloom? I don't think so. I can read between the lines, brother. You're wondering how many ears this guy whispered your personal info into before he went bye-bye. I bet Jerry loved your Kingpin of crime adjustment."

"Yes, he did. Jerry is a man who sees things in a more positive vein unlike you, my insidious sidekick."

"Insidious? Jerry only sees new limo, tools, and potential. I'm around you much more in the target zone." Gus put his hands to his temples, looking up. "I, the all-knowing Payaso see a hurriedly advanced road trip to Washington until the hometown fires burn down."

"Showoff."

"Heh... heh. The thug entries at dinner didn't sit well with the great El Muerto, huh? How close did you come to executing those two at the 'Grotto'?"

"That is of no concern to you, Payaso. I am thinking of moving the loyal El Kabong into your hallowed position as sidekick, and reducing you in rank to minion."

"Minions don't sail boats out on body disposal runs, Muerto."

"El Muerto has been contemplating the creation of a sacred thug burial ground in Carmel Valley. Muerto has all contingency plans in place to deal with disloyal minions."

Gus couldn't help humorous appreciation of the Muerto contingency declaration. "No way you dig potholes in your land in Carmel Valley for reformed terrorists and gangsters. Besides, you don't own a big enough piece of land. Enough of this minion stuff. When's Paul communicating with you on facts concerning the guy who very well might know about you: the NSA clown?"

"I know Paul. ASAP. When he knows, we'll know. We have to keep a low profile around here for the time being, because I have no idea how soon the cops will be asking questions about Formsby's whereabouts, or how many people he informed about his planned meeting with me."

"Did you believe the story Formsby meant only to entertain your family while he offered you the contract on Paul?"

"He planned to hold them hostage until I finished the job. The money he offered, and steady position as lead enforcer was bullshit. With twenty-five million, he could have hired a small army of mercenaries to kill Paul. Formsby wanted Paul gone, but I've pissed someone off too I don't know about. When I finished the job, I would have been killed or captured. Formsby would have then disposed of Rachel and Jean. I know you and John would have ripped the earth apart looking for us, but it would have been useless. We would simply have disappeared."

"Do you think it was Collister?"

"I doubt it. Formsby knew all about our Nassau hit on the water. That means someone was in my old boss Frank's confidence - someone who may have been in line to make a fortune from Stoddard and Fletcher dying, but only if Frank remained alive. We'll have to tear into Formsby's files Paul uncovers from the hits on Milty's holdings. I have all the memory cards from their phones and tablets. I uploaded the contents into the computer in my safe-room with no Internet or Bluetooth capability. I didn't want anything signaling outward during the transfer. I'll send those on to Paul this morning."

"Damn, Muerto, your ass is in the breeze on this one. We must have left a loose end somewhere on that damn op. It was a beauty. You knew Frank was going to nuke us from orbit. We certainly settled with him. He didn't look the type to give out info on a lark to anyone. Your boss Frank was a blackmailer to the first degree."

Nick kept silent, his hands clenching into fists. Gus noticed. "Uh oh. I don't know what you're thinking about, but it looks serious. Did you get a revelation?"

"I sure did, and I know exactly which two dodos in government to ask about the loose end I thought of. Thank you for that."

Five minutes passed without Nick saying another word, watching Jean skip along next to Deke. It proved too much for Gus. "Muerto! Are you going to tell me or not?"

"When I confirm it, I will. I'm trying to cool off my thermostat. Something like this requires a calm voice or I will get nowhere. US Marshals Stanwick and Reinhold will sense how pissed off I am if I talk to them now. They would instinctively know that if they were in front of me, I would shoot them in the head. They know me well enough they'd pack their bags and head for Fiji."

"That bad, huh?"

"Oh yeah. I have to talk with Jean's teacher about time off, and I don't want to talk to her after talking with my US Marshal buddies. The good news is I think we may have a candidate for loose end. This is what working with government agencies gets you. They seem all warm and fuzzy on the outside, but inside, they just don't give a crap. Details can kill us in this profession Gus – wrong details and left out details. Check out the school. What is this, mob day?"

"It looks like some kind of protest," Gus said. "Maybe I should hang back with Jean and Deke while you go in and chat with Ms. Kader. That way you can find out before we walk right into them with Jean."

"Agreed. Jean! Stay here with Gus until I sift through the mob, and find out why you have a crowd out in front."

"Okay, Dad. They don't look like parents. They're all shouting something."

"See Gus, even private elementary schools aren't exempt from dolts with nothing better to do. I wonder what the hell they're protesting. How's the lunch menu, Jean. Maybe they don't like the food."

Jean giggled. "The food's okay. Maybe I should take the day off."

"I don't think so. I'll be back."

"I heard that," Gus said. "Don't do any 'Terminator' stuff over there. You're in enough trouble as it is."

Nick waved off Gus. As he drew closer, the slogans shouted became clearer. Nick realized with confusion the crowd of about twenty people were protesting the American Flag on the pole in front of the school. He angled around the crowd with other parents dropping off their kids to see who was in front of the mob. A thin, dark skinned man, looking to be a couple inches taller than Nick's six foot height faced the mob calmly. Nick had noticed him taking his two boys to school before. He stood with his arms folded over chest in front of the flagpole, listening to the two men in front of him shouting in his face. Nick moved nearer to the flagpole exchange. The parent in front of the flagpole was blocking the crowd from cutting down the flag. The suited, olive skinned man arguing with him spoke with a distinctly Iranian accent, Nick recognized. The crowd edged nearer. Nick grinned. Sorry, Gus, he thought, I'll have to get a piece of this. Nick walked over next to the man in front of the pole.

The man glanced at Nick, ignoring his assailants. "Mr. McCarty. How are you, Sir? I've read all your novels. I thought about introducing myself a bunch of times. I'm Jim Amos. My boys attend school here."

"Just Nick." He shook hands with the parent. Nick raised his voice to be heard over the slogan shouters in front of them. "Nice to meet you, Jim. These people want to take down the flag, huh?"

Amos smiled. "Yeah, Nick, that's what they want to do. I read where you were in Delta. I'm still in the Marine reserves, and fought in the second Gulf War. No one tears the flag down here in front of my kids' elementary school unless they do it over my dead body."

"Our dead bodies, brother." Nick turned with folded arms next to Amos. "Do you know this idiot shouting at us in front, Jim?"

"Yeah... he's-"

"Did you just call me an idiot?!" The olive skinned man moved in front of Nick, poking his finger threateningly in Nick's chest, as the rest of the crowd quieted. "I am Dr. Habib Rashidi. We want this nationalistic symbol of oppression removed at once! America murders innocents all over the globe under this symbol of tyranny. It offends the undocumented immigrants, and progressive thinking citizens, who want nothing to do with the genocide committed under its obscene banner."

Nick smiled at the apoplectic Rashidi. "Gee, Doc, that's too bad. Maybe you should either stop looking at it, or get the hell out of our country."

A cheer went up from parents milling around the confrontational edges. Before Rashidi could speak, two women joined Nick and Jim. A slender brown haired woman walked in between Rashidi and Nick to shake hands with the two unmoving sentinels.

"Rita Gonzalez, Army, two tours Afghanistan."

"Welcome. I'm Nick McCarty. This is Jim Amos."

Rita continued over to stand at Amos's side, before facing the now nearly silent crowd. "No one messes with the flag... no one!"

The other auburn haired woman stood next to Nick. "Hi guys. Can I get a piece of this? I'm Ruth Gurkovsky, Air Force retired, Iraq and Afghanistan, brothers."

"Sure can, Sis." Nick noticed other men and women filling in around them.

Seeing his protest ripped away moment by moment, Rashidi began another finger poking session at Nick. Gurkovsky snatched his hand out of the air, and in seconds Rashidi was on his knees, face twisted in pain. "Didn't your mamma ever teach you it's rude to point? I assume she didn't. Take this lesson to heart, ass-wipe. Point again, and I rip it off, and shove it up your ass."

Ruth released him with enough of a push off to land Rashidi on his butt to the loudly cheering backers behind her. Police cars drove next to the confrontation with revolving light show, but turned off their sirens. Nick sighed, seeing Sergeant Dickerson approaching with five other officers behind him. Dickerson shook his head as the other officers strode in between the two groups. Nick gave him a little wave.

"I might have known. Would you care to explain this elementary school standoff, Nick?"

"Certainly, Officer Dickerson," Nick replied affably. "These people in front of us wanted to rip the American Flag down. My Marine buddy, Jim Amos, decided that could not be allowed. The rest of us agreed with his position, and joined him. Our kids actually go to this school. I have no idea who these anti-American, slogan shouting zombies are, except for the leader scrambling to his feet behind you. He told us his name was Dr. Habib Rashidi. The flag offends him."

Dickerson glanced at the surrounding flag sentinels. "Did Nick explain it correctly?"

A murmuring assent sounded in agreement.

"That's exactly how it happened, Sir," Jim Amos added.

"I have been assaulted in front of witnesses!" The raging Rashidi tried to brush by Dickerson, but was restrained by another police officer. "That woman attacked me!"

"That's a lie, Sergeant," Jim Amos said. "Big mouth was poking Nick in the chest, and Ruth restrained him. He fell on his butt. Boo Hoo! He's lucky I didn't adjust him like I wanted to. We wouldn't be listenin' to him crying like a two year old with a scuffed knee."

Laughter rang out, and Rashidi began shouting threats in Farsi. Nick called out tersely to him in the same language. Rashidi screamed and launched at Nick, his hands in claw form. Nick simply met him with a palm strike at diaphragm level, landing Rashidi once more on his back, but this time gasping for air in a fetal position.

Dickerson looked questioningly at Nick. "What did you say to him, Nick?"

"He was shouting threats in Farsi at Jim, and I told him that wasn't very nice."

Ruth Gurkovsky started laughing, patting Nick on the shoulder.

"Did you have something to add, Ma'am," Dickerson asked, reading between the lines.

"No... huh uh... I thought Nick was very restrained."

"Okay, I believe we've all had enough for one day," Dickerson said.

"Sergeant? Isn't it illegal to assemble in mob form for the express purpose of damaging private property? This is a private elementary school with children attending under twelve," Nick pointed out. "I would wager not one of these rent-a-mob people have ever had a child attend school here. I believe what they tried

86

to do here would fall under the category of reckless endangerment, wouldn't you say. I would like to press charges."

"Don't do this, Nick," Dickerson pleaded, as the other parents added their wishes to press charges.

Seeing Nick smile, but remain silent, Dickerson sighed and turned to the mob, some of whom had already slipped away. "I would like any parent of a child attending this school to step forward."

The mob remained motionless. "In that case, you will be charged for illegal assembly and child endangerment. None of you move! My officers will write citations for appearance later."

Dickerson then helped Rashidi to his feet, and hand cuffed the still gasping man, while reading him his rights. "Do you understand your rights as I have explained them?"

"Yes! This is not over!"

"You have the right to remain silent. Use it," Dickerson advised, turning toward Nick. "I see Gus, Jean, and Deke on the outskirts of the crowd, Nick. Can I have a word with you after you get done with school business?"

"Of course."

"Thank you. I'll deposit the instigator in the squad car. I'll meet you at the school entrance."

The sentinels remained, exchanging greetings and handshakes, with Ruth staying close to Nick.

"What did you really say to that guy, Nick," Jim Amos asked.

"Nick told him his mother sucked dicks in hell, and his father was a goat," Ruth answered for Nick, provoking wild laughter amongst the group.

"I was sort of hoping no one else spoke Farsi," Nick replied.

"Air Force intelligence." Ruth smiled. "Nice meeting you all."

The group said their goodbyes, and Nick joined Gus, Jean, and Deke.

"I'm impressed, Muerto," Gus said. "That was a relatively peaceful ending. I take it the Sergeant would like to talk with you."

"As soon as I get Jean into class, I'll have a word with him. I'm pressing charges against that flake leading this mob mess. Be right back, Payaso. C'mon Jean, we still have two minutes. It's a good thing we left early."

"Did those people really want to tear our flag down, Dad?" Jean followed Nick toward the school once again. "That's weird."

"The older you get, the more you understand human nature can never be fully understood. People will follow along behind something or someone for the most inane reasons imaginable, against all common sense and logic. I gave up a long time ago trying to figure it out. Aside from some of my known psychopathic tendencies, I do know right from wrong. I've been in enough places around the world to know this country and our flag deserve respect. If not respect, then you know me, I'll settle for fear."

"I'm going to join the Marines when I get out of school," Jean stated with conviction. "I'll need seasoning, and I can get that in the Corps."

Nick did a double take at the words, and saw Jean stifling laughter. "Good one. If you pull that on your Mom, you'll be in the Corps before you ever leave the house again."

"You'd let me join the Marines, wouldn't you?"

"I'd be forced to point out the advantages of a college degree, with which you could be anything you want, including a Marine officer, but I certainly wouldn't talk you out of serving your country."

"I thought you'd get a kick out of my Marine Corps seasoning piece. I put it together from a few movies. You probably think I'll join when I'm eighteen just so I can watch Mom's head explode, don't you?"

"Unfortunately, yes, that is exactly what I'm afraid you'll do. As a husband who has only recently stopped putting Jello in your Mom's slippers, it's bad form for me to lecture you on baiting your Mom in horribly creative ways. I do believe Quinn will be quite different than you, and will keep your Mom busy in a favorable way. Kids are usually polar opposites."

Jean waved at Nick as she walked by Dimah Kader, her teacher. "Don't worry, Dad. I'll train the little twerp to be a killer."

Startled, Nick took a step toward the classroom, but thought better of it as Jean turned, giggling while doing a touchdown celebration dance. Ms. Kader enjoyed the show.

"Jean is rather unique, is she not, Mr. McCarty?"

Nick shook the finger of fate at Jean while answering. "I guess you could use that word. I have to quickly ask you about taking Jean on another book tour with me in Washington State. It will probably be within a week or two. I promise to stay in touch and tutor her the entire time."

"It will be quite all right. You saved my life. I will make it all right. Besides, Jean was actually ahead of the class when she returned from your Boston tour. You followed my guidelines to perfection."

"Your class syllabus on-line is very clear with the assignments. I don't have to do much to keep Jean in line on her studies. If I could keep her from driving her Mom crazy, that would be nice."

"She is very well behaved and confident in class."

"So that's where all the good behavior goes. Anyway, thanks for your understanding. I'll let you know the dates we'll be gone as soon as possible."

"I...I saw what you did outside. That was very brave."

"Nope. My motto is, when in doubt, always follow the Marines. Your Marine should be coming home soon, isn't he?"

"Yes," Dimah replied with excitement. "I hope to hear when for sure in the next few weeks. He wants to meet you when he comes home."

"I'd be honored. I'll let you get to work. Thanks again."

"Of course."

Sergeant Dickerson met him at the school entrance as promised. "I see you've kept an amiable relationship with Ms. Kader. Killing that psycho relative of hers in the hallway of the school before he could do an 'honor killing' on her butt must have made an impression, huh?"

"She didn't deserve to die for being engaged to a Marine overseas, and I didn't kill anyone. His weapon went off during the struggle, part of which I was unconscious for, if you remember."

"I remember, Nick. I also remember you stopping the other two family members who tried to take you out at your home."

"Old news now, my friend. What's on your mind today? Did you get my musings on the muggers messing with our older tourist crowd?"

"Yep. Did you happen to hear or read the news item about four dead bad guys, whom we know by rushed DNA samples are the ones responsible for the muggings around here?"

"I've been writing my new novel, Neil. I have a book tour to prepare for in Washington State too. I barely have enough time to enjoy my usual beach walk, and help Jean with her homework. I don't have any spare moments for the news. Hell, half the time, the media makes it up anyway. That works out pretty well for you with those guys being found short of breath. Who popped them?"

"No one popped them. They were all killed with a knife."

"Kinky. Well... nice chatting with you. Thanks for the update. I'll erase my mugger notes if they're already out of the picture."

"Nick." Dickerson clasped Nick's arm. "I have a feeling if I could access your file, which I have tried to do, it would read expert in hand to hand combat with a knife."

"Probably," Nick replied. "I was also my team's sniper. Are you hinting at something, Neil? I realize since we've met, Pacific Grove has experienced more than its share of trouble, but don't you think all small touristy towns go through cycles like that. I certainly didn't entice four banditos into coming here to mug old people."

"True, but did you end them?"

"Oh, I get it. Now I'm like the Charles Bronson character in the 'Death Wish' movies, huh? Does this mean you don't want me to continue as Pacific Grove Police Department's 'Castle'? I did buy you the neat coffee machine."

"Much appreciated. I notice you didn't answer the question."

"Why would I bother typing profiles and musings about the muggers to send you if I had already killed them?"

"Because you're smart, and I suspect, one of the most deadly people I'll ever be around. I wanted you to know not to think I'm some braindead flatfoot without some powers of deduction."

Nick shrugged. "Gee, Officer Dickerson, if I'm that dangerous, maybe you shouldn't associate with me. And here, all this time, I thought we were becoming good buddies. I have to go write some pulp fiction. If there's nothing else you need to discuss, call me when the DA decides whether to pull on his big boy pants, and prosecute that idiot Rashidi and his crew."

Dickerson chuckled. "Although you couldn't know it, the DA is very much the type to shirk his duty in this case. It would not be a good idea, if our fearless DA punts this down the road, for anything bad to happen to Dr. Rashidi, Nick."

The Terminator surfaced for a moment, and Dickerson noticed. "What would be very bad is for Rashidi to do anything besides go away, and forget he ever saw me."

"I understand." Dickerson backed away from the entrance door. "Thanks for looking into the mugger case for me. I'll try not to bother you again. You wouldn't mind if I did ask for your opinion though once in a while, would you? With your connections to all the alphabet soup agencies, you're a handy informational source."

Nick was silent for a moment, studying Sergeant Dickerson. "I don't mind, Neil, but if I become the focus of police business, it will make me unhappy."

"I...I get that. Thanks." Dickerson held out his hand and Nick shook it. "I'll call if I need anything from you on the Rashidi mess."

"Until then... until then," Nick replied, walking off, still curious as to whether Dickerson was playing him or not.

While Deke sniffed at everything within reach of his extended leash's limit, Gus awaited Nick with grim visage. "That looked like a very solemn conversation, even through the entrance door window. Is your buddy Neil upset with you?"

"He's more than suspicious, as befits any thinking police officer. I knew the mugger action would push the envelope. Assholes maiming old people after they work their butts off all their lives so they can enjoy taking time to do things like visit the ocean really hit one of my hot buttons." Nick started walking home after taking Deke's leash, with Gus striding next to him. "Neil and I needed a cooling off period anyway. If the PD stays busy with the poor old muggers' tragic end, maybe we'll get some space between our new freezer guests from last night and me. That will get a little tricky, because I don't see any way Paul can thwart at least a preliminary investigation once Formsby's minions send out smoke signals their exalted leader is missing."

"I don't see Paul giving you problems on a sanction involving a guy trying to have him killed. He may be a bit more than amused if he needed to step into our vigilante business with the muggers. The beach really will be nice this morning. Are you still on the wagon?"

"After last night? I don't think so. We're still right on time too. After we load my writing utensils and our refreshments, I'll check on sleeping beauty. I'm glad Rach decided to start her maternity leave. I think the last month she's been running on empty. She was perky last night with our uninvited dinner guests. Anyway, I'd like to sip a couple down at Carol's beach before I contact my US Marshal nitwits. If I have a buzz going, maybe I won't say something rude when I talk with them."

"I know better than to comment on that attitude adjustment, but I will be interested in what the hell you think they did. Was it a sin of omission, or are they undermining you at the DOJ?

"We had an agreement about a player to be named later, and they didn't follow through on the deal. I won't accuse them of it, but I believe it's a dead bang certainty they never got the traitor at Los Alamos, Pence Didricson. Remember how I told you I'd let the FBI and the US Marshals deal with him? Well, that was a mistake. I keep telling you about loose ends, yet here I am dealing with my own."

"Didricson should be in a maximum security prison with no hope of parole, and no contact with the outside world." Gus paused, thinking along the lines Nick mentioned. "This is bad. I heard the mention of loose ends instead of end. You think someone else you let live has been painting a target on your back too?"

"I suspect that the other US Marshal target I helped Timmy and Grace capture to rat out the DOJ informer, named Uthman Sadun, is behind this Formsby mess. I haven't got the details worked out in my head, but those three networked somehow, and I'm going to find out how. It's always best to go straight to the source of suspected misery."

"You wouldn't kill Grace and Tim, would you?"

Nick met Gus's gaze as they walked. "No, but I'm glad you consider it worth asking. I don't want you thinking I'm turning into a Care Bear."

"Your reputation is safe with me, Muerto. You do attend Lamaze classes with Rachel though once a week. That threw my murder meter calibration off on the Muerto alarm."

"Those classes are a joke. I've delivered two babies, one in Afghanistan, and one in Morocco. When the pain hits, I don't care if it's Wonder Woman giving birth to Batman's baby, no amount of

huffing and puffing while ordering her to breathe works. It's a feel good thing like giving hugs – for a few seconds, the hugger feels important, and the huggee feels loved. The pain hits, and all bets are off."

"You delivered two babies? Good God in heaven. Why in the world haven't you ever told me that? The deadliest killer on earth bringing new life into the world. If that didn't give the cosmos a heart attack of imbalance, I don't know what would."

"One of them I delivered during a firefight, where I had to play sniper in between contractions. The Mom was the wife of an Afghan soldier we were training. The midwives of the village wouldn't come near her, because they figured rightly if the Taliban found out, they'd be toast. I got a twofer on that delivery."

"What the hell does that mean? What'd you get?"

"The Mom named the baby after me, and gave me the name of the head Taliban asshole in the region. I took off that night while little Nicholas Wardak slept peacefully in the arms of his Mom. I blew the head off Emil Balkhi when he popped out of his shack to take a whizz. When I followed taking poor old Emil out with picking his crew off one by one at night, they stopped fooling around with the villagers, and sued for peace with us. They logically figured if they didn't become allies, I would just hang around shooting them in the head until we didn't need any more allies."

"In case I've never mentioned this, Muerto, you are a very bad man."

"But Payaso, I brought little Nick into this world."

"Somehow, that loses its soothing effect when you kill how many?"

"Uh… fifteen."

"Madre de Dios!"

"Calm down, Payaso. Let's focus here. We were talking about Lamaze classes with Rachel. I'm telling you they don't work, but I know what to do that will: guaranteed."

"I'm afraid to ask what that might be, but go ahead, enlighten me."

"Pressure points. I know them all. When the contractions start making Rach scream, I'll apply pressure to the nerve at the base of her neck while huffing and puffing shouting 'breathe' in her face. She'll pass out, until Quinn decides to make his appearance. Easy-Peasy."

"Madre de Dios!"

* * *

Rachel met them at the door. "Guess what, Muerto, your school confrontation made the news. I was checking for a bulletin on your escapade last night as you asked for, and surprise, El Muerto defends the flag at our own little grammar school."

"In my defense, I backed the Marines. There is no downside to doing that. Plus, I met a lot of vets who had been keeping to themselves. If the clip goes national, I'll sell another million books. C'mon, Gus. Let's get our beach visit equipment ready. We can't keep John waiting."

"I'm going with you." Rachel followed Nick and Gus into their kitchen. "I need a good walk this morning."

"Okay, but I'm not running for the car today. Gus, can you drive our car down to the beach parking lot. Then we'll have transportation for emergency bathroom runs. The Princess can drive down the street to the golf course, and use the bathroom there."

"Good solution, Muerto," Rachel said. "I'll get dressed. Thanks, Gus."

"My pleasure," Gus said as Rachel turned to walk toward the stairs. "I exercised on the Dagger walk to school. Plus, as you know, there was entertainment this morning. I'm not required to do two more hours in the gym like Muerto does. Driving down to the beach with the chairs, and refreshments works for me."

"You talk like I drive somewhere. You can work out with me in my gym right here. I won't even charge you a fee."

"No thanks, Muerto. I'm good. I want to see Rachel's reaction when you tell her about your pressure point baby delivery scheme though, so I'll hang around until she gets dressed. Take your time, Rach."

Rachel's eyes narrowed. "What pressure point baby delivery scheme?"

Nick quickly goosed her in the direction of the stairs. "Never mind. It was a joke. Now hurry and get dressed, or the McCarty Express will leave without you."

"Okay, but I'm getting my answer some time this morning about what the hell a pressure point baby delivery is."

Nick waited until Rachel reached the top of their stairs. He then poked a forefinger in Gus's chest as his partner enjoyed the blindside hit on Nick. "Have you ever had a kidney transplant, Payaso?"

"You know I haven't."

"Want one?"

* * *

The weekday morning hosted only a few sporadic stops from tourists on Carol's beach. Off leash, Deke streaked up and down the beach as the usual scavenger birds arrived, screeching at the happily annoying dog. Deke stopped his beach patrol only if spotting the small creatures popping out from between the rocks. Settled into a comfortable beach chair, enjoying the light gray cast day with no wind, Nick sipped his Irish coffee while contemplating his beach companions' mood. He felt another rising tide of trouble on the horizon. Weighing his fascination with the violent comedy he had made of Gus's El Muerto label, Nick didn't think he could let go of it, exposure or not. Muerto haunted every mission he considered. He guiltily remembered nearly deciding to attribute the mugger action to El Muerto, endangering everyone in his small group of family and friends.

Gus kept glancing over at his friend with a perturbed look. "I know what you're thinking Muerto. You're becoming as predictable as an old comic book plot."

"Contrary to what I'm sure were evil thoughts on your part, Payaso, I am merely sipping my beverage, watching Deke romp around, and enjoying the grains of sand on the beach."

"Gag me… what you're thinking about is going on the tour, and taking on the 'Seattle Ripper' as El Muerto. It's not enough to take on an Isis terrorist group, you can't wait to don the mask for a 'Ripper' post mortem video."

Realizing among the other thoughts from a moment ago, that he indeed had been plotting action against the 'Ripper' as El Muerto, Nick frowned at Gus. "How dare you think such dastardly assumptions without evidence, Payaso?"

"I knew it," Gus stated with confidence, relaxing in his chair. "You pull the outrage card whenever I hit the nail on the head in predictions. Did you get the blood out of your mask from our excursion the other night?"

"None of your business," Nick replied, seeing Gus's nearly clairvoyant observation amused his other companions. I'm really getting sloppy, Nick thought. He stood, putting aside his empty cup. "I need to call the Marshals while I'm still in a good mood, only slightly ruined by Payaso's 'Mentalist' act."

"Take it easy on them, Nick," Rachel urged, leaning forward, nearly spilling her tea as she grabbed Nick's hand. "They were with us from the start."

"Only one thing wrong with your logic, my dear. If what I suspect is true, they came very close to ending us, and are now allowing the danger to exist without a warning. I simply wish to know why. Drink your tea. Tim and Grace will survive."

"Promise?" Rachel's features betrayed her bleak knowledge of exactly what her husband was capable of.

"I promise." Nick patted her shoulder, and walked away with his specially crafted phone for secure calls in hand. Tim answered the phone on the first ring.

"Nick? You must be telepathic. We planned to contact you today. The AG doesn't care how you stop the 'Ripper'. Let us know when you can get into the area with us."

"We need to talk over another unfortunate glitch in our relationship, Timmy."

"Ah… I'll put you on speaker. Grace is here with me."

"Hey psycho," Grace acknowledged the connection.

"We had a deal concerning Pence Didricson. He's still at Los Alamos, isn't he?"

Nick's mouth tightened during the silence on the line. "Yep. That's what I thought. There's been a very dangerous result from my not knowing Pence was still in play."

Nick tersely explained Formsby's attempt on his family. He also outlined his suspicions concerning a thread between

Didricson, Uthman Sadun, and Formsby. "What I suspect is Formsby footed the bill for a law team to represent Sadun. Then he connected with Didricson backed by a lot of money. In their small circle I'm sure my name circulated in reference to the name gathering foray I did on behalf of the DOJ with Sadun, and finding proof of Didricson's espionage acts. Now, I have an ongoing problem, kids. What do you think I should do about it, other than shoot both of you in the head?"

Tim was the first to speak. "We…we need to make some calls, Nick. Let us track some details concerning your suspicions."

"I'll allow that, Timmy. First though, explain why I didn't receive a warning, especially about Didricson. Make your answers concise, truthful, and to the point. You know I'll find out if I get fed bullshit. If you take that path, then let the games begin."

"We couldn't do shit to Didricson," Grace admitted. "Thanks to your info, we had him cold on espionage. What we didn't know when the FBI took him into custody is that he had gathered incriminating evidence concerning the DOJ, and the FBI's handling of over a dozen terrorist cases. All the convictions would have been thrown out if Didricson's blackmail file was revealed. The bastard even worked it so he gets an office, and although no classified information ever crosses his desk, he draws a six figure salary."

"And I was not told about this why?"

"We were ordered not to speak of Didricson to you under any circumstances. If we did, we were warned we'd be fired, and arrested for revealing classified information, which was exactly what we were trying to charge Didricson for," Tim answered. "We never dreamed anything like the Formsby scenario would surface. Grace and I would have quit rather than put Rachel and Jean's lives in jeopardy. Before we go on with this, let Grace and I investigate how and if Sadun actually did get involved in this."

"You could have trusted me to help with this problem, kids. I don't just think outside the box, I am outside the box completely."

"It's too late to say we're sorry, Nick," Grace replied. "We'll go find every thread, and call you back."

"Until then." Nick disconnected. He saw Rachel staring at him. The concern in her features reassured him Rachel had no illusions he had magically transformed into the Easter Bunny.

"How'd it go?"

"Pretty well, Rach." Nick accepted a fresh Irish coffee from John. "They're going to trace down connections between the imprisoned Uthman Sadun, Formsby, and the Los Alamos guy, Pence Didricson."

Nick explained the complications, and why they left him out of the loop. "The way I figure it, no one asked Pence in the correct manner. Once he understands the severity of what he's done, I'm certain he'll help us in any way he can."

"Sucks to be him," Gus said.

"Luckily, I did my homework on Didricson before I lost common sense, logic, and apparently my survival instinct. Pence is quite the social guy. He keeps his Facebook current, and Twitters everywhere he goes as if he's a Kardashian, and someone cares. In this instance, someone does care. Pence frequents The Ghostrider's Tavern three or four times a week. I know he owns a late model BMW. I'll hack the entry code, and get a key. Los Alamos is too tricky an interrogation site. I'll drive his BMW to Carmel Valley, where I'll have more time to find out all about the blackmail file scaring the crap out of the DOJ."

"If you don't need me on this one, I think I'll go to bed early," Dan said.

"I agree," Nick replied, while checking the Twitter feed on his phone. "We've been burning your candle with a flame thrower lately. This is a long drive there, and back. We might miss our window of opportunity too, but I'm feeling lucky today. Pence hasn't missed a Monday night at the Ghostrider's Tavern in over a month. He never went home earlier than eleven on any Monday night he's been there."

"Do you want Jean and me in the safe-room?"

"Absolutely. Pence is only the first loose end. I'll need to involve Tim and Grace in my next loose end adjustment. He doesn't know it yet, but Uthman Sadun will be receiving a transfer into US Marshal custody as an advisor on a cold case. I'm afraid he won't make it to his destination. That's in the near future. For tonight, anyone interested in a ride along with me, pack a bag. I'll need either Payaso or Kabong to drive my car home. I'll stick with the Uthman's BMW."

"I will go," John said.

"Count me in," Gus added.

Rachel sighed, leaning back in her chair, looking peacefully at the clearing sky. "It's a good thing I stopped at Walmart. We were running low on the big black plastic garbage bags and duct tape."

Her shopping restock statement drew appreciative laughter from Gus and John.

"You're getting to be quite the comedian, Rach," Nick commented. "I'm sure you recall how our supply of duct tape got low."

Rachel straightened again, pointing warningly at Nick. "You'd best not be contemplating any repeats of my being duct taped into bed, Muerto. It won't go well for you."

"Of course not, my dear. I have put such childish things behind me."

"No Jello ever again either."

Silence, except for the snorting amusement of Gus and John.

"Muerto!"

"You drive a hard bargain," Nick mumbled. "What's in it for me?"

"I'll forget I heard anything about 'pressure point baby deliveries'.

"Deal."

Chapter Five

Loose Ends

Gus thumbed at the parking lot behind them. "Uh oh."

Nick turned to see Sergeant Dickerson straighten away from the driver's seat of his squad car and signal for Nick. "Mentioning duct tape and Jello was a bad Karma move, Rach. See what happens when you throw the cosmos out of balance with accusations and innuendo?"

"Yeah, I'm really sure Sergeant Dickerson looks like someone shot his dog because of my mentioning horrible practical jokes from your past... oh wait... I hear the Karma train pulling into the station... maybe this is about your insensitive treatment of the poor woman who married you."

Nick enjoyed Rachel's upbraiding along with Gus and John, but kept his eyes on Dickerson as he handed over his Irish coffee to Rachel. "I bet I can guess this one. Formsby decided to haunt me one last time before Paul erases any thread connecting us. Don't throw away my Irish, Hon."

"I'll think about it, Mr. Jello. The wind tends to blow the sand around though."

Nick stopped. "There's no wind today, Rach."

"Just sayin'."

At Dickerson's squad car, Nick made a friendly wave gesture. "Neil. You must really like me today. Too much coffee from the new machine I bought the PD, huh?"

"Step inside my office for a moment, Nick. I have another matter to discuss with you about your dinner last night at 'The Grotto'."

"Sure." *Bingo*! Nick slipped into the squad car's front passenger seat, a questioning look on his features as he met Dickerson's gaze before closing the door. "You did want me in the front, right?"

"Close the door. Do you know a man named Milton Formsby?"

"You already know I do."

"Formsby's people said he had a meeting scheduled with you last night at 'The Grotto', and he never returned from the meeting. In their words, 'it's like he vanished'. Also missing are his two bodyguards, who you accompanied to his limousine. Would you like to tell me about it?"

"Absolutely. Two guys interrupted a very nice dinner I was enjoying with Rachel and Jean, insisting on all of us meeting with their boss in the parking lot. I explained that would not be possible, but I'd be happy to go along with them. They reluctantly agreed, and I followed them to the limo. Milton Formsby introduced himself. He then offered me a large amount of money to ghost write his autobiography. I explained I don't write any nonfiction under any circumstances. I hate that genre, especially autobiographies. He was disappointed, but Formsby could tell I would not change my mind. I had him drop me off at my friend John's place that I own in the Carmel Valley. Formsby mentioned he owned an estate somewhere in the Valley."

"Did he mention where he was going after he dropped you off?"

"No, but I assumed he was going home," Nick replied.

Dickerson shook his head, gripping the steering wheel. "This isn't going away, Nick. Formsby's people want a complete investigation. I was ordered to locate Formsby no matter what."

"Have you pinged his cell, or the limo GPS gizmo?"

"Of course. Nothing at all from either," Dickerson answered. "How does a limousine, its owner, and two bodyguards suddenly disappear after talking briefly with you about a writing assignment?"

"I don't know, Neil. Formsby never said what he did for a living, or why anyone would be interested in reading a book about him. Maybe I should have taken the gig. He probably wanted a lot of fiction thrown in as filler."

"When are you going on the book signing thing in Washington? Soon, I hope."

"Pretty soon. I still have to make a few more arrangements with my agent. Are you telling me to get out of town?"

"No. I know we won't be the only ones looking at the video footage from last night. If Formsby doesn't reappear soon, there will be others investigating his disappearance."

"Well okay, thanks for the warning. I'll be within reach," Nick said. "I'm only going to Washington State. You have my cell number. Call me anytime if you have questions, or some other organization needs to hear my story."

"Will do. I'm glad you have friends in all the government organizations. I think such connections will come in handy right now. It may be as soon as tomorrow if we don't find a clue as to where he is."

"I'll be here," Nick replied, wondering whether he could zip down to Los Alamos, snatch Didricson, stash him in the Carmel Valley interrogation center, and get home in time for unwanted company. Nick exited the squad car, trying to decide if he wanted to find out. "I hope you locate him, and all this is just a misunderstanding."

"I doubt it, but I guess we can hope. See you later."

Nick rejoined Rachel and friends, plunking down in the beach chair, and accepting his Irish coffee from Rachel again. He cautiously took a sip, hoping it was only cool, and not gritty.

"I didn't sand it down, Muerto. Was it what you expected?"

"Yep. The powers that be are climbing all over Neil a day earlier than I thought. I hope Paul gets to work on my cover up. I can't blame him for being slow on the draw with the cam footage gathered at the Wharf. If the PD moved that quickly and thoroughly on the muggers, El Muerto, Payaso, Ka Bong, and Geezer could have sipped cocktails on the deck instead of baiting traps to save old people. Where is the justice? Now, I'll have to really push on the Pence. The only upside to this travesty is if I can pull off this caper, there's no way they would tie in his disappearance with me, because of the degree of difficulty."

"You mean impossibility," Rachel replied. "That's over a three hour drive one way. It will take seven hours, there and back, if you don't want to be pulled over with him in your trunk. That doesn't take into consideration locate and snatch time. It makes my head hurt imagining the complications. Now I understand why I hate going to the beach with you bozos. I could be on the couch eating bonbons, and watching movies. No damn wonder I never see my bestie Tina down here in Depressionville."

By the time Rachel finished, her male companions, all but Dan, were humming violin concertos, while making gestures they were playing invisible violins. Nick stopped his violin playing pantomime. "Sorry, Rach. Now you know why we drink when we come down here."

"I'm glad to be out of this road trip," Dan said. "I think Rachel's right. You guys are nuts to try this. Nick can wait a few days before going after Didricson."

"You're forgetting the impossibility factor," Nick reminded him. "If Neil points somebody my way, and I answer the door at home, I'm golden for anything connected with Didricson disappearing. Don't sweat it though. I'll abort the mission if too many things happen messing with success. I admit I'm anxious to get Pence. He's the key between Sadun and Formsby. Anything Tim and Grace find for me, threading the names together, will give Paul more leeway to protect me. Pence is the daily double for me, selling out the country, while blackmailing the government. If he had been smart, Pence would have taken his ill-gotten gains, and fled into Mexico. He could have bought a new identity down there, and went anywhere he wanted."

"I wish you luck." Dan stood. "I'm walking to the house, and start my time off with a nap. Please call me tomorrow morning to let me know you goofballs made it back in one piece."

"Okay, Dan. I resent the 'goofball' tag though, partner." Nick watched as Dan didn't turn. He simply waved. Deke ran to him as if to find out where Dan was going. Dan petted him roughly, and told him to stay.

"Dan's okay, isn't he," Rachel asked.

"He's never going to be okay. Dan's been helpful, and we give him enough to do and worry about to fill some of his hours. For now, that's all we can do. I'm glad he wants to go with us to Washington. I know we'll keep him busy there. Plus, getting away from here won't hurt him any either. God only knows what it feels like to live in the house where he and Carol were together for over four decades."

Rachel stared off at the ocean. "You're right. I know I don't want to imagine it."

"Let's go home. I need to wash Deke off, and get to work on entry codes. Then I have to see if my man Jerry can use another car."

"When do you want to leave?" John began gathering their beach paraphernalia.

"We'll leave about 6 pm. That'll give us some leeway in case we hit any traffic. I'll get some sleep before I pick Jean up from school."

"Do you have an approach in mind at the bar?"

"We're going to use the Frank approach, John."

"The what?"

"He gets the entry codes to Pence's BMW, waits for him in the backseat, and sticks him with a needle after Pence gets comfy in the driver's seat," Gus explained. "Nick's old boss, Frank Richert tried to sanction us. He thought he was invincible too, until Muerto showed him the error of his ways."

"That guy was evil, John," Rachel added. "Not El Muerto level evil... but evil."

"Hey... I think I resent that."

* * *

"Are you sure you don't want me to meet you at closing. I can go into work anytime I want now," Pence Didricson explained to the blonde waitress serving his drink while putting a twenty dollar bill on the bar. "C'mon, Nat, give me a chance. I have money. I'm not hard to look at, and I have a great job."

Natalie Montrose spread the fake smile she reserved for annoying customers she didn't like across her features. The twenty-four year old developed a bad case of the creeps whenever she came near the man across the bar. She didn't know why, but there was something off about him. "I've heard your resume before, Pence. I'm glad you're doing well, but I have a boyfriend."

"Not like me," Pence said, pushing the change back at Natalie. "Keep it. Think about it. I'm not going anywhere soon. You and I could have a lot of fun together."

"I'm sure we could, but I really do have a serious boyfriend, and he's the jealous type," Natalie lied. "Thanks very much for the tip."

Didricson watched Natalie move to another customer at the bar, his eyes narrowing. The familiar tightness, rejection of any kind caused, gripped him in a fist clenching moment. Pence relaxed, recovering with a large gulp down of his drink, while checking his watch. It read nearly 11 pm. He glanced at Natalie once more, thinking he would settle with her one night after closing, when no one was around. She would learn all about fun. No one would miss one more bimbo behind the bar.

He finished his drink, and walked out of The Ghost Riders Tavern. There had only been two other customers, which was normal for a late Monday night. He unlocked his BMW using his remote. Didricson suppressed instant annoyance at the fact he was boxed in by two other vehicles in a nearly empty parking lot. Cursing as he slipped through the small opening possible without his door hitting the car next to him, Didricson's lanky form settled in comfortably. Pence ran his hands through his long blonde hair with only a hint of receding hairline, while checking his appearance in the lighted mirror.

"You look lovely, Pence," a voice said from directly behind him, as Didricson felt a sharp stabbing pain in his neck. "What... the hell?" Black shadows swept over his consciousness. An irresistible numbness seeped into his suddenly unmovable limbs. "Why?"

"Because you've been a very bad boy," the voice informed him. It was the last sound he heard for hours after.

* * *

Nick reached to the side of the BMW's driver's seat. He used the switch to power the seat all the way back, and then did the opposite to the passenger seat, leaving him enough room to slide onto Didricson's lap. After tilting the wheel all the way upward, Nick fastened the seat belt, started the car, and drove away, stopping only when he reached the darkened outskirts of Los Alamos. John parked at an angle behind him, hiding the trunk from view. Seconds later, Didricson had black plastic garbage bags over his five foot, eight inch frame, one over his head, and one drawn up over his legs with his mouth, arms, and legs duct taped. Nick added duct tape around the bottom, center, and chest high bag positions. Only then did he tear a breathing area around Didricson's nose. He hit the BMW trunk release. John and Gus helped him throw the bound body inside the trunk.

"Drive carefully, guys – not too slow, and not too fast. I'll wait ten minutes before I follow. I don't want us to look like we have a convoy."

"Payaso doesn't know how to drive any other way," John remarked. "He's driving home, so you have nothing to fear from us other than driving boredom, Muerto."

Gus clipped John in the back of the head as he stumbled toward the passenger side of their vehicle. "Smartass!"

"See you in the Valley, guys," Nick said. "John's right, Payaso. Not too slow, Grandma Gus."

Gus flipped him off without comment, and a moment later drove away as Nick entered the BMW once more. So far, so good, Nick mused, noticing he would have a few hours if they made it home shortly after 3 am to find out if he only needed one interrogation session. "I think I'll open you for interrogation in my special room. We'll even put our costumes on with the light show, and eerie music for you, Pence. You'll love it... at least for a few moments, when at last you'll realize the special room will be the last place you ever visit. I do hope you're smart enough to blurt out the truth for me. I might get a few hours of sleep before the Feds come knocking on my door."

Nick continued to talk with the unconscious Didricson most of the way home. By the time he reached his place in Carmel Valley, John had turned on the spotlight shining on the entrance to the hidden below grounds subbasement interrogation area. Nick and his crew made sure they didn't make any permanent paths forming to the stand of trees where the entrance was located. Nick had installed a decorative Gazebo structure half way between the house and his subbasement, so he could have a stone pathway part way to the subbasement. Nick drove the BMW into his garage, and John closed the door.

"Hi guys." Nick popped the trunk. "We made good time. I was telling Pence we would be getting into costume in my special room for him. I explained to him I had been informed by my US Marshal pals of definite threads linking him with both Sadun and Formsby."

Gus looked in the trunk. "You've been talking to an unconscious guy wrapped in black plastic bags and duct tape all the way from Los Alamos?"

"I was warming him up." Nick plucked Didricson out of the trunk, and shouldered his bulk with impressive ease. "Pence is very considerate too. He didn't interrupt me, or make smartass comments, like some of my friends tend to do."

Gus and John both enjoyed Nick's admonishment as they followed him out to the subbasement entrance. "I'm glad you guys think this is funny. I have to prepare and question Pence before I take the BMW to Jerry at 4 am."

"Don't rush, Muerto," Gus said as they descended into the lower level. "I can take it over to Jerry. How much do you want to give him?"

"It's another last minute rush job, so he gets the car, and twenty-five thousand. Lately, Jerry's becoming the most important outside contact we have. I can't wait until we get Pence situated on a gurney, and I bring him out of his snooze time. I bet he'll be surprised."

"Either that, or he'll have a stroke, and die right on the table when a vein in his head bursts like a water filled balloon," Gus replied.

"Don't ruin this for John, Payaso. This is his first time seeing the special room in action. It's a very intricate tool for obtaining information quickly, John."

"It's actually a horrifying nightmare of unending torment, birthed in a mind so twisted, you'll be glad we haven't eaten since early last night."

"I look forward to yet another new experience in the war against the forces of evil."

Gus patted John's shoulder. "Good one, John. Keep those happy thoughts in mind. You'll need them once Nick activates his insanity room."

Gus and John took Didricson's wrapped form from Nick, laying it on the nearest gurney.

"I am sure Muerto only uses this extreme solution for gathering information from very bad and deserving miscreants," John stated.

"Actually, the last two people treated to a special showing of the room were the parents of Jean's best friend. She directed Muerto to solve the problem of the parents dealing drugs out of their house. Muerto cured them of that bad habit in one therapy session here in the manmade Seventh Level of Hell."

"I think that's enough of your unenlightened perceptions of my holding facility, Payaso. I'll put Pence through his paces for an hour, and see what I can get him to share with us. You guys get him stripped down, and I'll start the music."

* * *

Didricson awoke in a sweat, his head throbbing. He couldn't move a muscle. Every movable part was strapped tightly to the gurney. Blinking at the images of torture and mutilation depicted everywhere by ultraviolet lighting, Pence called out loudly to be heard over the eerie music playing in surround sound around him.

"Hello... where am I? What do you want? Please... let me go." He watched as three men, two with black masks, and one with a hideous clown mask, approached him with white gloves, shining under the black-light. "Is...is this some kind of joke? Why are you holding me here? I have money. We can make a deal."

"No deals," Nick said. "We'll start with something simple. I've been informed you've been blackmailing the justice department. Apparently, you have information stored away, making some very important people nervous. You're using it, threatening to release it if you are bothered in any way. Like an arrogant idiot, you even made them allow you to continue working at Los Alamos. I want to know where the information is, and I want you to describe it to me."

Hope surged through Didricson. "You bastards think you can scare me. I have a deal. No one touches me. If I get killed, hurt, or even sick, every major breakthrough we've had at Los Alamos will be released around the world."

"I see," Nick said. "Let me explain something to you, Pence. When the DOJ gets in a hole they can't dig their way out of, they call me. Once I take a contract, I find out everything they want to know, and solve every problem in the contract. They don't

114

know where I am, what I plan to do, or whom I plan to kill. They want your blackmailing operation ended, the information safely in their hands, and every contact you've been selling the United States out to revealed for their viewing pleasure."

Nick walked alongside Didricson's gurney, within reach of the surgical instrument tray near the gurney. He held out his hand without looking away from Didricson, palm up. "Scalpel please, Payaso."

Gus moved next to him, and slapped a scalpel into the palm of Nick's extended hand. Nick deftly made a shallow incision from Didricson's ribcage to his groin. Gus took the scalpel as Pence screamed.

Nick held out his hand again. "Formula please, Kabong."

John handed him a bottle from the instrument tray with a large eyedropper top, and Clorox marked in black felt marker on the front label. Nick then used the eyedropper to dribble Clorox bleach into the open wound. By the time Nick finished covering the wound, no doubt remained as to whether Pence would help or not. In the next fifteen minutes, Didricson between cries of utter agony, explained every step to take in order to retrieve the drive. Instead of going on, Nick called Paul immediately after, leaving Pence to writhe on the gurney.

"What's that noise," Paul asked.

"Oh… sorry. Wait one." Nick moved away from Pence. "I found out exactly how to retrieve the drive Didricson is blackmailing the DOJ with. I know better than to hand it over to those boobs. Each of these steps must be followed precisely, or it triggers the release of materials. I'd tell you who, but Pence hired an anonymous contractor."

"Maybe he does know, and you haven't found the right method to get the name."

"Did you just insult me?" Nick glanced on the other side of the room where Didricson screamed and begged to be able to tell everything he knew.

Paul chuckled. "I'll get this done right now. Do you need confirmation?"

"Absolutely. My informant is anxious to help, and I don't want to let him go until I know he hasn't made any mistakes in explaining this to me."

"One hour. Thanks, Nick."

Nick rejoined his companions. By then, Pence had stopped screaming, and began sobbing unintelligible mutterings. Nick washed the wound off, and applied an analgesic from the tray in a thick salve over the open wound. The effect of greatly reduced pain brought Didricson out of his ravings. He gasped short aching breaths after his extended screaming session. Nick leaned over him and waved.

"Hi Pence. Have I made it plain how important it is for you to help me undo all your nasty complications and traitorous deeds?"

"Yes…yes… anything! Just ask… but at least give me enough time to answer… please!"

"Sure, buddy. The first question is do you know Uthman Sadun?"

"Yes! His lawyer contacts me regularly. Sadun was one of my biggest bidders before our mole in the DOJ was discovered. Lately, he's been in touch with a billionaire… uh… Formsby… Milton Formsby. Formsby was paying big money to find out the identity of the man who had recovered the chip I stole. Sadun told Formsby the name, because the same guy caught him. From what Sadun's lawyer told me, Formsby suspected the man to be a hired assassin, using a weird deep cover identity as a writer. Formsby was under investigation by the CIA for aiding and abetting terrorists. He wanted information on the writer's personal dealings without being tied in any way to the information gathering. I went to Pacific Grove, and found out everything about him. I thought Formsby was nuts."

"Let me get this straight, Pence. You trailed this guy yourself?" *No way in hell did this idiot get on my trail without me knowing it*, Nick thought. *If he did, I'm getting the hell out of the business.*

"No... Formsby was right. I waited outside his home after he walked his daughter to school with another guy and their dog. When he returned, there was something creepy about him. He seemed to feel me watching him. I started the car, and drove away before the asshole could focus on me. I turned over what I had to Formsby, and told him he'd have to do the rest himself."

Nick remembered numerous instances where he did his usual scanning for strange vehicles because of a feeling he had. At least you haven't lost your damn edge completely, Nick decided. "Give me the lawyer's name, Pence – the one Sadun uses as a go between. I also need to know where you normally meet the guy, and where he lives."

Nick held a glass with a straw for Didricson to sip water. "Think carefully. Don't spew a bunch of crap on a whim. We have your phone, so I'll check your contact list."

After sipping the water thirstily, Didricson nearly choked, sputtering out denials of ever having any intention of stalling or misleading. "His name is Brook Wargul. He has an office in San Francisco, and another in Washington, DC. Since Sadun is being held at the Federal Penitentiary at Atwater, Wargul's been staying in California at his SF office."

Satisfied with the threads Pence gave him, Nick ordered him to speak freely, concerning when he began selling secrets, his motives, and everyone connected to his subversive lifestyle. "Just talk Pence as if you were writing your autobiography of being a traitor."

Another half hour passed, where Pence finished, and Nick waited for confirmation from his boss. He answered the call on the first ring. "I was beginning to get worried, pal."

"We have it all, Nick – thank God. He had everything on it. The FBI is hitting his house in the morning. I assume he will be another one that got away without a trace, huh?"

"Yep. I'm about to send Pence on his last journey. I hope you haven't forgotten about my video problem with the Formsby mess."

"Already confiscated from the local PD through the Patriot Act, because Formsby is now under indictment for espionage. I already have the DOJ's release of the case into CIA hands, since most of the indictment encompasses his overseas interests. If anyone hassles you locally, you call me directly. I'll take care of them. I don't think the FBI will be snooping around on the Formsby case, but you never know. Great job, Nick. With this kind of success, the number of favors owed to us keeps piling in a bigger mound we can use in the future."

"Good, because I have a couple of other loose ends I have to work through. I'll be in touch with the logistics, Paul."

"I'm here to back your play, Muerto. Just give me some warning, okay?"

"Will do. You can get some sleep now. Thanks for staying in this to the end."

"Are you kidding? You prevented a major catastrophe. I am sorry about the exposure it caused where you live. I hope fixing the loose end problem shifts you back into relative obscurity other than your novel writing. Call me if you need me." Gilbrech disconnected.

Nick brought over a syringe with him to Pence's gurney. "You did real good, Pence. Here's your reward."

Nick injected the hotshot of heroin into Didricson's neck. Thirty seconds later, the pain faded completely, and soon after Pence's life followed. "Well John, what do you think? Pretty effective, huh?"

John took off his mask, as did Nick and Gus. "Although I agree with Payaso about this method being about the most twisted, horrifying end of a human being I've ever seen or imagined, it produces excellent results."

"That's all that counts, Kabong." Nick brought over a body-bag from the storage cabinet in the room.

"Only you would say such a thing, Muerto," Gus said, helping John shift Didricson's body into the bag Nick held open. "I have to admit it though. There wasn't any other way faster to retrieve the blackmail drive. What's next?"

"I have a rather intricate plan to use one loose end to help me tie up the other loose end, and as a bonus, make Timmy and Grace get their hands dirty in penance for causing this. Can you and John put Pence on ice while I go deliver the BMW?"

"Sure," Gus agreed. "I'll drive by Jerry's after we finish with the Pence interrogation cleaning. Did Paul tell you whether tomorrow will be a tough day with the PD or not?"

"According to him, I won't be bothered at all."

* * *

Nick managed three hours of blissful, dreamless sleep before his inner alarm awakened him to the day's duties. He rubbed his eyes, taking satisfaction in the fact the nightstand clock read one minute before seven. How refreshing, Nick conceded, the sleep of the psychopath. Before descending the stairs, Nick avoided waking Rachel as he fought off the already awake Deke, who knew the daily routine very well. He stopped outside Jean's room next, but hesitated, shushing Deke with a hand gesture, while listening intently. A slowly forming smile spread across his features, as Nick realized Jean was near the door, waiting to ambush him.

"Up early, huh Dagger?"

The door swung open to a perturbed Jean wearing a black body leotard and Muerto mask. "I didn't have a fragrance you could smell through the door, and I didn't move a fraction of an inch while lying in wait to pounce. How did you know?"

"I have a sixth sense for Ninja wannabes. Plus, you didn't control your breathing. I didn't smell you this time, but I heard you. Nice outfit."

Jean stroked Deke's head. "I'll remember. You're mine one of these days."

"It won't matter. I'll be too old to care. What do you want for breakfast?"

"Toast and tea."

"By your command." Nick bowed away from the door.

* * *

Jean finished off her toast and tea while Nick worked the next scene in the new Diego adventure. Rachel walking into the kitchen triggered a slurping of crumbs and tea. Jean reacted appreciatively when Rachel turned away with a disgusted look, by pumping her fist.

"Another horrible habit learned from the instigator, El Muerto. I asked you not to do that in front of me, young lady."

"I can't help it, Mom. Your face scrunches like a voodoo doll the second you see me eating toast and tea."

"That's the way my face reacts to evil, Daughter of Darkness." Noticing Jean concentrating on her iPhone screen next to her, Rachel turned in Nick's direction, opening her robe to reveal Nick's gift of a short silk, black, see through negligee. She also put on light makeup for the moment. Although very pregnant, Rachel knew the effect she had on Nick no matter what she wore in a provocative way.

Nick, who enjoyed the mother/daughter exchange without ever looking away from his scene, glanced at Rachel, his mouth tightening at seeing her pose. He knew the game. She would do this only minutes away from him walking Jean to school. Nick never questioned whether he was a killer psychopath. He did question the general opinion psychopaths pretended all their feelings, and everything in life was an act. Knowing he had tortured and murdered a man only hours before affected his lust for Rachel not at all, even in her last month of pregnancy. His problem was she knew how to play him as if she were reeling in a twenty inch trout. Nick checked his watch, promising a long period of payback the moment he returned. He then made gestures with both his hands and mouth at the still posing Rachel. He mimicked what was in store for her that she loved, but pretended disgust at, until in the middle of exactly what she professed to hate. Rachel gasped, blushed, and tied her robe at the same time.

"Go brush your teeth, toasty. We leave in five minutes. I'll clean your mess when I get back. Gus may or may not make it in time."

"Okay, Dad." Jean slurped a last crumb filled mouthful of tea for Rachel's benefit, and ran upstairs with Deke on her trail.

"You vulgar snot!"

"You teasing vamp!" Nick gathered the pretending to resist Rachel into his arms.

"Don't even think for a second you'll be doing anything of the sort to me, now or ever."

"We'll see. You may say no now, and yes…yes…yes later." Nick's hands roved gently over Rachel, nuzzling her neck, while listening with satisfaction to her moaning indications she might very well make a liar of herself when he returned. Then the doorbell rang. "Perfect timing, Gus… you prick."

Nick checked to make sure it was Gus on his kitchen monitor, and then went to answer the door. "I didn't think I'd see you here this morning, Payaso. Would you like a cup of coffee to sip on the way?"

"Sure. I couldn't resist coming along to hear your plans. Besides, Tina kicked me out of bed to get her a double latte at seven. After I collected my fee, I decided I may as well take a shower, and satisfy my curiosity." Gus sipped from the travel mug Nick handed him, while giving Rachel a wave. "Good coffee, Nick. Did you know if you order a plain black coffee at Starbucks, the robot at the register goes into massive brain freeze?"

Nick chuckled. "Yeah, I learned my lesson about ordering plain coffee in a specialty coffee assembly line place. To their credit, they actually sit you down, and make it for you. It's funny when you think about how hard it actually is getting coffee in a coffee specialty place. Then, I remember I'm a cement head, and if I wanted plain coffee, I should have stayed home."

"That's right, cement head," Rachel called over her shoulder from the teapot. "Deny that's the reason you do it too, Gus. I dare you."

Gus raised his hand. "Guilty. I do it only for the entertainment value, and if I have time to waste. I didn't this morning."

They moved to the door with Nick holding Deke's leash apparatus. Hearing it clinking around, Deke flew down the stairs, to take a position near Nick's feet. Jean, only a minute behind, hugged Rachel. "Remember, today's a half day for some goofy reason, so don't get to fooling around, and forget about me."

"Why you little..." Rachel barely missed snagging the backpack before Jean disappeared through the front door. "That calls for a room displacement visit. See you guys later."

"What's a room displacement visit?"

"Rachel disturbs everything in Jean's room as if she's doing a cell check at Folsom Prison. It drives Jean nuts. That's the reason we have a keyed deadbolt on our bedroom door, because Jean seeks revenge immediately. She caught Rachel by surprise when the Mommy didn't envision payback on the part of the Daughter of Darkness."

Gus shut the door behind him, and reset the security code. "Damn, Nick. I can imagine you feeding off this, poking the hornets' nest the second it settles down."

"I do no such thing. Rachel and Jean do not require any outside help to instigate an act of war. They light each other off at every opportunity. Deke and I are only neutral observers."

Jean skipped ahead with Deke as usual, leaving Gus with an opportunity to inquire about Nick's next steps, knowing from experience that ignorance was never bliss with El Muerto. "You hinted at drawing Tim and Grace into this. Do you have something vague in mind for this stunt, or are you playing it by ear?"

"We have two loose ends: Brook Wargul, Sadun's lawyer, and Sadun. Since Wargul's operating out of his office in San

Francisco, I'm going to track him, and shoot him in the head from long range. Then, I'll get Tim and Grace to argue a case for moving Sadun away from the Federal Penitentiary at Atwater. They leave the prison with Sadun in custody. I blow a tire out on their US Marshal mobile. Tim or Grace fake a crash off the road, just enough to fire the airbags, and I grab Sadun for a gab session at John's place. Easy Peasy."

"Will you for God's sake stop using that term? It's more annoying than your murderous assassin rampages."

"That's hurtful, Payaso."

"Speaking of hurtful, are you expecting trouble today at the school? We've had so much happen since yesterday, I'd forgotten all about the riot you instigated at Jean's school."

"I won't dignify that scurrilous accusation with any reply whatsoever."

"In other words, you think there may very well be more problems at the school. Did you catch a news flash the rent-a-mob would be back?"

Nick shook his head. "I haven't had time to listen to the news. We both know the media though. If they spied any opportunity yesterday to continue stirring the trouble pot, then we will have a contingent of them out there this morning. It could also be an ambush, where they'll try to make any pro American Flag folks look like idiots. Look on the positive side, Gus. There might not be anyone at the school other than parents, students, and teachers."

"I'm not putting any money on that sucker bet. You're right though. It may be a media protest today, where they arrive to get 'opinions' which they promptly edit into one line napalm taken out of context. I'll see if they have any trouble listed on the usual sites." Gus used his iPad to search through local newscasts for any indication of a planned smear job, but found nothing. "I don't like this, Muerto. There's no media outrage for the flag defilers. Instead of doing a half day, maybe they should have taken a full day off. The media has the attention span of a pack of gerbils. Make them wait a day, and it's old news."

"I agree, but I didn't get a vote," Nick replied. "You dropped our lawyer Wargul conversation with a cheap shot, but did you have a real objection to what I have in mind?"

"How do you plan on getting Tim and Grace on board this Muerto express into career suicide? Granted, their oversight on not informing you of the government's usual mishandling of a real threat nearly ended in..." Gus shut up for a moment. "Never mind... no matter how I try and underplay the dumbass move they went along with in not telling you about Pence, the more idiotic what I'm saying actually sounds to me."

"It's very simple. I'm not giving them a choice. They will help me with this. In fact, the turds will probably look like heroes, who knew the mob must be trying to kill Sadun, because of his lawyer's murder. It will be their job to sell the danger of a potential mob hit inside the prison by an unknown source. When I hit their vehicle outside Atwater, they'll look like visionaries."

"How could that work? Atwater's in the middle of nowhere. Any ambush in or around it, would cast suspicions immediately on an inside job, involving Tim and Grace."

"Not if they're found tied and gagged a city away in Merced."

"Madre de Dios!"

Jeaned glanced over her shoulder with a grin. "Uncle Gus?"

Gus waved her off. "It's okay. Your Dad told me something so out there in left field, my mind blanked." Gus reduced his audio signal to a whisper. "That is wrong on so many levels, Muerto.

What they did was wrong, but tied and gagged, and left for anyone to find… really?"

"That's not quite all, Payaso, my shortsighted partner. I'll have to wound one of them."

"Madre de Dios!"

"Sometimes, doing what's right hurts a little, partner."

"When do you get to explain their part in this obscene Kabuki play of yours, I want to be there. Is that possible."

"Sure. I have no objection. I think you're going to find Grace and Timmy to be very receptive to my so called 'Kabuki Play'. I'm interested in how they choose who gets wounded. I'm betting Timmy mans the hell up, and takes the bullet. On the other hand, Grace will probably browbeat him into allowing her to do it. They're sleeping together now, so they'll probably play some form of 'Alphonse and Gaston' vying with each other to make the sacrifice."

Gus shrugged. "You're sick, Muerto. I'm worse though. I'm like the rubberneckers on the freeway after a horrendous accident with body parts strewn everywhere. I can't look away. You've made me into a sick freak like you are."

"No, I didn't. You whine too much."

"Uh oh. Here we are again in the Muerto is always right bubble. Look at the damn news vans. You'd think we had a terrorist attack yesterday, instead of a statement made by common folk in defense of the flag."

Nick smiled, watching the parents stream by with their kids, looking up at the flag still waving proudly in the air for another day, but ignoring the media vultures completely. He saw Jim Amos go by with a glance at the flag, and a wave off to the press with his sons. "I see a few of my former compatriots doing exactly the right thing, ignoring the media. You remain here with Deke. Jean and I will thread our way through directly to school. Ready, Dagger?"

"I'm ready. I missed all the adult fun yesterday."

"No fun today either, kid. We're going to walk right by these clowns. No offense, Payaso."

"None taken."

Nick walked toward the school, holding Jean's hand. "I know you don't like me playing the overprotective parent as if you were a kindergartner, but I don't want to lose sight of you in this crowd, Dagger."

"It's okay. They look scarier close like this."

"The media are born bullies. It's a prerequisite for being a reporter. If you are a wildly annoying, arrogant jerk with no scruples, being a journalist seems like a wonderful career choice. It keeps them off the streets, but not out of rehab."

Jean giggled. As they passed the flag pole, Nick stopped and looked up at the only symbol he truly respected without exception. Jean followed his example.

"There he is! That is the man who attacked me!"

Recognizing the voice, Nick spun toward it, his right arm sweeping Jean behind him. Habib Rashidi was striding toward him with two other men in suits, who could pass for his brothers. The media, smelling blood in the water, circled the feeding area. Nick made a stopping gesture with his hand.

"That's close enough! Allow me to take my Daughter into school, and you can spew whatever nonsense you want at me when I come out."

"You will answer for what you did now!" In spite of his words, Rashidi slowed to a stop.

"No, I won't, but if you force the issue with your two buddies, I will put you all in the hospital."

"Are you threatening me?"

"No, butthead, I'm giving you the only logical alternative to getting hurt, badly: stay away from me until I take Jean in to school." Then, a growl sounded from next to him. Deke took a position near Nick, ready to launch, with Gus's intimidating figure at his side.

"That is good advice," Gus told them. "Deke doesn't like it when he senses danger to Jean. Anyone moving toward her will not enjoy the consequences."

As if to add an exclamation point to Gus's remark, Deke voiced a short violent bark and snarl with all his teeth showing, jutting ahead as if eager to begin. That startled the media and Rashidi's crew back a few steps.

"Thanks," Nick said. "I'll be out in a few minutes, Gus."

Gus smiled. "Deke and I will be here. Have a good day, Jean."

"I will, Uncle Gus." Jean hugged Deke, and led the way inside the school. "Were those guys going to beat you up right in front of the cameras and reporters?"

"Nope. They were about to get a lesson in actions have consequences. Luckily, Gus and Deke timed their arrival perfectly. If I had seen Rashidi, I would have asked Gus to bring Deke with us. I don't like to upset Deke. He doesn't like bad mouthing crowds, because he senses their mood. Don't worry, I won't let Deke get a piece of anyone. Even in self-defense, the stupid people in authority would insist on putting him to sleep. That ain't happenin' to my beer buddy."

"See that boy talking to Ms. Kader," Jean whispered, retreating a step. "His name's Tyson Salvatore. His family moved here from Washington D.C. He's in my class. His folks call him Sonny. I think he likes me."

A tall for his age, thin, dark haired boy spotted Jean. He waved at her. Nick grinned as the boy blushed when Jean waved back. "Yep. I think you're right."

"Are you okay, Jean? I was telling Ms. Kader that you and your Dad were stopped outside by the flagpole."

"I'm good," Jean said. "Sonny, this is my Dad, Nick."

Nick shook hands with the boy, noting his firm grip. "I'm glad to meet you, Sonny."

"Same here, Sir."

"We better get my class started, or I will be in trouble," Dimah Kader said. "Nice seeing you, Nick."

"I remember the half day, Jean. Bye, Dimah." Nick watched them enter the classroom, smiling as Jean playfully bumped Sonny into his desk. Oh boy, another detail of life I hadn't given a thought to.

Chapter Six

Ill Conceived Plans

Nick hurried through the entrance, but slowed his steps once he passed the doorway. He came abreast of Gus and Deke, as they maintained their positions. "Ready, Gus?"

"I'm on my last nerve here, so yeah, I'm ready. Deke was ready two seconds after you went inside the school. I don't speak these guys' language, so I have no idea what they said, but I would wager it wasn't anything good hearted, or nice. A few of the reporters left, so your buddy has been working himself up into a frenzy. What are you going to do?"

"Walk home." Nick turned away from the crowd, beginning his trek. Deke pulled Gus along to follow. Nick called Sergeant Dickerson while striding with Gus and Deke at a leisurely pace, gathering an enraged following with every step.

"Nick?"

"Yeah, it's me. I have a stalker. Remember the nitwit from yesterday, Habib Rashidi?"

Dickerson sighed. "Yes."

"He came to the school again, blasting away at everyone with news crews in attendance. He has a couple big guys with him that look like his brothers, and a few others chummy with him following along for the ride. I dropped Jean off. Gus and I, along with Deke the dog are trying to make good our escape without finding our way onto the evening news."

"On my way. Can you outpace them?"

Nick glanced toward his unwanted retinue, speeding their pursuit, because Nick wasn't slowing down to engage them.

"Nope. I'm not running either. I'll keep the line open. Gus, can you get your iPad out ready to film?"

"Way ahead of you. I've been taking clips of us moving away from them. Would you like to let Deke get involved."

"No. Sergeant Dickerson is on his way. If we keep moving, maybe he'll be in time to keep me from doing something violently incorrect. There's five of them, and you're filming it, including our attempt to leave the area without violence."

Gus did a video panning of the scene again with an added note. "The big guy who was with Rashidi is jogging forward toward you, Nick."

"Thanks. Keep Deke tightly to you."

A few seconds later, a huge hand gripped Nick's left shoulder with an order to stop. Nick spun, wrapping his left arm around the big man's extended arms, clutching them in an unbreakable grip. He then punched the helpless man in the groin, following the devastating blow with a knee to the man's face. Nick allowed him to drop to the sidewalk, continuing on without breaking stride. Gus kept filming, while controlling Deke with the leash and calming words. Sirens sounded on the squad car approaching from the opposite direction with Dickerson at the wheel. He steered to the curb near Nick, Gus, and Deke. The small gang had been slowed while checking their companion, left writhing on the sidewalk.

"Did you do something, Nick?" Dickerson hurried around the hood of his squad car to the sidewalk. His partner, a tall athletically shaped brown haired woman stayed at her passenger side door, one hand on the butt of her weapon

"Yep. You were a few seconds late to keep one of them from trying to yank me to a stop. Gus has it on video."

131

Dickerson watched the pursuit, and painful ending. "Ouch! That had to hurt. Nice speech before the action."

"It bought us enough time for the valiant Pacific Grove police to arrive in the nick of time to save Nick."

"Very funny. Here they come, but the one you put down isn't doing too well."

"Good, I want to press charges, so officer, do your duty."

"Oh boy... I was afraid you'd say that." Dickerson turned to his partner. "Call it in, Trina. We're going to need backup."

Because the group moved toward them, Dickerson and his partner stayed where they were. By the time Rashidi and his companions reached the squad car because of their limping comrade, two other squad cars arrived behind them. Four more officers exited those vehicles to surround the oncoming men.

"Arrest him! He assaulted my brother for no reason! I want him in handcuffs immediately!"

"Calm down, Sir, right now," Dickerson warned. "First off, I ordered you to stay away from that elementary school. You not only disobeyed my lawful order, you brought others along, and proceeded to stalk after a Pacific Grove citizen who actually has a daughter attending classes at the school. His friend filmed your pursuit of him as he walked home, including an attempted assault by your brother. Mr. McCarty is pressing charges. You, and your friends, are going to jail. Turn around and put your hands behind your back!"

"This...this is outrageous!" When Rashidi didn't follow Dickerson's order, Dickerson forced him around, and handcuffed the squirming Rashidi. He then read the men their rights.

"Do you understand these rights as I have explained them?" Dickerson kept repeating the phrase while his other police

132

comrades watched each other's back while restraining the men with Rashidi. After the third repeat of the question, all but Rashidi had indicated they understood.

"I will say nothing!"

"I filmed it," Gus said. "He heard his rights read to him in front of witnesses, and on video."

"Thanks Gus. Your refusing to acknowledge your rights isn't a problem anyway. I don't have any questions for you. Mr. McCarty, I'm sure, will be glad to give us a copy of your assault, and press charges at the station, right Mr. McCarty?"

"The moment I reach home with my dog and Gus, I will get in my vehicle and drive to the station," Nick stated.

"You will pay for this affront!" Rashidi began a screaming tantrum, which Gus continued to film, while the police loaded the men into the squad cars for transport.

"I don't think he likes you, Nick. I admit it. I don't mind this particular arrest at all. Rashidi really screwed the pooch returning to the school. I don't know for how long, but he's going to jail."

"I will testify. I guarantee you that, and I have solid witnesses from yesterday too."

"What I think will happen is the DA will offer them deals after Rashidi cools down, and his lawyer explains he isn't in Tehran under Sharia Law."

"They're pushing for it," Nick replied. "It's getting so we're not allowed to be Americans in America anymore. We have to remove our flags, piss on the Constitution, and allow Islamist assholes to enslave their own wives and daughters right here in America as if they were still in an Afghan cave. When Sharia Law becomes our law, I'll be dead, and every bullet I can get my hands on will have been fired."

"And I'll be dead next to him," Gus added.

"Save me a spot, guys," Dickerson agreed. "See you at the station, Nick. I think there were some suits getting ready to visit your house anyway on the Formsby matter. You'll save everyone some time coming down to the station."

"I'll be there. Thanks for showing so quickly today, Neil."

"It was my pleasure as it turned out."

After the police left, Nick, Gus, and Deke restarted their journey home. "Rachel will love this new twist in the simple school walk."

"I bet she'll start making you drive Jean to school pretty soon," Gus replied. "After the last couple days, I'd be willing to entertain the idea if I were you."

"Deke loves his morning walk to school with Jean. If I have to kill a few people to make it less of a trial, so be it."

"Speaking of killing a few people, when are you letting Tim and Grace in on the wonderful plan you want them involved in?"

"Tonight if they'll come down here," Nick answered. "I'll call them after I get back from the station and bring Jean home."

"I hope you can get a couple hours sleep in there somewhere. I know I plan to."

"The Rashidi mess fired me up. I'm surprised the press didn't follow him and his gang. That in itself is a bit disturbing. You don't suppose they wanted to keep my possible beating off the news, do you, Payaso?"

"The fact they were haunting the school makes me wonder about their sudden disinterest when we were followed," Gus admitted. "Nothing those jackals do surprises me though. You've made them look bad many times, amigo. If they had followed, you would have been blamed in some weird way, only the venerable fifth estate could fathom. I like this outcome. You didn't have to shoot anyone in the head, but that was a nice beat down you put on the Rasidi brother. Do you think they're going to survive this continuing escalation against the dreaded El Muerto?"

"Only time will tell, but if I have to hear that Rashidi voice one more time, I may be forced to make an adjustment. I hope to serve anything like that cold though. I have too many hot irons in the fire right now. We have a couple of big cases in the North. I don't want to get bogged down here, and miss a window of opportunity to play El Muerto."

"I will be cursed for all time in creating that comic book reference to compare you with," Gus admitted. "I hope your continued games involving us as the 'Unholy Trio' doesn't backfire with you ending your days in a prison cell."

"Not happening, Gus."

"Why not? What the hell could you do about it, chomp a suicide pill in your teeth?"

"I could, but I won't have to. I'm protected. When the government finds a killer, they don't let him go to prison unless he kills the wrong people, like a Senator. Now that adjustment in the congressional population might have put me over the top into liability land. Since I was already on an NSA hit list thanks to Frank Richert at the time, it didn't much matter. If I get taken into custody wiping out an Isis clan, or doing surgery on the Seattle Ripper, they'll grab me from the locals, and stick me in a military prison. From there, after a few months, I'll be quietly released into a new identity. That would be the death knell for my writing career, but I'd go to work somewhere else with Rachel and Jean. Damn!

I'd sure miss Pacific Grove though. It would be years before I could move into the area again."

"At least you'd be able to take the family. What about me, Muerto?"

"I'd send for you, Gus. Hell, I'm not letting John go either. He's perfect in these times for going after the real enemies of our country. We can't stop them with daisies fresh out of the garden. We'd start our operation again somewhere else with a coastline. We need to keep your boat in play."

"How about the Keys, or even near your friends in Sarasota?"

"I hope I don't have to live there. With the damn heat and humidity, all I'd feel like doing is fishing, and drinking ice cold beer."

"Maybe that means you should go there to live," Gus replied, holding his hands in a defensive gesture as Nick eyed him coldly. "I know... I know. It was me that talked you out of your retirement into full time writing. Look there, Muerto. Rachel's waiting for you on the porch. She's smiling, so I guess that's not a bad omen."

"Rachel is a surprise a minute since she hit the late term of her pregnancy. I have to fulfill my civic duty, so take off, and I'll see you later if you want to sit in on the Tim and Grace meeting."

"I do." Gus waved at Rachel, and walked away toward his house.

"Hello, Dear. You look happy."

"I was watching the news, and guess who had a starring role," Rachel asked.

"That was quick. I made it into the 'Breaking News', huh?"

"Yep. What's that do to our alone time?"

"I have to stop by the station, because I'm pressing charges, but after that, we'll have a short time before I fetch Jean."

Rachel invaded Nick's air space, edging Deke out of the way. "I bet we could do a short time now."

"Meaning my pantomime earlier has been haunting you?"

Rachel blushed, and bit her lip. "Damn you... yes."

"Well now, I may be able to delay the long arm of the law for half an hour. I bet that will be enough time for you to alternate between no...no...no and then yes...yes...yes."

"Quit gloating, and get inside."

* * *

The police did an admiral job trying to throw Nick off during a lineup of suspects, but he picked each out in seconds with their lawyer present. The lawyer tried to engage him in conversation while he did it. Nick finally turned to Dickerson, who was standing with them.

"I was under the impression the suspect's lawyer could monitor the procedure," Nick said. "I was unaware the lawyer could interrogate and badger me while I participated in picking out the suspect."

Dickerson turned to the lawyer. "Mr. McCarty is correct. You have been asked to refrain from speaking by the victim. If you continue to speak, I will have you removed Mr. Nagi. Do you understand?"

"Yes...yes," Nagi answered, waving Dickerson off.

The procedure went smoothly after the initial interruption. Nick signed the papers Dickerson had already made available describing the arrest details. By the time he finished with the arrest procedures, two men in suits waited for him to finish. Dickerson made eye contact with Nick and nodded.

"Are you finished here, Mr. McCarty?" The medium built man with thinning brown hair asked. He showed Nick his FBI credentials. "I'm Special Agent Remy, and this is my partner, Special Agent Johnson. We're here to discuss the disappearance of Milton Formsby."

"We'd like to know what happened after you went for a ride with him," Johnson said. The ebony skinned Johnson, stocky, and a couple inches taller than either Nick or his partner, appeared ready to slap the cuffs on Nick immediately.

"That's a tough one, Agent Johnson. I didn't go with Mr. Formsby after our initial ride. I turned the offer down he made me to ghostwrite his autobiography. We didn't speak anymore after that."

"Why is it you turned him down? Did he mention where he was going next after speaking with you?"

"He didn't say much of anything after I turned down the job. He was disappointed, but I don't write nonfiction... ever."

Nick's pleasant half-truths annoyed the two agents, and Nick began to wonder why. He knew the FBI were part of the operation to raid Formsby's holdings, Gilbrech had told him would happen immediately. Suspicions Remy and Johnson may have been getting a piece of the Formsby pie began seeping through Nick's consciousness.

"We're going to need you to come with us," Remy said finally.

"That's not happening."

"What makes you think so, McCarty?" Johnson moved into Nick's airspace. "You think because you're on the bestseller list that you can tell federal agents what they can or can't do?"

"Nope. I'm wondering why two FBI agents, asking about Formsby, didn't know all his holdings here and overseas were hit by your agency and the CIA abroad. Excuse me a moment." Nick took out his phone, and hit speed dial to Paul Gilbrech, while Agents Remy and Johnson stared at each other, trying to cover for the shock Nick's revelation caused.

"Nick?"

"Yep. I have two FBI agents here out of the loop. I'm thinking maybe for good reason."

"You're thinking right. Put them on with me."

Nick offered his phone to Johnson, who wouldn't touch it. After a slight hesitation, Remy accepted the phone. A few minutes later, Remy handed the phone back, all blood drained out of his face.

"Agent Remy doesn't look so good, Paul," Nick said, watching the two men in a frenzied huddle, whispering fiercely at each other.

"They're on arrest warrants being signed by the Attorney General, even as we speak. Formsby's people must have ordered them immediately to take over the case. They left DC on a redeye heading in your direction, and left their phones off. What did they want to do with you?"

"Take me somewhere."

"Can you keep them there until I fax a warrant to your contact in the Pacific Grove police department?"

"Did you just insult me again?"

Paul chuckled. "Meaning if you did, it could get messy. Let me speak to whomever you know there in the department."

Nick handed the phone to Dickerson, who was watching the interchange with growing suspicion. Nick waited while Remy and Johnson continued having a heated debate, forgetting where they were, or what was at stake for the moment. They looked unstable enough to try and shoot their way out. Nick felt the butt of his .45 Colt underneath his windbreaker, loosening it a bit. What he didn't want to happen was his friend Dickerson to be shot by a couple of fools desperate enough to get into a gun battle inside a police department. When Neil finished talking with Gilbrech he handed Nick back his phone.

"The Director of the CIA?" Dickerson whispered. "Good Lord, Nick. Who the hell are you? Mr. Gilbrech said to follow your lead."

"Unstrap your piece, and put your hand on the butt of it," Nick answered. "Tell them they are under arrest, and are to be detained on order from the Attorney General. I'll back your play. Do not get between me and them, Neil. Are you okay with this? Say so one way or the other now. We can let them walk. I'll take them into custody later."

"I might as well throw my damn badge in the trash can if I get afraid to arrest people. Is there any chance of me ever knowing who the hell you really are?"

"Most of my connections with the DOJ, US Marshals, FBI, and CIA are as a special consultant. Anything else is classified, Neil. Let's do this. Remember what I said."

"I will." Dickerson walked to Johnson's side, his hand on the weapon at his side. "I know Mr. Gilbrech explained your situation to you. I am detaining you both by order of the Attorney General of the United States. Please lace your hands behind-"

140

"The hell you are!"

Before Johnson could reach for his weapon, Nick was in front of him with the barrel of his Colt against Johnson's forehead. "Twitch, and I shoot both of you in the head. On your knees with hands laced behind your heads, and you can still live through this."

Johnson looked into a professional killer's eyes and knelt. Remy followed his lead, both men lacing their hands behind their heads. By that time, Dickerson had motioned three more officers over.

"Handcuff these men."

The officers handcuffed the FBI agents, and helped them to their feet. Without asking permission, Nick disarmed them, completing a thorough frisk of the two detainees. They had their main weapons, two hideaways, and two knives. Nick helped Dickerson bag everything, including the men's credentials and personal effects.

"Put them in holding," Dickerson directed. He watched them until they were out of earshot. "You weren't going to shoot two FBI agents in the head."

"First off, he planned to shoot his way out of the precinct, which is not as hard to do as you think when bad guys don't hesitate. Secondly, I had to take him in close. Never get in close with a weapon meant to kill from out of reach, unless you have every intention of killing at any movement. Let's forget all that. I knew Remy was watching his life pass in front of his eyes. He wasn't going to do anything. Johnson wised up and decided to keep breathing too. It's a win."

"How did you know about the bust?"

"I can't tell you that, Neil. I knew if Remy and Johnson were here monkeying around with me, then they didn't know what was happening with Formsby's holdings."

"What about you knowing the CIA Director? Is that a secret too?"

"I work for him."

"You have his number on speed dial."

"I have to go home, and see Rachel for a little while before I fetch Jean home from school. Can we shelve the interrogation for today? I have you on speed dial too." Nick shook hands with Dickerson. "I hope they don't let that nitwit Rashidi out. Two days in a row was enough having that jerk in my face."

"I know it's a day late and a dollar short, but I'll have a patrol car on hand at tomorrow's school day. I've had enough of the rent-a-mob bullshit too. We're going to make Rashidi's pack hurt financially. They're going to find out how much endangering the public safety actually costs, especially around a school. Believe me, they won't like it."

"See you later, Neil."

"I'm not comfortable with you knowing the CIA Director," Dickerson called out.

"You'll get over it."

* * *

Nick lay next to Rachel, his fingers moving over her forehead with a gentle back and forth motion. They were both bathed in sweat. Rachel's breath had only returned to normal a moment before.

"I hate you."

Nick smiled. "You always say that. Jean wasn't here for the wonderful little scream, so no blood, no foul, right?"

"I hate you." Rachel covered her eyes. "I'm so demented."

Nick moved over her, kissing her eyes, lips, and neck. "You were gorgeous today, and very erotic. I'm sure you weren't even close to demented."

"Don't Nick… you'll be late for the school."

"No I won't."

"Oh…"

* * *

The school appeared back to normal, with only parents meeting their kids. "See, Deke, it's all good. We'll meet with the US Marshals tonight. Then you and I can relax on the balcony. You deserve treats today for being so well mannered."

Deke glanced at Nick, his expression one of infinite patience. He hopped onto his hind legs in dance like perfection as Jean approached them with her friend from class. Jean hugged Deke, making him sit and shake hands with Sonny, which he did.

"Wow… neat dog. Hi Mr. McCarty."

"Hi, Sonny. Do you have plans for the day?"

"I was hoping Sonny could come home with us, and have dinner later," Jean answered for him.

"That's fine with me, but you need to let your parents know where you're at, Sonny. I'll talk to them if you'd like, but you have to get their permission." Nick wrote down their address and his mobile number. "Here's where you'll be, and a number your parents can reach anytime."

"I'll call them right now." Sonny called home on his iPhone using FaceTime. When he had talked with his parents for a moment, he gave Nick the phone.

"My son tells me you've been roped into feeding him," the woman on screen said with a smile. "I'm Clarice Salvatore."

"Nick McCarty, Clarice," Nick replied. "My wife's name is Rachel. "What time would you like Sonny home tonight?"

"By eight would be fine, Nick. Thank you."

"I'm always glad when Jean has new friends. I'll bring Sonny to the door later."

"Okay, bye."

"Start thinking about fast food, kids. I'm not springing a dinner guest on your Mom, Jean. Besides, I'm trying to get Grace and Tim to take a meeting, so we'll get some extra food, and your Mom won't have to do a thing."

"Pizza's always a winner," Jean said. "We can get extra stuff with it too."

"Sounds good to me. What about you, Sonny?"

"Anything but Sushi is good with me."

Nick nodded in agreement. "My sentiments exactly."

"Grace and Tim are US Marshals, and my Dad consults with the Marshals, FBI, and CIA," Jean explained with her usual excitement, watching Sonny's reaction. She wasn't disappointed.

"I...I... don't know what to say. Holy crap... that's awesome," Sonny blurted out. "I thought you were a writer, Mr. McCarty."

"He is," Jean stated before Nick had a chance to speak. "He was in Delta Force."

Nick gave Jean a furrowed brow Terminator stare when Sonny wasn't looking. "It's not as exciting as it sounds, Sonny. I'm a consultant because I've been in so many parts of the world, and I have an affinity for languages. They like to get outside opinions on some of their cases."

"It sounds exciting to me," Sonny replied. "Are you meeting with the US Marshals about a case tonight?"

"Possibly. It's a theory I've been working on for them," Nick said, while getting the kids and Deke moving toward his house. "Are you two working on homework together tonight?"

"Ms. Kader assigned a long math page. She said we're getting sloppy, and not checking our work," Jean explained. "We'll get it done before dinner. Can we practice with my throwing knives?"

"Ouch! Sure Jean, if you want the US Marshals to arrest me for child endangerment. What part of keeping that extracurricular activity on the down low didn't you understand?"

"I won't tell, Sir," Sonny said.

"Absolutely not. I don't do anything behind parents' backs," Nick stated. "I'm disappointed Jean even mentioned it to you."

"What if I got their permission?"

"I'd consider it, but I'd have to talk to them face to face about their permission on something like throwing knives."

"Could you show him the knives, and throw a few times, Dad?"

Oh this is wonderful – blending the assassin's lifestyle with family, Nick thought. *Rachel is going to blow a gasket.* "No comment until I talk to your Mom about many things, including your new sharing personality."

"I didn't know you'd throw me under the bus if I asked," Jean complained.

"Now you do. By the time I get through explaining your new propensity for sharing our home life, you'll have tread marks from the tips of your shoes to the furrowed forehead you're gracing me with."

Sonny turned away, stifling laughter at Nick's remark. Jean bopped him on the head.

"I didn't mean to get you in trouble, Dagger," Sonny said. "That was funny though."

"You're not supposed to call me by my secret identity either," Jean said.

"Let's shelve all this for now, you two. Stick to homework and what kind of pizza you'd like. I'll handle the entertainment part."

"Meaning movies or playing catch with Deke… boring."

"Actually, I was thinking of the exciting game of taking Sonny home right after dinner, and then watching you write 'I will not be a sarcastic little brat' a thousand times before you go to bed."

Sonny earned another headshot over excessive enjoyment of Jean's possible punishment.

* * *

"Wow." Rachel sat across from Nick sipping tea at the kitchen table. "This isn't like Jean at all. Even I admit that. You do understand what this is though with the sharing, right?"

"I do indeed. It means if she continues along this new path, they'll be sending a SWAT team to collect me for an extended lifetime visit at Leavenworth."

"It means she really likes this boy, Sonny."

"Yeah… that too," Nick admitted. "My reality thinking only goes as far as my new Leavenworth stay. Ten year old crushes lose their excitement for me in comparison."

"We'll work through it. I'll talk to her. The fact she's forgotten about our cross country jaunt, and the need for careful consideration of every word we share means she's got it bad. I think it's cute."

"Which part, my fifty year Leavenworth stretch or the crush?"

Rachel giggled, covering Nick's hand with hers. "Thanks for the act of debauchery you subjected me to this morning before you went to collect my new sharing daughter. Did you call Grace and Tim?"

"You're welcome, but I didn't consider it a duty. It's more of a lifetime calling. Yes, I called Tim and Grace. They'll be here around dinner time. They can have some pizza. I'll run a plan by them I've formulated, and they'll probably throw up the pizza. Oh… Gus and Tina will be over too, so I'll order a few big ones with the extra side dishes. I asked John, but he has a date he'd rather see one on one for now."

"You've made the US Marshals' visit sound ominous, but I don't want to know why. I took a nap, so I'll be fine for guests. I'll entertain the kids with Tina while you conduct your meeting. Are you going to demonstrate the throwing knives for Sonny?"

"Nope. Once he has the knife throwing conversation with his parents, I believe the crush will be over too."

"Boys are pushovers for stuff like guns and knives. Do the demo after they finish the homework. I've seen you with the damn knives. I've always been impressed as hell with the way you can shoot, but there's something about the way you work the knives that almost makes it seem like a magic trick."

"Yeah, it's a magic trick, made so by a thousand hours of practice," Nick admitted. "Okay, I'll do it, but remember I warned you. Want me to fool around a little with you under the table while the kids are distracted."

"No!" Rachel blushed. "Damn you. Now that's all I can think of. Get away from me."

"Heh…heh…" Nick slipped in beside Rachel. She made motions of fighting him off, but her breathing told a different tale. Jean took that moment to pop her head in the doorway.

"Hey, we're all done with the math. Come and check it, Dad. Did Mom talk you into the knife throwing demo for Sonny?"

"Why you little brat!"

"So, you just rolled me by preconceived plan," Nick observed. "This affront will not be forgotten, ladies."

* * *

Nick caught the knives Jean tossed in the air to him, immediately slinging them dead center on target. He then turned his back on target, spun right and then left, using both hands to throw, striking center target in each instance. He noticed the open mouthed, stunned observer, Sonny, watching with ever widening eyes. Nick also noted Sonny was filming the demo on his iPhone. Nick collected and put away the knives in their case. Tim and Grace walked out from the house to join the backyard audience of Gus, Jean, and Sonny. Nick could tell in a glance they had been watching from inside the house with Tina and Rachel.

"Well… that's just disturbing," Grace said.

"Um… very impressive, Nick," Tim added.

"Sonny, this is US Marshal Tim Reihold and the frumpy one is US Marshal Grace Stanwick. I'd like you to meet Jean's new friend Sonny Salvatore."

Sonny shook hands with each of them. "I've never met a US Marshal before. It's nice to meet you both. Mr. McCarty says he consults with you on cases. That's really neat."

"I'm not sure neat is the right word," Grace replied.

"Choose your next word carefully, frumpy," Nick warned, earning stifled amusement from Gus.

Tim grinned down at Sonny, nodding in assent. "Yes he does, Sonny. We're here to meet with him about a case today as a matter of fact."

"That's awesome."

"I'm not sure awesome is the right word," Grace continued poking.

"Say, would you kids like to see me throw a knife into an apple perched on Marshal Stanwick's head?"

"Sure," Jean said, giggling at the death stare she received from Grace.

"Uh... I don't think I'd like that, Mr. McCarty," Sonny answered seriously.

"Dad was joking, Sonny," Jean told him. "Let's get some veggies and dip before the pizza comes. She guided her guest inside.

"Would you two like to eat with us, and then talk?"

"I'd like to hear what you have to say before eating," Grace replied.

"Let's go up on the deck then."

When Nick offered refreshments, only Gus accepted a beer. "I've delved into our loose end problem. It's partially repaired, but we have two still in need of attention. One, I won't bother you with except as a card to play for the second loose end's repair. Here's what I have in mind which will require a little pain for a gain from you two."

Nick explained in detail how the soon unfortunate demise of Uthman Sadun's lawyer, Brook Wargul, could be used as a ploy by the Marshals to relocate Sadun because of projected danger to his life within the Atwater Federal Prison. He and Gus retained grim featured countenances during his explanation of what was needed to repair the damage done, caused by the Pence Didricson situation not being shared with Nick.

"I...I can't believe what I'm hearing," Grace stated. "You want us to be shot while transporting Sadun, so you can take him somewhere to be tortured and killed, but only after you put a bullet in his lawyer's head? Are you out of your damn psychopathic mind?"

"It's doable," Tim admitted. "How would you handle the shooting? I'm not at all enthused about taking a .50 caliber bullet anywhere on my body as a wounding ploy."

Nick chuckled. "I would wound your passenger side tire, giving you a reason why the car went off the road. We'd pull in behind you with a tow truck, as if I'm making a service call. I'll put a round right between Grace's eyes, and nick your shoulder. Then-"

"Very funny," Grace broke in, punching her amused partner in the shoulder.

"After I nick one of you, enabling an explanation of my having gotten the drop on you both, I'd inject something to incapacitate the valiant US Marshals while I take Sadun. An hour later, I'll call in an anonymous concerned citizen accident report from a payphone so the brave Marshals can be found unconscious. The authorities will believe his cohorts took him in a daring daytime snatch. Their search will prove to be fruitless, and hopefully I will be able to end this unfortunate blight on our relationship."

"I'll do it," Tim said. "Grace won't need to come along. I've escorted felons we had deals with from a facility where the other inmates were threatening their lives. It's a good plan."

"That's the spirit, Timmy," Nick said, as Tim took another shoulder shot from his partner. "That's so sweet. Tim's taking a round for you, Grace. What a guy."

"I'm going along with stupid, just to make sure you don't drill him between the horns. I think we'll skip the pizza feast after your hair raising solution to our error in judgement. Call us when you cement the threat into place." Grace stood and left the room.

Tim gave Nick and Gus a small hand wave. "I'll get her to remember we put ourselves in this situation. After what that double crossing jerk Sadun managed to do right under our noses, I won't lose any sleep over his exit from the planet."

"I wouldn't worry about it too much, Tim. It will be over before you know it. I won't mind having a chat with Uthman. I have a few questions for him."

"I'll bet." Tim left to follow Grace.

* * *

Nick arrived at the Salvatore home at 7:30 pm. Jean and Sonny were discussing the day's happenings with an easy tone of friendship. He and Jean accompanied Sonny to the door, where a woman in jeans, sandals, and red blouse answered the door before they reached the porch. Her dark hair tied back tightly at the neck, hung past her shoulders. Nick figured her to be middle thirties, about five and a half feet tall, and athletic. Nick held out his hand.

"Clarice?"

"That's me." Clarice shook his hand with a firm grip. "Come in for a moment, Nick. Did Sonny give you a bad time?"

"Nope. He was a perfect guest except when he and Jean talked me into a knife throwing exhibition. I was surprised you gave him permission."

"My husband and I know a bit about you, because of recent, shall I say notoriety surrounding some past instances this school year."

Oh boy. "This has been a very difficult year for us as far as unforeseen circumstances."

Sonny held his iPhone so his Mom could see the screen in landscape view. "You have to see this. Mr. McCarty is really good with the knives."

At first Nick saw a resigned look on Clarice's face, then shock, concern, and finally uneasiness in one showing. Nick smiled. He figured that should take care of any further interest in the McCarty household. The video finished, and she patted Sonny on the shoulder.

"Go show that to your Dad."

"C'mon, Jean. You can meet my Dad while I show him the video."

Jean glanced at Nick uneasily, as he sensed she was beginning to notice a bit of strangeness. He nodded at her. "Go ahead. I'll be in to meet Mr. Salvatore in a moment."

"That was better than a circus act. Where did you learn to throw knives?"

"It was something I took an interest in while I was in the service. Jean has a real passion for it, and now that it's a widely accepted sport, I've been teaching her how to throw. She's a natural."

"Were you really in Delta Force? My husband hates pulp fiction, but when he found out you were a bestselling New York Times author of an assassin series, he bought your first one: Diego's Way. He hated it, but I thought it was interesting."

"My assassin series is definitely not for everyone, and yes, I was in Delta."

Clarice crossed her arms over chest, leaning back slightly, a classic body language negative. "When Sonny called me about the knife exhibition, he said you're with the FBI, CIA, and the US Marshals. He said you had two US Marshals at your house tonight. Is all that really true?"

"Yes. I'm a consultant with all of those entities, and even with our local police department. The two US Marshals are in charge of our Northern California area. They sometimes need an opinion on a case, as do the other agencies mentioned. I have a propensity for languages. I've also been all over the world when I was with Delta, and doing research for my novels. It's not a big deal. I have an active imagination, and real life combat experience. I helped the Department of Justice with a leak problem they had, and it led to my consulting position. I became involved with the CIA during my time in Delta."

"Don't you have to kill me, now that I know your secrets?"

Nick enjoyed that adlib. "No. I consult only, so I don't really have to sign any nondisclosure contracts or anything, except during the time I'm consulting on a particular case."

A man a couple inches taller than Nick stepped into the room, also wearing jeans, but with a gray t-shirt and loafers. Dark haired, dark eyes, and with an easy smile, Nick couldn't picture him ever being anything but relaxed. They shook hands.

"This is my husband, Phil."

"Glad to meet you, Phil. I'm Nick McCarty. I see you've met Jean."

"Nice meeting you too, Nick. If Sonny hadn't shown me that knife exhibition on video, I wouldn't have believed it. It must have taken many hours of practice to achieve that level of expertise."

"Finally, someone that knows it's not a magic trick." Nick grinned. "Yes, it took many, many hours of practice. Jean has taken an interest in the sport."

"So she told me. Sonny wants to try it too, but I have concerns. I've never pictured throwing knives as a sport. It's deadly, and throwing them the way you do does almost seem like a magic trick."

"Jean and Sonny seem to hit it off well, so I'm sure they can find other interests. I'll curtail any further demonstrations," Nick promised. "They worked their homework in solid harmony. That's a nice start."

"For now, I think it would be better for Sonny to stay away from the knife throwing. I'll give it some consideration though. I read one of your novels."

"Clarice said you dislike pulp fiction, and that is what my assassin series amounts to. As I mentioned to her, it's not for everyone."

"Small doubt about that," Phil agreed. "Wouldn't you agree though that even pulp fiction should be a bit believable?"

Nick grinned, knowing each one of Diego's adventures were based on his real life sanctions; that were both bloodier, and even more violent. "Oh, I don't know. I read all Edgar Rice Burroughs' novels like Tarzan of the Apes, and John Carter of Mars. Later, I read many of Robert E Howard's novels and stories with Conan the Barbarian, Solomon Kane, and El Borak. They're larger than life pulp fiction type heroes."

"Yes, I guess it is a matter of taste."

"Exactly," Nick agreed. "I never hype my novels claiming they're anything other than pulp fiction. I'm definitely not writing Shakespearean prose."

"I see your point. I work for the State Department, so I know it's impossible for you to belong to all the agencies Sonny told me about. What is it you really do with law enforcement?"

Nick shrugged. "I answered the question truthfully. You can choose to believe anything you want, Phil. Well, tomorrow's another day starting early, so Jean and I will off to prepare for our adventures in the morning. Nice meeting all of you."

Phil followed. "Sorry. I didn't mean to offend you. I wanted you to know I'm familiar with what can and cannot be in federal law enforcement."

"I'm not offended at all, Phil. As I said, you can believe anything you want. You're mistaken in my case, but it's not worth getting into a debate over. Goodnight."

"Ah… yes, goodnight."

Jean and Sonny exchanged waves as Nick led the way out. In the car, Jean gave Nick the silent treatment. "Okay, what did I do?"

"You let that Phil guy call you a liar."

"He didn't call me a liar. Phil cloaked it in very considerate language," Nick replied, grinning over at Jean while he started the car. "What did you want me to do, beat him up?"

"Yeah… but I see what you mean. You could go back over there with all your ID's," Jean suggested, "or have your CIA boss call him. That'll make his mouth drop open."

"There's something a bit off about Phil. When he mentioned working with the State Department, my alarm bells went off. I don't know of any State Department jobs on the West Coast. In regard to your suggestion, I'm not doing that. I'd rather you remain friends with Sonny, and stay away from the adult business. I've probably already given Phil enough mystery that he'll be poking around where he shouldn't as it is."

"What happens if he does?"

"Nothing. He'll simply find out he can't access my records at his level. That will be enough for him to drop any further inquiries into my business. He and Clarice seem like real nice people, and I can tell Sonny's a good kid."

"Sonny's going to join the Marines like me," Jean said. "He liked my line about getting seasoned in the Corps."

"I'll bet he did."

"Did you ever have a best friend when you were a kid?"

Nick hesitated. He wanted to assure Jean he had lots of friends, but he had never lied to her about anything, and he didn't plan on starting now. "No. I was a loner. I had buddies in the service I was close to, because our lives depended on it. I never did meet anyone I cared to be around much. Let's face it, psychos don't make very good besties. If we need something from you, we'll pretend to be a bestie until we get it. That's as close as we come though."

"You love Mom and me."

"I'm older now, and getting soft in the head."

Jean giggled.

Chapter Seven

Until Guilty

Rachel waved from the couch, where she and Tina were watching a movie. She paused the show. "How did the parental meeting go?"

"Not so good," Nick admitted.

"Sonny's Father called Dad a liar, and he's still breathing," Jean inserted, garnering surprised laughter.

"Gomez," Tina said. "Are you turning over a new leaf?"

"Phil didn't call me a liar in so many words. He… sort of hinted at it. As I tried to explain to the Daughter of Darkness what bothered me were some of the questions both he and Clarice asked, and the fact they moved here from Washington, D.C. He questioned the veracity of my being a consultant for the CIA, FBI, and US Marshals, claiming he worked for the State Department. I think they were going to interrogate me further, but Sonny showed them the video he took of my knife exhibition. I think it dissuaded them from pushing the envelope. I could tell Clarice was shooting over some raised eyebrows at Phil. I think it would be best if Jean and Sonny tryout their friendship without we adults becoming involved. We don't have to be rude, but we can avoid another interrogation."

Rachel jabbed a finger at Nick from over the back of the couch. "I know you. Mr. Salvatore is about to become the subject of intense scrutiny."

"Maybe."

Tina sighed. "Same old Gomez, different day. Don't make this Clarice a single Mom until you gather more evidence."

When no one spoke, Tina glanced at Nick's slight smile as he watched her. All frivolity disappeared from her features instantly. "Uh… I may have had one wine too many, Nick. Sorry."

"Inside the Addams' Family living room is the place to do it," Nick said. "I don't think it would be a good idea to do so anywhere uninformed ears can hear those witty one-liners, Cousin Itt."

"Understood."

"Is Gus on the Deck?"

"He didn't want to watch 'Malificent' with us, so he adjourned upstairs."

Jean sat down with them instantly. "I'll watch that one again."

"I'll keep Gus company. Has Deke been out lately?"

"He's been in and out a few times," Rachel answered.

"Good. C'mon Deke. I'll spring for a beer. You were a-"

Before Nick could finish the sentence, Deke was staring down at him from the stair landing. "That's a very unique way of finishing my sentence, Deke."

* * *

Tina gulped some wine down, and motioned for Rachel to wait a moment while she went to pour another portion from the bottle on the living room serving stand. "I sure stepped in it for a moment there."

She sat down again. "You two could have giggled a little to take the edge off the silence."

159

Jean hugged Tina. "Don't worry, Aunt Tina, Dad would never hurt you… unless he had to."

Tina frowned at the smiling Jean. "Not funny. You're getting to be a scary little girl, Miss Wednesday Addams."

"I hope so. It's the only way to survive in this family, Cousin Itt."

"Wednesday's right," Rachel agreed. "The good part - it's never boring. The bad part – it's never boring. Take for instance this book tour to Washington with the added ingredients of serial killers, and terrorists."

"I have to keep in mind, Cousin Itt was a visiting character, and sometimes disappeared for long periods. Someone throw Cousin Itt a lifeline if you see her heading for the quicksand."

"We will," Rachel said, patting Tina's hand.

"Give us a chance though," Jean advised. "Don't dive into it before we can throw."

* * *

Gus was laughing as Nick and Deke came out on the deck. "Planting that bug in the living room was pure genius, Muerto. Tina's worried she'll get a quick burial at sea if she doesn't watch her mouth."

Nick sat down with a shot and beer after pouring Deke one. "I thought to record a few insights from my surprise visitors like Sergeant Dickerson. I see you've found a dangerous form of entertainment. If Tina ever finds out you're spying on her, it's the doghouse for you, Payaso."

"Duly noted. I heard about your visit with the Salvatores. That sounded a bit ominous. I see you've brought the satellite

160

notebook on deck. Does that mean you're going on a fishing expedition?"

"It seems like the right thing to do. Paul gave me unfettered access to the CIA infrastructure. I may as well use it."

"The Salvatores' arrival from D.C. does seem too much of a coincidence while Formsby's empire is getting smashed, especially with the people we know he's been paying off."

"That's my take on it too." A moment later, Nick cursed under his breath, downed his shot, and chased it with half the beer. "Guess who worked under Nancy Pettinger for a few years at the DOJ, before being promoted to the State Department. He also ran across Ken Schilling more than a few times while in his liaison position."

"Oh boy." Gus filled his shot glass. "You're turning our hometown into a hotbed of government minions who seem to be pursuing a course unfavorable to our survival, Muerto."

"It gets worse. He's the head of the liaison office at State which deals directly with the CIA. I'm not certain I'm the only one fishing in these waters. Would they move a State Department Chief into a West Coast town without an agenda, or a job cover of some kind? You would think they'd figure out something other than sending him here with his family in tow. There's a note in here about Phil being on assignment. Maybe that's the clue we need to follow. I'm alerting Paul first, so if there's a plan in the works to screw his Formsby moves, he'll at least know where it originated."

"Nick?"

"Yep. I have a guy out here slipping into my personal life with a wife and son, named Phil Salvatore. He worked with Nancy Pettinger, and brushed shoulders with your traitorous buddy, Ken Schilling. I see in his file he's listed as on assignment. His last job title was Chief at State's CIA liaison office."

161

"He's in Pacific Grove?" Gilbrech's surprised tone worried Nick.

"Yeah, right in my backyard."

"First off, I didn't know they had reassigned him to the West Coast. Everyone who ever knew Pettinger or Schilling was demoted, including Salvatore. He ain't the chief of anything. I've seen his file, because of his circumstances, and connection to CIA. He's clean, but apparently a bit too trusting. Hold on… I'm almost through the… yes… Phil's been demoted to the San Francisco Passport Agency. They probably let him work out of anywhere he wants on the coast. That he picked where you live is a bit disconcerting. How did you run into him?"

"His kid goes to school with Jean – same class. They're friends, which seems genuine, but Phil may have guided his Son into the friendship. With all the crap flowing around from Didricson, Sadun, and Lawyer Wargul who has an office in San Francisco, I'm wondering if my pal Phil knows something about me he shouldn't. I talked to him tonight. He made a point of letting me know he didn't believe I could be consulting with multiple government agencies. Now I'm curious to know what he does believe. You know me and coincidences."

"I can make a call, and he'll be filling out forms in a cubicle at the Passport Office."

"Let's leave him be for now. I'm changing modes for fixing my Lawyer Wargul problem. I'll be calling soon. Thanks for the update, Paul."

"Anytime, Nick." Gilbrech disconnected.

"This is becoming a regular chess match with all the pieces materializing out of nowhere on the board. I have to make the Wargul sanction look and feel like a professional hit, or Timmy and Grace won't get permission to move Sadun. With this unknown rogue bishop scampering here from Washington D.C. assigned to an office in San Francisco, I'm hesitant to plug Wargul from afar as I planned. Salvatore knows too much about me."

"Damn, Nick. It would be the shits if you have to whack the Dad of Jean's friend."

"Tell me about it. His questions seemed too off base. Anyway, I'll hack into Wargul's office, and get his day planner for tomorrow. Maybe he has something on his schedule where I could snatch him, take him somewhere quiet, and put a .22 caliber bullet in the back of his head, gangland style. That should make the US Marshal ploy to move Sadun work. I think we'll have to cut our ties to Sergeant Dickerson. He's a jinx. We have some down time, kicking back on the beach with Irish coffees, and he calls me in for a consult. Then, before you can blink your eyes, we have traitors, assassins, gangsters, flag protestors, terrorists, and a serial killer all for attention on our horizon. If that isn't a jinx I don't know what is."

"I doubt Dickerson's a jinx," Gus replied. "More likely, these days of danger are due to your Karma train steaming into the station, late on arrival."

Nick's head thudded on the table. "Not you and your damn Karma train again. You only play the Karma train card when you've had too much to drink. That's what comes of guzzling booze while creepily eavesdropping on your wife's conversations – out pops the Karma train."

Nick straightened while Gus enjoyed the Nick's slam. He lanced into Wargul's office network without a glitch, chuckling a little in appreciation. "Thank you, Brook. Guess who went smartphone nuts, and had his security system wired into his network so he can check on everything from anywhere?"

Nick's chuckle turned to laughter. "Well what have we here? It looks like my new good buddy, Brook Wargul, has an eye for the ladies, Payaso. Then, he allows his other body parts to reap what the eyes doth desire."

Gus moved around behind Nick. A man, Gus knew to be Brook Wargul, was in the middle of a carnal act on top of his desk with a woman bent over it face first. Her face was turned toward the side angle camera Nick had accessed. "Oh man, this goes to show, there really can be too much technology. I know what you're thinking, Muerto, but there are too many security cams in those buildings. You can't waltz in there, pump a round into Brook, and disappear."

"We need to find out if this is a regular thing, or a one timer with a client. Keep an eye on the door, Payaso. I need to turn this up a little so I can hear their after sex chatter."

When the sex act ended, Nick increased the volume, listening intently to the participants' conversation while they dressed, and straightened the office. Before they left the office, Wargul embraced the dark haired woman with passion.

"I love this with you. I can't wait for the end of the day. Watching you parade around at work drives me crazy. All I can think about is this time we have before the cleaning crew gets in here. I hope to God you're not thinking about ending us."

"Why would you say that? I'm here. This is so kinky. I can't believe I'm doing it. I have to go. My husband will be home soon. I can only stretch the delay business so far. I'll see you tomorrow."

"I can't wait."

Nick and Gus watched Wargul gather his briefcase, and leave, locking the place before he left. "I'll find out who she is from the employment records. Now, we have to wait and see how long it actually takes for the cleaning crew to hit his floor."

The professional cleaning service began on Wargul's floor twenty minutes later. "Oh, this will be sweet, Payaso. I'll hack into their building security, and avoid most of their cams. You'll have the easy work. We'll use my downstairs safe-room, where I have the multiple monitors in place for this kind of op."

"You can't break into the building without being seen, Muerto. You'll be on video somewhere approaching the building. They have cams everywhere."

"Who said anything about breaking in? I'll drive to SFO International, stash my gear in a locker, and then take BART (Bay Area Rapid Transit) into the city tomorrow morning after we walk Jean to school. I'll have my lawyer Muerto disguise on, complete with briefcase, three piece suit, long coat, and hat. I'll find a quiet place to wait for day's end, drifting into position somewhere near his office. At the proper moment, I'll come in with Muerto mask in place, zap Brook, and administer a sleepy time shot to his paramour adulteress. I'll duct tape Wargul into a chair, and shoot him in the head with my .22 auto with stainless steel titanium noise suppressor. I'll let the janitor discover him while I hightail it to BART for my ride to SFO. I should be back home before ten."

"You rattled that out of your psychopathic mind in seconds after noting Wargul nails his secretary after hours. You are a very bad man, Muerto."

"Thank you, Payaso. I try to be thorough. Your job will be to watch everything around me on building security. I'll be observing their security people during the day. I'll let you know if I spot anything funky that could disrupt my exit from the building. The important check will be watching me on their cams as I avoid them, going all the way to his office in the morning."

"You'll need to note down how well I do at each checkpoint," Nick continued. "I can probably do it a few times without arousing suspicion in the morning with people arriving for work and appointments. After that, I don't think it would be a good idea. If I can find and disable any type of alarm at an emergency exit door, I should be able to disappear into the night without even a stir from security. You'll be watching for exactly when the body is discovered, where I am at that time, and when the police finally arrive in relation to my journey home."

"One thing's for sure," Gus replied, "if you can pull that stunt off without a hitch, it will definitely rate as a cold blooded professional hit. Tim and Grace should have no problem requesting and being granted a change of venue for Sadun. Do you want me to fetch Jean home from school too?"

"No. I don't want you moving from the screens. I'll have Rachel drive over for Jean. She won't have to explain where I am, but if she does, the answer will be writing my new manuscript. That is exactly what I'll be doing all day tomorrow, while avoiding excess scrutiny."

"It will be one stress filled day. You are going to ask John to come over on this too, right? I don't want to be the only one on the monitors.

"Of course." Nick poured another half beer for Deke, and sipped from what remained in the bottle. "I need John in on this too in case I have to go to ground for a while, and avoid all public places. If that happens, I'll find a spot along the docks on the Embarcadero to wait until he can make his way into the city. I plan on making sure that safety valve doesn't get opened though."

"When you steamroll one of these suicidal ideas into motion, do you ever get even a slight twinge of anxiety?"

Nick met Gus's curious stare with a malicious looking grin. "Here's the deal, Payaso. As you know, I kill people as a vocation, and I'm good at it. I'm good at it, because I don't hesitate. I don't care what the mark does for a living, what brought him or her to a position where I'm ready to execute their asses, or who will be wailing in sorrow at their funeral. Sure, I may have an assortment of reasons why I decide to kill someone, but once it's decided, it's a done deal that either the mark or I will be dead. Wargul's going to die tomorrow, or I am."

"I sure picked the right comic book character for you, Muerto."

"Remember who talked me out of retirement, Payaso."

"Believe me, you haven't let me forget that for a day since I did it. I shouldn't have bothered. You were only about a week away from a rampage or going back to work on your own. Even your fictional psycho, Diego, on a killing spree mimicking your own real life adventures while earning you a fortune wasn't enough. Admit it, and take me off the blame list. You used me."

Nick chuckled. "Yeah, you're right, Payaso. I'll stop needling you on that point. I was done with retirement. Even going back into the sand was preferable. When you hit me with the Muerto thing, it came at a great time. I hate when I can't wear the mask and make videos now. I want to do the hit tomorrow as El Muerto, and it's disappointing I can't."

Gus held his beer for a toast, which Nick clinked with his own. "To Muerto."

"And Payaso, and El Kabong," Nick added.

"We are lunatics. You know that don't you?"

"We're deadly ones though, and I can't wait for the road trip to Washington. I want that 'Seattle Ripper' guy. I have some ideas for his doubtful longevity. He will be going out in style with El Muerto's tag on him. Don't worry, I haven't forgotten about our Isis compound problem either. All in good time, Payaso. All in good time."

* * *

167

After parking his car in the short term parking at SFO International Airport, Nick exited in his three piece dark gray suit with dark tan long coat, lapels up, and pinch front gray fedora hat. His leather briefcase held Nick's .22 caliber automatic and noise suppressor under a layer of reinforced leather at the bottom. He also carried a syringe kit, laptop, foldable black windbreaker with hood, and a black scarf. He had studied the layout of the security system within Wargul's building until he knew where and what triggered the moveable security cams.

The exit Nick decided on for his escape from the Wargul building was a first floor fire exit he needed to be certain would not be locked. The building also had a break room with every conceivable vending machine, along with tables and chairs. Nick planned to spend the day there writing in a corner, out of security cam sight.

Leaving on the BART (Bay Area Rapid Transit) train out of the terminal inside the airport, Nick arrived in San Francisco's downtown Market Street BART station by shortly after 9 am. He checked in with Gus and John before walking the mile to Wargul's business location, testing communications, and cam signal.

"It's all good, Payaso. I'll text you from the break room inside the building. It will be in your hands after that to let me know when Wargul plays around with the office help. I'll proceed directly to his office the moment I get the all clear sign from you."

"I'll send you the video from all cam's perspective at the moment you enter the building. I'll work on erasing you while you move from one station to the next. We should have plenty of time while you're in the break room to go over what we have to keep or change. John wants to know if you're going to check the make of the office door lock. Once in there, you won't be able to simply pick up and leave."

"Tell him I have that covered. I've picked countless locks like this office has. After all, they don't have a nuclear weapon in there, Kabong."

"We'll get off the line then, and attend to our business here, stalking the 'Seattle Ripper'," John joked. "Gus explained the intricacies of finding out a few starting threads 'in the Ripper's life. By the time you get back home, maybe we'll know who the 'Ripper' is in reality."

"Fine by me," Nick replied. "We'll simply confirm it when we get to Washington, and then lay in wait for an opportunity to catch him red handed. One thing at a time though. We have a Wargul to teach his last lesson to, followed by the infamous Sadun. How's our after-hours lady doing today?"

"She's hot, Muerto. Our little Heather Durst dressed to the nines for Brook. Short black skirt, and a red silk shoulder-less blouse. She's working it too. Ms. Durst and our buddy Brook really have the office erotic romance going for them. I'm sure Heather plans to walk on the wild side again after work."

"I'm depending on you guys to make sure I come in at that wonderful moment of release, when our Brook will be enjoying those flowing endorphins of happiness. It will then be a special moment for his lady friend adulteress, Heather. Let's concentrate on making it memorable for all of us. Get busy, and keep me informed. We don't want to disappoint our lovely couple."

"He's a sick man, John," Gus stated. "Admit it."

"Sorry, Muerto, but you are a sick man."

"Taking pride in what you do, and doing it well, should not be a target for critics who do nothing but bitch and moan, Payaso. I'm very disappointed in you, Kabong. This insidious mutiny within the ranks of the Unholy Trio will not be forgotten by El Muerto."

"We have to go, John. When he starts talking in third person, my teeth start aching."

John chuckled. "We'll be working it, Muerto. Good luck."

"Good luck? That's blasphemy, John," Nick replied, maintaining his outrage.

* * *

Brook Wargul locked the outer office door, his heart pounding in anticipation. Watching Heather the entire day, Wargul fought down his nearly debilitating desire for the woman. Since starting the affair a month ago with his office manager, he endured the monotonous daily workload with a careless attitude toward business he never experienced before. The inadvertent smiles, touches, and whisperings acted only to draw his illicit attention to each day's ending tryst. The fact they were both safely married to inattentive partners made their pairing easy, and urgent, without worry about pressure being brought to bear making more of the affair than there was. To Wargul, it was the best of all possible worlds. He and Heather acted out their lovemaking foreplay all day long in exciting doses made all the more erotic by the presence of their coworkers. By day's end, their desires could only be satisfied in a short, nearly violent romp, the ecstasy of release their only mutual goal.

Heather awaited Brook, sitting on the corner of his desk, her legs crossed with skirt riding upwards past her thighs. He grunted approvingly, noting her panties and bra were tossed in a ball onto an office chair. Her unbuttoned red silk top opened slightly as she hunched forward provocatively, her breasts pushing against the material. She allowed her long blonde hair to hang loosely over her cheeks, untethered from the restraining tie during the work day.

Brook moved toward her after closing his inner office door with slow deliberation. The moment before he initiated contact,

170

acted as the catalyst each day to end their mutual foreplay, and begin the much anticipated coupling each sought release in. His hands framed her face, lips brushing together at first in gentle acknowledgement, turning into a writhing urgency, hands kneading and caressing all within reach. Heather moaned, arching to meet his busy hands.

"My God, Heather... you drove me insane today! I couldn't think of anything else."

Heather allowed Wargul to push her skirt up while she unbuckled his pants. "I want you inside me now! Don't you dare come either for a few moments. Then, I'll turn... then I'll want it hard, fast, and final with everything you've got, baby!"

"Anything... anything," Wargul whispered against her mouth.

* * *

"How far are you away, Muerto? John and I may have misjudged the climax of this sinful union," Gus said.

"I anticipated it somewhat from past times we studied. I knew I'd need to avoid the cams we had gone over location for on the way to his office. I'm approaching his outer office door now."

John sighed in relief. "Good, because I think you should enter the office now. Then move to his inner office door."

"Believe this," Gus added, "Wargul will not hear you open the inner door. Open it slightly, and wait for our cue. I hate to say it, but I believe you may have predicted yet another horrific moment to be logged into the El Muerto file of the sacrilegious and profane."

"I must agree with my brother, Payaso," John added. "It is a good thing this is not St. Valentine's Day. Cupid would arrive to avenge this travesty you're about to attempt."

171

"Cut the comedy act!" Nick whispered, while bent to his task with a smile.

The final tumbler moved on the outer door lock as Nick pulled open the door in a quietly rapid motion as he pushed down on the door handle. He slipped inside, closing and locking the door once again, his black Nitrile gloves keeping a firm grip on the handle until the door was completely secured in place. Nick approached Wargul's inner office door with a grin. The sounds of the office's occupants made it plain to Nick they would not hear him open the door, even if it did make a little noise. He quickly put on his El Muerto mask, and then retrieved the syringe destined for Heather's journey into unconsciousness. As he gripped the handle, Gus gave him a warning.

"Get the door open, and syringe in hand, Muerto. The final stage in this play is how should we describe it, John?"

"Shooting to a conclusion?"

"That's the one," Gus confirmed.

Nick shook his head with Gus and John chortling in his ear. He retrieved the syringe from his long coat pocket after pushing the door open slightly. Listening intently to the last stages of an energetic lovemaking session, Nick waited behind the door with patience practiced and perfected over the years, his heartbeat nearly the same as if he were eating an apple while sitting on a park bench. A distinct crescendo was reached in loud mutual gratification by its participants.

"Now, Muerto," Gus directed.

Nick slipped inside, closing the door behind him silently. He hurried to where Wargul lay partially atop Heather's back, panting nearly in cooing harmony with his paramour. Nick reach around Wargul's flank, and used the syringe on Heather's right buttock.

"Ouch!" Heather tried to push away from the desk in reaction to the sharp pain.

Wargul remained where he was, not sure if he heard her right or not. "What did you say, Hon?"

Heather's movements to break free of her lover merely hastened the drug's effect, rendering her unconscious seconds later, her last sound a sleepy groan. Wargul massaged the unconscious Heather's shoulders, while straightening slightly, still coupled to her.

"Oh baby, that was the best." Brook smacked Heather on the butt, grinning at her completely relaxed state. "Wore you out, huh?"

The stun-gun electrodes catapulted Wargul against the desk, and then into a vibrating heap on the floor. Nick roughly dragged him into an office chair with armrests. As Wargul tried to keep from passing out, Nick duct taped him into place on the chair at his wrists, ankles, knees, and chest. He stuffed a small ball into Brook's mouth, and sealed it with another piece of duct tape. Nick checked Heather's pulse before transferring a white cardboard sign with newspaper clipping headline letters reading 'ADULTERESS!' from his briefcase onto her back.

"That's cold, Muerto!"

"If you're offended, Payaso, look away and do your job of watching for building security. The sign will give the cops numerous other false avenues to follow."

Nick slapped Wargul into coherent thought with light, sharp, smacks. When Wargul was fully aware of his surroundings, with wide staring eyes, and blubbering speech, Nick waved a hand in front of his face.

"Hi, Brook. Your days of dealing with terrorists are now over. I know you've been doing naughty things, passing your client

Uthman Sadun's notes to Milton Formsby, and Pence Didricson as a traitorous gopher. I have only one question for you; but first, I need to let you know I'm like a human lie detector. I'll notice what we call 'tells' you won't even know you're doing. Then the bad times start happening, like this."

Nick stun-gunned Wargul's balls. The man jackknifed against his restraints, the intense high pitched squeal emitted in an unending sound of horror around the ball in his mouth. Once the pain subsided, Nick leaned down to stare into Brook's eyes. "Did you get the message of what will happen if I detect any lie at all?"

A violent up and down affirmation of his head indicated Wargul's complete understanding.

"Good, because if I detect a lie, the ball goes back into the mouth, and you get three more doses of electro testicle treatment." Nick removed the duct tape and ball. He positioned himself to look directly into Wargul's eyes once again. Nick shushed the whining Wargul. "Quiet. This will all be over shortly. Did you share the information you received with any other human being?"

"No!" Wargul stared back at Nick unblinkingly, terrified his answer would not be accepted. He wanted to plead, but the cold darkness in the eyes gazing into his made him fearful he would be tortured for added sound.

Nick grinned. "Good. I'll fix you for the janitor to find."

Nick stuffed the ball back into Wargul's mouth with sealing tape over it. He took out his .22 caliber pistol with noise suppressor from under the false bottom in his briefcase, and shot Wargul in the back of his head three times. Nick checked over the room with care, along with his additional scene structure.

"I'm leaving. How's it look, Payaso?"

"All clear. The security guard is out front taking a smoke break. The moment you leave, John and I will wipe all trace of you away. Call if you need us."

"Will do. I should be home at a decent hour, probably in enough time to discuss the deadly danger ahead for Sadun. Someone murdered his lawyer – a truly heinous deed. We must make sure our buddy Uthman is safe."

"Oh yes, we must make certain of that, Muerto," Gus replied, with John laughing in the background. "Are there any suspects in the death of that poor lawyer?"

"I'm thinking the butler did it."

"You're in a law office. They don't have butlers."

"Maybe they should. Then, something like this could have been prevented."

"Get the hell out of there, Muerto, before the janitorial staff arrives," Gus ordered.

"On my way, Payaso. Your attitude tonight has not been very professional. I found you to be disrespectful and sarcastic in our interaction. This will not look good on your record."

"I'll survive. You would have to physically find the Twilight Zone to recruit someone to take my place."

"That simply isn't true, Payaso." Nick slipped out the emergency exit he had disarmed while passing the day in the building until it was time to keep his appointment with Wargul. "I could pay someone off the street a few hundred dollars per week to insult me when I have a mission."

"Oh barf!"

"Did Rachel pick up Jean okay?"

"Yep. I sent John with her anyway, in case there were any holdovers from the flag bashing idiots. It seems that particular bunch have decided to curb their baser tendencies, since you influenced a lot of the parents to file complaints against the instigators."

"We took Sonny home, and Rachel went in to meet the Salvatores," John added. "She said it turned from a 'hi, and how are you, pleased to meet you', into an interrogation. Rachel said Mr. Salvatore wondered how they met, what she did, what you did when you weren't writing pulp, and what you used for inspiration. Then, according to Rachel, he snuck in a grinning joke about all your supposed badges from different federal entities."

"Oh boy," Nick muttered. He stopped at the corner of a building nearly three blocks away. He stuffed his long coat and bowler hat in the brief case, changing into the Giants ball cap and black windbreaker from the case. Nick drew the hood over the ball cap, tightening it in place before proceeding on to the BART station. "As long as everyone survived, we'll stay away from the Salvatores, and let Jean develop her friendship with Sonny on her own. I'm headed to the BART station right now. All quiet on the Western Front. Start tuning into the news, and keep me updated."

"Will do," Gus replied. "That scene you left them should be enough of a mystery to keep them busy for a long while. We'll let you know when the janitor discovers the bodies. How long will the woman be out?"

"Probably until midnight or so. She'll definitely be on display for the janitor. You guys go ahead and watch the monitors, and news. I have a ways to go."

Nick made it to the Market Street Station in good time, amongst a crowd of people at the normally busy station. At SFO International, he retrieved his car, and headed for home without anything happening on his way that would call attention to his trip.

A couple of hours later, Nick walked in the front door, having made great time. John greeted him.

"They only just discovered Wargul and his girl. The janitorial staff had to make due with two fewer workers from the snatches of conversation we heard between them and the security guard. The police arrived a few minutes ago. Rachel and Jean are in Jean's room. Go say goodnight. Gus and I will keep track for you.

"Thanks, John." Nick fended off the excited Deke who flew down the stairs to greet him. "Easy Deke. Have you been taking care of our women folk? Let's go check in with them, and then I'll give you some exercise."

Jean rushed over to give Nick a hug as he cleared the doorway behind Deke. "Dad! You made it home before ten. Nice."

"Yep. My small business trip was good, and I'll have a favorable report for Tim and Grace. I heard you and your Mom had quite the meet and greet at the Salvatores."

"That's an understatement." Rachel came over to embrace Nick. "I handled the interrogation pretty well. You're right as usual. There's something going on we are not aware of. I'm certain Sonny doesn't have a clue. He was giving his old man the fisheye at some of the questions. The Mom is in on the game though."

"I'm not messing around with Sonny anymore," Jean stated. "His parents are weird. Heck, we're weird, but we mind our own business."

"True, but you don't have to stop being Sonny's friend," Nick said. "Your Mom and I will continue to be polite, but I think we'll stay away from the Salvatores. They want to know a lot more than a couple of regular parents would want to know. His ties to a couple of very suspect people in government, and then being demoted to the West Coast might mean he's a bit upset with me."

"Sonny's really nice. He apologized for his Father today at school. Like Mom said, he was confused at the way his parents were acting. I could tell he thought they'd be nicer."

"Get some sleep. The Dekester and I will be escorting you to school. I'll say hello to Tim and Grace for you."

"Goodnight, Dad. I'm glad you're okay. I was worried. I knew tonight was important, and I saw Uncle Gus and Uncle John's faces. I could tell they were worried."

Nick kissed her on the forehead. "Thanks for worrying. See you in the morning."

Rachel kissed Jean goodnight, and followed Nick out. "I'm going to bed, Nick. That Salvatore guy wore me out. It's lucky I didn't have my stun-gun with me. I would have lit him up. Are you going to walk Deke tonight?"

Nick glanced down at Deke, who cocked his head quizzically as he walked next to Nick. "Yeah, I'm taking him out. I have to stay awake for a while until I see how my business does in the media. If it's not on the late night news, I'll have done real well staying under the radar."

Rachel bumped against Nick, grabbing his hand. "Wake me when you come to bed."

"I will do so, would you like a little of this?" Nick stepped away, trying to launch into the pantomime Rachel did not like, but she jumped him.

"Don't you do it!"

Nick instead played roving hands for the next few moments until Rachel pulled away breathlessly, at which time Nick completed his hand pantomime with Rachel slapping his hands.

"Damn you!"

"You won't be able to think of anything else now. I won't have to wake you. You'll be lying awake waiting to be ravished in your favorite manner."

Rachel blushed, and gave Nick a push. "It's not my favorite. Get away from me."

Nick backed away, holding his hands in a surrendering gesture. "Okay... but I warned you. Only a loving husband could make his very pregnant wife so sexually aroused."

"Revolted would be more descriptive, Muerto," Rachel replied in a hissing whisper.

Nick spun away from his planned perusal of the news with his unholy trio partners to quickly repeat his revolting tagged gestures, drawing a gasping intake of outraged breath from Rachel, much to his amusement. He continued on his way down to where his friends monitored both internet and mainstream news.

"Nothing yet, Nick," Gus said. "John and I exited surveillance at the scene. The homicide detectives are probably just arriving now. The moment the janitor gets released from questioning, he'll be outing the whole experience to the news media. How much you want to bet he took camera phone pictures of your scene too. If those get leaked with the executed Wargul, the coverage will be all over the place, blaming the husband, the mob, and even getting it right by blaming it on a serial killer."

John turned away, enjoying Gus's pronouncement the media would be right if blaming Wargul's death on a serial killer. "Very funny, Payaso. I'm going to sip one, and then take Deke for a walk. I think we're done for the night. It doesn't matter what they fantasize about now. They'll have to wait for our adulteress to awaken, and for the initial CSI results. You two can take off. I'm calling Tim and Grace on the walk, and let them know to begin suggesting Sadun's transfer."

"I do not like to mention these messy details, but we need to empty our special freezer. I know the Sadun thing is a priority. If you plan to also make Sadun disappear in line with the escape being planned by Sadun's friends, we need to clean our body vault."

"Agreed. I haven't been considering details lately concerning our room temperature guests in the Valley. You're right about Sadun. I need to make sure no one ever finds him. I'll fill you in on my Tim and Grace call tomorrow. Let's meet on the beach."

"At nine?"

"Yeah. I'm escorting Jean to school. It's getting late. I think I'll sip one when I get back. C'mon Deke. Let's walk our buddies out." Nick grabbed Deke's leash. He set his security system after the men cleared the doorway.

"I'll walk with you, Muerto. I need some air," Gus said. "See you tomorrow, John."

"Okay, Gus. That op was very well done, Muerto," John said, waving as he walked to his car.

Gus and Nick started out walking Deke with Nick calling Grace and Tim. He heard Tim's voice. "It's done, Tim. After the news hits tomorrow, you and Grace can start making your case to move our friend."

"We'll be watching the news then, Nick. Grace and I will push for the move immediately after the news gets out, and I'll let you know exact time and date."

"Good enough. Talk to you then." Nick disconnected. "Well Gus, did you enjoy today's action? I figured you didn't walk Deke with me because you wanted to hold my hand."

"That was insanely good luck, Muerto. I really did want to get some air. You pulled off the hit exactly as you planned, and even managed a janitorial problem postponing the discovery of Wargul's body."

"But… I feel a but coming."

"Why not let it end without taking a chance on getting Sadun? You've eliminated the go between. Sadun doesn't have anyone to spread his poison to."

"True, but I don't take those kinds of chances, Gus. Sadun would eventually replace Wargul with another traitor. He has the outside money and means."

"I wanted to make sure I pointed out an option I thought was better than the snatch and grab outside the prison."

"Acknowledged, Payaso."

"Here." Gus handed Nick his flask. "It's full."

"God bless you, Sir!" Nick took the flask, and downed a large gulp. "Man… that hit the spot. You were reading my mind. I was already sorry I didn't throw one down before we left."

"What you did to the coworker was a cold piece of work."

"It will be a bit of an embarrassment, but also a life lesson for the woman. Adultery is not a victimless crime."

"Madre de Dios!"

Chapter Eight

Attempted Bombing

Returning from the walk, Gus related some ideas of when they could empty their body freezer at the Carmel Valley house. Nick grabbed his arm suddenly, making shushing sounds. He drew Gus down the hill slightly, and into the darkness cast by the trees lining the property owner's lawn. Deke sat at the nearest tree, watching the two men with him curiously.

"There are two guys in black fooling around my house. Can you stay here with Deke while I go collect them for the cops?"

"Are you sure about this, Muerto," Gus asked while taking Deke's leash. "We can call the cops on them."

"I have my stiletto, stun-gun, pepper spray, and my Colt. I have a damn good idea who these two are, and I have dibs on them before the cops."

"The flag guy, right?"

"Yep. I'm betting it's Rashidi, and his dimwit brother. I've been wondering why I haven't been contacted by the DA or someone. The DA's office probably wants to treat this as a catch and release deal. The brothers think I'm home. I'm not sure about their plan, but they disabled my motion sensor lights. Where they are right now, it should look like daylight. I'll call you when I get a conference with my banditos."

"Please don't get killed, Muerto."

"Okay, but only because you asked nicely."

* * *

"Quickly, Akim," Habib Rashidi whispered. "Attach it right here under the eave."

Akim Rashidi did as his brother ordered. "Do we really need to attach two more, brother?"

"Yes." Habib handed Akim one of the remaining charges. "Attach this at the back corner where I showed you on the house plan. I will put the final charge on the other side of his house."

"Very well. I will meet you at the front when I am through." Akim stayed near the house, stopping every few moments to listen for any noise out of the ordinary. He heard nothing. As he attached the explosive charge to the ash-block base at the left rear corner of the house, Akim heard a sharp electrical crackling noise. The pain in his back proved excruciating enough to cause Akim to momentarily blackout. When his eyes fluttered open, Akim saw Nick smiling at him a moment before Nick pressed the electrodes against Akim's neck for an extended period.

On the other side of the house, Habib heard the crackling noise. He hurriedly set the charge on his side of the house before he heard yet another crackling sound. Making sure of his charge's attachment with a tug, he set the charge, and went to join his brother. Habib hurried around the picket fence on the corner house's front boundary, only to jam against the electrodes of Nick's stun-gun. Habib dropped as if struck by a baseball bat in the head. After an indeterminable time, Habib regained his wits, trying to move his hands, but they were restrained at his back, along with his ankles.

"Hello, Habib," the dark form Habib squinted at patted his cheek. "I've already called the police. They'll be here shortly to collect you, your brother, and your bombs. While we're bonding, I'm going to teach you something about me to take with you to prison."

In the next instant, Habib heard the stun-gun discharge a split second before the worst pain he had ever felt lanced through his groin. It was so bad, the only sound that emerged from Habib sounded like a tea kettle on the boil. The discharges continued at

183

short intervals, where he did not pass out, but stayed in a constant state of unimaginable pain. Sirens in the distance ended the torturous regimen. Habib was dragged to the front of the house with his brother.

* * *

Nick found the cell-phone detonator in Habib's bag, but left it untouched. Rachel and Jean were in the safe-room upstairs where he had told them to go. The safe-room was bomb proof, and although he had inspected the bombs they had planted, he made sure if there were a mistake, Rachel and Jean would not pay for it with their lives. Gus joined him with Deke a moment before a squad car with Sergeant Dickerson arrived.

Dickerson and his partner, Trina Helmgrin walked carefully with hands on the butts of their weapons. "Jesus, Nick, what the hell happened now?"

"Did you request the bomb squad like I told you?"

"Yes. They're in route from Monterey. These guys actually planted bombs on your house?"

"I'll show them to you. I caught them in the act. Gus and I were walking Deke. When we returned, the Rashidi brothers were attaching bombs to my house. I stun-gunned them, and called inside to my wife Rachel to take Jean into our safe-room. The bombs are activated by a cell-phone detonator inside Habib's bag. It's still turned off, but I waited for you and the bomb squad."

"He…he tortured us," Habib croaked. "He…"

"Shut your mouth!" Dickerson squatted down to look into Habib's eyes. "I don't know how the DA ever let you two jackasses out on the streets again, but I can tell you this, you and your brother won't be seeing the outside of a cell for the good part of your lives. Listen closely while I read you your rights again."

When Dickerson finished, he and his partner cut the restraints off, and handcuffed the Rashidi brothers. Once they were in the rear of Dickerson's squad car, Nick showed him the bomb placements while Dickerson filmed it. Nick noticed how nervous Officer Helmgrin was when they returned to the house front.

"The detonator is off," Nick explained. "We can wait on the street for the bomb squad. It wouldn't do any good though. There's enough C4 in those charges to wipe out everything in a hundred yard radius."

"Did they say anything at all about this?"

"I didn't ask, Neil. Would you like me to interrogate them for you?"

"Uh... no, but thanks for the offer. What was Habib mumbling about torture?"

"Well... I didn't find them attaching bombs onto my house structure, and then decide to let bygones be bygones. I disabled the Rashidi boys. I did so with a stun-gun, and I toasted them until they stopped moving. Then I restrained them. I had every right to shoot them both in the head, but I didn't."

"No argument there. I'm really sorry about these two getting out with no warning. When you told me on the phone who you were holding captive, I couldn't believe it. There's no way the DA should have turned them loose before they were arraigned."

"Don't beat yourself up over it. They would have done this sooner or later, and you can bet this isn't the first time they've done something like this. I'm damn lucky we walked Deke tonight or half my neighborhood would be gone."

The bomb squad arrived minutes later. Dickerson handled everything from then on, with Nick joining Gus and Deke across the street, and out of the way.

"We could have found room for those two in the Valley, Muerto. I'm frankly shocked you didn't gut them."

Nick took a deep breath before speaking. "I thought about it, but as I told you before, we have too many things going on right now. The Rashidi boys will be on my radar from now on, along with their families. I didn't see anything like this coming. The most that would have happened to them for the stalking business is some jail time. They were cocky enough to believe they could blow a city block to hell, and get away with it. When they get out, they die. I would imagine they'll be in prison so long I may die first though."

"I believe you've overestimated our justice system, Muerto. Instead of being transferred to Gitmo, they'll probably get a fine."

"You're right, but either way, I'll take care of them. I'm going to get my lawyer to find out what kind of deal could possibly have been done to let them out without informing me."

"You have a lawyer?"

"Sure, I have a lawyer. He's dedicated to me too. His names Justin Khole. I normally don't leave my personal business in the hands of police and our court system. I've used Justin only for mundane law issues like copyright hassles, and property problems. He has people to handle every kind of law problem from estate law to criminal law. He handles the high profile criminal cases."

"I'll bite. How did this gentleman lawyer find his way onto your tab?"

"He defended the wrong criminal."

"Out with it, Muerto. Don't short shrift me on the story."

"It will have to wait for the beach tomorrow, Payaso. Here comes Neil. I need to go inside, comfort the girls, and get some sleep. Thanks for doing duty all day on the monitors."

Gus handed Nick Deke's leash. "It was a classic. That's for sure. Are we sippin' the Irish tomorrow?"

"Bring it, and I'll let you know when I get a US Marshal update. I'll bring the coffee. If you show for the school walk, I'll tell you the Lawyer Khole story on the way."

"If I'm not here by the regular walk time, take off. It will mean I'm in Tina's doghouse, and I'll be trying to make it up to her."

"Understood. See you tomorrow." Nick watched Gus give Neil a quick wave on the way by. Nick walked forward to meet Neil. "How's it going, Officer Dickerson?"

Dickerson showed a pained expression. "I know you're upset about not being informed when those two terrorists were turned loose, but there's not much I can do now but apologize."

"That's okay. I was telling Gus I'm going to have a lawyer friend of mine look into the reasons behind such an oversight. I'm wondering if I have an enemy in the DA's office."

"In your position I'd be doing the same thing. Whatever asshole ordered their release without warning you could have gotten your family plus many in the surrounding houses killed. It can't get swept away under the rug. Homeland Security agents have been notified. They will be here tomorrow morning. Speaking of families, you can rejoin yours now."

"Thanks, Neil. I'll be on my routine tomorrow: walk Jean and Deke, write, and have coffee at the beach. My iPhone will be on if you need to talk with me."

"I'll have to say, Nick, you don't seem very upset about all this. These two terrorists… because that's what they are, attached bombs to your house, and I haven't even heard your voice raise in tenor."

"I'm screaming on the inside."

Dickerson chuckled, and shook his head. "Okay Nick, I'll be in touch."

"One other thing before you go. Did you find that Formsby guy who offered me the ghostwriting gig?"

"Nope. It turned out the CIA and FBI were doing a massive raid on Formsby's holdings. He was dealing with terrorists, and I guess the raid was very successful. They believe he's in hiding. It's a good thing you didn't get mixed into his business."

"That's why I don't do anything but fiction. Real life is a drag."

"If that Formsby ever does contact you though, string him along, and call the feds."

"Will do. Goodnight, Neil."

Nick did an in depth perimeter search just to be safe before going in the house and testing his alarm system. Only the motion detector lights outside weren't working. After giving Deke water and food, Nick went to the upstairs safe-room and let himself in. Rachel and Jean were both sound asleep. He backed out quietly, thinking they must have the utmost trust in him to drop off to sleep with bombs attached to the house. Nick opened a beer on the deck, sat down with his laptop, and immersed himself in his assassin Diego's new adventure. Deke joined him at his feet as his laptop warned him of the approaching third hour of the morning.

"C'mon Deke. Let's go to bed. It's going to be the pits getting up for the school walk. You know how it is though when they attach bombs to your house, it takes a little time to relax. I wrote another thousand words though. I had my man Diego get into a beef with a mobster who reneged on a contract. Then the jerk threatened to blow Diego to hell. Guess what I did then, Deke?"

Deke looked at Nick questioningly, his head tilted to be ready for a command. Nick gathered his laptop and walked toward the bedroom.

"Diego went away laughing, Deke, and then he put a bomb in the mobster's house first. I don't know if I'll leave the scene in the story, but I sure enjoyed writing it. All in all, my canine friend, that was one hell of a day."

* * *

Nick patted Deke's backside which was parked near his head on the bed. "The least you could do when taking Rachel's place is put your head next to my face instead of your butt. I don't mind if Rachel sleeps with her butt in my face, but you... no thanks."

Deke snorted.

"Yes, I know it's only six-thirty in the morning, but I have to shave and take a shower while riding herd on Jean to keep moving. You can stay here a while longer. I'll be back to get you."

Deke glanced at Nick, and then flopped into place again. After quickly showering and dressing, Nick went to the safe-room. Jean didn't budge when Nick jiggled her shoulder gently the first couple times. She groaned on the third shake, turning with squinting eyes toward Nick's smiling face.

"I don't want to get up, Dad."

"Assassins do not sleep. They abide until morning."

"Really?" Jean rolled quickly out of bed. "That's why we can't ever beat you out of bed in the morning. It's a Jedi mind trick, right?"

"Yep. Assassins have inner clocks, which cannot be fooled. Fifteen minutes can be like a full night's sleep to an assassin."

"Wow... okay... I'm awake, and ready," Jean stalked around the room in her pajamas as if waiting for a ninja attack.

"That's the spirit. Get your shower, and I'll have your breakfast ready. What would you like?"

"I'll pick out a cereal when I get down to the kitchen. You can make me some tea though. It's okay if assassin's get a caffeine jolt, right?"

"Oh yeah, no rule prohibiting that."

"I'm hearing all of this ridiculous assassin talk," Rachel mumbled. "You two do know that, right?"

"You're dreaming, Mom. We're a figment of your imagination," Jean whispered over the closed eyed Rachel. "It was just a dream... a dream."

"Get away from me, Daughter of Darkness." Jean giggled, and ran out, headed for the shower. "How many dead, Muerto?"

"None. I let the police and bomb squad have them. It was an instance where a case could be made for God looking out for fools and assassins."

"Or a combination of the two," Rachel replied, sitting against the headboard.

"Or that," Nick admitted. "You know if I had seen that coming, it would never have come close to happening. Those two would have been in the freezer in the Valley. The flag confrontation, and the brothers trying to scare me later was one thing, but bombs on the house? I'll have to live until I'm ninety to be around when those idiots get out. I'll have to add the Rashidi family to our other enemy family combatants to be watched: the Naders."

190

Rachel covered his hand. "I know. Go make the Daughter of Darkness some tea, and I'll be down in a few minutes."

"Remember though, you still owe me this." Nick made his obscene pantomime, eliciting the hoped for gasp of fake revulsion.

"Get out of here, Muerto." Rachel covered her eyes. "You're disgusting."

"You say that now. We'll see."

"No... we won't!"

* * *

Gus rang the doorbell as Nick kissed Rachel before walking out with Jean and Deke. "I didn't think Payaso would make it this morning."

"Maybe after last night, you should drive over to the school."

Nick cupped Rachel's chin while Jean answered the door, and hugged Gus. "I'm better if I don't have a steering wheel in my hands. I don't hesitate, and I have an open target range. We'll be looking into this Rashidi angle for more than two pissed off jerks."

"I picked my course, and you're in it, Muerto. I trust you, but I can't help sneaking in a wifely warning or suggestion once in a while."

"They're always welcome, partner. See you in a little bit. Would you like to go down to the beach today?"

"I'd better. I'm getting too stiff fooling around only at the house. I'll make some hot mulled wine for myself."

"It's a date."

Outside, tendrils of ground fog clung to the road down the hill. A chilling sea breeze blew in from the ocean, and coupled with the overcast sky to make a gray scenic Pacific Grove morning. Jean skipped ahead with Deke, but stayed closer than her usual walk to school. Nick and Gus paid attention to every vehicle noise, or movement near the houses. It was a morning of heightened senses, and acknowledgement all was not quite right in El Muerto's backyard. The men remained observant, but quiet until arriving safely at the school with Jean. Nick walked Jean to the classroom, noting he did not get any curious looks from the other parents. He rejoined Gus and Deke with only smiles and waves.

"It looks like the news hasn't hit," Nick said. "I'm wondering if Homeland Security arrived, and put a clamp on everything to do with last night."

"I wouldn't blame them for doing so," Gus replied. "I assume they have the Rashidi's in the interrogation rooms this morning. There's no doubt in my mind those pricks lawyered up the moment they entered the station. Too bad we couldn't get them down in the Valley for a chat with your theme music playing."

"I could tell last night those two would be begging me to let them talk inside of ten minutes. They'll be wasting their time trying to question that arrogant asshole, Habib. He's probably having his lawyer cite religious persecution as the reason he was arrested while planting bombs. I wish they'd let both of them go. I'd fit them into my schedule. I got caught relying on plain old naked luck last night. I'll be glad when we take care of Sadun, and get the hell out of town for a while. I think we need to let our home base cool off for a while. It's getting toxic, and I don't like it."

"What would you have done differently though?"

"Put the Rashidis through the CIA database wringer. If they're only idiots, then so be it. If I find a link I shouldn't have missed, then I have to file that one away as a blessing I probably won't see again. I'll take my satellite laptop special down to the beach today. We'll conference with John, and I'll do what I should have done before I had bombs planted on my house. Rachel's walking with us. I'll check in with the Marshals, and my lawyer. He'll be getting into his office about the time we get to the beach."

"Want to tell me about your lawyer?"

"Khole defended a killer in Sacramento. As I told you, he's one of the best criminal attorneys in the country. Justin believed the accused killer was being framed. This Carter Mulligan guy moved down from Oregon. He worked construction in and around Sacramento. A woman was raped and murdered who had been seen with Mulligan at a bar the night she was murdered – no DNA, or anything tying Mulligan to the murder. The cops knew they had the right guy, but couldn't prove it. Mulligan fooled Justin right out of the gate. He told me he'd handled a lot of liars, but none as accomplished as Mulligan. Khole convinced him to take a lie detector test which he passed with flying colors. The DA had no choice with what they had for evidence but to let him go. If it had ended there, we wouldn't be talking about my friend Khole."

A car came up one of the streets running perpendicular to their route, and both men turned, putting hands on weapons because of the engine roar. When it passed, Nick went on. "Part of the problem was the cops didn't have a DNA sample for Mulligan. They couldn't trick or obtain it from Mulligan without evidence, and he refused any cooperation, playing the outrage card. Khole got him released before the cops were able to get a court order. Then, one of Justin's law clerks stumbled on the fact Mulligan never existed until five years prior to the Sacramento murder. My buddy didn't want to drop an actual killer on the street, because he got stupid. Justin invited Mulligan in to sign papers, treated him like a king, and then sent the DNA sample from his coffee cup to be tested by a private firm."

"Be careful about curiosity, huh?"

"And then some, Gus. Justin turned the report over to a friend in the DA's office. The very next morning, he had Sacramento police swarming his office there. Mulligan was in the wind, but not before linking him to four kidnapping, rape, and murder cases in Maine. Mulligan's real name was Seth Darboe. Then the FBI was called in because of the serial kidnapping, and across state lines business. I have to hand it to Justin. He was no dummy. He knew the police and FBI would swarm around like a hive of African bees, but do nothing other than launch into a massive circle jerk. Justin put his wife and two daughters in hiding. Then he went looking for someone to handle Darboe. It turned out Justin defended an old service buddy of mine, Jake Watterston. Jake knows a lot about me, and Justin had defended him successfully on a counterfeit ID charge. Jake has my personal mail drop. I was between jobs, writing the third Diego novel. Since there was a lawyer playing a large role in my novel, I thought it would be a kick to get involved with Justin."

"I stopped thinking about it as a humorous endeavor when I found out the facts. I know we joke about me being a serial killer, which is true, but I don't kidnap, rape, mutilate, and murder innocent young women."

"True, although you kidnap, mutilate, and murder many other not so innocent people, hence my point about you being a serial killer, Muerto."

"Oh good, thank you for clearing that up, Payaso."

"Go on with your story."

"No. You've hurt my feelings, Payaso."

"You don't have feelings, Muerto."

"True. Where was I when you insulted me? Oh yes... I looked into this Darboe guy. I didn't like what I found. After meeting with Justin, I sent him into hiding with his family, but showed him in detail how to not be found. He thought I was sending him into hiding for years. I found Darboe in three days. He crossed the country to Maine again, where he had old connections. Seth had a drink at an old hangout in Bangor one night, left at closing, and disappeared. I told Justin that although there would be a nationwide manhunt ongoing for Seth, it was a formality, but to accept any police protection offered to keep our forces of justice busy. He reads all my novels, and we get together a few times a year when he's in his Salinas office."

"That story doesn't sound like the pre-Rachel, Jean, and Deke Nick."

"I've told you before I take risks occasionally when I meet someone real. If not for Paul, I would have never taken on his Marine buddy who was avenging his niece's death. I knew if he was let in on the details he'd screw me. That is not the case with my lawyer buddy. He never calls me. He never writes me. He posts a short blurb on my mail drop that he'll be in Salinas, and what time. That's the other plus sign about a guy like him. He knows I hunted down, murdered, and made disappear a serial killer no one else could handle. Yet he still likes having lunch with me, never mentions what I do, and always wants to talk about the novels."

"So what are you going to ask him to do for you?"

"Poke a stick into our DA's office, and find out the details behind the scenes as to how a set of brothers capable of blowing people to hell and gone get to walk out of lockup without a single word to the civilian they have a grudge against. Justin annoys the hell out of people when he wants to, but he does so with a professional flair. I want a face and identity without my having to get it personally. Justin will get it."

Gus pointed ahead as Deke stiffened. "It looks like you have federal company already. Heh… heh… they actually think Rachel will open the door to chat with them."

"Rach hasn't called, so she's seen them on the security monitor and decided to ignore them. She's seen enough frauds to know taking a chance on opening the door to strangers is a bad idea in my household."

"So, you think they're frauds?"

"Take Deke. I'll let you know."

The two men in suits on Nick's porch turned, saw Nick, and went for their weapons. Nick's .45 caliber hollow points, pulped their heads before they could do more than begin to draw. "Get Deke down behind the tree, Gus!"

Nick turned in a crouch to the black SUV parked in front of his house, which started, and shot forward. Nick put four rounds into the area of the tinted windshield where the driver would be. The engine idled forward with wheels turned into the curb. Nick ran to the door, and shot into the driver's head once more. In seconds he was inside, checking for other gunmen, while reaching behind him to turn off the engine. He backed out, set the parking brake, and ran to his porch. There was no doubt the two men on the porch were dead.

Nick used his iPhone to take pictures of both men, and his portable fingerprint digital ID app to quickly gather fingerprints. He ran to the van, and repeated the process before sending evidence on to Paul Gilbrech. Nick then called inside.

"Hi honey. No beach today. Road trip."

"How many, Nick?"

"Three. Did they try to get in, showing ID's."

"Yep, and they looked real good. I didn't like the looks of the one with glasses, not that I would have opened the door anyway after having bombs attached to the house last night. Someone put a contract out on you, didn't they?"

"Affirmative," Nick looked at the faceless men. "Uh… what color suit did the one with glasses have on, dark blue?"

"No, black."

"Thanks, pack some things. We're moving into the Valley house for a while. I'm afraid Jean will have to miss a little more school than we figured."

"On it. Want me to take Deke?"

"Yeah. I'll let him in, and then I'm going with Gus to collect Jean from school. I hear sirens, so I better go get Deke inside before they get here, and declare a crime scene. Oh… good, here's Gus and Deke now."

Nick turned off the security system, opened the door, and reached down to where Gus stood holding out the leash. Nick picked up Deke, and slipped him into the house, and reengaged the security system. "Hell of a start to the day, huh, Deke. See you in a little while."

Nick then backed carefully off his blood and brain spattered porch. He glared at Gus. "Well, Payaso, this is a fine mess you've gotten me into."

"Yeah, Muerto. I'll go watch the school until you get free of the cops. You'll be coming to get Jean, right?"

"Yep. Call John. Tell him he's going to have house guests. He'll be getting ready to come to the beach anyway. Better get moving, Payaso. Those sirens are sounding close."

"Be seeing you, Muerto. Like you told Deke. Hell of a start."

Nick placed his .45 caliber Colt on the porch, pushing it away from him. He then called Paul Gilbrech. The moment Gilbrech answered, Nick briefed him on the prior night, and morning's adventure. "No, I don't know how much is connected, but this porch assassination attempt was the real deal. Someone put out a contract on me. I'm betting it's related to Formsby. The police are driving up now. I have to go Paul."

"I received the pictures and fingerprints. I'm pulling strings right the hell now, Nick. Get your family safe, and I'll find some answers. I saw the lawyer on the news. That was one cold piece of work. Are you still planning on the Marshal end of it?"

"I sure am. Thanks, Paul. Talk to you later."

"Indeed."

Nick put away his phone, and laced his hands behind his head. He took a deep breath. It was Dickerson and his partner. "Hi Neil. Hi Trina. It's cool this morning, huh?"

Dickerson stared at the porch scene in silence before turning to his partner. "Call the meat wagon, Trina, and the coroner. I guess we'd better alert those Bureau guys who moved into our office over last night's party at Nick's house too."

"Do...do you want me to cuff Nick?"

"There's no need. If he was a danger to us, we'd already be dead. Go make the calls, partner." Dickerson waited until Trina returned to the squad car. He sat down next to Nick. "I won't say anything so inherently stupid that you'll give me the silent treatment, but do you know if last night and this morning are connected?"

Nick had already made a decision about Dickerson. "I'm not much on coincidence, but I didn't get a chance to investigate the Rashidi brothers this morning as I planned. I'll let you in on this part. My other boss at CIA with the title of Director will be calling in some favors. He's worried about this series of events too. I don't want you thinking I'm sitting around with my thumb up my ass. There's no use in playing this charade game with you, Neil. I work for the CIA, the Department of Justice, and the US Marshals. I also have FBI credentials. Yes, part of what I do is consult. The other part would not do you any good to know about. We have some very big problems involving national security that we're trying to solve. I believe you'll find the Bureau agents sent for the Rashidis have been briefed to some extent."

"You're right about that," Dickerson admitted. "I offered to bring them over to meet you this morning, but they told me it wouldn't be necessary, and took the Rasidis. I already know the Director of the CIA takes your calls. Tell me how this went down."

Nick explained what happened, and how quickly. "Rachel knows what I do. After last night, there was no way she'd ever open the door to anyone. The moment those guys noticed me, they went for the guns. Their getaway driver is in the van wheeled against the curb. Right now, that's all I know. If it's just you and Trina, why not give me a pair of gloves, and let me see what their ID's look like. Rachel said they flashed some very impressive ones."

Dickerson nodded. He stood, and handed him a pair of Nitrile gloves. He retrieved Nick's Colt from the porch. "Here. I normally would have to take it, but what's the use. I know where it will be, and what it was used for. I'll let you know if anything is requested, like turning it in."

"Thanks." Nick holstered his Colt. "I do write novels, Neil."

"So I hear, Castle. I can't even call you that anymore. That writer pussy on TV doesn't do this type of work," Dickerson said while searching the man Rachel told Nick she hadn't trusted.

"I liked that guy in 'Serenity', but he let his weight balloon up, and his part is kind of wimpy, like he sits down to pee." Nick went through the blue suited man's pockets, smiling at Dickerson's enjoyment of his backhand putdown of the 'Castle' TV show star."

199

Nick inspected the FBI ID and wallet he found. No other hint of the man's identity was on his person. "This is very good. I would have probably opened the door to this guy."

"His buddy has a good one too. I guess it would be racist to note they look Middle Eastern in nationality, although the holes in their heads make it a little tougher to determine anything for sure. My question would be why didn't they try to play it out as FBI agents until you moved closer?"

"Frankly, I think they have a shoot on sight order, and they figured I'd hesitate. They figured wrong. Also, they planned to ambush me inside the house using Rachel, I'm sure. If they had gotten in the house, there would have been a bloody shootout inside. Why they had a shoot on sight order is the more important question. I need to get Rachel and Jean somewhere safe, and do some research in conjunction with my boss. I know you'll be here a while. Do you mind if I go collect Jean from school? I need to move her and Rachel out of here."

"Go ahead, but keep your phone near at hand, Nick."

"I will."

* * *

Fifteen minutes later, Nick explained some of what was going on to Dimah Kader in the school hallway, stressing the urgency of the danger. "I know how weird this all sounds. I will keep Jean in good shape academically, but for now I need to protect her physically. Until the threat passes I have to keep Jean with me."

"That is horrible! Of course you must keep Jean safe. I'll bring her out to you." Kader went into the classroom to help Jean gather her belongings, leaving Nick thankful for someone not interested in playing twenty questions.

In their vehicle returning home, after sending Gus ahead to the Carmel Valley house, Nick explained what had happened the best he could. Jean listened intently, perceiving far more than a normal nine year old. "I bet you're glad Mom made you get this Grand Caravan with all the cargo room. Do you have the Escalade in Las Vegas now?"

"Yep."

"You should trade in your old Chevy Malibu for one of those special James Bond cars."

"Yeah, that's what I need, a James Bond car, just in time for Quinn's baby seat."

Jean giggled. "He'll be fine. We'll put little sunglasses and a turned around baseball cap on him, and he'll be rockin' it."

"Hey... your brother isn't a little Mr. Potato Head to try different accoutrements out on."

"Sure he is. I'm getting him a mustache and different plastic noses, and ears. He'll learn how to deal with pain too. Those things will probably hurt when we slam them into place."

Nick tried to hold onto a look of outraged horror, but lost control in seconds. After many moments, he finally said something decipherable. "You do know if you repeat anything you just said in front of your Mom, the police will be dredging the water for your body, right?"

"I know. The Momster has no sense of humor right now... absolutely none. Did you forget something when planning to escape with us to a safe-house?"

Nick sighed. "No, I didn't forget about volunteering to chaperone your dance on Friday. Despite multiple attempts on my life, and bombs attached to my house, I know better than to use my real life danger to wiggle out of your dance."

"Good. Just checking. Sonny is going to be there. I'll make him dance with me. He says he can't dance, but I remembered your story. He's not escaping to the wall of shame like you did."

"Playing hard to get, huh?"

"I can't let him become a hopeless wallflower like you. In any case, you have to take care of business before Friday."

"You do know today is Wednesday, right?"

"Yep. Get busy." Jean crossed her arms, leaning against the seat. "Wow, look at all the people and yellow tape. I'm beginning to lose hope for my dance."

"Don't give up hope yet, Dagger. I'll be working on solutions the moment I get you, Deke, and the Momster into the Valley house with John. My friend at CIA is looking into this personally for me, and I haven't begun to check on the threads I've already found." Nick drove around the block, opened the garage remotely, and drove inside.

"Stay here for a moment while I talk with these approaching suits."

"Okay, Dad."

Nick met Dickerson and the two men he figured were federal agents with his hands in plain sight. He held out his hand. "I'm Nick McCarty. Sergeant Dickerson was kind enough to allow me to bring my daughter Jean home from school."

Each of the men shook his hand, and produced FBI/Homeland Security ID's. "I'm Special Agent Glen Rogers," the dark haired man nearest Dickerson said. "This is my partner, Special Agent Jarrod Agnew. We have orders to leave you out of this investigation, but to keep you informed of any progress on the case."

Agnew chuckled. "The orders came from so high up, we weren't even allowed to ask why. Maybe you could give us a hint."

"I believe it's because of a case I'm consulting on. We don't know what involvement the Rashidi's or the fake agents who tried to kill me had with the case yet, but we're working on it. If you give me your cards, I'll contact you with anything I'm allowed to divulge during my research into this. Here's my card."

Nick handed them one of his cards with mobile phone number, and accepted theirs. "May I get my family ready to move to another location?"

"Yes, of course... one other thing" Rogers said. "We know you were with Delta, but we can't access anything in your record other than that, and a vague note about being a consultant. I've read your novels, so I also know you're a bestselling author. What the hell would guys be blowing your house up, and gunning for you in broad daylight about."

"That's what we're trying to find out, gentlemen. If I find a definitive answer, I will pass it on to my chain of command, and if they give me permission, I will call you right away. Thanks for reading my novels, Agent Rogers. Are you a fan of my character, Diego?"

"Yeah, it's entertaining pulp. There's not much realism, but I've read some of the replies you've made to people you call 'Book Killers' because they do one star hit pieces on novels when it is clear they haven't read them. You admit they're pulp."

"Most of the BK's are funny. They change tactics the moment they're called on a false accusation they make about the novel they're doing a book killing on. I've often wondered if other readers can tell."

"I can now, but until I read a few of the ones you confronted, I don't know if I would have noticed. That's neat the way you have me talking about your novels, and away from the subject of the investigation."

"I don't know anything more about the why in your investigation. If I find something I can share, I will. Sorry if that's repetitive, but that's all I have for now."

"I hope you get a call allowing us some answers," Agnew replied. "The Rashidis are not talking. They were caught red handed though, and we are charging them with multiple felonies, including domestic terrorism. Please call us if you can."

"Will do." Nick noted Dickerson did not walk away. "Trouble, Neil?"

"How in the hell do you have the juice to ward off Homeland Security?"

"Because it's a matter of national security, and in this case, there are people in governmental high places who understand the importance of finding out what the hell is going on. I'm sure I'll be talking with you soon. I get into bad spots with my consulting work. Sometimes, for a period of time unwanted attention is focused back on me. Then things get dicey for a while. I admit I may have stepped in it somewhere along the line on this case I'm unaware of. It smells on my shoe, but I'm uncertain where it originated."

Dickerson nodded. "Okay, Nick. Be careful. If you need something, give me a call. We're all under orders to support your 'consulting case' status."

"Thanks." Nick walked around to let Jean out. "Let's go get a couple bags, and get out of here. I have work to do if I'm going to get you to the dance on Friday."

Chapter Nine

Contract Kill

Rachel brought in coffee to Nick's away from home office. Gus, John, and Nick poured over databases for any thread connecting the Rashidis with the names they worked on in the last few days, Wargul and Sadun. They also ran the names related to Formsby's empire, along with Formsby's connections with Tanus Import/Export conglomerate.

"Any luck?"

"Not yet, Rach," Nick answered. "We haven't heard from anyone yet. I have a call in to Tim and Grace. If they get anything set in motion with Sadun, I know they'll call me. Paul's working on the faces and fingerprints I sent him from this morning's uninvited guests. He knows how important this is. He had a hit put out on him. We haven't ruled out the Salvatores moving into our area either. This puzzle needs a couple more pieces put in place. I know Sadun is at least partially responsible; but without his lawyer Wargul passing notes in class, he should be irrelevant in this situation."

"It's early though," Rachel pointed out. "That was great you getting let loose like you did. Paul really greased the rails for you there."

"I doubt he was the only one. I have a feeling he has some close confederates in the DOJ who like what we've accomplished. I don't want to ruin the backing we've garnered by making enemies due to name dropping. I'm glad Dickerson knows some of the story, and he doesn't think I'm a bad guy."

"But you are a bad guy, Muerto," Gus chimed in to Rachel and John's amusement. "Every horrific reference they can think of would fit you like a glove."

"Gee… thanks, Payaso, you prick." Nick's phone dinged. Nick turned on his scrambler. "Oh good. Here's Paul. Hey buddy, we've been waiting anxiously for your call. We're having trouble with tying all the players together on our end."

Gilbrech wasted no time on small talk. "It's Lee Collister, Nick. You were right to wonder about Salvatore. I'm sure he doesn't know why, but he was sent to keep an eye on you, and your movements. Collister promised him a way back in after his demotion, if he did exactly what he was told. Word is Salvatore is proving he had nothing to do with Nancy Pettinger, but in doing so through Collister, he's working under a traitor."

"All that puts the corner pieces of the puzzle together. How about the would be assassins from this morning?"

Paul was quiet for a moment. "Black op NSA. Collister restarted where Frank left off, Nick. Those three exist nowhere on any government payroll. They're private contractors just as you were under Frank. Collister is the one who ordered Formsby to try and hire you to take me out. It was to be a test run with the objective of getting you on the hook, and back in the Black ops business. I was the bonus, because of the hit on Formsby's operations. When Formsby and his men vanished without a trace, Collister knew exactly what happened to them. I'm not sure how long he's known about you for certain, but I believe Sadun and his lawyer explained how you took down Sadun's ring, and exposed Nancy Pettinger. If you had not rigged Pettinger's death the way you did, he would have went at you with prison time, trying to implicate me."

"The scandal would have been enough. How are we with the DOJ?"

"Solid. They have the right people spouting the 'bring them to justice' crap, but they want more of the 'ends justify the means' operations, including Sadun. I held off calling you, because orders have been issued to move Sadun. US Marshals Reinhold and

Stanwick are to take custody of Sadun at 4 pm today from Atwater Penitentiary. What will you need to get this done?"

Nick's mind raced, picturing the Atwater facility. "Unfortunately, a little luck. I'll call Tim and Grace right now. Do you have eyes on Collister?"

"Every minute of every day at this time."

"Where will he be tomorrow?"

"In hiding would be my guess. Those three men you took out today were his go to guys. As you know, he can't simply walk outside, and hail a few more down like calling a cab. He knows what happened to Frank Richert. We're making all kinds of noise, shooting out queries from FBI to CIA to DOJ, getting to the bottom of who hired three outside mercenaries. Since he's going way beyond what Frank ever did, Collister contracts mercenaries from overseas. Two of the three you dealt with were ex Egyptian Secret Police, Ammar Sobhi, and Mando Morsi. One was ex Iranian Ministry of Security, Adel Nassiri."

"That's smart in a way. If they had been successful and caught, nothing could fall on his head. If they had been successful, and slipped away, no one would have ever touched them."

"Yeah, but he sent them after you," Paul stated. "Now, they're dead. We know who they are, and Lee Collister knows who killed them. You can bet he suspects you know his name because Formsby knew it. He's sweatin', Nick. After you take Sadun, would you want to hold off on Collister?"

Nick's features spread in a grim smile of anticipation. "I don't think so, Paul. Does he have family in DC he stays with, or does he move from the family homestead to DC when he has to?"

"He's divorced, but he's not dopey enough to have a mistress anyone knows about. Collister lives in the 'Congressional

207

Village' apartments. That place has surveillance cams everywhere."

"Does he have one specific driver for taking him around Capitol Hill, and does he employ bodyguards?"

"Yes to the first question. No to the second. He may scramble a couple of bodyguards fearing you're on the loose," Paul replied. "You're killin' me here, Nick. What do you have in mind that wouldn't involve assassinating the sitting National Security Advisor?"

"I'll need a flight in and out of a small airport we won't attract attention at, like Monterey Regional. I'd like to do it tomorrow, so I can be with my buddy tomorrow night. I will also need some eyes only files to take to our pal Lee under the guise of a special messenger. Can you put together everything you have on Formsby, call Lee, and tell him he needs to see the information you've gathered on Formsby's overseas holdings? Use the excuse you want to brief the President in person, and you want Lee read in on it. I'll arrive at his place with a handcuffed briefcase. Don't worry, I'll look good in full military dress uniform. Also, can you make me an ID with everything needed in case he asks for it, along with a nametag?"

"I'll fly in myself. We'll go over everything together on the way to DC, Nick. You're not going to just shoot him in the head, are you?"

Nick chuckled. "I thought you read all my novels."

"Sorry. I know you not only write plots for assassins, but you also are one. The job you did on Frank Richert was incredibly good."

"Yep, and I have some special juice left for Lee. I'll call you after today's activities."

"By the way, how is your writing doing?"

"I'm down to only about fifteen hundred words a day since I've been having to clean up all your messes, Gilbrech."

Paul was still laughing when Nick disconnected. He looked around at his wife and companions with a big grin. "Well, the good news is I know who has to die. The bad news is it's going to be a busy couple of days. You know what to do, John. After Gus and I leave, batten down the hatches, and shut off all communication devices except for the burner phone I gave you for emergencies. Throw some things together for a road trip, Payaso. It's a little over two hours to Atwater Penitentiary. I'll call Tim and Grace. They already have their orders, but I need to spell out a couple things for them."

"Okay, Nick. Do you have what you need here, or will we have to stop by your house?"

"I have what I need here. No more house visits until Sadun is taken care of. How's Jean doing?"

"She's out back throwing knives," Rachel answered. "Deke's with her. He loves this place. I think he's marked the entire territory. Can I go on line to get Ms. Kader's school assignments?"

"Sure. Don't interact with anyone, though. Do you remember the safe-room code here?"

"Of course. You don't believe we'll need it though do you?"

"We take no chances. If John says get in the room, you grab Jean and Deke, and head into the room. El Kabong has enough firepower to hold off an army until we get back, but I'm certain that won't be necessary. I have to handle the yucky part now. Excuse me."

Nick called Grace's phone.

"Hey, Tim, did you order a killer?"

"Ha, ha. I heard you have your orders."

"We transfer Sadun out of Atwater at 4 pm," Grace answered. "Any other alterations?"

"Yeah. Rent an SUV with a real spare tire, and room in the back cargo area. I'm going to drop you two off on the outskirts of Merced. I'll call in an anonymous tip about an SUV rocking around on the side of the road when I'm a half hour out of Merced."

"I hate you."

"Don't make me have to remind you who it is that's responsible for this cluster fuck, Gracie. You and Tim will be heroes, hijacked, and stripped of a prisoner, obviously set up by a leak in the department."

"I hate you."

* * *

"Where are you taking me," Sadun asked.

"We told you," Grace answered. "It's not safe for you here. Someone killed your lawyer. It was a professional hit. We're moving you to a safe-house in Sacramento until other arrangements can be made."

Sadun chuckled. "Is that what you have been told? We have another plan which will work much better for me. Perhaps you two will live through it."

"Oh shit," Tim mumbled. The highway they were on was desert, with no traffic. What looked to be a California Highway Patrol car was angled across the road with a uniformed patrolman waving them to a stop. Behind them, an SUV type vehicle was speeding toward them from the rear. Tim pulled his 9mm Ruger, while Grace followed his example. "We're screwed."

"Put down your weapons, fools! My men will not shoot you unless they have to!"

Tim glanced back at Sadun. "They're going to have to."

"Idiots!"

Tim gauged the approach of the vehicle behind them in the rear view mirror, figuring on ramming the patrol car ahead, and taking their chances in the gun battle that followed. At that moment, the windshield on the trailing vehicle shattered, and the SUV pitched to its side and rolled. Tim focused on the patrolman in front of him, who had now brought a machine pistol to bear on them. The patrolman's head seemed to explode toward them. A large caliber, high velocity round burst from his forehead, expanding as it exited, and taking most of the man's upper face with it. Two other men began exiting the patrol car, firing wildly. They took shots to the chest.

"Wha...what has happened?" Sadun stared from front to back in stunned shock, his eyes wide, and unblinking. "Why are you laughing, woman!"

"It's like this... idiot," Grace replied, watching the scene tensely in front of her. A hooded figure in tan fatigues approached the patrol car, and fired a round from a pistol into the heads of each man only wounded. The figure looked at their SUV, smiled, and waved. Tim waved back. "You planned an escape, which means we have yet another damn leak somewhere. You must have had a warning the moment we were given our orders. A very professional bunch hustled into place to free you from our clutches. Unfortunately for you, we have a stone cold killer watching our backs. Remember the guy we told you not to mess with after he questioned you in the van before we turned you in?"

211

Sadun began thrashing around in the back, "You cannot do this! Take me to the safe-house. I will tell you everything!"

Tim grinned at him with a sigh. "That ship sailed already, Amigo."

Another vehicle skidded to a stop next to them as the hooded man approached. Tim holstered his weapon. "It's Gus."

"How do you think he knew?" Grace put away her weapon too, and opened the door.

"I guess we'll find out."

"Hi guys," Nick said. "Nice ambush. Uthman… boobie… pal… how the hell are you? Long time, no see."

"Stay the fuck away from me!" Sadun scrambled into the far corner of the rear seat.

Nick waved a finger at him. "That's not nice, Uthman. Well, kids, I have good news for you. Thanks to the unsuccessful Uthman ambush, I'll only have to put you two to sleep. This will be a wild one for them to figure out. I took pictures and fingerprints of the three in the front, but I don't have time for the guy in the rear. C'mon, Uthie. We have to go. Don't make me have to shoot you in the dick."

When Nick took aim to do exactly that, Sadun worm crawled to the door Nick held open for him. "Good boy."

Nick put him into the backseat of his escape vehicle with Gus guarding him. Nick gestured at the back of the SUV while taking out two syringes. "Get comfortable in the back after you put your pistols on the ground. I'll give you something for a couple hours rest, and put your weapons under the front seat."

212

Tim put his Ruger on the ground, and curled inside first. Then Grace put her weapon on the ground, and climbed into the SUV cargo area in front of Tim. She muttered, "I hate you."

"Another leaky/leaky, I see. You two are lucky I got into position long before Uthman's wild bunch showed. Anyway... sweet dreams, kids. I'll text you who it is that tipped off Uthie."

"Thanks, Nick," Tim said.

Grace turned away as Nick pressed the syringe to her neck. "I hate you."

* * *

Instead of the original plan, Nick called Paul as Gus drove away from the scene. "They have another leak, Paul. Sadun's men ambushed them nearly in the place I had picked out. I'm sending pictures and fingerprints of all but one. I didn't have time to gather info on the guy driving the backup vehicle."

"Shit! They would have had to of been tipped off nearly the moment the transfer was approved. Does Sadun know who the leak is?"

Nick glanced at the cringing Sadun, curled into a fetal position on the rear seat. "Hey Uthie. What's the name of the leak that received the info about your transfer as fast as the Marshals transferring you?"

Sadun remained silent, turning away from Nick.

"Sorry, Paul. We're having a failure to communicate. Do you need to know before Gus and I get Uthie further along the road?"

"No. Get to your destination safely, without police intervention. Since the ambushers have gone bye/bye, I'll scan everyone in on the transfer info up and down the line. They'll get word about what happened, and then I'll see where the rat scurries."

"Don't worry, if that avenue doesn't pan out. Uthie needs a reeducation lesson about hiding things from El Muerto. I have to move fast to catch my buddy Collister before he does any more damage. Are you still planning on flying into town for me?"

"I'll be there at 8 am your time. Does that work for you?"

"Yep. I'll be at Monterey Regional from 7:30 on."

"I'll have a guy looking like James Bond meet you at Departures. He'll have a bored expression, and an arrogant attitude. His name's Clyde Bacall, and he looks like Will Smith. He's the only one right now I trust around me. He's been in combat with the Rangers. CB believes he knows everything about everything, but I like him, and you can trust him."

"We'll need a guy like that on this. The logistics on me being a courier have to be perfect, including the driver I arrive with. Make sure he spit shines his shoes, and presses off his Ranger duds. I'll talk to you in a while after I introduce Uthie to my new propane torch."

"Ouch. Until then, my friend."

"You…you cannot simply torture me! I…I am a prisoner. Take me back to Atwater!"

Gus sighed. "Oh for God's sake, dummy. Tell Muerto what he wants to know. He has time to double check anything you give him on our way. If he finds out you've been truthful, your journey into hell will be painless. You can't be stupid enough to think we'll allow you to walk away no matter how Muerto has to obtain the facts. Do yourself a favor, and start talking. Keep in mind Muerto is like a human lie detector."

Silence.

"Okay. I tried, Muerto."

"I am unimpressed with your good cop, bad cop act. Take me back to Atwater at once!"

"Remember, Muerto, this is one of Jerry's favorite loaners: untraceable plates with no GPS tracking. He won't like it if you redecorate the interior."

"Paul's working another angle. He's cool with us taking Uthie to the Valley. I hate to ask this, Payaso, but can you empty out the meat locker while I'm gone? Have John put my girls in the safe-room when you're ready to leave. With Uthie, we're going to have standing room only. I kept meaning to do it, but it's been one thing after another."

"I know. Maybe this would be a good time to call in Geezer. He can help John and me with loading chores, and then watch the house while we go for a cruise. We'll need to get out there a long ways this time, Muerto."

"I'll give him a call. I meant to check on him last night until the Rashidi brothers planted bombs on my house." Nick took out his phone, but held the call when Sadun spoke.

"Habib and Akim Rashidi?" Sadun sat and leaned forward.

Nick chuckled appreciatively. "How many Rashidi brothers do you think we all know, Uthie? Want to tell me how you know them."

Sadun dropped his head dejectedly. "Those jackals blew a simple plan to follow your every movement, draw you into the open, publicly discredit you, and reveal your true profession. Then Collister felt you would only have one way you could survive, by taking his offer of employment. When Formsby and his men disappeared while sent to recruit you, Collister contacted me. He explained Formsby had to go into hiding suddenly, but that he believed he had another way to force your cooperation. He wanted your CIA boss out of the picture, and he believed you to be the perfect tool to get it done. When I heard his plan involved the Rashidis, I had my lawyer Wargul get a message to Collister not to use those two dolts. I know them. They are hotheads, who believe we can browbeat anyone into compliance with silly tricks and outrage. I have used them before where a simple propaganda task was to be performed, never on an important mission. Now, all is changed."

"Nice start, Uthie. Tell me the leak Collister is using in the DOJ now, and tell me if the name Salvatore means anything to you."

"Can I buy my life with the name?"

"No," Nick answered, "but you can buy your death. Ten minutes into my partner, Mr. Propane Torch's interrogation starting at the bottoms of your feet, and believe me, that name will seem like the greatest bargain on earth."

"I can help you bring down Collister! I can testify against him. I know what you're thinking. I-"

"No!" Nick interrupted with a hand wave. "You don't. If you knew what I was thinking, you'd be singing the name I asked for as if you were doing an aria with the Hallelujah Chorus."

"Douglas Cameron..." Sadun muttered, after seeing in Nick's eyes only the immediate and absolute fulfillment of what Nick threatened. "Collister influenced your DOJ to replace Nancy Pettinger with another of his dupes. Collister knew of my transfer before your US Marshals did."

"Sit tight, Uthie." Nick called Gilbrech. "Douglas Cameron."

"No way... it can't be! He's the son of Senator Diane Cameron from Maine. Why in hell would a... oh never mind,

Nick. Let me put my people on ripping his life apart in the next instant. I'll call you with what I find out."

"No problem. We're still an hour away from either a happy faced Sadun at room temperature, or an absolutely twisted faced, horrified Sadun screaming for death. I hope for his sake, Douglas did the deed."

"Please forgive me for praying it's not true." Gilbrech disconnected.

"You didn't make my boss very happy with that name drop. I'm not familiar with his Mom, Payaso. Do you know who Senator Diane Cameron is?"

"Only by typical East Coast political hack reputation – the usual anti-Second Amendment, pro-abortion, and climate change polar bear hugger public stances."

"That wouldn't explain her offspring selling out his country. How does Collister immediately replace one traitor with another so fast, Uthie?"

"With Nancy Pettinger it was money. The one time I crossed paths with the woman, I was to deliver a file and a payoff. When I tried to engage her in conversation, she cut me off and said, 'show me the money'. Collister blackmails others who have become embroiled in gambling or sexual indiscretions, and he has at least four layers between him and the action."

"I'm impressed," Nick admitted. "People do not fool me often. When you gave us Nancy Pettinger's name as a last resort to having me make alterations on you until you did, I did not suspect you of hiding a name. I understand why you took such a gamble. You thought Collister would free you some way, and I wouldn't torture the shit out of you because I went away happy to get Pettinger's name. He almost did succeed in freeing you. It makes me suspicious of you possibly having another name in reserve."

"I know you will kill me no matter what. I would not be in this car driving to my death if Collister had listened to me about the Rashidis. Admit it. If not for those two imbeciles invading your life so stupidly, would you have ever found the connection between me and Collister?"

"Although you knew Collister planned to have Formsby recruit me, did he tell you he suspected Formsby didn't disappear mysteriously?"

Sadun stared at Nick with dawning realization. "You killed Formsby and his men! You had Collister's name already! Why then... shit!"

Nick and Gus enjoyed Sadun's obvious recognition he had been played. "I see he didn't share with you that he suspected I had indeed retired Formsby, and while doing so, I likely extracted his name from Formsby. The people he sent to intercept the transfer were to kill you and the Marshals. I think Collister suspected you to be the last link endangering him publicly. He probably thought there was a chance to nail me too. Today's botched mess will really shake his tree. I think you're telling the truth, Uthie. One other thing, are you familiar at all with the name I asked about earlier: Salvatore?"

"I don't know that name, but I didn't know everyone Collister had on his string. If I did, I'd tell you. Are you going to kill him?"

"Hopefully tomorrow."

"Good. Will you torture him?"

"Sure," Nick lied. "Would you like me to spend some extra time with him since he sold your butt down the river?"

Sadun relaxed against the rear seat his head tilted back against the head rest with a faraway look in his eyes. "Yes... as much time as you can spare."

Gus and Nick packed away Uthman Sadun in a body bag, and placed him on their gurney for transport to the meat locker.

"It's only 7:30," John said. "You guys really made good time, and we don't even need to interrogate him. I've been watching the news. It's a media mystery. They have dead fake highway patrolmen, drugged US Marshals, a missing terrorist, and no clues."

"We had to alter our plan a bit when the unscheduled ambushers arrived," Nick replied. "It all worked out in the end. Uthie filled in the missing pieces to our puzzle. Tomorrow, I'll go with Paul to jam the last piece into place. It's a good thing Paul has eyes on Collister. After he confirmed Douglas Cameron's appointment to the Department of Justice job held by Pettinger was indeed influenced by Collister, there will be someone on Lee's tail from now on until I can deliver his final message."

"It's too bad Sadun didn't know one way or the other about Salvatore," Gus said, as they walked the gurney toward their horror interrogation room and freezer. "What's your feeling about Salvatore, Nick?"

"No matter what he's into, I'm not killing him, except in self-defense," Nick stated. "My take on him is he gladly took what he thought was simply an information gathering security matter. Phil probably thinks he was assigned to watch me as another step in shutting down problems related to Nancy Pettinger's department."

"Killing Jean's boyfriend's Dad would be very bad, Muerto," John said. "Besides, you have too much going already. You must fly to DC, kill Collister, and then fly back here in time to chaperone Jean's dance on Friday. Add in killing her dance date's dad, and that is one bridge too far, my friend."

"Tell me about it. Once Collister's gone, we'll allow justice to work its incompetent magic, and nail the Douglass Cameron leak. In the wake of all that, we'll see where Salvatore winds up on our persons of interest list. "I'm going to bed after we tuck Uthman in for the night. I'll have to get an early start tomorrow. I'm glad I had my uniform cleaned and bagged after I used it last."

"We've never seen you in uniform, Muerto," Gus said. "Will there be pictures?"

"Oh sure, Payaso. I'll get Collister to do a selfie with me. Maybe we can get Paul to photobomb our wonderful meeting."

"There's no need to be sarcastic, Muerto."

* * *

"This is Clyde Bacall, Nick. He'll be driving you to the Congressional Apartments with your briefcase and eyes only files on Formsby."

Nick smiled at the tall man in a black suit, and held out his hand. "You do look like Will Smith. I guess Paul told you we can't wear our MIB suits to this wingding. We'll have to be dressed to the nines in our uniforms."

Bacall shook Nick's hand. "So you're the big bad? You're a legend where no one can read your file, and all we have about you is rumor, and urban horror tales. Even Mr. Gilbrech speaks about you in a whisper. What makes you so bad?"

"I eat spinach mixed with lima beans," Nick answered with grim featured seriousness. Gilbrech laughed while Bacall frowned at his boss's enjoyment of Nick's reply. "Anyway, you don't have to call me 'big bad' – just Nick will do. When we get in the air, let's do a quick review of how to proceed from the time we arrive at Collister's place to how we make our exit."

The three men took their seats aboard the private jet's spacious interior seating, complete with table between them. Nick noticed Bacall staring across the table at him. He could tell the man was a killer. Nick knew the look. *I wonder what this guy has a hard-on for me about*, Nick thought. Once they were in the air, they unfastened their seat belts, relaxing slightly. Gilbrech sat next to Nick. He seemed surprised at Bacall's attitude as well.

"Do you have a problem I don't know about, Clyde?"

"Yes Sir. I was in the Rangers with Carl Stou. I'd like to know why the Big Bad felt it necessary to murder him along with Formsby. I'm assuming, of course, Formsby and his two men didn't disappear into thin air after meeting with you, McCarty."

Nick smiled across at Bacall, but said nothing. *What was the use of explaining the unexplainable? What am I going to say to him, tough break for your friend, wrong place, wrong time, or maybe he should have taken a job at McDonalds?*

Paul Gilbrech gave Bacall a dismissive gesture. "I told Nick I trusted you. Maybe that was a mistake on my part. It may be you're in the wrong department, Clyde. Unfortunately for you, we have numerous leak problems already."

"Meaning what, Sir, he kills me too? Carl never had a chance, did he?"

"Do you mean did I say one, two, three, draw. Uh... no. Everyone has a chance, and choices," Nick answered. "Carl made a bad one working for Formsby."

"Carl was a war hero. What the hell are you, McCarty?"

Nick shrugged. "I'm a killer. I don't draw, paint, or quilt. I kill people, many in cold blood without thought, hesitation, or mercy. You're right. Carl never had a chance."

Gilbrech leaned forward. "Why am I only hearing of you serving with one of Formsby's men now? I read you in on the files, and you never mentioned Stou to me. You're a problem for me, Clyde. Nick will be wondering what the hell you'll be doing if he runs into trouble. So will I. We're going after a traitor in a very high position. I can't have you on the fence as to our mission. I needed you behind this action one hundred percent now, during, and after."

"You're going to have me killed." Bacall reached for his weapon, only to be staring into the business end of Nick's .45 Colt.

"Don't do this, Agent J," Nick said calmly. "Paul's not going to have you killed. He's trying to make you understand how important it is for you to do your job on this mission, and shut everything else in your head off. After it's over, you do your next job the same way, only in a different department, and you keep your mouth shut. This is a black op. You signed on to do this type of work, but you're not cut out for it. There's nothing we can do about that today. Calm down, kid. You'll live through this if you remember who you work for. You don't work for a traitor like your buddy Carl did. Take your weapon out with two fingers, and hand it to your boss. Then we'll go over this mission in straight forward terms. I will explain exactly what you are to do. Am I clear?"

Bacall did not see Nick's draw, nor did he see any sign there would be even an instant's warning before Nick killed him. He opened his coat slowly with his left hand, reached inside with thumb and forefinger, and drew out his Glock 9mm. Gilbrech took it from his finger hold. Paul looked to Nick. The Colt was back in its holster. Nick clasped his hands in front of him on the table.

"Here's how we do it. Paul will set the drop-off time with Collister, so he knows exactly to the minute when we'll be at his door. You'll park in the complex, and walk with me through the complex to his apartment. If he has a man outside, watching for us, we will wait with him until Collister allows entry. You will remain next to his man, whether he goes inside the apartment, or stays outside the door. I will deliver the file, allowing Collister to enter the code Paul will give him for the briefcase lock. Collister will open the case, take the contents, and close the case. Then, we leave. Clear enough, Agent J?"

"What happens to Collister?"

"He dies. That's not your concern," Nick replied. "Do you understand what you are to do?"

Bacall nodded. "Yeah. Watch the guy I'm with."

"Exactly. You do not take your eyes off him. Collister is my problem. If he has more than one man with him, they will both be your concern. You will then drive me back to our plane, and I go home. What do you want Agent J to do after I catch my plane ride home, Paul?"

"Go home, and start thinking about other jobs he'd like to do in the CIA," Paul said, putting the Glock into his own suitcoat pocket. "If you need direction, I'll think of something for you, Clyde. No matter what though, you will forget about today forever. There is a term we use for men and women who don't become actively involved in black ops. It's not an insult. It's just a simple classification. We call them Snow Whites. We don't have whistle-blowers at this level, my young friend."

Bacall noticed Nick again smiling at him. "I understand."

"Good. What next, Nick?"

"Did you bring your dress uniform with you, Agent J," Nick asked.

"I have it."

"Let's get dressed, and then we'll do a couple of walkthroughs with Paul acting as Collister. You and I must be military from the moment we leave the car until the moment we slide back into it for the ride to the plane. Every movement must be precise as if we were delivering nuclear codes to the Pentagon. We will be stern, no nonsense, and stiff. We'll repeat our performance until Paul thinks it looks good. He was a Marine, so I have no

223

doubt he'll take great pleasure in pointing out any discrepancy in our performance."

"You got that right you army pukes," Gilbrech joked. He handed Nick an envelope. "Here's your new nametag and ID set, Major Gibbons. Get dressed. Let's see what you got."

Nick checked the ID packet. "My first name is Alvin... like the chipmunks?"

"Get over it. What were you expecting, Stone Cold or Razor Reddig."

* * *

Lee Collister opened his door when the coded knock from his driver and bodyguard sounded. He had been working steadily behind the scenes trying to get on scene information about Uthman Sadun's disappearance. What he knew for sure was his men were all dead, and the US Marshals were alive, although found drugged in the back of their transfer vehicle. Word from Pacific Grove was Nick McCarty went into hiding with his family after the botched bomb attempt, and morning after gun battle. Phil Salvatore proved to be a solid asset in the area, a simple dupe who thought he was an undercover agent. He had called with what he could find out from the police, claiming to be a friend of Nick's. Collister began to have hope McCarty had not found out his name.

That hope increased exponentially when Paul Gilbrech called him with a request to read in on the Formsby investigation for a meeting with the President. He had been unable to find out everything CIA and the DOJ knew about Formsby's operation. His being read in on the case for a formal Presidential meeting meant Gilbrech knew nothing about his involvement behind the scenes. Also, no one had bothered his man on the inside of the DOJ, Douglass Cameron. Collister now felt the removal of Gilbrech could not be done unless he found a way to get a prime scapegoat like McCarty to do it. With yet another botched attempt on his family, McCarty would be nearly impossible to approach. Sadun had been right about the Rashidi brothers. They were insane. Collister shook his head to clear thoughts of how close he had come to possibly being linked to the devastation of a bomb blast in a California coastal town.

He opened the door to a Delta Force Major, looking to be a lean six footer with grim visage, and stiff demeanor. His beret perfectly positioned with locked briefcase cuffed to his arm, the man exuded an uncompromising military bearing Collister hated. Behind the Major, stood another uniformed sergeant, equally precise in bearing and demeanor. The two of them saluted in sync. Collister waved them off. "Major Gibbons?"

"Yes Sir! Special envoy from CIA Director Paul Gilbrech, Sir!"

"Come in. Leave your man outside though."

"Yes Sir!" Nick spun to face Bacall. "Sergeant Bacall. You will wait here at the door with National Security Adviser Collister's man. I will be out shortly."

Bacall saluted with perfect snap and flair, which 'Major Gibbons' returned. Inside the apartment, Collister waved the envoy over to a table cleared for the occasion. The briefcase was positioned facing Collister with the envoy turning studiously away. Collister entered the code, and opened the briefcase, noticing a slight oily residue on his right fingers. He took out the envelope marked as being highly classified documents.

"Please sign the top form inside the envelope, and place it inside the briefcase, Sir. That will acknowledge the file is now in your custody.

Collister did as requested, and shut the briefcase. The envoy grabbed the handle, shifting the briefcase to his side. "If there is nothing else, Sir, I will leave you to your duties."

Collister nodded, happy to be soon rid of what he considered yet another arrogant uniformed puppet. He opened the apartment door, stepping aside for the envoy. "Thank you, Major."

"Thank you, Sir. Please enjoy your evening, Sir."

Collister shut the door, poured himself a Scotch, and sat down in his favorite recliner with stand next to it. He sipped the Scotch, noticing a slightly metallic flavor. A half hour later, with his drink gone, Collister began feeling hot. Sweat formed on his brow, and upper lip. He set aside the file he had been scanning. Pushing himself to a standing position from his chair, he felt a slight tightening in his chest, and a small bit of vertigo. Inside the kitchen area, Collister poured another Scotch, but added ice this time. After turning the thermostat down to sixty-eight degrees, he returned to his chair. This time when he sat down, a grainy vision of his room made him wipe at his eyes. They cleared for a moment. He gulped a large swallow of iced Scotch, set the glass down, and closed his eyes for the last time. The file fell from his hands to the floor, his last action a panicked grab at the falling file with a suddenly very numb feeling hand.

* * *

At the plane, Nick shook hands with Bacall. "Thanks for the lift. I'll see you on the other side."

"Not if I see you first."

Nick chuckled. "You'll do great, Agent J. Not everyone is cut out for this killer crap. Take my word for it. We're damn lucky we have a CIA Director who knows we're going to all be dead if we keep allowing these assholes to use our laws against us. The law was never meant to protect terrorists and traitors."

"You still didn't need to kill Carl."

"Yeah… I did. I like you, Bacall. Please don't speak of anything you have done here today, or acknowledge any part of it to anyone."

"Or you'll kill me?"

"Someone probably will," Nick answered.

Bacall grabbed Nick's arm as he turned to board the plane. "Would you take the sanction on me?"

Nick glanced around at Bacall with a grin. "Nope. They don't send me after Snow Whites, kid. Be careful out there."

Bacall watched Nick board the plane, his mouth tightening for a moment. He took a deep breath, and returned to the black SUV he had driven McCarty in to catch his private flight. Before driving on, he turned to his passenger. "Where would you like to go, Sir?"

"Take me home, Clyde," Paul Gilbrech directed. "I could use a driver. Are you interested? It would mean some courier type work, and research."

"Courier work like today's delivery?"

"No. You won't be doing anything like the courier work today again."

"You seem to think a lot of McCarty, Sir."

"Unless I send you with a file to be delivered to him in person, or to assist him behind the scenes, we won't be speaking of Nick again. Is that clear enough for you?"

"Yes Sir. McCarty just seems like some dude you meet at a baseball game."

"Last word on Nick. If I knew he was after me, I'd put a bullet in my own head."

"I'll take the job as driver, Sir," Bacall said.

"I'm very happy to hear that, Clyde." Gilbrech put the syringe in his hand away. "I need someone close to me I can trust implicitly as a driver, courier, and in certain situations, a bodyguard. I hope that person will be you, Clyde."

"Yes Sir, I believe I can handle that."

Chapter Ten

Road Trip

"Knock… knock!" After paying the cab driver, Nick called out to the house. Gus came out to greet him.

"You look real fine, Muerto. Did you keep the uniform on just for us?"

"I took a military flight back, so Paul thought it would be best to stay in uniform until I reached home," Nick answered. "How are things here?"

"Dad!" Jean ran out to hug him with Rachel, Dan, and John trailing. She backed away after a moment while still holding onto his jacket. "Nice uniform… not as sharp as the Marines, but pretty good."

"Thanks, snob." Nick hugged and kissed Rachel. "Let's go inside. I believe a small celebration is in order. I wrote nearly three thousand words on the plane in my new Diego adventure 'Dark Interlude', and I think all the leaky loose ends have been plugged. Paul will handle Douglas Cameron through the DOJ. Cameron doesn't command anyone anyhow. His only connection is his Mommy the Senator from Maine. She won't be happy with the black eye he's about to give her all over DC. According to Paul, the DOJ is going to make sure Douglas will be the poster child for being blackmailed in public office."

"We do have some news to share about the Salvatores," Rachel said as the group locked the front, and went into the kitchen. "Neil called to tell us Salvatore was trying to find out where you were, saying he was a concerned friend of the family. Neil told him he thought you were in a safe place with your family until more is known about the assaults on our house."

"Your lawyer checked in too," Gus said. "He turned the DA's office inside out over letting the Rashidi brothers loose without even calling you. He said he wants to talk with you anyway, but guarantees the Rashidis will not move an inch without all of us knowing about it for the rest of their lives."

"Yes," John added. "The Rashidis do not know it, but they had better get their prayer rugs out and petition Allah never to allow them out of prison. El Kabong wishes to be on hand with his Unholy Trio brothers Payaso and Muerto if they ever do get free."

Nick busily passed out beers and shots to his Unholy Trio brethren. Jean received a soda while sitting on the edge of her seat, hoping for more in roads into the very strange and dangerous existence she was part of. Rachel wanted only ice water. Nick considered what he'd heard while hanging his uniform coat and beret on his chair. He drank half his beer before speaking, following the thirst quenching with half of his shot.

"Oh my... that was good. Yes, Brother John, there will be no court dates for the unfortunate Rashidi brothers should they ever see the light of day. I hope Neil wasn't caught in the pounding on the DA's office, but that had to be done. I did manage to question Sadun about Phil Salvatore. The name meant nothing to him, so I'm figuring Paul's right about him being a dupe of Collister, trying to be an undercover agent. He was an easy target for Collister to use because of Salvatore's ties with Pettinger. Tomorrow morning will be an interesting journey into the news coming out of DC."

"How did it go in reality?"

"Very well, Rach. I had a little trouble with one of Paul's minions, but we worked it out, and Paul will make sure he stays on our side. Collister was pretty much what I expected, and we delivered the file to him. Flying to and from DC in one day does not make me happy. Not having to worry about that guy in the position he's in raining terrorists and assassins down on me, definitely improves my mental outlook considerably to make up for the air flights."

"You're in a good position now to move on the Washington gig," Gus said. "This is perfect timing to leave the area for a while. By the time we get back, the hotplate will have cooled down. John and I also emptied out our storage unit while Dan watched the house. It was a beautiful day on the ocean too, Right John?"

"Oh yes, Payaso... it was simply wonderful. Payaso sped out of the Bay at a pace guaranteed to make a dolphin throw up." John finished his shot and beer as he shook his head at the sea cruise he had been forced to make. "I refuse to go on any more voyages with Captain Hook."

After much enjoyment of John's less than shining review of his day at sea with Gus, Nick turned to Dan. "We haven't seen you for a few days, Dan. Was it a problem for you coming to the Valley for the day?"

"Oh hell no. I was just moping around, trying to give you guys a break from the Geezer. I know you're heading to Washington soon. I visited with my kids, and stayed out of trouble by doing all the crap I should have done on the house a long time ago. When I heard about the bombs being placed on the Muerto homestead, I began to wonder about your more open endeavors lately. Do you really think you have a handle on it now, Nick?"

"I believe so. Did Gus tell you about the unfortunate US Marshal adlib I had to do?"

Dan chuckled. "Yeah, he did. I could picture Grace Slick curling into the back of that SUV to go sleepy-time."

"Oh, she was thrilled," Nick replied. "Hey... I didn't have to nick either one of them to make it look good. I should have sent Jean to bed before I asked you about it."

"The sneak eavesdropped on the conversation already," Rachel explained. "Unless we're going to tie a bell around her neck, there's not much we can do about her. I've thought of getting one of those perimeter collars, like they have for dogs. We can set it to zap her the moment she leaves her room."

"Mom!" When she noticed everyone else was laughing, Jean relaxed, pointing a warning finger at Rachel.

"Don't point that thing at me. Deke's lying on his mat out in the yard. I can smack you around like a red headed stepchild without intervention."

Jean dropped her hand comically the moment she noticed her canine protector was absent. "Uh... no fair. You can't mark me up before the dance tomorrow afternoon."

"I'll mark you, and then cancel your dance engagement. No blood, no foul."

"Dad hurried everything so he could chaperone at the dance," Jean replied with some smugness. "No way he allows the Momster to ruin our day together."

"I'll give you a Momster!"

Nick watched the ensuing race around the table, but intervened by grabbing the Momster. "I'm sorry, Momster, but I'd rather keep you out of the emergency room tonight. We'll do what we always do when the Daughter of Darkness acts against your wishes."

"Heh... heh... yes! We will collect all electrical gadgets for a week!"

Jean gasped. "Noooooooooo... you're kidding, right? That's not funny, Momster. I have to check in with my peeps during and after the dance! I'll be exiled to uncool land where outcasts go to be tortured and ridiculed for their entire lives."

Jean giggled as her list of passionate protests and punishment drew wild amusement even from the Momster. Nick poured his partners another beverage along with getting them another beer.

"I have to admit, Daughter of Darkness's vocabulary is very impressive, Momster," Nick said. "Were you thinking about going to the dance too?"

Rachel bowed her head, slowly shaking it as if in anguish. "I have been exiled from the dance by The Daughter of Darkness who fears my girth and possible water breaking on the gym floor are too horrifying as possibilities to allow me to accompany you. She would rather I didn't become a biology lesson in the midst of her dancing elves."

"Is that true, Dagger? Are you really sacrificing your Mom's attendance at your first dance for fear of embarrassment? I am shocked," Nick said.

"Oh come on. Boo hoo." Jean was not falling for the martyr cloak being thrown over her head. "You'll take movies, and we'll all watch them later on TV and laugh. Mom knows she doesn't want to pop Quinn out on the gym floor in front of a bunch of preteens, some who will be laughing while others are throwing up."

Rachel shrugged. "She's right, Nick. Take movies. It would be just my luck to have exactly what she described happen. Then not only would I become the subject of ridicule, but I'd have to listen to her chanting 'told you so' until Quinn graduates from high school. Every time she'd get mad at him, Jean would be saying 'yeah, well at least I wasn't born on the gym floor next to the dirty tennis shoes'."

"After listening to your acceptance speech of possible retribution, I'm beginning to understand where she gets those dark thoughts," Nick replied.

"Guilty," Rachel admitted. "She's like a clone of the way I was. I'm glad we were so involved in staying alive while visiting down South with my Mom that Jean didn't get to hear about all my adventures torturing her Grandma Mona while growing up. Okay, I'm tiring a bit, so this is last call. Finish your drinks, and let's hit the road you lushes. Jean and I have our bags packed in the Ford already. We'll leave John all alone again, and sleep in our own beds tonight. Put on your coat and beret, soldier. The Momster wants to have a military escort tonight.

"Hey... kid here," Jean objected. "That's enough of the X-rated promos."

Jean didn't move fast enough to avoid the Momster ear hold. "Oh sure, now you're a kid. Being in on murder and mayhem is old hat, but suddenly your precious sense of decency is in danger over the mere mention of adults loving one another, huh?"

Jean yelped as the Momster shook her ear a bit. "I...I need that ear for the dance, Momster! G.I. Joe! A little help here!"

Dan stood, while motioning to Gus, as negotiations went on between Momster and the Daughter of Darkness. "C'mon Payaso, throw the rest of your drink down. You'll need it with the Momster driving your new Ford home."

"God help me," Gus said. "John, get my blindfold."

That was enough for the Momster to switch targets with Nick enjoying the whole show while never moving from his spot. "Oh... you did not just insult my driving skills, Geezer! I haven't had a ticket in decades!"

"The police can't be everywhere," Dan replied. "Let's go, Nick, before the Momster makes a play for my ear next."

"Keep talkin', and you'll be riding on the end of a chain at the back of the Ford into Pacific Grove," Rachel warned. "What are you laughin' at, soldier boy? Get that coat and beret on."

"We better do as she says," Nick stated, putting a guiding arm around Jean's shoulders. "It's been a long day. I'd like to go on our balcony deck, and have a beer with my buddy, Deke."

"We'll see about that," Momster said.

* * *

Gus's smirks as they walked Jean to school finally provoked an accounting from Nick. "Okay, what has your mouth twisted in that annoying way of yours this morning."

"Seeing you, natural as can be, on the usual morning walk after Rachel's very humorous explosion last night. Did you finally get her talking coherently?"

"She was fine. The Momster and Daughter of Darkness have to fry each other's bacon two or three times a week. I usually miss a couple episodes. Rach has been confrontational. I believe it's her hormones and pregnancy. I think she's funny. I play along if I'm not in danger of getting a fry pan to the back of my head."

"That sounds like a dangerous game. Speaking of dangerous games are you going in to see Dickerson this morning?"

"I called Justin last night. He says I'm square with the police, and the DA's office has the real Homeland Security/FBI guys breathing down their necks for letting the Rashidis go in the first place. They're taking over the investigation into those three shooters with fake FBI ID's too. That one is solved with the death of Collister. Once they go into his place, and do the usual scouring for data a National Security Advisor's death would warrant, there may be a quiet storm in DC. I like our chances of moving on to Washington by next week. I plan on ignoring Salvatore. He'll have a hard time getting any job in DC with Collister gone."

"Sounds like yet another reason for him to be bitter," Gus pointed out. "I didn't think you'd care much for a guy watching you like he's doing."

"I didn't say I wanted to be his BFF. If I ignore him, what the hell harm can he cause? He won't have anyone to report to anyway. Jean and I like his kid." Nick paused as Gus began chuckling. "Yeah, I know, I'm getting careless again just when we've taken care of some bad problems. Is John meeting us at the beach today? I guess he can pounce on me too."

"He'll be there, but he agrees with you. I don't have any answers for Salvatore. Do I wish he wasn't in our backyard? Yep. I don't want to rain all over Jean's new squeeze, but I think she'll get over it by the time she's ten."

"I heard that," Jean had drifted within earshot while Gus and Nick were talking.

"Sneak!"

"I don't want Sonny's Dad to disappear, Uncle Gus."

"He won't," Nick said. "Gus's job is to tell me stuff I don't want to hear. He needed to point out our Phil Salvatore problem. With everyone else out of the picture, I believe we can simply ignore Phil. I'm glad you didn't get behind in your schoolwork. I'll talk to Dimah today and make sure we're okay for the Washington trip. Chaperones for the dance arrive at 2:30, so I'll make sure I'm there in plenty of time for the big show."

"It only lasts until four. We could go get some ice cream afterward with Sonny. I don't know if his parents will be there or not."

"You can ask him. I'll have my writing and workout done for the day before the dance, so you and I can go even if Sonny can't. We'll bring your Mom home something she wants too."

"Okay, but I already know what Mom wants. Pick out something with the most chocolate and calories, double it, and she'll be fine."

236

"You are so lucky I don't rat you out. You might not be so lucky with blabbermouth Payaso."

Jean stopped in mid stride. "What happened to what goes on the walk to school, stays on the walk to school?"

Gus smiled at Jean's hands on hips pose of annoyance as she waited for his response. "This is getting to be like walking a thirty year old to school, Nick. Don't worry, your secrets are safe with blabbermouth Payaso. Don't be surprised if your Mom tricks it out of Muerto. He's an easy target."

Nick bowed his head, scuffing at the sidewalk with his shoe. "I'm so weak."

"Perhaps a few stories about the young Moms eyeballing the famous author would make for good dinner conversation too," Jean replied.

"You little wart. That's blackmail!"

Jean giggled and skipped ahead with Deke again.

"I've created a monster."

"I won't pretend to know kids, but I believe they get worse when they hit their teens."

"Gee, thanks for that happy thought, Payaso."

"That's Blabbermouth Payaso to you."

"I stand corrected."

* * *

Nick walked Jean to her classroom. Dimah Kader waited outside the classroom to greet her students and a few of the parents. She seemed glad to see Nick and Jean. After a quick wave hello, Jean skipped inside to where Nick saw Sonny Salvatore.

"I'm happy to see you are both well and safe. I heard many rumors about bombs, gunmen, and your family going into hiding. Mr. Salvatore seemed to know quite a bit of what actually was happening. I believe he questioned the police as to your safety."

Yeah, I'll bet he did. "That was thoughtful of him. We did have trouble, but it's over now, and we want to make sure Jean stays ahead in her studies before our trip to Washington."

"I'm certain she will be fine. I saw your name on the chaperone list. It is nice you can come today. It should be fun. Will your wife be coming along?"

"No, she's a bit uneasy about some events because of her pregnancy being so far along. I'll be taking movies though. I guess I'll see you there." Nick turned to leave, but Dimah grabbed his arm.

"Nick, I want to speak with you, possibly at the dance where we'll have more time. My cousin from New Jersey will be visiting on her next vacation. She wants to escape our family's primitive and violent clutches as I did. My separation from the family out here has been an angry topic in the East."

Uh oh. "I'll be happy to talk with you about it, but won't your fiancé be coming home soon?"

Dimah grabbed Nick's hands in hers excitedly. "Yes... that is the other subject I wish to speak with you about. I wish to have a small wedding, but there will be close to fifty people there. I...I have nothing to do with my family anymore. Would you consider giving me away at the wedding, Nick?"

"You really don't have anyone else, Dimah? I mean... I'd be honored, but-"

"Oh thank you, Nick. I am so blessed to have a friend like you! I will talk with you more this afternoon." Dimah gave his hands a firm shake, and turned into her classroom.

Wonderful. Wait until Rachel hears about this… and Gus. I just got rolled.

* * *

"You did what?"

Gus laughed while watching the Rachel hands on hips show as she reacted to Nick's update on the Dimah Kader wedding.

"I'm assuming that was a rhetorical exclamation," Nick answered. "I got rolled. Don't act like you've never seen it happen before. You and the Daughter of Darkness roll me quite frequently. Are you pissed off because an acquaintance did it?"

Rachel took a deep breath, and let her arms slip to her sides as she straightened. "Maybe. I'm shell shocked. You only last night returned from ending an incredibly dangerous threat. I heard you wake to tackle Diego's continuing adventures, all happy-go-lucky. Then, you walk Jean to school, and return with us as the main ingredients in Dimah Kader's wedding, including you giving away the bride – at a wedding her family will probably send suicide bombers to. How am I doing?"

"Pretty fair, except you forgot to mention my agreeing to help Dimah's cousin from the East, also running from her psycho family," Nick replied.

"Madre de Dios!"

"I'm getting a lot of that lately." Nick turned to the very entertained Gus. "See, Payaso, I told you Rach would be calmly tolerant of my newly acquired duties."

"I want my husband back! You know… the one I married. The one who shot a woman right between her horns while petting her dog. Let's see… what was it you said when I asked you if she was bad? Oh yeah… you said 'she was to someone'. You probably

239

ate the dog later. That's my husband! Where is he! What have you done with him?"

By that time both Gus and Nick were engrossed in amused appreciation of Rachel's verbal tantrum. Rachel plopped down on a kitchen chair. "I'm glad you and Payaso think this is so funny, Muerto. You could have pointed out the fact there is such a thing as elopement to Dimah. You could have written them a check for a Las Vegas special with an entire hotel wing for her fiancé's Marine detachment."

"Is there something you don't understand about the admission, 'I got rolled'."

"Never mind. I'm going to fix this for you. When you chaperone the dance, have Dimah call me. I'll make some polite suggestions, and add an offer to help with a planned Vegas special. They have some great package deals I'm sure she'll enjoy. I don't think she's considered the unintended consequences of having even a moderately attended wedding with her whacko relatives anywhere around."

"That sounds good to me, Rach. I'll punt that ball out on her one yard line the moment I have a chance to discuss things with her during my chaperone duties."

"Sometimes, it takes a woman's light touch in these matters."

"By the way... I didn't eat the lady's dog, you Philistine."

* * *

Nick was stationed near the older kids at the dance. The principal rightly assumed with the reputation he had garnered, there would be less likelihood of any trouble with the students nearing their teenage years. Having accidentally on purpose killed a gunman in the school hallway went far beyond making gang signs with fingers, and wearing pants at the thighs. He was the real

240

deal, and the dancers under his supervision respected that fact with relatively good behavior.

Nick could see Jean interacting with her friends, and dancing with whatever boy was courageous enough to ask her. When she did, he recorded it with his small zoom lens digital cam. Since she didn't turn anyone down, more of the boys gravitated to her. Sonny danced with her a couple of times, but seemed more taken with her conversation between dances which Nick also recorded because he knew Rachel would think them cute. Nick had already relayed Rachel's request to Dimah, who promised to call her before she and Nick talked. He saw Dimah approach hurriedly with a big smile as the song ended.

"Rachel is so happy for me! She agreed to be Maid of Honor if Quinn is born on time. You two are the best! I have a beautiful spot picked out near 'Lover's Point' amongst the trees there."

"That is a beautiful area. Well, what a nice surprise," Nick said. "Rachel never hinted to me that she would be interested in being part of the wedding. I thought perhaps she had some other suggestions for you. I guess it's all set then. It's good you weren't shooting for an April wedding. I will need most of this month to handle the book signings in Washington."

"I can't possibly do it until June, which will be perfect. I believe Rachel hopes Quinn is early. She mentioned being very tired of her pregnancy."

"It would not be good for her to have Quinn on our trip, but what happens… happens. As long as he's healthy, inconvenience means very little."

"Yes, so true. How do you like our April dance for the kids. I bet you pictured all manner of scenes with your imagination."

"I think it's great," Nick agreed, motioning at the kids dancing. "I told Rachel and Jean, boys mostly stood along the wall, and girls danced with each other when I was a kid. These kids are all dancing, and they seem competent doing it."

"They dance all the time to their iPods and phones. I can always tell when they are listening to something by Bluetooth when they should be paying attention in class. They cannot keep still. I have confiscated many electronic gizmos this year. I of course give them to the parents. In the old days teachers probably confiscated only chewing gum, and comic books. We are well beyond those days."

"Agreed. You mentioned your cousin. Will she be visiting in time for the wedding?"

"She is trying to arrange her escape so she doesn't attract attention. I don't know if she will make it for the wedding. Her name is Cala. I believe she plans to drive, so she can simply disappear. Once Cala settles here, and gets a job, it will be very difficult for my family to pressure her back. I will find out more soon. Thank you for asking, Nick."

Nick spotted Phil Salvatore entering the gym, dressed in a dark gray suit, and looking formidable in a banker type manner. Sonny intercepted him, but Phil patted his shoulder, and continued on toward Nick. "I think Sonny's Dad is heading our way. By his expression, I hope he wants to talk with you."

"Gee, thanks Nick. Pardon me, but I am hoping he wants only you. Sonny is a good student, and apple of the teacher's eye, a wonderful-"

"Suck-up," Nick interrupted Dimah's comical listings of Phil Salvatore's son's good qualities. "You should be ashamed of yourself, Ms. Kader."

Phil was approaching too fast for Dimah to get in a last retort, so she elbowed Nick, while smiling at Salvatore. "Hi, Mr. Salvatore. I'm glad you could make it. Nick has been policing the older kids for us."

"Call me Phil." Salvatore smiled charmingly while shaking Dimah's hand, and then Nick's. "Yes, I'll bet Nick has been policing these kids very well. I was wondering if I might have a word with you, Nick."

"Certainly."

"I will get closer to my bunch of young rebels. I will talk with you both later. Nick, I will discuss my cousin's situation with you after this weekend if that is alright with you."

"Of course, Dimah." Nick and Phil waited until Dimah moved across the gym. "What can I do for you, Phil?"

"Have you heard the news from DC?"

"I'm working on a new novel I'm titling 'Dark Interlude'. With book signings in the state of Washington this month, I've been trying to get as far along with my new novel as I can before the signings. We authors have to hawk our wares past, present, and future at every opportunity. The novel so far is going very well, and I admit I am out of touch concerning current events away from my keyboard. My wife Rachel didn't mention anything out of DC. What happened?"

Salvatore stared at Nick, obviously trying to gauge whether he was indeed as innocently ignorant of the recent news or being deliberately obtuse. "If you had come up for air from your keyboard you would have noticed the National Security Advisor to the President, Lee Collister, died of mysterious causes last night."

Nick furrowed his brow in an award winning look of questioning concern. "My condolences. Was he a friend of yours?"

243

Salvatore's mouth tightened into a thin lipped clamp on something it took control not to disgorge. "No... he was one of my mentors... a boss, if you will. I had some trouble at my previous posting in DC because of a woman I worked for named Nancy Pettinger. She was accused of being a traitor, and died rather ignominiously in a sex scandal. I was caught in a web where the powers that be decided we were all tainted. Collister aided me in getting the posting here, and a way to earn my way back to DC. All I was to do besides grunt work in the office was report on happenings concerning your actions."

Nick smiled. "My actions. You mean writing novels?"

"No. I mean finding men planting bombs on your house, and hitmen sent to your house you killed in cold blood. I know you were a consultant on the Nancy Pettinger case. Now she's dead. A man I greatly admire had me looking into your adventures on the coast, and now he's dead. Maybe all this is just a big coincidence, but I'm wondering if I'm going to be found dead of mysterious causes soon."

Nick shrugged. "I don't know, Phil. Have you done anything that would warrant someone killing you? You said yourself Pettinger died in some kind of sex thing gone wrong, and you don't even know yet what caused this Collister guy's death. It doesn't seem like you've done anything to get killed for yet... according to what you've told me."

Salvatore's face took on a flushed appearance as rage seeped into his features. "Are you playing with me, McCarty?"

Nick allowed the Terminator to surface, not to impress Salvatore, but because he was getting awfully tired of talking to him. "Believe me, Phil. I don't play with anyone. I'll tell you what though. I will do you a favor. Wait one."

Nick took out his iPhone, and called Paul Gilbrech.

"Nick?"

"Yep. I have Phil Salvatore here at our kids' dance with lots of curiosity. Would you talk with him for me so I'm not forced to make an adjustment?"

"Put him on. Thanks for calling me first."

"Happy to do it, my friend." Nick handed the phone to Salvatore. "This is for you."

Salvatore took the phone. "Who is it?"

"Paul Gilbrech, the Director of the CIA."

Salvatore nearly dropped the phone. He put it to his ear tentatively. "Hello."

Nick watched him cringe as he heard Paul taking Salvatore through a litany of louder than normal voiced conversation. After a few minutes, Salvatore said, "Yes Sir, I understand, Sir."

Salvatore handed the phone back to Nick. His face had much less color. "I'm glad you called anyway, Nick. I knew you wanted to know. Clyde took the job as driver."

"Outstanding," Nick said, pleased the kid didn't take one for the team. "Thanks for letting me know. I liked him."

"The feeling is not mutual. Be talking with you soon," Gilbrech disconnected.

When Nick put away the phone, and turned his attention to the dance floor without commenting any further, Salvatore could only stay silent for a minute. "I have to ask. What did 'forced to make an adjustment' mean?"

"Let's leave it with an old school cliché, Phil. Curiosity killed the cat, and satisfaction did not bring it back. In fact it ate the cat's nine lives like chocolate covered Cheerios. Through no fault of your own other than trying to get ahead in DC, you crossed paths with the wrong people. Take this to heart. Enjoy your time here in this beautiful place. Work your present job with distinction, and live within your means. I'm afraid you won't be returning to DC any time soon. Please don't make mention of me to anyone, for any reason, or in any reference. Is that clear?"

Salvatore nodded. "Clear. I don't think it's a good idea, or a safe one, for my son to visit your house. Is that a problem?"

"Nope. I understand completely. They're nine, and going to school together. They'll be okay. Does that mean you don't want Jean to visit your house either?"

"Can I get back to you on that? My wife is upset over everything to do with my being sent here. I believe she figured Collister's chance for me to get my old job back was a sure thing. She loved the Washington D.C. scene."

"You mean the parties, and socializing?"

"Exactly."

"Do you or your wife golf?"

"Ah… yes. It's kind of a must in DC social circles."

"Good," Nick said. "I have a connection with Corral de Tierra Country Club in Carmel. It's a private club. I'll have a friend of mine, Julius Danvers, invite you to join. It's by invitation only. I'll take care of the fees. It will please your wife."

"That's very generous of you, but I-"

"Don't say no, Phil. Take the offer home to Clarice."

"Okay… sure… thank you. Are you a member?"

"I have a membership because Julius is a big fan of my novels, and I did a favor for him once. He has a shipping line. He

246

asks me in for a consultation once in a while, and we meet at the Corral. My Rachel doesn't care for golf or country clubs, so other than having dinner with Julius once in a while at the Corral, we're not active members. You won't have to fear running into me there."

"Why would you do this for me?"

"Jean likes Sonny, and I want you to know there aren't any hard feelings about getting into my business, just so you never do it again. Leave everything at 'our kids go to school together' and we won't have any problems."

"Don't worry about that."

Nick grinned at Phil. "Believe me. I'm not worried."

* * *

"Hello? Rollover Rachel... we're home." Nick briefed Jean about the sudden inclusion of their entire family in Dimah Kader's wedding on the way home. "Jean and I want to hear all about Dimah's wedding plans from her Maid of Honor. Hello?"

Rachel walked out of the living room to join them. Deke streaked through the dog door to dance around his human housemates. "Okay... get it out of your systems. Even Deke has been avoiding me. Make it fast because I'm feeling my Princess Bump inner monster surfacing. Believe me, you don't want that."

"We wondered if you managed to explain everything to Dimah. Instead of an open wedding with guests in danger of the Kader family's murderous nature, you had planned to suggest a nice wedding in Las Vegas. After Dimah talked to you, she seems to think you meant a Las Vegas type spot under the trees at Lover's Point. I thought you meant the place in Nevada with casinos and lavish hotels. Were you going to put in a roulette wheel and a slot machine for the day at Lover's Point, Hon? Oh, and I thought you were getting me out of being in the wedding party, but according to Dimah, you meant to get into the wedding party."

"Am I the Flower Girl now in Ms. Kader's wedding, Mom," Jean added. "Hey, Dad, maybe Mom means to put one of those little saddles on Deke so he can be the ring bearer too. We'll have the whole ceremony covered if we can talk Uncle Gus and Uncle John into being ushers."

"You two are just too cute for words. Are we done now? There's no sense in sugarcoating my complete failure at interventions. What would you two like for dinner?"

"Italian Wedding Soup," Nick replied.

"And wedding cake with ice cream," Jean finished.

Rachel spun away, her right hand alongside her face in a classic shunning gesture. "Dead to me. You are both dead to me."

* * *

Nick and Deke led his group of Gus, Tina, Rachel, Dan, and Jean aboard the private jet, put at his disposal by Paul Gilbrech. Clyde Bacall greeted them on board the plane, distastefully checking Deke out with a jaundiced eye. Nick introduced him to everyone, including Deke, who sat and raised a paw on cue. Bacall ignored it.

"Don't leave my dog hangin', Clyde."

Bacall reluctantly crouched to shake Deke's paw as the other members of Nick's crew proceeded to their seats. "An entourage and a dog… really?"

"I shouldn't have introduced you to my family," Nick replied. "We should have walked by you without even a look, like we'd do with any other rude-ass flight attendant. Let's stick to business. My other partner left for Washington under the radar a week ago with a specially designed GMC Yukon programmed so it can't be tracked. He joined the Masjid Al-Nur in Olympia after checking out a few Islamic sites. He has already made contact, and been recruited to meet with some of the founders at the suspected Isis compound in Onalaska."

Bacall looked shocked. "How in hell did he work his way in so fast? The FBI has been trying for over a year to infiltrate the compound with no luck at all."

"John's my secret weapon. His real name is Ebi Zarin. All of the terrorists he once was associated with are dead. He was trained overseas, and infiltrated from Canada. I caught him and turned him. I trust John with my life. His name can be checked by the locals in Olympia. They will treat him like a hero for surviving. His cover story is solid. I'm telling you this because we will be the only ones who know about him. If anything happens in a police roundup, or action by the FBI, I need you to be on top of it. Paul said you would have a liaison working with us, so we wouldn't be seen together much during this operation."

"She'll be coming on board any moment. Her name is Robyn MacEachern. She works with Homeland Security, and coordinates operations on the border with Canada Border Services Agency. Mr. Gilbrech says you can trust her with anything. She's one of ours inside HS, so anything you need that you don't have, she will get you locally."

A slim woman of medium height, in jeans, tennis shoes, and a black windbreaker boarded the plane. She waved at the pilot before walking over with a big smile. "Hello. You must be Nick. I recognize you from your book jacket, and of course your file."

Nick shook her hand. "Clyde filled me in on your liaison duties, Robyn. He says if I need anything, you can get it."

MacEachern lowered her voice. "The Company has more than a few assets in the area because of border infiltration, and that viper nest in Onalaska. It beats me why they don't simply send a Reaper over it, and erase the damn place from the Northern Hemisphere."

"Good question. I have a trusted friend on the inside. By the time we're ready to make a decision, he'll be able to tell us what they're actually doing at the compound. C'mon, I'll intro you to my 'entourage' as Clyde calls them."

MacEachern tugged on Nick's sleeve to delay the introductions for a moment. "I'll be working with you closely. I booked you in at the Great Wolf Lodge Grand Mound in Centralia. It has everything, including an indoor water park for your daughter. It's twenty-five miles away from Olympia, but it's an easy drive, and Centralia puts you closer to Onalaska. I have a GMC Yukon at the Lodge now, as per your request for personal use. The keys are with the desk clerk. We'll take a limousine to Centralia from the airport as befits your bestselling author status. I will be with you the entire time when you have book signings, or simply in transition from one place to another. Mr. Gilbrech read me in on your other operation in Seattle. I can coordinate that for you too. It seems like a bridge too far with this Isis gig, Nick."

"I know. It provides cover for my leaving the area though officially with another book signing in Seattle. We don't know how explosive our interaction with the Onalaska compound will be. It may be bad. I like being settled in closer to the compound, but we still have to deal with local police fallout. We're heading for the area early because as I was telling Clyde, I have a man on the inside now. I'm his backup. The book signing party in Olympia won't take place for another week. I'm going in tonight to recon the coordinates my man gave me, and every night until we know one way or another what the hell is going on inside."

"This is straight from Mr. Gilbrech, McCarty," Bacall stated. "If you find out this is an actual Isis infiltration base, he doesn't want them brought to justice, or to see the inside of any courtroom. The crap they're pulling overseas has even the usual

Islamic apologists worried we're likely to taste the same thing here. I don't want to know what you have in mind, but my job is to help you make it happen. He said one other thing I didn't understand – Mr. Gilbrech said you can use cartoon characters if you have to."

Nick laughed. "You've made my day, Clyde. Anything else before you meet my people, Robyn?"

"Nothing serious. I'm glad you're getting into place early. This Lodge I picked out is perfect for staying out of the public view. I know you have an agent named Cassie Sedwick, who handles all of your publishing endeavors. Has she been read in on anything other than your author business?"

"No, and I'd like to keep it that way. Paul sending you in as an extra liaison is a perfect fit right now. It will make everything much less complicated. Cassie's easy to get along with, and she usually packs it in early once the signing gets off the ground. She won't get in your way. It will be great having someone familiar with this entire area and assets along."

"I have to say McCarty, your reputation hinges on the proverbial lone gunman template. What the hell is all this mixing family, friends, pets and other hobbies into national security operations?"

"Don't give it a thought, Clyde," Nick replied. "You know the old saying, 'if it ain't broke, don't fix it'. I'll add one other thing you need take to heart – don't presume to know me, what I do, or how I get it done. If I ever catch you working at cross purposes on a mission I'm on to undercut me, I'll introduce you to a side of me you'll only see once."

"I wouldn't be doing my job if I didn't point out weaknesses in your mode of operation."

"Yeah… you would, and you'd be less annoying. Remember what I said." Nick took Robyn's arm. "This way to the bane of Clyde's existence."

Chapter Eleven

Terrorists No More

"Damn, Nick, it's darker than the black hole of Calcutta out here." Gus drove slowly along Spencer Road to the loop Nick programmed into the GMC before they started out. At the late hour, no traffic or even the far off glow of headlamps could be seen. "I realize you need to know exactly what terrain you'll have to traverse to stay away from a frontal assault, but what if these guys have the surrounding area booby-trapped? You couldn't see a trip wire to save your soul in these woods."

"Oh, I'm sorry, Payaso. This isn't the Las Vegas Strip. Even the Isis death cult freaks won't take a chance on blowing some unsuspecting hiker to kingdom come. If anything, they'll have motion sensors, and networked cams to protect their tunnel entrances. They don't have fences because a fence would be like an arrow pointing at the place from orbit."

"You do remember," Nick continued, "the little factoid John was able to share with us about these assholes having an entire network of tunnels underground, right? There aren't any doors to knock on, or assault for that matter. Like John says, this place is a training facility and halfway house for infiltration from Canada. They don't need housing and a community so they can pretend they're practicing religious freedom away from the Islamophobic populace. They're training soldiers. They're also stockpiling weapons, explosives, and they have a sealed lab, John was warned to not even go close to."

"Fine. Since we know this complex is all underground, how are they hiding power, and utility use?"

"Generators and wells, and probably even solar panels in protected spots where they can catch rays from an other than horizontal position. With what they had to construct for the tunnels, I doubt they had any trouble at all finding water wells here in the Pacific Northwest. I think there will be questions to be answered about how this place was built without the government knowing it. I can see a construction firm being paid to do a job, and protecting the secrecy of it by claiming it's a military defense project. Where an installation like this runs into trouble is their ventilation. They can camouflage the vents, but they can't hide them completely. If we had the time, I'd get Paul to send a bird overhead. With the exact coordinates John gave us, we could get a heat signature from the vents, along with an outline of the complex."

"You have a week to pull this off. What did we need Dan for if you were going to shit-can our original plan?"

"Dan was going to be our distraction around their main entrance on the day we moved on them from a different direction. That's not going to happen. They don't have a community or a main gate. John said they even have their vehicles drive down inside."

Gus checked their position. "I'm almost afraid to ask this. We could have driven around the area, and went in hiking. We could have taken pictures, movies, and tested what they do when their perimeter is breached. Why the hell are you doing this in the pitch dark?"

"Because I'm going in to get John. I didn't say anything, but he missed his check in earlier today, not that it mattered. I briefed him before he left. We already know what these Islamo-Fascist tools are doing. If I spent a week scoping out the place, someone would burn me, and we'd all end up dead. Paul gave me the code we worked out. He told Clyde to tell me I could use cartoon characters if I needed to. That meant he was worried somehow the mission would get compromised, and for me to do anything I wanted. I pretended for Clyde and Robyn I'd be doing a recon on the compound for the next week. We're taking care of business tonight, Payaso. It will throw them into a panic when I use the EMP gun at one of the entrances, and then go inside for an assault."

Gus hit the brakes, driving to the roadside shoulder. "You did not just say you are going into the Isis tunnels to assault the compound tonight! No! Uh uh… that did not happen! If it did, I'm leaving you right here, and I'm going to the Lodge and rat your ass out to Rachel."

Nick chuckled, expecting to get an outraged condemnation from his friend. "I'll need you at the coordinates I have on our satellite laptop on the backseat. I brought your com gear so we'll be in touch every second. It's the badass tech without peer. Tunnels, scramblers, barriers – nothing will cut us off. The EMP prototype I have will wipe out anything I point it at. John said there were twenty-two soldiers, facilitators, and infiltrators. That's a big cell for El Muerto and his merry men, Payaso and El Kabong. I'm afraid they may be messing with our brother the Kabong. We can't have that, Payaso. He left a tracker at the entrance they took him into initially. It's working, so I'll have a target entrance to check on."

Gus stared across at his friend's smiling countenance, remembering the rescue Nick did to bring his brother Phil out of Kingston, Jamaica. "Tell me what you need, brother. We're not leaving without Kabong. I know how you assault places by yourself. Is that what those bags are in the back cargo bin?"

"Yep. I can tell you're thinking Kingston, huh?"

"It's the only way one lunatic pulls off a one man assault on an armed compound, and you certainly did that to get Phil away from the Jamaican Posse. You knew where Phil and the Butlers were being held, so you didn't kill them too. What about John?"

"He activated his tracker two hours ago, which was the sign he was in trouble, as well as unable to contact us. His signal is on the laptop too. He was supposed to activate it, and swallow it. John laughed when I told him if it took me longer to get to him than it did the tracker to make its way through his digestive system, he wouldn't need it anyway. This is a good place to stop. I'll get my gear on, and you can ready the laptop."

"You are one crazy guy, Muerto."

"So I've been told." Nick started out of the GMC, but then ducked his head inside again. "We both know what I am, Gus. I'm either going to kill a lot of people, or I'm finally going to get popped myself. I'm betting they don't have enough guys to take out El Muerto. If they do, John will be with me, so drive to the Lodge, call Paul, and tell him to take the place out with a 'bunker buster'. That should be safe enough, even with the unknown stuff they're fooling around with in that lab down there."

"If El Muerto does win this lunatic assault, what do you have planned for the lab then?"

"Nothing. I'll bring you down with the equipment bags, and we'll have some fun. We dress in costume, rag the crap out of Isis, and then we get the hell out of there. I'll call Paul with all the particulars. He'll put our liaison to work. I'll let him handle the cleanup. I imagine the video of the cartoon brothers will drive everyone nuts while they find out what's been going on right under their noses. Robyn seems competent enough to simply proceed with her duties. Once Clyde finds out I took care of business without him, I'll let Paul deal with his minion outrage. If he gets in my face again, I may have to make an adjustment."

"He's an asshole. Go on, and get ready, Muerto. I'll check on John's signal."

Fifteen minutes later, Gus drove toward their original coordinates. He glanced over at Nick sitting sideways in his seat. "You look like one of those guys in the G.I. Joe movies. Is there anything you don't have on? In Jamaica, all you had on were shorts and a pack. How many did you kill that day, a hundred?"

"No, I didn't kill a hundred people. We're high tech now Payaso. They make lightweight full body armor. The spot I picked to start my approach is only a couple miles away from the complex."

"Yeah, through the densest woods I've ever seen."

"If anyone could do this we'd be sitting in the Lodge bar throwing down shots and beers."

"If we live through this, I don't care if it's 5 am, I'm throwing them down until I'm blind."

"Seriously, these guys will be asleep. If my EMP gun doesn't disable their alarm system, they'll be jumping out of their racks not knowing what the hell's happening. I'm hoping to get John with me before I have to really get serious. Even with you letting me know where I am in relation to him, I'll feel better when I have him in sight. Although I won't be broadcasting every moment, I want you to keep talking every few minutes, so I know our com is good."

"Here we are, brother." Gus stopped at the spot Nick picked out. "I won't say good luck or any of that crap. At least you're not wearing your Muerto mask going in. Another thing – don't start talking to me in third person either."

"El Muerto never does that, Payaso. El Muerto away!" Nick disappeared into the woods.

"Asshole." Gus turned off the GMC. He had no other task than to watch both of his friends' tracker signals. "I wish I could see into that stupid complex so I could tell you what to do when you're in there."

"Coming through loud and clear. We'll have to settle for I'm getting warmer or colder. He may be a straight shot from where I go down at. His tracker at the entrance is on my GPS screen. The terrain's solid, so they must not have had their usual flood of rain lately. I figured I'd be sloggin' in the mud by now. My short wave infrared prototype night vision goggles are the best. I'd be movin' like a snail without them."

"What all are you packing?"

"El Muerto has his trusty silenced MP5 this time on mission, my Colt .45 with silencer, razor sharp stiletto, and a backup MP10 for Kabong. I brought along enough grenades to level the complex too, along with gas masks in my pack for Kabong and I."

"You should have told me what the hell you had planned before, Muerto. I could have went in with you. Dan could have driven the getaway vehicle."

"Dan's a Luddite. He's about as computer savvy as Deke. Also, this assault is not a job for my trusty sidekick and enabler, Payaso. You are the deadly Payaso, facilitator of the psychotic Muerto. El Muerto must this time combat the forces of darkness alone. El Muerto must-"

"I have your favorite Giants baseball cap with gold lettering in my hands right now. One more third person El Muerto outburst, and I puke in it. Then I'll seal it in a plastic bag."

Silence.

"Heh… heh."

"I'm telling Kabong about this," Nick muttered.

"Heh… heh."

Nick picked his way through the dense woods as a lifetime stalking prey dictated. The wetness of spring in the Pacific Northwest muffled his footsteps while he listened to Gus insulting him in humorous ways at three minute intervals. Nick acknowledged each voice check with a whispered 'Yo mamma'.

Although telling Gus the men he hunted would never set traps to blow up unsuspecting hikers, Nick paid close attention to his every step once he passed within a three hundred yard range of the compound. His cautionary approach added an hour to his reaching the compound entrance, but greatly reduced the noise level to nothing more than a slight rustling breeze. Nick found a razor wire perimeter trap at ankle height when he reached the fifty yard mark, and another at twenty-five yards. A familiar smell then drifted to his nose: tobacco smoke.

"Smoker," Nick whispered.

"I remember the lesson," Gus replied, remembering the men Nick had stalked in the past with Gus along, and how far the smell of tobacco smoke could reach. "You sure made those guys pay for their up until then innocent habit, proving that smoking is indeed hazardous to your health."

Nick went to a crawl, picking each hand and foot advancement with care and patience. As he neared the sentry's position, Nick watched a billowing cloud of tobacco smoke waft upwards into the air. Flipping his night vision goggles upward Nick allowed his natural night vision to work. He couldn't take the chance the sentry might be in constant communication with someone inside. Nick waited until the red glow of his cigarette brightened as the sentry inhaled, and fired two silenced hollow points into the face behind the glow. The sentry dropped with very little sound.

The approach remained a careful time consuming task as Nick covered the remaining distance to the dead sentry. He breathed a sigh of relief, finding no evidence of anything relating to a communication device. The sentry had nothing of an electronic nature on him. Nick confiscated the Uzi and extra clip from the guard. Removing his small pack, Nick extracted his remote viewing video cam at the end of an extendable cable. He propped the entrance hatch quietly to allow him to snake the video cam into and down the stairs. No one was in sight, which was not unexpected at nearly 3 am. With pack in place once again, Nick entered the compound entrance with noiseless steps. In the entry tunnel, a constant underlying noise of generators provided cover for his steps. A red glow from corridor lights made maneuvering an easy task for Nick.

"I'm by myself in the entrance tunnel," Nick whispered. "Guide me to John."

Nick hugged the corridor wall, his silenced MP5 at the ready. He moved forward slowly, to give Gus time to react to his movements.

"Look for somewhere to go right."

Fifty feet ahead Nick came to intersecting tunnels going in both directions with still no one in sight. He went right. After moving ten feet, Gus affirmed the right direction.

"You're getting close," Gus said. "There should be something on your left soon."

* * *

Hanging on a chain, naked except for his undershorts, John tried to balance on alternating feet, cringing each time as his feet were cramping. They had received word from the East with conflicting stories, one claiming Ebi Zarin died during an operation in Boston. The other source claimed Zarin had been killed near the Canadian border. John denied the stories, joking he was standing with his contact, Yuri Aman. Therefore he could not be dead. Aman showed his lack of humor by chaining John in the position he was now in.

Only his toes touched on the cold bare floor. He grinned through the pain, remembering he had just seen a TV show with the main character hung in such a way. John had been left alone since shortly after midnight. The man who originally brought him to the compound returned with a second man. His original recruiter stood directly in front of him, staring at John with his hands clasped behind his back. The man who came in with him arranged surgical implements on a side table.

"You don't need to torture me, Yuri," John told the man. "What is it you wish to know?"

John's statement surprised Aman. His eyes narrowed, and his lips pursed in a tight line. "You think this is funny. That is good. When my friend Hadi shares his passion with you, I am most certain you will tell us everything you know. Who are you in reality?"

"I am Ebi Zarin. I did not lie to you about my name."

"Ebi Zarin died. That, we do know."

"I know that is the story. I faked my death with help from the man who told me to tell you everything if I was caught."

"Who is this man?"

"His name is El Muerto. He killed my entire cell, and another with my help near the Canadian border. We made movies of it. Have you seen them on YouTube? They are very popular, almost with as many hits as a cat video. Muerto wants you to know everything I know, because he said he would kill you and all of your men here soon anyway."

Yuri smiled then. "You think much of this Muerto. I hope you like him as much when we cut pieces from you slowly."

"Why would you do such a thing," John asked, trying to buy as much time as possible. "Take me down, and give me a notepad. I will write everything out for you. All that I have experienced since I faked my death will be in writing."

Hadi walked over with a scalpel. "This Ebi is very funny. Let me cut his dick off, Yuri. He will be serious then."

261

Yuri waved him off with disgust. "Too much blood. Get the surgical sheers. You may cut off the first joint of every finger one at a time. We will be sure of the truth soon about this Muerto."

"I am trying to tell you about him," John insisted, reciting the mantra Nick had suggested to try first if they did not believe him. "He is the 'Dead One'. His hallowed sidekick, the deadly 'Payaso' named him because of his horrific manner of dealing torture and death. What do you wish to know? I will tell all."

"Cut off his finger joints," Yuri instructed. "I am sick of hearing about this fantasy character."

Yuri heard a thud and gurgle, as the scalpel hit the floor with a clatter. He turned to see Hadi's hands grasping the knife handle protruding from his throat with panicked eyes wide as saucers. "What has-"

"It is El Muerto," John explained.

* * *

"You should be at a room," Gus said. "It looks as if you are standing very near John."

"There is a door ajar on the left," Nick whispered. "Hang on."

Nick heard voices, one of them John's. He grinned, hearing John speak of El Muerto. He slipped into the room behind where he could see John hanging by a chain. The grin went away to be replaced by his Terminator mask of concentration. In the split second Hadi looked questioningly toward the figure near the room door, Nick's stiletto flew unerringly to its target. Nick strode to the man staggering with blood pumping around his hands. Nick's left hand held the MP5 trained on Yuri, who stared in disbelief at Nick, raising his hands in surrendering form. John chuckled, knowing Yuri's surrender meant little to El Muerto. The man with the stiletto in his throat collapsed, his body gradually relaxing into a final death spasm as life blood pooled around him.

"El Kabong. I'm very happy to see you, my very good friend. Payaso. Kabong is alive and well, but I don't much care for his new position though. Did this guy put you up there?"

"Yes, Muerto."

"Payaso says hi. You there. Get my friend down."

Aman rushed over to John, bear hugging him around the waist, and lifting him so he could free himself of the hook holding the chain. He then fished in his pocket for the key to John's manacles. Once John was free, he flexed the blood painfully into his hands once again while gingerly working his feet and toes.

"Put the manacles on your buddy, and put him on the hook if you can, Kabong."

John smiled at the horrified Yuri. He swiped his captor across the face with the manacles, driving Aman to his back clutching his face. "Hold your hands out, Yuri, or I'll smash you in the head again. If you make noise, I will smash you for that also."

Yuri held his shaking hands away from his bloody face. John put the manacles on his wrists, and helped him to his feet. "Put your arms up with hands held apart."

Yuri did as ordered. John lifted him easily to his own former position on the hook. Nick handed John a piece of duct tape, which John placed over Yuri's mouth. "Sorry, Muerto. They received word from the East I was dead much faster than we figured."

"It's a small thing, brother." Nick poked the swinging Yuri back and forth while John dressed. "I am unhappy finding you in such a position, Kabong. It's a good thing to have your new pal waiting on the hook while I take care of his Isis recruits. How are the living conditions, John?"

"They have three living quarters. They feel invulnerable. If you dealt with the man at the entrance I marked he was the only one watching outside. They do not have anyone below on watch. Very sloppy terrorists. In their defense, they do not know the crazy Muerto."

"Here, Kabong, you can listen to Payaso laugh at your disrespect of the fantastic El Muerto." Nick handed John an earwig to network with Gus.

"Payaso! I am here."

"If you can, hurry Muerto along. He wants to do cartoon movies too."

"Yes! It will be the return of El Kabong. It will have a million more hits than the closest cat video. Kabong may even pass the laughing baby ones."

"C'mon, John. We better get moving or Payaso will start whining steadily until we want to rip our own ears off." Nick plucked his stiletto out of Hadi's throat with a towel from the utensil table Hadi had been preparing for John's torture.

Nick gave John the MP10 he brought with extra clips along with the gas mask. "Show me the quarters, and then we'll decide how we want to do this. We'll recon quietly, take a quick look, and come back here. Is the sealed lab and weapons stockpile you spoke of in a corridor away from the living quarters?"

"Understood. Yes, it is on the far end of the complex in the opposite direction of the way you proceeded to find me from the entrance I marked."

John led the way. All quarters were along the center corridor with bathroom facilities opposite of the quarters. John checked the bathroom while Nick peeked into each open doored bunk room, making an instant decision. He checked with John, who indicated no one was using the bathroom.

"The hell with it, John," Nick whispered. "Put on your gas mask, and retreat toward where we left Yuri. I'm going to blow this place now.

John nodded in agreement. "I like it. You are a very bad man, Muerto. Is that not so, Payaso?"

"Don't get him started, Kabong, or it will be ten in the morning by the time he stops talking about himself."

Nick pushed John on his way. "Go on. Get into position to fire from about a hundred feet down the corridor. Best cover your ears."

Nick placed two grenades by each doorway. He then went to the first doorway, pulled the pins and rolled the two grenades inside. Nick in precious seconds repeated the action two more times as the grenades exploded in the first room, shaking the entire corridor. By the time Nick ran towards John the third set blasted the weakened section apart, causing a massive cave in at the living quarters section. Nick tossed his last two grenades down the corridor into the rubble. The entire corridor gave way after the explosions, forcing the two men around the corner.

"Put on your mask, John. Do you know this place well enough for us to do a methodical search of the remaining compound? I will get Paul to send a special team in for handling the lab, but it will take time for him to do it through the FBI and HS. Lastly, I want to open their vehicle entrance, so Payaso can bring the GMC down inside. No prisoners. We'll take care of the guy on the hook for the movie ending. How did we do on video footage, Payaso?"

"Horrifyingly clear HD," Gus replied. "I'm timing you guys. Quit gabbing and get moving. I'll start down the access road now, so I'll be in position when the vehicle entrance is open."

"On our way, Payaso. Take your time, John, and let's be thorough. You lead. Blast anything or anyone in your path. I'm on your six."

With John leading, the two men spent the next forty minutes covering every square inch not impacted by the grenades. The weapons stockpile was locked. Nick fired on the locking mechanism until the door swung inward.

"Wait until you see what we're allowing to be stockpiled under our noses, Payaso." Nick and John walked amongst the weaponry in amazement. "This, my brothers, is insane. Hey... here's a safe. I love surprises like this. Let's recon the lab, and then go get the combination to the safe from our hooked helper."

"What if he doesn't know the combination?"

"Gee... I think it will really suck if he doesn't," Nick replied. "I'll have to make certain he's not lying, and that process will definitely hurt more than his feelings."

When they reached the lab, the door was ajar. "Uh oh," Nick whispered. "I think we left a live one at our backs. Shout at the door who you are, John. Then tell him 'we're under attack', and get him to come out."

John grinned and moved to the side of the open doorway. He shouted out in Arabic, "I am Ebi Zarin! We are under attack! Come! I must get you to safety!"

A clean shaven man wearing a white lab coat, and appearing to be in his middle thirties peeked out the door. John grabbed him by the hair when he saw the man clutched a briefcase, and a metal case in his arms. "Get on your knees!"

The man did as ordered. Nick took away the briefcase and metal carrier case from him. "This doesn't look good. Who are you?"

"I...I am Malik Handal."

"Have you seen this guy before, Kabong?"

"No. What is your duty here? We can see you operate in the lab."

"Research only," Handal said.

"Get up," Nick ordered. "Search him, and we'll let Malik show us around the lab. What's in the cases, Malik?"

John frisked Handal thoroughly after helping him to his feet. Handal remained silent.

"Come now, Malik," Nick spoke in Arabic. "This is not going to end well for you no matter what. If you cooperate, we won't have to persuade you."

"You cannot make me talk! I have rights!"

John grabbed Handal's ear, yanking him to his tip toes. "Listen closely. This man will make you beg to tell us everything you know. We will find out anyway. Come. We will take you into the lab, and make this easy for you. I do all the light work for El Muerto. When you are uncooperative, I will break one of your fingers. When I run out of fingers, I will move up your arms. Then El Muerto will take over."

Handal stared at Nick in horror. "I recognize the names now! You are El Muerto and El Kabong. I saw the videos of what you did to that kidnapper. It was unholy to do such a thing!"

"Yes," Nick agreed. "When I finish with your unholy evisceration, I will stuff pig guts inside of you, before sewing your belly shut again. We will then bury you for eternity, unclean and cursed by Allah."

"No!" Handal turned as much as his captured ear permitted toward John. "You would allow such a thing? You are not an infidel!"

John smiled. "I will help him stuff you."

Handal's body sagged, and John released his ear. "The briefcase contains my notebook computer and flash drives. The metal case contains the biological strains I have been working on."

"Good," Nick said. "Show us around your lab, and we will take you to where we are holding Yuri. Do you know the combination to the safe in the weapons storeroom?"

Handal shook his head no while leading Nick and John inside the lab. "I have never went inside the weapons room. Yuri is the only one who knows the combination to the safe there. He has brought me money when I needed to travel after going in there."

Thirty minutes later, Nick took Handal into the room where Yuri still hung from the hook they placed him on. John went to the vehicle entrance to allow Gus to enter with the GMC. Unlike John's silent endurance, Aman sobbed, screaming out weakly when he balanced from foot to foot. When he saw Nick enter with the now restrained Handal, he began to beg.

"Please... I will tell you anything you want to know! Take me off this hook! I will tell you all!"

Nick plastic tied Malik to a chair in the room at the ankles, hands behind the chair. Then duct taped him in place at his waist, shoulders, and calves while Aman continued to plead. He then walked over in front of Yuri with a smile.

"I'm glad you want to cooperate, Yuri. I was afraid I'd have to get tough with you. Let's start with the combination to the safe in the weapons room."

"Yes! I will tell you. Take me down!"

"Nope. That's backwards, Yuri. First, you give me the combination, then I go open the safe. Then I come back here and take you down. The longer you keep asking in this backwards manner, the longer it will be before you are off the hook as it were. Let me show you how it feels to be moved slightly just to get you on board."

Nick gripped the chain holding Yuri's wrists on the hook, and began yanking on them, causing the frantic screaming man to dance in agony. "Are you seeing this, Payaso? If only I had some white face paint. This would be a true Kabuki dance moment."

"I see it. I just puked in your Giants cap, but I won't seal it in plastic yet. We're heading towards you. I have my tablet on with your psychotic prisoner handling on screen, Muerto. Let the man tell you the combination! I swear... every cell in your body is rotten... every cell!"

Nick could hear John's appreciative chortling in the background. Nick stopped shaking the chain. "Fine! I'm sorry I upset your delicate nature, Payaso. I hope you brought the bag with you I told you to bring from the GMC."

"I have it. We'll be with you in a couple minutes. You're lucky the ventilation is still working in here."

"Luck had nothing to do with it," Nick lied. He bopped the sobbing Yuri on the forehead. "You should have had a V8, Yuri. Okay... calm down and tell me the combination."

Nick passed Gus and John on the way out with Malik's briefcase and metal containment case. "I'm opening the safe. Don't take whiney down until I see if he gave me the right combination.

By the way, get your uniforms on they're in the bag Gus has in his hand. The Unholy Trio strikes again! For now... El Muerto... away!"

Nick danced out of the door with Gus waving a fist at him. "You're damn lucky I don't have your Giants cap with me!"

Nick returned with his pack bulging. "Oh my. This has been a profitable assault. Get my buddy Yuri down while I become El Muerto. We'll film the ending to our mission, and get the hell out of here. I called Paul, and told him to give us a two hour window. He knows about the lab. I left Malik's gear inside the door of the lab. Yuri, my hanging man, tell me what all this buildup is for. What the hell are you guys training to attack?"

Yuri sobbed nonstop now, unable to endure any position on the chain. "We have not... received our orders for anything. Please... I'm telling you the truth! The safe opened, did it not? Let me down!"

"He is telling the truth. We know you will kill us. What happens now matters little. We are dead men," Malik said. "We won't be receiving orders for another month, because of delays in the East from strikes on our cells there."

"That fits." Nick went over and lifted Yuri off the hook. "I liked the contents of your safe, Yuri. Very nice."

John took charge of Yuri with rough enthusiasm.

"We could just skip the cartoon movie, Muerto."

"No, we could skip your birthday, Payaso. We can't skip the video. Duct tape Yuri next to Malik while I arrange the camera."

Ten minutes later, the Unholy Trio in full costume hovered around Malik and Yuri with camera recording. Both men had their mouths duct taped shut, but their eyes reflected the terror of their situation more effectively than any words. Nick as El Muerto with both mask and cape strode in front of the camera. Gus and John stood in the shadows behind their prisoners with arms folded over chests. Nick positioned a light so Gus's clown mask, and John's eerily highlighted El Kabong mask glowed in the darkened room.

"This is El Muerto! The Unholy Trio of El Muerto, the dangerous Payaso, and the deadly El Kabong struck early this morning to obliterate another small army of saboteurs, hell bent on the destruction of America! They worked right here in our own country, stockpiling weapons underground like jackals, experimenting with biological weapons, and training guerilla soldiers. The Unholy Trio killed them all, except for these two. El Kabong infiltrated this deadly cell, and was nearly tortured to death. He will deliver the end to these two saboteurs. Our hallowed government agencies will be directed to this site so all cleanup of hazardous materials can be done."

Nick stepped aside, gesturing at John. "Take out these last two in cruel and horrific form, El Kabong, so that our enemy knows we will not hesitate to match their brutality!"

John immediately slit the throats of Yuri and Malik, their arterial blood spraying in horrific fashion. The chairs they were duct taped to crashed to the floor and splintered under the violence of the men's death throes. Nick moved in front of the camera once again, pumping his fist.

"Death to the enemies of America! Beware the Unholy Trio! We are everywhere!"

Gus walked around to turn off the camera. "Well, Muerto, that was a ghastly movie, especially when you edit in the exploding burial of over twenty men in there, coupled with your find in the lab, and weapons room. Even you must be satiated after this adventure."

"Less talk and more packing, Payaso," Nick said while stuffing his costume into the equipment bag. "I should take some of the hardware in that damn weapons room, but I don't want anything traceable with us by error. That bio lab is a bad thing. If these assholes are building bio weapons stockpiles in these supposed privately innocent 'Muslim Communities', we are in trouble. This one was a secret underground seed of destruction. Think about these bozos building labs under Mosques, using them as shields as they did to kill our soldiers overseas."

"That is why this strike was so important," John added. He followed Nick and Gus into the corridor. "They believe they are untouchable. We at least put doubt into their minds, and our video will make their heads explode."

"Right you are, Kabong," Nick replied. "The government doesn't allow the kids we're sending overseas to die in some sand toilet to fight a war, so we'll have to give the enemy small glimpses of what will happen when we finally do decide to fight this like a war."

"If we ever do," Gus said. "Do something about your people, Kabong."

"I did. You were standing next to me during the video. It is embarrassing to admit this to two infidels, but my people are not peaceful religious followers of Allah. We have been third world, small minded monsters for centuries. We breed like rabbits, and refuse to assimilate into any culture other than murderous Sharia Law driven kingdoms of death. You infidels are doomed."

"He's right, Muerto."

Nick grinned. "I just thought of an idea how we can combat this plague Kabong speaks of. I'm starting my own backfire with Pacific Grove as the fire line."

"This is going to be good, Kabong." Gus threw his bag of equipment inside the GMC. "Spit it out, oh oracle of death."

"Dimah Kader has a cousin escaping the East Coast wing of the crazy Kader family. She asked me to help. I will introduce the cousin to our suave, sophisticated, and deadly El Kabong. They will fall in love, marry, and have so many children raised as likeminded Kabongs, the Islamists, who are dumber than a bag of rocks anyway, won't stand a chance. We will have Kabong Law instead of Sharia."

"Did you let Muerto run around without his gas mask on, Kabong?"

"I would hear more of this cousin, Payaso. I did not know you had a hidden skill as a matchmaker, Muerto."

Nick shut the rear hatch after throwing his pack and equipment bag in the back. "Muerto has many skills, Kabong. You ride shotgun next to the doubtful Payaso. He doubts the skill of El Muerto until he sees with his own eyes the skillful conclusion of yet another Muerto miracle."

"Great. He's launched into third person El Muerto again. Hand me the Giants cap out of the glove compartment, Kabong."

"I won't kill you, Payaso, but I will shoot your kneecap off," Nick warned.

John passed the Giants baseball cap over his shoulder to Nick, enjoying the interaction, some of his celebratory feelings due to still being alive. "You were not joking about the cousin, right Muerto?"

"Nope. We may have to cull a few of your in-laws out of the herd, but other than that, we should have you married off in less than six months. You don't want a long engagement, do you?"

"I trust your judgement in all things, El Muerto."

"El Muerto is definitely promoting you from minion to sidekick, Kabong. Payaso has disrespected the compassionate matchmaker, El Muerto, once too often. He is as of this moment reduced in rank to minion of El Muerto."

Gus made gagging noises as he steered onto the highway toward the Lodge. "Oh barf!"

"Don't be hatin', Payaso."

* * *

Nick woke at 10 am, grateful Rachel had shielded any sleep intervention by either Jean or Deke. Five hours sleep felt like heaven, especially with everything of a violent nature taken care of, and days before his book signings. He got out of bed, and right into the shower. Although he had taken one earlier in the morning, Nick thought he could still smell cordite and death. He had sealed his outer clothing in a garbage bag, as had Gus and John before splitting apart for the morning. John was to get checked into a suite and meet with his Unholy Trio companions, and Dan in the bar at 11 am. After a shave and shower, Nick felt as if he could write all day, and into the night, but he knew that would never happen. His best chance would be a 10 pm night, and then a 4 am date with Diego's 'Dark Interlude' adventure. Rachel stuck her head in the bathroom door.

"The gentleman and lady from the plane are here to see you. I banished them from the room three hours ago when they were set to invade. Shall I tell them to hit the road again?"

Nick walked to the door, and gripped his wife's hand. "Thanks for that, babe. I'll take the meeting with a bit of the Irish if that's okay with you."

"With as steamed as the guy is, I think that's a great idea. I'll make it for you."

Nick kissed her – a long, lingering, meeting of lips and souls. "You are the best."

"Don't you forget it, Muerto," Rachel replied, closing the door.

Moments later, Nick came out of the bedroom with his tennis shoes, jeans, and black t-shirt on. Robyn MacEachern and Clyde Bacall sat at the suite's kitchen table, drinking coffee. Rachel put his doctored coffee in front of him as he sat down, placing his iPhone in front of him. Deke ran over to jump on his lap for a hug. Jean followed Deke with a heartfelt hug.

"I'm glad you're back safe, Dad," Jean whispered. "You won't have to kill these two, will you?"

"Nope. Are you and your Mom taking Deke for a walk in the countryside?"

"Yeah, we figured to leave you some sorting out time. They really do have a great indoor waterpark. I want us all to go together this afternoon around one, okay?"

"It's a date, Dagger. Can you talk Momma into putting on a bathing suit?"

Jean giggled as Rachel gasped. "Yep. She has a special tent for swimming."

"We'd better walk Deke before I start smashing electronics gear," Rachel said, grabbing Jean by the back of the neck, causing the Daughter of Darkness to hunch her shoulders comically for Nick's appreciation. "We'll be back to break up the meeting soon."

"Okay, Hon." Nick sipped his Irish coffee with relish, the at least two shots Rachel had doctored it with shooting right down to his toes. After a second long sip, Nick put down the cup, and smiled at his guests. "How we doin' this morning, kids?"

Robyn smiled back. "You certainly took Clyde and I out of the picture, and considering what the team found there this morning, I'm glad you did. We are so screwed."

"That was our take on it too, Robyn," Nick replied. "We're allowing this infiltration to reach the point of suicide. From what I've seen on the East Coast, we're constantly playing a deadly game of catch up."

"What would you suggest, McCarty, exterminate all Muslims?"

"I have a Muslim working with me, infiltrating these nests, idiot. He knows how dangerous it is allowing 'No-Go' Muslim zones like the Europeans do, where anything can be stockpiled without fear of discovery."

"He's right, Clyde. This is war. We have to fight it with our hands tied behind our backs," MacEachern added. "The other side took heavy casualties. Boo hoo."

"Did you see that video he made? That was obscene! It makes us no better than they are."

"If you believe that, you're too stupid to be in this business, Clyde. We were much better. That was our side with the knife in the video. I'm not debating this with you. I thought you had promise. I'm beginning to think you're more of a liability than an asset. I hope you keep your mouth shut, Clyde, and do everything Paul tells you to without hesitation or comment. Otherwise, I don't like your chances of staying in government service."

Nick stood. He reached out and shook hands with MacEachern. "Pleasure meeting you, Robyn. Anytime we need a hand here in the Northwest, I'll give you a call. Thanks for the Lodge setting. It's beautiful."

She held out a card, and Nick took it. "That's my private number. You call, and I'll help in any way you need, on the books or off."

"I appreciate that."

"No problem. Thanks for freeing me from the book tour deal. It's not exactly my line of work. I feel the same way as you do about this ridiculous 'War on Terror' they claim we're fighting. If you need an extra hand in my neighborhood, don't hesitate to call. Bye Nick, bye Clyde." MacEachern walked to the door.

Bacall gave her a wave, but stayed silent.

"Bye Robyn," Nick said. "You and I have nothing further to say to one another, Clyde. If we need you, I'll call. Don't forget to keep your mouth shut about all of this. Let the story play out. With what they found in that lab, there will be plenty of cover for us all."

Bacall stood, pushing his chair back with his rage on a short leash. Nick grinned. "Don't say anything that I have to cut your Adam's apple out for, Clyde. Get out, and have yourself a good day, alive and well."

Bacall left without another word. When Nick heard the door slam shut, he slipped his stiletto inside his front jeans pocket again. He sat down, enjoying his still warm Irish coffee. Nick called Paul Gilbrech.

"I didn't expect to hear from you this early. I just had a short call from your protégé, Clyde though," Gilbrech joked with Nick.

"Good one. You may have been right about Clyde. I'm trying to keep him alive, but he's not helping. How's everything looking from your viewpoint in DC?"

"Fabulous for the Republic, but not so good for the 'Terrorists just need jobs' crowd. They were a bit shocked by the video you cartoons filmed. It went viral in an hour. YouTube knocked it off, but it was pirated with our help to hundreds of outlets worldwide. The Middle East is on fire with indignation and outrage. In America, they want to give the Unholy Trio a tickertape parade. People are sick to death of watching our people get butchered, and genocide done without a single response other than crocodile tears."

"It was a large body count, and you've seen the armory they had underground there. These suckers were training for a huge hit somewhere. They were delayed by our strikes on the East Coast. I was hoping you'd get some indication as to who or what they're planning to hit out here when the briefcase with Malik Handal's laptop and flash-drives arrive in DC. Although I'm certain Aman and Handal didn't know a specific target, they don't have the other puzzle pieces you do in DC."

"They're on the way by special courier. I believe you're right, and the strike will be in the West somewhere, but I'm hoping for something more specific once we plug in the data from Handal. It may be you goofball cartoons delayed another major attack with the hit this morning. Once they dissect the info from Handal's briefcase I'll let you know if a targeted area becomes clearer."

"Goofball cartoons? I think I resent that. Just wait until the 'Unholy Trio' flush out the 'Seattle Ripper'. Have my unfortunate US Marshal friends contacted you after their Sadun ordeal? They knew than to call me even on a secure line."

"Yep. They're fine, but now involved in a manhunt for Sadun, whom they already know is beyond anyone's reach here on earth. I put in a word at the DOJ their consultant will need them in Seattle soon to work on the Ripper case."

"Good. I need them to run interference for me with the 'Criminal Minds' FBI serial killer wing. Grace is caustic, but she has talent as a liaison with the federal and local people and their sometimes comical task forces."

"I'm a little concerned with you consulting officially on a case where El Muerto takes part on the physical end."

"I know, Paul. I'm getting the same static from Payaso. He's become the Unholy Trio's official wet blanket. El Muerto has reduced him in rank from sidekick to minion."

Nick grinned and swallowed the last of his Irish coffee while listening to Gilbrech's enjoyment of Payaso's punishment.

"Call me... if you need me... Muerto." Gilbrech disconnected.

Chapter Twelve

Ripper

Rachel and Jean with Deke came in the door, followed by hotel management. The man, a well-dressed executive type in his middle forties had a stern look on his face. Just under six feet tall, slightly overweight, but robust looking with short cropped hair, the man clasped his hands behind his back as he entered. Rachel crossed her eyes when Nick looked questioningly at her.

"Mr. Bingham would like to discuss Deke with you, Nick. I explained Robyn MacEachern handled all of our accommodations, and made sure to get an exception to Wolf Lodge's pet policy, but he wishes to speak with you."

"Mr. McCarty. I'm Fred Bingham, day manager for Great Wolf Lodge."

Nick stood and shook his hand. "Robyn did tell me about your no pet policy, and said she had made sure to obtain a waver for Deke."

"I did get that note. However, I was wondering if I could ask you not to parade Deke around in the public areas when avoidable, Sir. I have no idea how Ms. MacEachern maneuvered around our policy, but we will get complaints from other guests I'm sure who will be upset because they were not able to bring their pets."

"I understand completely, Mr. Bingham. Hang on just a moment." Nick went into the bedroom. He retrieved two thousand dollars out of his plunder from the early morning raid. He rejoined Bingham and handed the money to the shocked manager. "This is for you, Mr. Bingham. Smooth over Deke's stay, and there will be two grand more when we leave. Deke means the world to us, and we don't go anywhere without him. We won't take him anywhere he will attract attention."

"I...I don't know what to say."

"Say you'll help us with our Deke problem."

The manager pocketed the money and shook Nick's hand again. "What problem? Good day, Sir."

"Bye, Mr. Bingham."

After Nick closed the door, he fought off his outraged women, with Deke trying to rescue his drinking buddy with growls and nips. "Why am I being attacked? I see a problem. I solve a problem. Thanks, Deke... my only friend."

"I thought you'd waste him on the spot, Dad, not pay him off."

"He was rude to us," Rachel added, trying to free her heel from Deke's mouth as he dragged her back.

"Definitely a crime punishable by death. I see no reason why we can't keep Deke on the down low during our stay. I'll walk him twice a day. Mr. Bingham seems properly motivated to make our stay hassle free with Deke. I bet you two were wandering around that huge lobby, gawking like a couple of rubes from Parma with poor Deke trying to be inconspicuous, weren't you?"

Rachel turned away with arms folded. "Maybe."

"Okay then, Deke's walked now. I'll give him one of his beef bone treats, and he'll be good for the rest of the day. I'm meeting my confederates in Grizzly Rob's Bar for a business meeting, so I'll see you two in a little while."

"Don't you get tanked before the water park, Muerto!"

"I am not going to get tanked, Dear. A relaxing beverage after saving Western Civilization is not too much to ask. Add in saving my drinking buddy any further hassles with the local hotel management, and I'd say at least two relaxing beverages would be a small but pleasant reward."

"Go ahead, but remember we're heading for the water park at 1 pm."

"Bring your harpoon though, Dad. There might be a whale sighting in-"

Jean ran for it with Rachel in hot pursuit. Nick sighed contentedly, and brought Deke his beef bone treat. "Don't let this conflagration go on too long, Deke."

Nick grabbed his wallet while listening to the sounds of chaos in Jean's bedroom. Deke took his bone with him and ambled into Jean's room too. Nick took the opportunity to make good his escape. It was only a brief journey to Grizzly Rob's Bar, which he could see had only just opened. John, Dan, and Gus were already seated inside at a large table. Nick walked over to join them, trading the usual greetings. Nick sat down, seeing beers and shots in front of Gus and John, but iced tea for Dan. The waitress came over right away.

"I'd like a Long Island Iced Tea," Nick ordered.

"Sure. Be right back."

"Going heavy on the celebration, huh Nick?"

"It was one of those after assault stressful mornings. I had to handle numbskulls like Clyde, who will be lucky to live out the year, and then hotel management because it is official lodge policy that pets aren't allowed. Robyn fixed it for our reservations, but a manager didn't like the way my ladies were flaunting the Dekester around in the lobby."

Gus covered his face as the waitress left off the Long Island Iced Tea for Nick. He peeked out at the amused Nick. "Please tell me we don't have a body to dispose of, Muerto."

"I'm hurt you would even think that, Payaso. I bet that unkind thought never even passed through the minds of Kabong and Geezer, right guys?"

Silence. Nick took a gulp of his drink. "No one died."

"What happened then," Dan asked. "Is he in a hospital somewhere with his memory wiped?"

"Oh… very funny, OG. I worked the logical and common sense solution to the problem. I paid him off. Man, we hit the jackpot this morning, guys. Toast."

Dan held back while the others toasted. "Don't you have to give over anything taken in a raid to the government?"

"You bet I do," Nick said, lowering his voice. "As soon as it's the government that infiltrates a terrorist underground training center filled with soldiers, weapons and biological plagues, I'll be the first to drop off the booty on their doorstep. Since it was only the Unholy Trio, I don't see the government connection for the payoff."

"Agreed," Gus said.

"I was hung on a hook for a couple hours, left to fend for myself," John added. "I get an extra cut for my new lady love, right Muerto?"

"Excellent points, Kabong," Nick replied. "You shall indeed. As matchmaker supreme, Muerto must provide an ample dowry for his sidekick Kabong."

"Matchmaker, dowry, lady loves? Boy, I missed out on a lot not being bait this time."

"We're saving you for the 'Ripper' operation. Thanks to Kabong's quick infiltration, we had to move fast, especially since he screwed up and got put on a hook like a big guppy."

John, who had been taking a gulp of beer when Nick made the guppy remark, nearly shot it back out through his nose. Gus pounded on his partner's back while John coughed his way into control. "Not... funny!"

"That did sound serious about a matchmaking. What the heck did I miss there," Dan asked. "Did you meet someone while infiltrating the training center, John?"

John shook his head no. "Muerto is trying to choke me out, but also introduce me to Dimah Kader's cousin, who is escaping from her murderous family back East. Kabong will be the hero who makes her safe, and later weds her so as to have a huge family of loyal American Kabongs."

"Have you seen your soon to be bride, Kabong?"

"No one has yet, but I am certain she is most beautiful."

"I'm not very trusting of Muerto, but I hope it works out for you, John," Dan said.

"What is this about not being very trusting of Muerto? El Muerto is completely trustworthy, Geezer. How dare you call into question El Muerto's ulterior motives?"

"Now you've done it, OG," Gus said. "You've launched him into third person El Muerto. Snap him out of it or we'll have third person El Muerto for the rest of the day."

"I have been watching the news since early this morning," Dan said. "They only played small bits of the video you characters put together. That was impressive. It caught the media assholes by surprise. They tried to frame it as a brutal murderous rampage by insane men no better than the terrorists. The people laughed in their faces, saying stuff like it was a great start, and they can't wait for the next El Muerto attack. How did your boss like it?"

"He loved it. He knows there will always be fallout over an action like that, but he's in for the long haul. I trust him with my life. Paul will back any play we make to get the 'Ripper' too. I'm sorry we didn't get to Seattle before he got the fourteen year old runaway, but we didn't have a choice. This is how I think we can use OG. We're going to get our own harem of prostitutes, and OG is going to be their pimp."

"Oh...my...God... you are nuts, Nick," Dan replied. "Who in hell would ever buy me as a pimp?"

"Damn, Nick," Gus said. "That's not bad. We'll have to recruit some tough ladies to pull this off though. You'll be great as a pimp, Dan. We'll dress you to the nines. You'll have three or four very high class ladies of the night, and we'll back your play. I've read the 'Ripper' has cleared the streets of prostitutes, just as you told us you joked with the Marshals about, Nick. The 'Ripper' will be ripe for finding a new victim. He won't be getting anymore runaways. The police are doing roundups of all indigent girls on the streets that have nowhere to go, and no means of support. It's too bad they don't do it everywhere, and it's a shame it takes a murdering monster to fix aspects of social problems no one wants to deal with."

"I agree with you on that," Dan said. "How tough would it be for the cops to have the security people at the bus and train stations collect these kids that scrape together enough to get a ticket into town. They already know the kids will eventually commit crimes to survive, end up junkies, or dead. Pimps protect their meal tickets, so how would I fit in? I'd scare off the Ripper."

"We have studied the victims," John said. "After his first attacks, it forced the prostitutes who were plying their trade on their own to seek out a pimp. The Ripper stepped up his game. Although they don't get the same treatment either by the Ripper or the news media, three of the pimps had their throats slashed. No one cares about a pimp, and because the pimps weren't eviscerated like the women, the cops can't say for sure it's the Ripper doing it.

Nick predicted the less than compassionate populace's reaction. Regular folks read about prostitutes and pimps getting killed, and they shrug their shoulders. The fourteen year old runaway changed that perspective, hence the police round up of indigent girls."

"I don't want to make this seem like a crusade," Nick added. "I realize this guy is taking not so innocent lives. I've seen and met pimps and prostitutes in our big cities, and in many places around the world. The prostitutes don't have hearts of gold, and their pimps aren't knights in shining armor protecting them. We're going after the Ripper because I'm slightly nuts, and I liked the idea of going after him as El Muerto. That said, we did El Muerto and the Unholy Trio here on a large scale. I may be satisfied with taking on the Ripper in a different guise."

Gus chuckled. "Believe me, Nick. We didn't think you were going after him out of the goodness of your heart. You made that clear when you told us about what you said to the Marshals. Admit it. You love screwing around with the task forces with their text books and profiles like a... wait a minute! Oh no... you are not doing the 'Mentalist' in the Ripper case. If you try that all seeing oracle crap, you'll get everyone but the Unholy Trio in trouble."

"You mean like he did in Charleston? I thought that was funny when you told me about his doing the Mentalist in the middle of a police station," John said.

"Yeah, but this is an FBI task force," Gus replied. "Muerto already pissed off the FBI in our hometown."

"I did not. I called both those FBI/HS guys, and let them know the Rashidis and the fake FBI dupes I killed in front of my house were indeed connected, but it was an ongoing investigation taken over by DC authorities. I'll have you know Agents Rogers and Agnew were very appreciative. When I arrive in league with my US Marshal pals, this FBI task force leader, Kaitlin Anderson, will be pissed as hell. Grace hates her, so I'll be able to play those two off against each other like in Charleston with Grace and the police lieutenant. When she tries to screw up our plan, I'll get a recommendation from Rogers and Agnew."

"I have to hand it to you, Nick," Dan said. "That is the most convoluted caper I've ever heard of. Carol and I used to watch that 'Mentalist' show until it ended. You've really decided to bring in this Ripper guy alive?"

"I would have to if my scenario works out the way I plan. That's the only downside, but it shelves El Muerto while we're doing the book signings in the same city, and still appeases my refined, compassionate, criminologist side."

Nick's three companions began making gagging noises all at the same time.

* * *

Rachel examined the smiling Nick closely. "I don't know, Jean. He's awfully good at hiding whether he's tanked or not. I definitely smell booze though."

"I didn't go to Grizzly Rob's for orange juice, Dear. We accomplished quite a bit at our business meeting too. I revealed my plan to catch the 'Seattle Ripper'."

"He sounds sober to me, Mom. Get on your bathing suit, Dad. I have to say, Mom looks pretty cute in her Princess Bump suit."

Rachel jetted her right hand with thumb and forefinger in a pinched position only a centimeter apart in front of Jean's face. "You're this close to not reaching double digit age!"

"I want you two in neutral corners until I get my suit on. You come with me Princess Bump."

"No," Jean said, pushing Nick toward the bedroom. "If you two go in there alone, I'll never get to the water park."

"Brat!"

"Momster!"

Nick was out with bathing suit, sandals, and t-shirt in only a few minutes. He found Rachel and Jean having a staring contest with Deke refereeing. "Who's winning, Deke?"

"It's a tie so far, but I have her on the ropes," Jean said.

Rachel then crossed her eyes, and vanquished the Daughter of Darkness in a split second of devastating eyeball comedy.

"No fair!"

"Oh waaaahhhh…" Rachel intoned, with fists up in victory. "Let that be a lesson to you young muffin."

"Let's go, I have the beach bag. Watch the room, Deke. I'll walk you when we get back if I survive the clash of the titans at the water park. Luckily, it's right by Grizzly Rob's."

* * *

"This is nice with the cabana, Nick," Rachel said. "Jean went right for the slides. I'll bet she's on that for a while. Are you going in? You're not really thinking of drinking all day, are you?"

I was. "Of course not. Take off the robe, and let me see how you look in the new Princess Bump suit."

"Don't start picking up every cast off dig the Daughter of Darkness slams me with." Rachel took off her robe, turning coyly to the side while Nick watched with interest.

"Very nice. I like you in black with the strapped top, and low cut cleavage look."

288

"Do you think the top covers Quinn attractively?"

Nick came over to embrace her from the back. "It does indeed. The creator of the 'Princess Bump' term will be here shortly with Tina. He's a bad influence on me though. Payaso claims he's going to sit here and drink beer all day... the cad!"

Rachel slapped Nick's wandering hand. "Stop that! Yeah, I bet that was his idea. It sounds more like something that cad Muerto would do. Is John and Dan joining us too?"

"It's possible. I think John said something about lying around in his room today, drinking and snoozing after his ordeal. Dan said something about communing with nature on his own. Here's that cad, Payaso already. Uh oh. Look what he's brought with him. He didn't even ask or get a waitress. He raided Grizzly Rob's on his own... the cad!"

Gus had a tray with beers, shots, two wines, and a soda.

Rachel sighed. "Fine. I'll sip a wine, but I am going in the water today, and you're coming with me, Muerto."

"Of course, my love. Hi partner. Hello Cousin Itt."

"Gomez... Princess Bump."

"Not you too, Tina."

"You look great, girlfriend. Sit back down with me, sip your wine, and we'll talk about the horrendous plot against America on every news program, foiled by a bunch of masked cartoons."

"Uh oh. I think Cousin Itt may have had a wine or two before arriving here at the cabana," Nick observed. "It sure has seemed like that kind of a day though. Thanks for the refills, partner."

"I figured you'd be ready for another round." Gus sat down opposite Nick at the cabana table, while Tina and Rachel sat on the lounge chairs. "I'm sorry I tagged you with the Princess Bump label, Rach."

"Don't worry about it, Gus. I slip myself and use it. Quinn will be joining us pretty soon, and then I'll be hiking down to the beach every day, throwing down shooters, and carousing like the rest of you pirates."

"No. You'll put a guilt trip on yourself, and be back working at the Café with Quinn riding your back," Nick said. "What you should be doing is hiking to the beach and throwing down shooters with us carousing pirates."

"Gomez has a point," Tina said. "I saw it in your eyes at the mention of the Café. You're already contemplating a return to waitressing."

"Joe needs me, unlike Muerto. He appreciates my steadfast code of honor and hard work. I am not taken for granted at the Monte Café as is the case at the Muerto homestead."

"Oh, you poor thing!" Nick ran around to massage Rachel's shoulders and neck, slipping his hands accidentally on purpose under her top until Rachel was squealing, and slapping his hands to the enjoyment of their companions.

Nick took off his t-shirt. "I'm going in with Dagger, and see how she's doing. I'll come back to get you in a little bit, Princess."

"Damn, girl," Tina said, watching Nick walk around hunting for Jean. "Gomez is looking good. He's getting checked out by all the female lurkers."

"He works out like a gladiator every day," Rachel said, smiling as Nick found Jean, and the two headed for the top of the slide together.

"I've worked out with him," Gus said. "Rachel's right. He works the heavy bag, weights, and cardio stuff until you think he'd drop from sheer boredom. Then he does the punching bag with forearm and elbow shots mixed with punches so fast you can't follow what he's doing. I can't do that crap more than a couple times a week with him. I'd burn out like an old lightbulb. And then of course he walks Deke and Jean all over creation. I doubt those calories from the Irish coffees even touch him."

"You look good, baby," Tina said, reaching from her lounger to pat Gus's leg. "Gomez looks like he's cut. His damn six pack looks like one of those Batman costume tops. Spill it, Rach. He's doing steroids isn't he? Inquiring minds want to know. I thought his head looked bigger lately. It's swelling like a ripe melon. Is his dick shrinking like the steroid warnings say? Does he stay cranky all day, and want to smack you around. C'mon… we're your friends. We'll help. You don't have to go through this alone."

By the time Tina finished with her 'Steroid Nick' routine, complete with gesturing hands, Gus and Rachel were enjoying the show loudly. It took more than a few moments before Rachel could respond in coherent form.

"He…he's not on anything. I'll tell you something else. He's so damn calm, it's freaky. I don't have to tell Gus that. I watched the fake FBI guys meet their maker on our HD porch cam. They never had a chance. They reached first, and none of them cleared a holster. We have a wide angle cam on the front sidewalk too. Nick's expression never changed. I couldn't tell for sure, but I think he smiled."

"There's a reason a guy like Paul Gilbrech backs someone like Nick all the way," Gus added, "and it has nothing to do with any kind of employee/employer agreement. Paul knows what happened to Frank Richert. Paul and Nick have an understanding. Nick says he trusts him with his life, and other than we minions of Muerto, there aren't any people listed in that small group."

291

"Was that his plan to do everything under the radar this morning, Gus?"

"Nick didn't hear from John, and that was it. He hit the place. As usual, he was right as rain. They had John chained on a hook getting ready to toast him. Instead they got Muerto. He has some funny plans for John. Did he tell you he's going to play matchmaker for John with Dimah Kader's cousin who will be fleeing the East Coast soon?"

"No!" Rachel sat straight in the lounger, taking a gulp of wine. "He never said anything about it.

"We've been laughing and insulting him about his matchmaking abilities ever since he mentioned it. John loves the idea, but he's a Muerto groupie anyhow."

"My Muerto, matchmaker supreme." Rachel took a deep breath. "That's just... disturbing. I'm going to get Muerto to swim with me. Don't let anyone touch my wine. That's the only one I get for the day."

"We'll guard it, girlfriend. Hey... remember that old movie 'Hello Dolly' about a matchmaker?"

"Sure Tina," Rachel answered on her way out, launching into a swaying dance step singing, "well, hello Muerto, you're lookin' swell, Muerto."

Rachel glanced around to see both Gus and Tina enjoying her rendition of 'Hello Dolly. "Is that the one?"

"Oh yeah... that's the one," Tina agreed.

Rachel found her 'Dolly' and the Daughter of Darkness in a comical discussion, feeding each other funny lines. "What's so funny?"

The two quieted quickly, which provoked furrowed eyebrows, and thin lipped angst in Rachel. "I feel my Princess Bump rising to devastate her surroundings. If you don't want that, I better get an answer as to why I'm once again the object of derision."

"You're not," Nick said. "Jean's raking me over the coals for leading women on around us. She seems to think as she does while blackmailing me during our walks to school that I'm flirting. I was reminding her that wallflowers do not grow up to be flirts. We delicate flowers grow to be circumspect and conservative. Jean was of course making gagging noises while I tried to explain it wasn't possible for me to flirt."

"Not everything is about you, Princess Bump," Jean added, immediately hiding behind Nick before Rachel could react. "No hitting. You asked."

"Who is Muerto flirting with?" When Rachel looked around, she saw more than a couple of women trying to glance Nick's way without being noticed. "Never mind. I see a few likely candidates. We'll have to put him in a burka."

Jean giggled.

"Let me know how that works out for you, Princess. Jean's hungry. I was going to let her take some money over to the snack restaurant over there called 'Buckets Incredible Craveables'. She wants a cheeseburger."

Rachel saw the restaurant was in plain sight, and she knew Jean was no naïve little girl. "Looks okay to me. Go ahead and get some money from Muerto's stash in the bag. Be polite and ask Gus and Tina if they want anything."

"I will, Mom. Do you want anything?"

"No, I ate too much at our brunch in the room."

"Yeah you did." Jean hurried off toward the cabana.

"One of these days… one of these days," Rachel muttered. "I'm ready for a swim. I'm uncomfortable with how good you look in that black bathing suit, Muerto. Can't you stick your belly out or something?"

"We'll be in the water, but I can go put on a t-shirt to soothe your sensibilities."

"No, then I wouldn't be able to enjoy the view." Rachel ran a hand over Nick's chest down to his trunks.

"You need to make up your mind, Princess. Besides, I think you look wonderful in your bathing suit, and I'm already picturing removing you from it."

"In olden days, when a woman got pregnant, she didn't have sex again until after she had the baby."

"That's a lie. Now, let's go swimming before you decide pregnant women weren't allowed to swim either." Nick took her arm, but their path was blocked by a big guy with dark brown beard, wild looking hair, and Hawaiian print bathing trunks. "Oh, sorry Sir, I should have been looking where I was going."

When Nick tried to guide Rachel around the guy, he stepped in their way once more.

Rachel glared at the man. "Hey, Kong, we're trying to get over to the pool."

"Your boy here's been checking out my wife for the last twenty minutes." The man's hands clenched into fists at his side. "I want to know why."

"It's your imagination, Sir," Nick said with a smile. "I don't even know who your wife is. The only woman I've ever loved in my life is standing next to me, nine months pregnant with my son.

Before she came over to join me by the pool, I was going on the pool slides with my daughter."

Nick's matter of fact accounting threw the man off. He kept glancing to the side where a blonde woman in a red bikini stood with arms folded over chest, and an angry look on her face. When she saw the man Rachel tagged as Kong looking at her with confusion, she stormed over to his side.

"He wasn't looking at you, Hon," the big man told his wife. "This is his wife, and she's nine months pregnant."

The blonde pointed at Nick. "He was staring at me, and making lewd gestures, while you were in the room."

Jean arrived gripping Nick's arm. "What's wrong, Dad."

Nice timing, Dagger. "The lady here claims I was staring and making gestures at her the last twenty minutes. Would you tell her husband what we were actually doing the last twenty minutes?"

Jean smiled up at Kong. "My Dad and I were riding the slides until Mom came over to swim with him."

Nick could tell Jean's arrival had completely disarmed the guy. He moved behind his wife, whispering to her. Nick had a suspicion this wasn't the first time the wife had put him in this situation. For her part, the wife shifted her glare to Jean, who put the lie to her jealousy gambit for attention. The woman spun away from Kong and headed for one of the other cabanas.

"Sorry about that," the man mumbled before following after his wife.

"Gus said to tell you he can't take you anywhere. Now that I've saved your life, can I go finish my cheeseburger?"

"Sure, and thanks for the save." Nick shoulder hugged Jean. "I think maybe your Uncle Gus is right. That was very smart sending you when he did."

"I was thinking about saying something like, 'wow Dad, this is the lady you've been staring and waving at', but I resisted." Having said that, Jean skipped off toward the cabana.

"Well, it's nice to see she recognizes a target rich environment," Rachel said.

"As of today, I'm taping everything to play back when she's sixteen."

Rachel smirked, yanking Nick toward the pool. "It won't matter. By then my head will have exploded. What were you going to do with Kong?"

"Nothing. He wasn't going to attack me. We may have had to call for security if he kept blocking our way to the pool. Kong was the real victim. He's married to that shrew who will eventually get him maimed or killed if he doesn't wise up."

"That was really sweet what you said about loving me."

"My life was in danger."

Rachel hugged his arm. "A life was in danger, but it wasn't yours. That was so sweet."

"If you knew how much I really loved you, I'd get taken advantage of, so I try to keep it to myself. It's too late now though. I may as well admit it. You're the best thing that ever happened to me. If something happened to you, and the kids were grown, I'd probably be looking for a way to cash out like Dan."

"I'd haunt you. I'd be in your thoughts so much, you wouldn't be able to think of cashing out. Besides, Jean will have

296

you committed to a padded room if she sees even a sign you're getting mushy in the head."

"Mushy in the head? Really. Just for that, I'll go out looking for a young Mom to ravish the moment something happens to you," Nick said.

"In that case, I'll let you rot on the vine in your own rancid thoughts until you can't think of anything else except death."

Nick began looking around. "Where is that blonde in the bikini Kong's married to?"

* * *

Nick heard the slight knock on the door at 7 am sharp. He looked longingly at the laptop screen where Diego parlayed with Fatima, the Black Widow type anti-heroine. Grinning as he went to the door, Nick plotted the final surrender of Fatima's attraction to the enigmatic Diego. She knew they existed in opposite realities, her mission to gain his complete trust, and betray him. Each time Fatima thought to have gained Diego's complete trust, he somehow thwarted her efforts at the last moment. She... the light knock sounded again, as Nick realized he had been in suspended animation on the way to the door. *Damn, Fatima, I don't know about Diego, but you sure have me going.* Nick opened the door to his comrades in arms, with Deke next to him.

"Yesterday and this morning have been wonderful, guys. I'm thinking of abandoning the 'Ripper', kicking back here at the Lodge, doing a little home schooling with Jean, hitting the water park, running Deke around in the woods, sipping a-"

"The Ripper sliced apart another prostitute early this morning," Dan interrupted.

"Shit!" Nick walked toward the kitchen with Deke, leaving Gus to close the door.

Nick poured coffee for his friends, having already set out sugar, and creamer. "How old?"

"Middle twenties, rap sheet a mile long, been in trouble since the day she was born, and still didn't deserve to die like that," Gus said. "It's not our fault. We can only move on this so fast. It's just as you said yesterday when we returned. There's a firestorm out there with government teams, cops, hazardous material/biological weapons specialists, and media vultures. The vultures are looking for any way possible to make the extermination of the terrorist enclave a travesty against humanity. The Wolf Lodge is a perfect place to lie low with wives, kids, and the Deke. If we can keep you from getting into throw-downs with the local civilian guests, we'll be fine here until things cool down."

"Payaso is right, Muerto," John added. "Even with Mr. Gilbrech's background help, there will be government people looking for any sign of the Unholy Trio. I'm sure he would appreciate it if we stayed out of the limelight for the time being. I wish I could have seen the faceoff at the water park. I always miss the good stuff."

"You didn't miss anything, John. This guy's wife was bored, and decided to stir her husband into a fist fight in the middle of a kid's water park. Luckily, Payaso ended the threat by sending Dagger over to quell the possible altercation. Like I told Rachel, I would have called security. We were already getting eyed by a couple of them for sure. I'll be watching out for that goofy woman from now until we leave. I think Kong understood what she was doing though."

"Kong?"

Nick smiled. "Yeah, Dan. Rachel called him Kong when he blocked our way to the pool. Do you guys want a shot?"

"Wait a minute. Was Rachel in danger? Did the great Muerto allow his wife and unborn Quinn to face a deadly mugger in public? It's a lucky thing the Daughter of Darkness tag-teamed with the Momster to scare away this scoundrel."

"Not funny, Dan." Nick frowned as everyone else but him, and possibly Deke, found Dan's pronouncements funny. "You guys are mean. Muerto acts with restraint, and this is the reward he gets."

Nick stood and made his coffee Irish. He brought the bottle back to the table, where John and Gus also poured in a taste of whiskey. "Before I heard about the unfortunate woman's demise, and then was held up to ridicule, I was in the midst of telling you guys how great this place is. I got up at 4:30, and took Deke out for a great run around the woods before dawn. He loves this place. Then, I came back here, and wrote until you ingrates arrived with bad news and bad attitude."

"We gathered intel while the great Muerto wrote pulp fiction scenes. Did you get a chance to find candidates for Dan's pimping project?"

Nick entered into his iPad, and handed it over to Gus. "I did indeed. There's our three crews to recruit from. They all work from the Dark Web. Key people in the city such as hotel managers, taxi drivers, etc. give out a card with phone number or Dark Web address. The interested party can peruse the different girls on the Dark Web site, and arrange a date. The pimps handle commerce right on the web without sending the girls out on the streets. This 'Ripper' has hacked the Dark Web, which is no easy task. His victims so far have all been taken in route to their meeting with a 'John'... I mean customer, including the pimps he killed. Here's the kicker – the FBI task force isn't looking at the Dark Web at all. They're focusing on profiles, and street prostitution which the Ripper has nearly ended."

"You seem to know a lot about this Dark Web, Nick. How the heck did you get the idea about looking there?"

"Remember when you and Carol used to see me down at Otter's Point with my satellite laptop, and I told you I was writing."

"Sure. We used to bring you coffee when we knew you were down there."

"Most of those beach visits were journeys into the Dark Web, where I conducted my freelance assassin business. The rogue NSA outfit Frank Richert ran kept all of our sanctions done on the Dark Web. Any entity interested in a sanction the NSA felt would be in our interests were dealt a connection on the Dark Web where they found me. That's how I received all sanctions not given out by Frank directly, and where I made contact with Hayden Tanus and his import/export business, eventually leading me to Rachel, Jean, and Deke."

Gus, John, and Dan traded surprised looks before Gus spoke. "Damn... there's always something related to you we find out in small doses. I've heard a little about the Dark Web, but never thought of it as a conduit for assassins."

"Let's concentrate on the prostitute business. I looked through all the cases. Every one of them was from a referral to the Dark Web. I found pictures of all the victims that haven't been taken down yet by the pimps running the show. The fourteen year old runaway was taken off Craig's List. She was opening her own business off her cell-phone. There was no mention of the Craig's List ad she took out, which the FBI would have had to actually pursue to find. They started on the wrong end – from the scene of the crime. I cut them some slack for the runaway though, because she tried to go right into business."

"Fourteen," Dan said, shaking his head. "She gets a bus ticket to Seattle, launches herself on some Internet predator site as a prostitute, and gets hacked to pieces. I don't want to think about her last moments, knowing her short life ended with a bus ticket and an Internet ad."

"It sounds like all you would need do is introduce yourself to the FBI task force, school them on the Dark Web, and let them have the Ripper," John said.

"True, John, but they would never run an operation like we're going to. If they listened to me which is doubtful, they would form an offshoot from the regular task force to study the Dark Web, and a myriad number of incidentals unrelated to the case. Although useless, the minutia they found I'm sure would be vital to their task force information gathering bullshit. In the meantime, the Ripper stays on the down low, carefully enticing targets of opportunity where he can get them."

"If for no other reason than to erase the thought of that fourteen year old girl's last moments I'm in. We should get this guy if we can. I assume you have more of a plan formulated for me and my pimp Geezer assignment."

"That's where this will be a bit tricky. I'm letting John and Gus ferret out three or four really high end girls, but with the toughness to take the money I'll be paying them, and risk their lives to get the Ripper. I plan on them being protected every step of the way, but they won't know to trust me, so they'll have to believe they're tough enough to handle a confrontation with the Ripper. We have a lot of money from the Isis score, so we don't have to touch our own funds or Paul's. We'll make the girls we pick an offer I doubt they'll refuse."

"What's the specifics for your confrontation and trap," Gus asked. "I see where you're going with the contacts and such, but once the Ripper is on the hook, he'll be hard to spot and handle."

"We need to get this set into motion today. Luckily, it's only an hour and a half's trip from here to Seattle. That's what makes the Wolf Lodge perfect as our base of operations. The book signings in Olympia are way closer than Seattle. We won't have to stay in either city. As to the physical part of the operation, I have a pattern we'll follow every time out. Once an interested party contacts our Dark Web ad, only one of our girls will go out at a time, and we will insist on at least a two hour window. I'll get into position with my silenced .50 caliber Barrett with a view of every step from the vehicle to the meeting place. Dan will accompany the girl with Gus driving, and John in the shadows, all well in advance of the meeting. I'll call Grace and see if she and Timmy are in Seattle yet. I've been putting that call off because she's still a bit raw I'm thinking from my Sadun snatch."

"If you reach her this morning, are we going there today?"

"There's no reason for all of us to go, Dan. I'd like you three to narrow down some prostitute candidates. I'll contact any of them that seem promising while I'm in Seattle. Besides, I can't have you guys with me anyway in case I have to meet with this Kaitlin Anderson."

"How much trouble can Anderson make? Hell, you've got a great track record with the DOJ."

"Aw… you're so cute, Gus. Plenty of trouble. If not for Grace, my last collaboration with law enforcement out of state would have been futile. They don't listen. They don't reason, and they don't abandon any guideline in their goofy manual, even when it doesn't work. I swear. I don't know if they get their guidelines from TV or TV gets them from the FBI. Another plus to not staying in Seattle is I don't want the Ripper spotting me with the Feds, and then seeing Rachel and Jean."

"Hey," John exclaimed, seeing Nick get another Irish coffee. "Are you driving to Seattle, Mr. Hemingway?"

"Nope. I'm taking a limo for the day, including any prostitute visits I have to make. I'll have a driver who knows to keep their mouth shut and drive. I'll write Diego scenes all the way to Seattle and back again."

"You don't mean Clyde, do you, Muerto?"

302

"Why yes, Payaso, that's exactly who I mean. Clyde and I are just like brothers."

"He hates your guts."

"Okay then… step brothers."

Chapter Thirteen

Seattle Safe Once More

In front of Seattle's West Precinct building, Nick exited the black Lincoln Towncar dressed in a dark gray tailored suit, giving Bacall a wave. "I'll call you when I need a ride to our next destination, Clyde. You can get something to eat or hang around here. I don't know yet how long I'll be."

"I'll get something to eat." The moment Nick closed the door, Bacall sped off.

Kids today... ungrateful weasels. Nick spotted Tim and Grace walking toward him. Tim smiled, but Grace gave Nick the death stare. "Hello, my fellow Marshals. How have you been? Anything frightful happen in your negotiations with the Great Kate?"

Grace relaxed as Nick mentioned someone she despised more than Nick. "Great Kate? Heh...heh, good one. We just left a meeting with her. She bitched when we were here trying to help her before, and she's bitching because we came back. Great Kate can't catch the Ripper, but without someone else around to blame, she's stuck taking calls from the DOJ and media for nonexistent progress reports. Great Kate hates your plan, but she's been told in no uncertain terms you'll be running the show with the prostitutes entrapping the Ripper. The Attorney General himself told her on a conference call she is to tell no one about the operation. He warned her if he hears one thing in the media or from another source about anything to do with the operation, he's going to have her signing visitors in at the Washington Monument."

"You can only imagine how much Grace loved that conference call," Tim added.

"Watching Great Kate's head nearly explode made me get that lovin' feeling back for you, my little Muerto," Grace said.

"We're uneasy with this deviation from your normal operation plan of killing everything that moves in and around the target. Tim and I munched popcorn in front of the TV news seeing the Unholy Trio's actions in Centralia. That YouTube video was horrific, but I'll bet effective. What's with the new bring them back alive deal? We figured you'd wave your magic wand, find the Ripper, and put his head on a pike at City Hall with an accompanying El Muerto video."

"Even Muerto must cool his trail a bit. I'm afraid Mr. Ripper will not get through this unscathed, but I'll deliver him. I'll run the show away from the task force. All I need from you two is some interference, and possibly facilitate something I get into the middle of on the street."

"That works for us," Tim replied. "We like your plan. I pray to God you can keep your bait alive and well or the Great Kate will throw us all under the bus so fast the driver will think we were speed bumps."

"Let's go meet the Great Kate, and get this initial crap storm out of the way. My buddy Paul put in a word with the FBI Director. I have him on speed dial. I'm sure the pep talk from the big boss set Great Kate on a helpful path, but in case she forgets her place, I have someone else closer to her paycheck to talk with."

"Well c'mon then, Muerto," Grace said. "I'm hoping she shoots her mouth off so I can listen to the resulting call to the FBI Director."

"That's fine, but remember to not lose your head and start spouting the Muerto tag. You did good with that Lieutenant Moragado in Charleston. Let's try to get Great Kate on board with this even though she can't stop it anyway. She might be vindictive enough get fired over leaking our operation just to screw us over at any cost. I don't have to tell you that would go badly for her. The good guys and gals under Muerto's protection do not suffer casualties because of ego maniacs in authority."

Grace glanced over at Nick. "Understood."

* * *

Agent in charge Kaitlin Anderson listened to the introduction from Marshal Stanwick with arms folded over chest in classic defensive body language. She ignored Nick's outstretched hand. "So you're the savior novelist they flew in to dump on me with, huh McCarty?"

There goes the kill them with kindness gambit. "That's US Marshal McCarty, Agent Anderson. One more word out of you other than professional help offered on the case, and I have a direct line to the FBI Director. I have been told he will deal with you personally if you get in the way of my operation."

Anderson turned toward Grace, who bit her tongue to keep from smiling.

"US Marshal McCarty also has credentials from FBI, and the CIA, Kate. He has extensive experience in combat situations. He has also consulted on numerous cases where his help led to the solution of terrorist and criminal threats, including the terrorist mole in the Department of Justice. Nick has the juice to put you on a street corner directing traffic. Please don't force him to use it. Marshal Reinhold and I will assist him in this. We will not hamper anything your task force is in the process of doing. You will not discuss this with anyone. We needed to let you in on the details, so your task force doesn't inadvertently sabotage Marshal McCarty's operation. Is that clear enough?"

A much subdued Anderson studiously kept from looking at Nick. "Yes, I understand. What do you need?"

"Just an office where we can operate from," Grace answered.

"Follow me," Anderson said. "You can have my office. I'll work out of the task force area. May I have a word with you in private after I get Marshals Reinhold and McCarty settled, Grace?"

"Sure."

* * *

"Who the hell is this guy, Grace?" Anderson stood in an interrogation room with Grace. "When I heard he was coming, I tried accessing his records. My computer access was red flagged immediately with a warning. I have Top Secret clearance."

"Not at Nick's level you don't. I can't share anything with you about Nick other than he is a special troubleshooter the Department of Justice, FBI, and CIA call in under certain circumstances. He has credentials with all of them, but works as a special consultant so as not to be handicapped by restrictions put on CIA assets working within the United States. Look, Kate. I know we didn't get along. I used to think like you that everything I did had to follow stated guidelines. Since working with Nick, I've come to understand he recognizes situations and solutions with a unique perspective. Give him a chance. He gets results."

"And if I don't? What then? When he breaks the law right under my nose, what do I do with him, look the other way, and pretend I'm not a federal law enforcement officer?"

Grace disliked nearly everything about Anderson, but she knew the sacrifices made by a woman to get as highly placed in the FBI as Anderson. Great Kate's body language and facial features worried Grace the woman would do as Nick warned against: put his crew in danger. Knowing that would end badly, and it was her job here to prevent it happening, Grace adopted the same stance she had in Charleston with the police Lieutenant there, Irene Moragado.

"I'll level with you about something you need to take to heart, Kate. Nick is the most dangerous man I have ever encountered. If you put him or his crew in danger, your job, the FBI Director, or even the Attorney General will be the least of your worries. Back off and forget any idea you may have about impeding or discrediting him."

Anderson's mouth tightened as Grace watched the woman's hands clench and unclench. "Is that a threat, Grace?"

"No. It's great advice, Kate. Nick doesn't do this stuff for fame or name recognition. He has that. He'll let your task force take all the credit, and will simply go away after he gets this Ripper guy without a word or a single press conference. Mess with his operation and there will be consequences you've never dreamed of."

"And if he fails to get the Ripper?"

Grace smiled for the first time. "That, you won't have to worry about."

* * *

Nick waved at Grace as she walked into their assigned office. He and Tim worked at their respective computers investigating the list of prostitutes sent from Gus and John as likely candidates. They used the Seattle police department's files for the women to narrow down their choices to pursue.

"How'd it go with Great Kate?"

"Fine, I think. It was good for me too. I don't despise her as much as I did. The pettiness, and arrogant remarks are different than when I handled the Charleston woman detective. Lieutenant Moragado was frustrated with corruption she wished didn't exist. Kate's in so far over her head she can't breathe. You were right. I'll keep an eye on her. She may indeed be dumb enough to wreck this plan just to see it fail. I'm going to reach out to some of the task force members I've seen that showed as much disgust with Kate as I have. I'll keep my concerns in general terms about letting me know if Kate starts undercutting us before we even get started."

"I'm counting on you, Grace. There's no way this works if the Ripper gets tipped off in any way. If that happens I go on the hunt. The DOJ and my boss have backed me completely. They would like this to be a win for law enforcement in public perception. I'm willing to deliver, but I'm not letting Ripper keep killing after Great Kate ruins my law enforcement plan for 'bringing him to justice'."

"I'll help Grace with this," Tim promised. "We won't have much to do while you're recruiting your new operatives. When you're all set to start though, Grace and I will be right here networking with you."

"She did give us her office, and it has a bank of monitors you can tap into street cams with for us anytime we go out to a prospective client. I think I have enough names here. I need to get out recruiting. The biggest problem I see right now is the pimps. I'll be honest. A couple of them who try to block me, or I get bad vibes from, probably won't survive my recruiting process unless I can bring them in to be held by my US Marshal buddies."

"Bring them in, Nick," Grace said. "We'll stash them under federal interdiction. I hope you can get the show on the road quickly. Our base here will rapidly degenerate into an armed camp if this drags on very long. It doesn't matter local and federal law enforcement couldn't find a solution to the Ripper. After a few days without results, they'll be howling that they were on the verge of solving the case and bringing the Ripper in until we interfered."

Nick chuckled. "Yep. I believe you have the situation outlined perfectly, Grace. You two do understand why my name and part in this have to remain unknown so the Ripper doesn't hear about me, right?"

"Of course," Tim answered. "If he finds out who you are and what you're doing, he could possibly locate Rachel and Jean while you're away."

"Exactly, Tim. I've trained them well enough, they'd probably survive, especially since Rachel will be on the alert any time I'm away. That won't be the only danger once I find out someone was stupid enough to do something behind my back endangering Rachel and Jean."

"Believe me. We understand that, Nick," Grace replied.

Nick patted her shoulder on the way by. "Just checking kids, so there aren't any dangerous misunderstandings. I'll call you later in the day before I return to the Wolf Lodge. One other thing… no hanky panky on the job. We must keep up appearances."

Nick grinned as Tim chuckled and Grace gave him a one finger salute.

* * *

Clyde Bacall watched Nick enter the room where he had asked for a meeting with six prospective candidates for his seraglio of women to be used as bait to catch a serial killer. He had listened intently as Nick explained what his job was during the recruitment process. Clyde was to interfere only if an unexpected threat mixed in which meant Clyde acted as a glorified doorman, or at least that was what he thought. The women were not worn out hookers on their last leg. Their ages ranged from twenty to twenty-five. They were all white, Hispanic, or Asian, because the Ripper's victims had all been of those races. Nick paid them immediately for one night's work for attending the meeting he had made under false pretenses. His money turned the meeting immediately from confrontational to bored arrogance.

"First off, this is Clyde, and I'm Nick. What are your names? After each one had told him her name, Nick repeated them.

"What's this all about," a blonde hooker named Bonnie asked. "Are you and Clyde wanting to get into a competition with all of us? That might be extra."

"No, Bonnie. I'm here to catch a killer. You six matched some specific features I had to have in order to offer contracts. You've all heard of the Ripper I'm sure."

Nick had their attention. "The Ripper is bad for my business, so I brought in an out of town crew to take him out of circulation. We know you ladies work with two different pimps, Freydo Juarez and Dominic Calhoun. We also know they've been less than kind in their professional dealings with their employees. In fact, I know Dominic put you in the hospital two months ago Ivy."

"Been there, done that," the dark haired Hispanic woman named Ivy said with a grin. "Old news. Not the first time Dom whacked me around. So what?"

"Nothing at all," Nick replied. "For a few days Calhoun and Juarez are going to be taken off the job. I'd like to know if it would bother any of you if they disappeared permanently."

"You mean killed?" This from another brunette named Connie. She stood and looked longingly at the door where Clyde was standing. "I don't want any part of that. Freydo's no saint, but he's okay. I sure don't want him killed."

"There were murmurs of agreement to Connie's statement from the other women, involving both Calhoun and Juarez."

Bacall noticed the grim look of understanding spread over McCarty's features. Bacall knew in an instant McCarty wanted the two pimps dead and out of the way, but now accepted he would have to put them in federal control until the operation ended or pay them off.

"Very well then, life it is for those gentlemen. Now that we have that out of the way. I need at least four of you young women to be bait for me to get the Ripper. You will be protected at all times, and the hazardous duty pay will be ten thousand in advance, and ten thousand upon capture."

"This sounds like bullshit! Show me the fuckin' money, Stanley," Bonnie said.

"Fair enough." Nick walked over to retrieve his briefcase. He opened it on the room bed. "There is two hundred thousand dollars in the case, all unmarked old bills. Check it out yourselves."

Bacall enjoyed the stunned looks as the women sifted through the packs of money. A red haired woman named Ellen was the first to speak. She did so with obvious annoyance.

"Don't mean much if we're dead."

"True enough. If you want out of it, you can walk right now," Nick said.

One of the women not yet heard from named Sarah walked over to Nick. "Are you going to kill this Ripper dude?"

"I'm going to maim him. Then he goes to prison for a long time or I'll kill Ripper the moment he walks, only he'll be a long time dying."

"He hacked my bestie to pieces," Sarah said. "I'm in to the end."

Ivy, Bonnie, another blonde named Deb, and Connie all agreed with Sarah's decision. Ellen walked toward Clyde. "I'm leaving now. Let me out."

"Wait a moment." Nick handed her another two thousand dollars. "Keep your mouth shut about this offer Ellen or there will be consequences. Take my advice and stay home for a few days."

Ellen stared into Nick's eyes with the world weary arrogant hooker grin Bacall had seen many times. "What the hell do you care whether some psycho carves up hookers?"

Then Bacall saw it again as on the plane when McCarty drew his Colt faster than Bacall could think. He recognized it now, seeing McCarty from another position. It was death. The man reeked of death, and it filled his body and soul, spilling out of those dead eyes of his when he allowed it.

"I don't, Ellen. I'm a killer. I contracted to take care of the Ripper in a certain way, and I'll do it. If you interfere in some way, your interference will have consequences. Am I clear?"

Bacall opened the door for Ellen as she gulped audibly, and nodded. She backed away from Nick and out the door. Bacall closed it behind her.

"Do we get any of our money tonight," Bonnie asked.

"Five thousand each." Nick went to the briefcase, and passed the money promised to each woman. "I know everything there is to know about each of you. I want you all to take the money, go home, and stay there. I will contact you with any jobs I need you for. Tomorrow, you'll meet my associates, and we'll get started early. Be here by noon. For now, we wait for your pals Calhoun and Juarez. They'll be here shortly."

"Why the hell are they coming," Ivy asked.

"Business," Nick replied. "I'm going to make them an offer they can't refuse."

Nick passed out refreshments while they all waited. Fifteen minutes later, there was a knock on the door. Clyde opened the door, keeping to the side, and out of McCarty's line of fire. It was Calhoun and Juarez. Each of them had a man with them Clyde figured wasn't there for window dressing. The two pimps looked around the room at Nick and their ladies of the night with confusion the main ingredient on their features.

"What the hell?" Juarez, a medium height, dark complexioned man with slicked back black hair and black leather coat, made an encompassing gesture with his hand. "Is this a party?"

"I'm Nick. This is my associate Clyde. Thank you for coming. I'm taking the Ripper out, and your ladies have agreed to help me. They didn't want either of you to die, so each of you get five thousand dollars to go home for the next few days and keep your mouths shut until I can eliminate the man killing your business."

Nick walked over, and took out ten thousand dollars from the briefcase. He handed Juarez and Calhoun the money. "If we have an agreement, my associate will see you all out."

Dominic smirked and made eye contact with his man. "I like the case. I think I'll take it with me too."

Bacall saw Dominic's man reach inside his coat, and started to reach for his own weapon. In the next split second McCarty pistol whipped Calhoun to the floor, and shoved the barrel of his Colt under Calhoun's man's chin. Then Nick made a buzzer noise. To his credit, Juarez merely backed away with his money, a restraining arm on his companion.

"Wrong answer, Dom. Clyde, please be so kind as to put this man on his knees with a plastic tie restraining his hands behind his back while I consider shooting him in the head." Nick kicked Calhoun in the groin as he lay rolling around on the floor, provoking a scream of agony.

Bacall forced Calhoun's companion to the floor, roughly jerking the man's hands behind his back while Nick held the Colt barrel against the man's forehead. Bacall disarmed him as Nick confiscated Calhoun's five thousand dollars. He then waved the Colt at Juarez.

"Do we have a deal, Freydo?"

"We do." Juarez handed Nick a card. "That's my private number. Let me know when I can get back in business."

"I will. Thank you for your cooperation."

Clyde opened the door for Juarez and his man. He kept it open as Nick then gestured to the ladies. "Thanks for coming. See you all tomorrow."

"Are you going to kill Dom," Ivy asked, edging around her whimpering pimp.

"Nope. As promised, he and his buddy are going away for a few days, but without any money. Once we have the Ripper, I'll have him released. I'll give you and Dom's other ladies a number to call. If he retaliates in any way, call me. I will come back here and cut his dick off, and shove it down his windpipe. I know none of you will take my advice, but the twenty grand you each get would make a nice start for you in a new line of work, and a new place of residence."

After the ladies left, Nick turned Dominic over, restraining his hands behind his back. He roughly disarmed him. "I'm going to get you on your feet, Dom. If you don't help me, I'm going to kick you in the nuts again."

It took only seconds to get the moaning but very cooperative Dominic to his feet. "Let's deliver these idiots to my US Marshal cohorts, and then head for home. You did real good, Clyde."

"You really think this'll work, don't you?"

"I know it'll work. He may take a day or two before he bites on the bait, but we'll get him. Ripper's been hacking the Dark Web for hooker appointments. If we don't get enough real appointments, we'll make them ourselves. Patience Clyde – we'll get this sucker."

"You wanted to kill the pimps. I could see it in your face."

Nick grinned at Calhoun and his man. "I'm still considering it, but the ladies made the decision. Dom better be a good boy. If I get a call from any of his ladies about him being a bad boy, I'm going to show him some knife tricks in the middle of the night after he thinks he's all snuggled in. We'll have some fun then."

The terrified look on Calhoun's face convinced Clyde the man believed Nick. Bacall breathed in deeply while bending to pick up their equipment bag. *So do I.*

* * *

Dan, dressed as if he were going to a London opera, looking every bit the part of a well-dressed pimp with his merchandise, escorted Sarah along the walkway toward the Seattle Hilton Hotel near the airport at 2 am. It was Dan's sixth appointment in two days. Each time, they had set in place their plan, but the appointments were completed without a problem.

"You sure look nice old man," Sarah told him. "Maybe you should get into the pimp business full time. I'd work for you."

Dan laughed. He enjoyed interacting with his supposed seraglio of women. "I'm afraid this is not my line of work, Sarah, nor should it be yours, young lady."

"This Ripper guy had me thinking about getting out of the business or at least relocating," Sarah admitted. "You do know that asshole carved up three pimps too, right?"

"Yep. He ain't carvin' this one up though," Dan replied. Then he saw movement in his peripheral vision to the right in the spacious and quiet parking lot. His body language betrayed him.

"I see him, Dan," Nick's voice assured him. "Don't tip Sarah off, Geezer."

Dan simply nodded his understanding while he heard Gus and John talking about their positions. A black hooded figure with matching mask nearly six and a half feet tall angled in front of them. Sarah cried out in surprise as Dan arm swiped her behind him.

"Hello there, big fella," Dan said. "Nice early morning, huh?"

"Don't reach for anything, Gramps, or you die." The black masked giant showed Dan the 9mm automatic Glock in his hand. "I've been watching your new operation, old man. You're pretty slick. You two are coming with me this morning."

"Are you the Ripper," Dan asked with a big grin.

"Whatever would make you think that, Gramps? I'm not the Ripper. I'm having some fun. I don't want to kill either one of you. Now, come along with me."

"I don't think so. I think you're the Ripper, and I bet my buddy does too."

"What buddy? Your driver drops you off at an appointment, and you walk the girls to their date. I ain't seen no other players, although why an old pimp like you didn't hire some muscle is beyond me. I'll just tie you up, have a little fun with your girl, and then let you both go. Nobody needs to get hurt."

"That's where you're wrong, Ripper. You're going to get hurt."

"That so? You first." The man raised the Glock, and the .50 caliber hollow point projectile from Nick's Barrett sniper rifle five hundred yards away took the man's hand off at the wrist. The impact slammed him to the parking lot surface. Shock gave way to mewling screams a second before the Barrett fired twice more. This time the projectiles smashed into his right ankle, leaving the shoed foot dangling by a couple pieces of skin.

"Stay right here, Sarah," Dan said to his charge. "I have to ask the big, bad, and ugly a question while he's still conscious."

"Ah...ah... sure, Danny. Go...go ahead."

Dan walked over to the writhing figure, and crouched next to him. "I need to ask you again if you're the Ripper. If you don't answer truthfully, my buddy is going to shoot off another piece of you. My advice is answer truthfully so we can enter the factual round of proof, and then get you to a hospital."

"Take me to the hospital! I...I'm bleeding to death!"

"Answer the question."

"Yes! I'm the Ripper! Take me-"

"Shut up! The Ripper took a souvenir from each victim. No one knows what that souvenir was, not even the media. Only the task force knows. What was the souvenir you took?"

"Their tongues... I took their tongues!"

"That concludes our business, Ripper." Dan walked away as John arrived from where he had lay in wait near the hospital with a pack. Gus drove alongside with his window down. "Come along, Sarah. Your job's done. You can wait in the car with me until our law enforcement people and ambulance arrive."

"Okay, Gus." Sarah walked over and kicked the Ripper in the groin on her way by.

Dan, John, and Gus all chuckled at the new sound of pain as Sarah got into the vehicle. John applied a tourniquet to the Ripper's arm and leg. He then covered the wounds before collecting the detached hand and foot. Nick arrived on scene a moment later, and put his Barrett sniper rifle in the trunk. With black Nitrile gloves on, Nick removed the Ripper's mask. While Nick held the man's head still, John took different angled photos. Nick then used his digital fingerprint scanner to send Ripper's fingerprints to Paul Gilbrech and his US Marshal contacts. He waved at Sarah in the backseat, holding Ripper's head so Sarah could see him plainly while John held a light on his face.

"Nice work, Sarah. It's all over now. Have you ever seen this guy?"

Sarah leaned over the open window frame peering at the face without recognition. "No, but I won't forget him. You weren't kidding about maiming him."

Nick released the Ripper, and removed his gloves. He patted Sarah's hand. "I never kid. Who won the pool, Gus?"

"John did. He picked the morning of the third day."

"Ratshit! I thought I won it," Dan said.

"You said midnight, Geezer," Gus replied.

Grace and Tim arrived first, looking as if they had not been sleeping well. Grace jumped out almost before Tim could stop the car. "We came as soon as we could. Did you get the right guy?"

"Yep. He knew about the souvenir tongues," Nick answered. "He was slick. I can see why he nailed so many victims. Wasn't he, Dan?"

"Yeah. He didn't claim to be the Ripper or anything. He's a damn giant. He talked convincingly he wanted to have a little fun. The women probably took one look at his size, and figured their only hope was to go along with him. He staked me out during our other appointments. He knew right away there was a new game in town."

Grace and Tim looked over the two appendages in plastic bags.

"Did you have to shoot his hand and foot off," Grace asked.

"You do see what's still clutched in his right hand don't you?"

"Pay no attention to her, Nick," Tim said, "We figured Great Kate would be howling for our heads by the end of the day. Now, we get an entirely different agenda for our day. We didn't know if you could pull this off, and bring the 'Ripper' in alive or not. On behalf of this US Marshal, I thank you."

"This guy is bad," Nick stated plainly, looking down at the still moaning Ripper. "I'm glad I had a chance to help. I may have taken a hand in this anyway even if not asked in."

"Hey… you two are US Marshals?" This from Sarah, now with a very confused look on her face. "You work with killers now? I think it's great."

"Sarah? Remember our chat about sticking to only the facts of how Ripper approached you, and the threat he posed?"

"Oh… sure Nick… sorry. I just wish they had brought you in sooner."

"Facts only, kid," Nick replied. "Don't worry. I have someone arriving today to help us with the task force who will be questioning us. Sometimes they forget who the criminal was, and begin trying to bury the innocent helpers of law enforcement."

"You? Innocent helper of law enforcement? Gag! Nick… I swear-"

"Grace!" Tim's exasperated interruption silenced his partner. "Your testimony and cooperation is appreciated greatly, Ms. Burns."

"Yeah, Sarah, pay no attention to the frumpy Marshal with bad hair. We think she's going through early 'change of life' problems, and gets confused easily about what the hell her job entails."

Another one finger salute was the only response from the frumpy Marshal.

* * *

Dan continued to do stretching exercises while a task force agent tried to get him to repeat his part in the apprehension of the Ripper. "Please, Mr. Lewis, sit down and answer my questions. The faster you do, the faster you get out of here."

Dan kept stretching. "I saw this in a movie with Harrison Ford called 'Hollywood Homicide'. When Ford and his movie partner, who are detectives, don't agree with their continued internal affairs interrogation, they start doing yoga and real estate business. I explained in detail what happened twice. That's all I have to say."

"I don't think you realize you could be charged with hampering a federal investigation. I am trying to get at the underlying facts and details leading to the so called Ripper."

"Although I lost a betting pool I thought I won earlier, I'd be willing to wager there is no way in hell you'll be able to charge me with anything. I'll still testify at Ripper's trial, but I'm done talking to you about underlying anything."

"But surely you see-"

"Done now." Dan sat and clasped his hands. "I want my lawyer when he gets here."

* * *

Agent Kaitlin Anderson sat down with a smile across from Sarah Burns. "I understand you participated in an operation to entrap Gerald Kensky, allegedly the Seattle Ripper. Is that true."

Sarah smiled back, remembering Nick's coaching about testimony. "I helped catch the Ripper before he killed me and Dan. I kept an appointment at the Hilton Hotel. Dan Lewis escorted me to the appointment with a client. A man in a hood and mask stopped us. He tried to force us at gunpoint to go with him. We refused. When he tried to shoot Dan, Marshal McCarty had to wound him."

"What provocation did McCarty have to shoot?"

"The Ripper aimed a gun at Dan's head."

"Will you be able to identify the suspect in court?"

"Yes. I know he couldn't stand at a lineup, but I could have picked him out of one. Long dark hair, thin face, pug nose, and he has a cleft lip scar."

"I thought he had a mask on." The investigation was not proceeding in the manner Anderson anticipated.

"Nick removed his mask while he was on the pavement. I saw him real good."

"Yes, but when you testify in court, the defense attorney will ask how you could know the man on the pavement was the same man who stopped you."

Sarah began to laugh, but stopped when Anderson didn't crack a smile. "I thought you were joking. How many huge wounded men did you think were on the pavement?"

322

"That was not the point of my question. I have to determine if your testimony could be impeached easily in court, and our case thrown out."

"Are you stupid? The Ripper faced us, pointed a gun, was wounded, and then unmasked. No one switched him out with an innocent bystander with the same wounds."

"I'm not sure you understand the countless questions an entrapment operation like this can generate in a court trial. You will-"

At that moment a man entered the room with a briefcase. He wore a black pinstripe suit. He had a friendly smile on his face, nondescript in appearance, angular in form, medium in height, and bright blue eyes which did not project friendliness. He handed Anderson a card.

"I am Justin Khole, Attorney for Nick McCarty, Dan Lewis, and Sarah Burns. I will be sitting in on every conversation from now on until you end this very strange pursuit of facts not in evidence."

"Ms. Burns is a federal witness. She will have to answer the questions asked of her for the trial involving the suspected Ripper, Gerald Kensky." Anderson's face did not reflect her confident tone.

Khole put a hand over Sarah's clasped ones. "Do not answer anything Agent Anderson asks. Her agenda here has nothing to do with your attacker."

"You will not get away with this, Khole. I don't care who you think you are."

"That's where you're wrong." Khole opened his briefcase and extracted a paper. "Mr. McCarty knew you would try to pull something like this immediately after the apprehension of the Ripper. Although the official word will get to you shortly. Let me assure you that your attempt to discredit Marshal McCarty's invaluable help in solving these heinous Ripper murders and bringing the perpetrator to justice has not gone unnoticed at the Department of Justice, nor with the Director of the FBI. Marshal McCarty tried to allow you full credit without any mention of his part other than a generalized note indicating he was acting as a S.W.A.T. team sniper charged with protecting the operation's participants. Ms. Burns, Mr. Lewis, and Marshal McCarty will be leaving with me right now. US Marshals Reinhold and Stanwick have been assigned the procedural completion of the case, including any contact with the media."

Khole handed Anderson the paper with the letterhead of the FBI Director. Anderson's face lost all color. Khole stood. "Let's go, Sarah. The people now actually in control of this case have your contact information when they need to get in touch with you. Good day, Agent Anderson."

Sarah gave the shocked Anderson a wave. "Bye."

* * *

Outside the precinct building, Tim and Grace waited next to Nick. They decided any conversation with Nick needed to be done somewhere off site.

"How did it go with my publicity exposure on this?"

"Thanks to your lawyer, very well," Tim said. "When Kensky comes to trial, we'll gather Dan and Sarah in for testimony. We'll submit yours as a deposition. You'll only have to testify as a last resort."

"Dan's eager to testify. He'll be a key witness. Dan was part of the operation, and being threatened at gunpoint on video cam," Nick responded.

"You sure called it right with Great Kate," Grace said. "The damn woman went after you the moment she had the Ripper in custody, trying to actually discredit you and the witnesses. I doubted she'd actually sabotage the arrest for some weird payback scheme, but that's exactly what she was attempting. My two acquaintances on the task force figured Kate thought since she knew who Kensky was now, even if they lost him temporarily, they would be arresting him later on an ancillary charge. It's a damn shame after getting warned, she still couldn't let it go. Now her entire career is in jeopardy, and maybe it should be. That bastard Kensky could have been released and then went on a rampage."

"That lawyer of yours is impressive," Tim said. "Great Kate walked out of the interrogation room after he got through with her in a numbed trance. I suppose part of it had to do with the people you contacted the moment you had Kensky."

"I knew I would need help to keep from getting mired in this. Kate's loss is your gain. The US Marshal Service gets credit now along with the task force. It looks like I get to go do some book signings in Olympia, Seattle, and some smaller ones around the area before heading home without any worries. I guess you can let that punk Calhoun loose along with his buddy. Anytime you two get a break, call me. We'll have dinner together at the Wolf Lodge, or here in Seattle when I do a signing. That reminds me. I brought you a first edition of 'Assassin's Folly', Grace."

Nick put his briefcase on the walkway, and extracted the hardcover edition. He handed it to Grace. "Don't worry, I simply signed it with a small note."

Grace examined the cover, with a grin. "This would be worth a fortune once you're dead."

Nick smiled back. "Read the note inside."

Grace frowned, opening the book. The note read 'To Grace. I ain't dead yet'.

Tim started laughing the moment he read the note over her shoulder. "Nick can predict what you'll say or write before you even announce it, partner. Are you going to ask him before he goes full bore into vacation land mode?"

"I refuse," Grace said. "Rachel will kill me if I get him involved in something else close to home."

"Yeah, I'm really sure that's eating at you," Nick replied. "Spit it out before Gus, John, and Dan get back from paying off our helpers, and cautioning them all to stay low key. One thing you'll have to realize is I'll be meeting obligations for book signings in four different venues between here and Centalia. I will not be in Pacific Grove for two weeks."

"We have a problem in Santa Cruz with a mob guy opening a protection racket down on the Boardwalk area motels. You've been there I'm sure with as close as it is to you. The motels in the area are old, and have a seedy worn out look about them. One of our people in the Witness Protection program works as a manager at one of them. She claims this guy, Chino Salermo is using one of the gangs in the area to shake down the small independent motel owners. We were told to stay out of it, and let the local police handle it. The only problem is our witness is due to testify in the murder case they built in New York City against Lino Verducci. Tim and I figured we'd yank our witness out of Santa Cruz, but she has a couple of teenage boys who love it there. She says if we move her, she won't testify."

"So give her a stipend to stay on a vacation leave until she testifies against Lino. Nice catch by the way. The East River in New York probably has at least a score of weighted bodies who crossed Lino. If you minions of justice would think about using... hey... wait a minute. I smell a rat. Why would you two be fretting over a WITSEC problem? You two are head district honchos now. After this Seattle Ripper exposure, you two will be golden at the DOJ. Why aren't you ordering full time US Marshal protectors for this sweet-pea in Santa Cruz from your staff of minions? C'mon, tell Uncle Nicky the whole story or Uncle Nicky walks away right now. I'm tired of being fed this crap one factoid at a time."

"I told you Grace. Tell him."

"I should turn in my badge for even thinking it. That's why," Grace admitted. "This is the first time Salermo has surfaced in two years. We think he was hiding out in Columbia. Salermo worked for Verducci as a mob enforcer a few years back. He killed my Uncle Joe in New York when Joe wouldn't pay protection money on his bakery in Queens. Salermo ordered the hit through a street gang near Joe's shop. The cops got the 'banger that did the killing, but couldn't indict Salermo even though they got the 'banger to point the finger at him. The kid was shanked at Rikers while waiting for the DA to make up his mind whether to deal for Salermo. The prick disappeared until now. Word was he's been in Columbia making contacts for Verducci."

"You have my attention," Nick replied. "I don't like coincidences either. Are you thinking Salermo's staking out the Santa Cruz area for Verducci, and possibly taking out the key witness against Lino? That would mean either you have another leak in the program or your witness screwed up. Which is it?"

"One of the damn teenagers called his old girlfriend back in New York on a burner phone, so he thought he was cool like in the movies. Chino doesn't know who the witness is yet, but it's only a matter of time. We did exactly like you advised, and had our witness take a leave of absence. She'll probably have to make a decision – die in Santa Cruz or let us relocate her to New Mexico or some other desert spot." Grace pointed at Nick, who was smiling. "I know what you're thinking, you prick."

"No you don't. If you knew what I was thinking, you'd probably try and arrest me."

Grace gestured with her hand in a come on fashion. "Lay it on me, Muerto."

"I'm thinking of the look on Rachel's face when I tell her I'm going to Santa Cruz when we get back to Pacific Grove, and kill Chino Salermo. Then, I'm going to New York and kill Lino Verducci just so I can do it, tell you I'm doing it, give this woman's life back to her, and turn the justice system upside down."

"Works for me," Tim stated.

"Tim?" Grace turned on her partner with a look of shock.

"Oh come on, Grace. Get the stunned look off your face. If you didn't want Nick to do exactly what he outlined just now, or something very close to it, what the hell did you expect him to do – go to Santa Cruz and hold the woman's hand?"

"He's doing it again! He's spewing out killer solutions outside the law, and rubbing our noses in it."

"He's rubbing in a whole lot of payback for your Uncle Joe too. I don't mind pretending the law works," Tim said. "When crimes are committed by run of the mill people, the law works pretty well. Where gangs can reach into our prisons, kill witnesses, terrorize potential witnesses, and do whatever the hell they want, I get a little tired of mouthing the mantra of working within the law. The people who wrote the laws never imagined the day where organized crime would simply kill anyone who made the laws work. If Nick hadn't brought in his own crew to trap the Ripper, we would have never gotten him either."

"We've sold our souls to the devil," Grace muttered, her head down.

"That's the spirit," Nick said. "Hey… I think I resent that."

Chapter Fourteen

Book Signings and Justice

Rachel watched Nick's cohorts ambling around their room, making drinks, and stealing glances at her when they thought she wasn't looking. For his part, Nick stayed in the kitchen, helping to make and pass out refreshments, avoiding her since saying hello upon his return. She knew they sprung the trap earlier in the day, and were mostly without sleep for the better part of two days. To her, The Unholy Trio and their Geezer mascot seemed far too cheerful. Jean was sipping a soda, staying near Nick so as to accumulate information with Deke next to her.

"Okay, this has gone on far enough. Who am I going to have to beat the story out of? John. Don't look away from me. What the hell is going on?" Rachel invaded John's airspace, grabbing his chin and shaking it. "Tell me! You are in my power. You will tell me everything."

"Muerto took another hit for right after we get back to Pacific Grove. He was supposed to tell you as soon as he walked in, but when he didn't I knew you would try and torture the information from us. Unhand me, woman! Muerto! Do something, you spineless jellyfish."

"Nice one, John," Nick replied. "It took you only five seconds to throw me under the bus. I'm demoting you back to minion for this horrendous lack of fortitude and loyalty."

"Don't blame John, Muerto," Dan said. "We've been listening to your new gig, and how you were going to sell it to Princess Bump all the way from Seattle. The moment you get in the door, you head for the liquid courage, and clam up like a sprung bear trap."

"Et tu, Dan?" Nick borrowed and reworked the famous line of Julius Cesar to his supposedly loyal friend Brutus when stabbed by said friend during the Ides of March.

"You're the fearless, El Muerto, not Cesar, you spineless jellyfish." Gus piled on. "We could have left you to face Princess Bump alone, but risked the wrath of the Bump out of compassion and eagerness to watch the aftermath. Grow a pair, drink some booze, and give her the outline of yet another outlandish commitment to the Muerto ego supreme."

"El Muerto was merely winding down a bit after saving Seattle from the deadly clutches of a wicked mass murderer, stalking, torturing, and killing young ladies of the night. Does El Muerto even get a few cherished moments to enjoy his incredible accomplishment? I think not."

Rachel enjoyed the continuing roast and professed outrage of Nick. She sat down at the kitchenette table. "Come sit down and tell Princess Bump all about it. At some point today, you guys will need some sleep."

"I can't bail Muerto out of this one anyway," Dan said. "If you gentlemen will excuse me, I'm going to go sleep for the next twenty-four hours."

"See you, when we see you, Dan," Nick waved at him. "You were a great pimp."

"Thank you… I think." Dan shook hands with his battery mates Gus and John as he made his way to the door. "Don't let the Bump tear Muerto apart too much guys. He still has to show for the book signings."

"We'll take care of him, Dan. We took down the Ripper. The Bump will cut him a little slack for that," Gus replied.

The moment Dan closed the door behind him, Rachel ordered the other two thirds of the Unholy Trio to the table. "Sit down you two so Muerto can quit stalling. Can you put this in a way so the Daughter of Darkness can stay, or does she need to go to her room?"

Jean knew better than to plead.

"She can stay. With all that's happened in the last few weeks there's no use in playing pretend, not that it ever worked after Jean's experience on the cross country flight from the Tanus mobsters," Nick admitted. "There's a situation Grace and Tim want me to handle in Santa Cruz a bit like you and Jean had, only with a personal thread tied in with Grace. A woman and her two teenage sons are in the WITSEC program. One of the boys made calls back to an old girlfriend, giving away their general location. A killer has moved into the area on the hunt. He's the same one that ordered Grace's Uncle Joe killed in Queens. She never mentioned him before. This Chino Salermo recruits local gangs to do his dirty work in protection rackets and killings. He's a soldier for the Lino Verducci mob in New York the woman is testifying against at a murder trial."

"Did Grace mention she'd probably catapult to number one on my shit list for dumping this on you?"

Nick chuckled. "She may have mentioned that in our conversation."

"Good. I can see you've already made up your Muerto mind to do this insanity. I know you can't pull this off as cartoons, so let me think." Rachel leaned back in her chair, eyes closed, rubbing her chin in deep comical contemplation. She leaned forward again after a moment hearing Gus and John stifling amusement in varying degrees while Jean giggled. "I see all now. The great Muerto wants to unmask the quirks in our justice system once again, while using the justice system's own minions to willingly help him carry out and cover up his heinous acts."

"Maybe."

Rachel sighed. "No maybes about it. I can't say I don't support you in this, but are you going to do the book signings too?"

"Yep. I have to. Cassie prompted my publisher to push a special print run for these signings. Cass will be flying into Olympia today. She's decided to stay halfway between us and Seattle. She called me while I was on the way home. The first signing will be tomorrow at 11 am in Olympia. I told her to send a limo for us on my dime which she's handling. Gus will be accompanying us on the book tour since his character Jed in the novels is so popular. I have a huge seafaring scene in this one just released, Assassin's Folly, and Jed played a prominent role in Caribbean Contract too. No critics dare challenge my seafaring plots with the ancient mariner Payaso at my side."

"John and Dan are flying home tomorrow," Nick continued. "John will check on our places, do preliminary visits to Santa Cruz to scope out the situation, and introduce himself to Dimah Kader. I'm calling Dimah today to prep her for meeting with my associate El Kabong, who will be taking the lovely cousin escaping the East Coast Kaders under his protective wing. Dan's going back because he's a geezer, and he's already homesick. I don't blame him. In any case, that's the scoop for the future while we're here enjoying the great Northwest."

"And after you solve the Salermo problem in Santa Cruz, Muerto?"

Nick shrugged. "What can I say, 'Doin' right ain't got no end'."

"You know I hate that 'Outlaw Josie Wales' quote, right?"

Nick reached across the table, and clasped Rachel's hands. "Yeah... so what's your point?"

"It means you're planning on going to New York after one of the most dangerous mobsters in the country."

"Like you admitted, Rach, in some cases the justice system misses the mark. I don't. If that woman and her kids ever hope to be safe again, Lino Verducci must be persuaded to leave them alone."

Rachel smiled for the first time. "I bet this outlaw intervention makes Grace mental, huh?"

"Oh yeah."

"Good!"

"Although I will be missing this glorious book signing event because I need to meet my future cousin-in-law, and assure her I can keep my future love safe, Gus has consented to wear a cam for my viewing pleasure. I wish to see the great El Muerto and Payaso handle the infamous 'Book Killers'."

"Sorry, John," Nick replied. "They don't show at signings. Some of the more intense book critics arrive to lecture me on grammar or plot twists they hated, but the BK's love their exalted positions working to cause chaos on the Amazon marketplace from the shadows."

"Gus? I thought you said I would see 'Book Killers'," John turned to his fellow Muerto minion.

"The great Muerto doesn't foresee everything," Gus replied.

"Yes I do."

* * *

Gus discussed nautical questions with nearly every reader in line, as the fact he had been Nick's inspiration for the seafaring Jed in the Diego novels became public knowledge after the book signings in the East and South. Since Jed threaded into many scenes in both Caribbean Contract and Assassin's Folly, people at the book signing asked about the dangerous boat maneuvers in the novels. Nick based his characters Diego and Jed's seafaring scenes on real life missions he and Gus crewed together. Since incorporating Gus into the book signings, the interactions improved with each new venue. The rumors and news headlines concerning Nick's consulting with local and federal law enforcement entities on important cases also improved the interactions with readers. With Tina, Rachel, and Jean shopping together in Olympia, Nick and Gus were on their own.

Nick loved watching the people in line waiting their turns. Most within hearing range listened intently to the conversations between Nick, Gus, and the person at the line's front. Nick signed quickly any way he was directed by the fan, then allowed for conversation and more signings while conversing. Nick's affable manner, and relaxed style discussing multiple plot points or scenes drew small groups around the signing table. If someone felt uncomfortable sharing in a small discussion, the reader could wait for a one on one Nick signing. The book signing was definitely not an author speed signing books without even looking up. Nick noticed the small group did not slow the line. In fact the fans seemed to know when their time should end. They moved on without incident. The few exceptions were spoken to quietly by the bookstore attendants.

A man gripping a copy of Caribbean Contract waited until the cluster of fans in front of him left so he would have a one on one signing opportunity. Nick noted the grim expression on his face as he approached the signing table. Slender of build, middle thirties by Nick's estimation, dressed in jeans and navy blue windbreaker, he threw the Caribbean Contract novel aside on the table.

"I don't want a signature," the man stated in a tenor voice loud enough to be heard by nearly everyone in the store. His statement quieted the chatter nearby as other store patrons stopped what they were doing. "I only grabbed a book because I figured they wouldn't let me get near you without one."

Gus tensed, and one of the security guards moved closer. Nick grinned at the man with his hands flat on the table in front of him. "Well... uh... what can I do for you then?"

"I read strictly on my Kindle. Your novels suck. It's incredible you've held any position on any bestseller list with the garbage you write."

Although a murmur of discontent rumbled through the crowd, a hush as everyone seemed to wait for Nick's reply led to a silent moment before Nick began laughing. Gus looked on somewhat uneasily, while many in the crowd laughed too because Nick did.

"Oh... you think this is funny?"

Nick responded after a few more seconds of enjoyment. "Yeah, I guess I do. Thanks for stopping by."

"I'm not done with you yet!"

That statement drew the security guard to the man's side, but Nick waved him off with a smile. "It's okay, Ken. I have this."

"I'll be right here, Nick," the security guard replied.

"Have you reviewed any of my novels, Sir," Nick asked the man.

"Of course I've reviewed the trash. I'm Bongo97. You've taken it upon yourself to insult my reviews in the Amazon reviews and comments section. I'm here today to face you in the flesh."

Nick turned to Gus. "You were right, Gus. We attracted a Book Killer for John's enjoyment." He faced Bongo 97 again. "I recognize your handle. I'm always polite with you, Bongo. You're what we call a 'Book Killer'. For some reason only you know,

335

instead of reading the preview Amazon supplies and avoiding novels you find beneath you, like mine, you engage in one star hit pieces in hopes of killing sales. Since Amazon allows such practices in spite of the lengthy 'Look Inside' preview feature they supply, which should eliminate one star hit pieces altogether, I choose to interact with my BK attackers. It's kind of neat to have one attend in person to a signing."

Bongo pointed a finger at Nick. "Your comments held me up to ridicule from your troll supporters. How dare you attack a reader's honest review!"

"I take it you're referring to my reply to the latest one you did on Caribbean Contract where you stated you had read all my novels, but couldn't get through two chapters of Caribbean Contract. You also claimed it was a waste of money, my writing sucked, and you had read better prose from high school kids. Then you claimed I was no Hemingway. I merely pointed out once again as with all your other one star hit pieces, that Amazon gives you three chapters for free, so why not read the preview, and avoid the novel. Lastly, I agreed with you that I was indeed not Hemingway, but that I did know how to spell his name, which you misspelled."

A ripple of laughter went through the crowd in appreciation of Nick's Hemingway comment. Nick could tell Bongo hadn't intended for the details to be heard. Nick sliced away while watching Bongo's head threaten to explode. "Coming here in person really wasn't very smart, Bongo. Any derogatory remark you spout off about I can answer with a simple plot question, which you won't know the answer to, because you've never read a single novel of mine. Think before you dig a deeper hole for yourself. Just saying I suck as a writer only works in the anonymous Amazon comments section. Here, I can ask for particulars, including plot points, which you won't know. You've been somewhat entertaining, Bongo. Let's part friends now while you can. Folks! Can we give Bongo a great sendoff? Bye Bongo. Bye Bongo."

In a split second everyone in the store was waving as Nick did, singing Bye Bongo. Ken, the security guard, moved next to Bongo. With a guiding hand, he escorted the red-faced Bongo to the exit.

Nick stood for a moment as everyone calmed down. "Look folks. I'm the first to admit my pulp fiction is not for everyone. There is graphic violence, romance, humor, and politically incorrect speech incorporated into every novel I write. Those ingredients are fully on display in the preview chapters Amazon provides for the novel free. Anyone having read the other novels in my Diego series, and is now disappointed in either the flavor of what I'm doing, or the character interaction, that is legitimate criticism. I probably won't change the way I write, but I appreciate the honest feedback. What Bongo and the other BK's do on the Amazon marketplace is laughable, but their hit pieces do kill sales. Contrary to my fellow authors' advice to ignore all reviews, I read them, enjoy them, and interact when it's a BK, or there is a question I can answer, because I never get mad, but enough speech. Step right up to the Un-Hemingway signing table and state your case."

Nick bowed comically at the smattering of applause, and sat down again next to Gus. The next lady placed her copy of Assassin's Folly in front of Nick.

"That was a very entertaining conversation, Mr. McCarty. I would like a special signing if that's okay."

"Sure." Nick opened the book and prepared to write.

"Write this - I'm so sorry, Mary."

Uh oh. Nick could feel the jaws of Karma closing around him. He wrote down the dictation. "Okay."

"I will never use a comma before a dependent clause again – signed Nick McCarty."

Oh boy.

* * *

"You guys have been uncharacteristically quiet," Rachel said. "I can tell even the Daughter of Darkness is waiting for some interaction about bookstore day."

"That's right, Gomez," Tina added. "Usually, you and Payaso are raving about one thing or another happening in the bookstore. Did something bad happen?"

"Gus and I are merely enjoying this quiet limo ride to the Lodge. I'm beginning to think a spot of the Jack Daniels I saw in the limo bar may be needed, brother Payaso."

"I know it's needed." Gus began fixing two large glasses with ice and Jack Daniels. "I was just waiting for the starting gunshot. Here, Muerto. Salute."

Nick toasted with his glass, and drank deeply. He grinned and sighed with contentment. "Oh my Lord, that was so good. I'm glad they don't have an open bar at these events. I believe Payaso and I would not make it past 2 pm."

"That bad, huh?"

"Not bad, Dagger," Gus said. "Customer interaction is a blast, but it does have its highs and lows. John called me to rave about his video with you handling the Book Killer. The little Muerto Sock Puppet said he nearly laughed himself into a coma when you led the goodbyes to Bongo."

"Yeah, but then I was knifed in the back by a dependent clause/comma Nazi," Nick complained while refilling his glass. "She's right, but I don't even know if I did it or not. She scared me. I figured if I asked for proof, she'd whip out her list of a thousand or something."

"The fearless El Muerto afraid of a grammar editor? Say it isn't so," Rachel pleaded comically. "That makes me want to read your novels all again with my red pen."

Nick hung his head. "Editing is the most humbling experience on earth."

"I thought you said admitting you were wrong was the most humbling experience."

"That too," Nick replied without raising his head.

"The inspiration for Diego's seafaring sidekick Jed had a good day though. I answered many questions about my scenes in the books. Would you like me to tell you about them?"

"I'd rather see the video clips of the Book Killer and the dependent clause/comma Nazi," Tina said. "I've heard all about your little boat cruises."

"Fine... I know when I'm underappreciated. Here." Gus turned his tablet so the females could all see.

When the video reached the dependent clause/comma Nazi, loud appreciative laughter erupted.

"Oh my God, she made you write an apology for something you don't even know you did or not. That settles it. If the signings are going to be this good, I'm going," Rachel declared.

"You're forgetting the hours of mind numbing boredom while we listen to Captain Hook tell sailor stories all day, and Gomez get his panties in a bunch because he doesn't know where to put a comma. You're on your own, girlfriend."

"Right, Tina," Rachel said. "What was I thinking? We'll scan the video for choice moments to enjoy in a luxurious setting."

"At least you didn't have to kill anyone today, Dad," Jean piped in.

"The day is five hours from midnight. There's still time. I've heard in the new Addam's Family they're thinking of writing a scene where Gomez goes mental, hacks Cousin Itt apart, puts the Itt pieces on the barbie, and then serves them for dinner."

"They do not," Tina said, startled at Nick's word picture.

"In my screen play they do."

"Don't be hatin', Gomez," Tina mumbled while her companions stifled amusement of Cousin Itt.

* * *

"You're certain he goes in along the railroad track?" Dominic Calhoun stared with tightly controlled rage at the single track running into the huge wooded area near The Great Wolf Lodge. "Today is perfect. It's overcast and drizzly. We'll be alone with him in there."

"Are you sure you can trust what that FBI broad mentioned? It seemed like she was setting us up the way she talked with the other agent when the cops escorted us out. She did sound pissed off though."

Dominic nodded at his two cohorts. Rafe Lansing had been on the receiving end of Nick's temporary adjustment to the pimp population. He was raw about the way Nick took them down too, but uneasy with the expertise he had done it. Jess Boyer freelanced collections, strong-arm extortion, and keeping the prostitutes in line. Boyer thought it funny they were out trapping some Fed because he roughed up Dom and Rafe.

"Instead of watching him, you should have paid me to kill him," Boyer said. "He's a damn dog walker. I could have followed him into the brush and been done with your Wyatt Earp wannabe without you driving here."

340

"The guy's no joke, Jess," Lansing replied. "Dom and I have been around the block. That sucker is fast. I'm glad we brought the Uzis. They have range as a rifle. I want to do this clown, but I don't want to be close for it. I figure all we have to do is follow a mile in along the tracks, and then ambush him when he returns from his dog run. He must go a long way in there. Jess and I didn't see him for forty-five minutes yesterday when we staked him out."

Dominic gestured for his men to follow him. "It's a good plan, Rafe. With the silencers, the asshole and his dog will be dead without anyone hearing it a mile in. He won't be able to spot us with these camouflage rain slickers. We'll drag their bodies into the brush and leave 'em. It's supposed to rain and drizzle for the next week. No one will find the bodies for weeks probably. I wanted a piece! That's why I had you wait until I got here, Jess. You're getting paid. What do you care?"

Boyer shrugged as he followed Calhoun while grinning back at Rafe. "The three man ambush works for me. This will be fun. We'll need to split up so we have three nests in case he is armed, and is as fast as Rafe claims. We take no chances. That okay, Dom."

"Perfect. We spread out at the spot with maybe fifty feet between us on each side of the tracks, far enough in the woods so we have cover. I'll shoot first. I don't want him getting near enough so there's a chance we'd hit each other."

"The guy did stop that Ripper bastard," Lansing pointed out. "I know he punked us in the hotel, but we were going to steal his money. Now, the girls are back workin' and business is good. I'm not sure payback is such a great idea, Dom. This could bring a lot of heat down on us killin' a famous novelist with a US Marshal's badge. You know damn well they'll be checking out anyone having a beef with him in the area."

Calhoun spun on Lansing angrily. "Fuck you, Rafe! I ain't letting bygones be bygones after what he did! Look at my face! He nearly took my eye out, and I'll have a damn scar for life. Then the bastard kicked me in the nuts! He dies today! You got that?"

"Yeah, boss, I got it," Lansing agreed with placating motions. "I'll cover him over with brush. Maybe they won't notice the bodies for months with spring rain hitting."

"That's what I'm talkin' about," Calhoun replied, turning again to the tracks. "I'm going to shoot that motherfucker right in the dick first. Let's get to our spot. Nobody does that shit to me and gets away with it."

Following at Calhoun's fast pace, they arrived at a spot on the tracks where they curved enough so the woods on either side of the tracks hid approaches. Calhoun pointed on the right side of the tracks.

"You go straight that way, Jess. Go in about twenty feet. We'll watch you."

Jess gave Calhoun a mocking salute, and entered the woods to the right, stopping at what he figured to be twenty feet. He crouched down. "How's this? I have good vision on the tracks ahead too without any big obstructions."

"We can barely see you. Hold position. C'mon Rafe." Calhoun positioned Lansing only slightly inside the wooded area, having him crouch down. "How's Rafe's spot?"

"Real good," Jess called out. "I can only spot either of you when you move."

"Will it be a problem if I stay close to the woods' edge, but ten feet further along than you, Rafe? I don't want in your line of fire," Dominic said as he high stepped to a spot to the left of Lansing, but further toward the track clearing. He crouched. "How's this?"

"You're good, boss. I'm not going to spray anyhow. I'll get him, but I'm aiming. You're in the clear with no chance of hitting Jess or me, so go full auto on him if you want."

"Yeah… maybe I will." Calhoun felt the drizzle turn into light rain a few minutes later. He smiled under his hood. "It's a good thing we hurried, Rafe. He'll be cutting short his dog trot for the day."

Rafe Lansing did not respond. Calhoun at first figured Lansing was being cautious about noise carrying. After ten minutes went by, he swore under his breath. Turning slightly, Dominic called out in a hushed voice. "Rafe?"

When he didn't get an answer, he checked the tracks for any sign of his prey. Seeing none, he straightened from his spot, and moved to Lansing's position as quietly as he could. He spotted Lansing in a sitting position, with knees braced against his chest while leaning against a tree. His arms rested between his legs. Rafe's head was tilted slightly as if listening for something. His posture seemed off to Dominic.

"Rafe? Damn you. Answer me," Calhoun hissed. He creeped closer, crouching more while turning from side to side, watching for strange movement. Reaching out, he grasped Lansing's arm, shaking it.

Lansing slowly fell away from the tree, crumpling to his side in the leaves and mud. His head flopped back against the ground. The rain slicker hood fell away from his face. Seeing the wide sightless eyes staring at him in the dusky light, Calhoun stumbled backwards, his hands shooting out to catch his fall. The Uzi strapped over his shoulder slipped into the mud. Lansing watched Calhoun's descent with uncaring eyes, the huge open slice at his neck still seeping rain thinned blood onto the bloody shadows beneath him.

* * *

Nick jogged to his usual turnout to the left along the railway tracks. Since discovering the tracks on the first day, he and Deke explored the wooded area on both sides of the track for miles along it, enjoying the trek in rain or sunshine. The day before, Nick had spotted the out of place men wearing rain slickers as they waited in their vehicle – a black Mercedes with license plate matching one of three vehicles owned by Dominic Calhoun. He grinned as he ran with Deke beside him considering the deadly mistake made by his freed pimp acquaintance. Ever since he was alerted by Grace and Tim of Calhoun's release, Nick waited to find out if Grace's contact had been right about Agent Anderson mouthing off about Nick's whereabouts while Calhoun and his minion Lansing walked by. Anticipating the worst case scenario, Nick had been prepared for an open gun battle or a more clandestine approach.

Pausing as the tracks wound out of sight from the turnoff with the road, Nick and Deke circled back into the woods. With range finders in hand, he waited for his prey to follow him. They parked their vehicles at the turnoff, getting out in their rain slickers, and standing at the turnoff like three fatted calves waiting for the butcher's knife. When they committed to following, Nick grinned, and petted Deke.

"Wait until you see old Gus's face when I hustle you out of here. C'mon, Dekester. We have to get a faster than usual sprint going, not so fast I fall and break my Muerto neck, but fast enough to get you to the awaiting Payaso. El Muerto has his deadly work cut out for him today."

Nick jogged at a pace twice the speed he normally did for the next mile, then angled up the slope toward the road in the distance. Gus was parked in the GMC fifty yards from where Nick and Deke exited the woods. He drove alongside, stopping while his passengers boarded.

"Don't say a word," Gus warned. "I see that smirk on your face. After you take care of this nasty business, how the hell are

344

you going to handle the bodies and vehicles? Why don't we call Tim and Grace?"

Nick shook his head. "They have Uzis. You and I can't arrest them without a gun battle. Great Kate gets away with her tipoff because I'll have to try and bury the unknowing accomplices. Think of my angst at being set up for the kill by that idiot Anderson. Calhoun and his boys could have went after Rachel and Jean. Drive on, Payaso. Let me off fifty yards before the track turnoff."

"What are you packing?"

"Sitletto and a folding shovel."

"Are you out of your Muerto mind? Get something big out of the back with a silencer."

"Nope. El Muerto must seek justice with his blade of darkness."

Gus drove away, making gagging noises for Nick's amusement. When they reached the position Nick had mentioned, Gus stopped on the roadside. "I'll be at the same spot with fresh clothes when you call… if you're still alive."

"Gee… nice pep talk, Payaso." Nick exited the GMC after petting Deke.

In a matter of moments, Nick angled fully into the woods after stripping off his pack, slicker, and making certain the black t-shirt he kept on was tucked in tightly. He also tied his shoe laces leaving no loop or loose end dangling. After tucking his pants' legs into his socks, Nick continued to the right, figuring the ambush they planned for him would not be with the three of them together. He knew they would not want to chance being too deep into the woods where they would be risking bullet deflection, Nick paced stealthily on the wet ground, loving the covering rainfall. He slowed drastically as he passed what he thought was a half mile in.

345

Ten minutes later, Nick nearly laughed out loud. He heard the sound of a video game being played. With silent precision, Nick picked his way on all fours to where he saw glimpses of a lighted phone screen. He had to pause, clamping hands to his mouth in smothered amusement.

In control once again, Nick began his deadly silent final approach. So absorbed in his video game was Jess Boyer that he never looked away from the screen until a hand gripped his face powerfully, shutting off his mouth and nose while the razor sharp stiletto blade sliced through his neck. The hand continued holding him in the frozen horrific pose as his arterial blood shot forward onto the leafy ground, taking his life with it. Nick allowed Boyer's body to relax through its death throes before releasing him to the ground. He listened intently, filtering out the rain and slight breeze. Nick heard nothing on his right, but definitely a distinct rustle of leaves to his left as if someone repositioned themselves.

Nick took no chances. He backtracked through the woods until he knew it would be safe to scurry over the tracks to the wooded area on his left. Once in the woods, Nick resumed stalking his targets. Rafe Lansing knelt on his other knee, brushing against the bush on his right. Watching the man shift uncomfortably as he came within sight, Nick figured his target had bad knees which made it painful to either kneel or crouch in a waiting position for any length of time. With Lansing, Nick made his final death lunge as Lansing once again switched knees. He yanked Lansing's face back with vicious proficiency, while clamping the man's body between his knees. They shared the sight of Rafe's life blood spurting in pulsing heartbeats of eternity. Nick then posed him against the tree while listening to Calhoun calling out for his partner.

As Dominic approached, Nick moved into the shadows on the opposite side of Lansing. Calhoun focused totally on Lansing and the area around him while Nick waited calmly without movement barely out of sight. He enjoyed Calhoun's discovery of

Lansing's demise. When Dominic fell back, Nick moved on his prey, stabbing him with three rapid strikes to the hilt of his stiletto under Dominic's ribcage. Shock paralyzed Calhoun, the stab wounds a mere burning discomfort compared to the Nick's smiling face as he removed the Uzi strap from Dominic's shoulder, yanking it away. Calhoun fell to his side, clutching his wounded midsection, screaming as he glimpsed the blood oozing out around his hands in the fading light. The pain from the wounds silenced his screams as they caused needle like shooting points of agony from his belt into his brain. He curled more into a fetal position sobbing uncontrollably.

Nick wiped his stiletto blade on Calhoun's jacket. He crouched next to his victim. "Hi Dom. In one way this is your lucky day. You only came after me instead of my wife and daughter. Secondly, I wasn't called in by one of your girls because you retaliated against them. Either of those acts would have earned you the repulsive reward of having your dick cut off and shoved down your throat while you were still alive. The unlucky part of your day is you did come after me instead of simply resuming your pimp duties. First off. How did you know where to find me?"

Calhoun twisted pleadingly toward Nick. "I'm sorry! I...I made a mistake. Don't do this! I have money! You can have it all! I overheard that bitch from the FBI griping about you living the high life at the Wolf Lodge at Grand Mound loud enough for the whole precinct to hear. It was like she wanted me to know. Did she set me up for this?"

He groaned, hugging himself tighter as his pleas caused sharper pains.

"Nope. She set me up for this," Nick replied. "Give me your account numbers, and I'll check what you have on line."

"Sure!" Calhoun turned slightly with hope. "Get me to a hospital. I...I'll give you everything."

"Gee, Dom, I thought you were smarter than that. See, the way this works is you give me access to your accounts so I can transfer all your money into my accounts, or I do this until you bleed out."

Nick stabbed the stiletto into Calhoun's upper arm, watching and listening to the resulting horrified movements and cries. "I figure I can probably stab you hundreds of times before you bleed out, but that's up to you for now. See, I figure I should be compensated for having to drag you and your dead buddies deeper into the bush for a shallow burial. I'd give it to your girls, but I'm not inclined to reward bad behavior."

When Calhoun continued to sob and cry while writhing around trying to find a position without pain, Nick plunged the stiletto in again through Calhoun's calf. That was enough prompting to get Calhoun's complete cooperation. As he stated, Nick checked accessibility to Calhoun's accounts, both locally and abroad. When he was certain he had the correct passwords, and account numbers, Nick slit Calhoun's throat. He then jogged along the tracks until he could retrieve his pack. After putting on his rain slicker and tying the hood in place, Nick put on his pack, and returned to his victims.

He dragged each one deeper into the woods on the left to a densely wooded spot with soft and loose ground surrounding the trees. With his folding shovel, Nick dug three shallow graves, stripped his would be attackers of everything on their person except clothing, and planted them in the graves. With the bodies covered completely, Nick concentrated on finding rocks and dead wood to cover the ground over the graves, lastly adding leafed branches. The rain pounded down as Nick finished his task, and shouldered his pack with Uzis and personal effects.

Gus answered on the first ring. "Payaso the pawn, how may I help you?"

"Drive to the spot. I'll be there shortly after you arrive. Bring some towels to cover the seat in. Did my absence draw much attention?"

"Just the usual complaints from the Bump and Dagger show. I bet you'd like to get dry, get comfy, write, and drink until nightfall wouldn't you?"

"I assume that isn't in the cards or you wouldn't be tantalizing me with it, you prick."

"Heh...heh," Gus replied. "It looks like the indoor water park for Muerto today. No rest for the wicked."

"There will have to be a slight delay in the water park mission. After I get dry clothes on we'll drive the bad guys' vehicles into Centralia and park them on the other side of town where there's no street cams. Rachel will have to drive us back to the Lodge. You can leave with Calhoun's car right away, drive across town, and park it a couple miles out of town toward Olympia. I'll pick you up, and we'll drive a couple miles further on. Rachel can swing by then, and pick us both up."

"Who gets to tell the Bump about your car disposal plan?"

"I do. I'll have to return the GMC to her before walking back out to get the minions' mobile for my drive through Centralia. Don't forget a garbage bag for my clothes, and our wipes and gloves for cleanup on the vehicles."

"Get moving. I'll be there soon."

Forty-five minutes later. Rachel and Jean stopped to get Nick and Gus. "Oh look, Jean. It's the infamous El Muerto and his sidekick Payaso. Whatever are they doing out here?"

Nick hung his head while allowing Deke to jump all over him as he got in the backseat with Gus. "No tongue, Deke. I

349

already apologized for this late in the day operation. Gus and I were one minion short."

"The Momster's only kidding, Dad." Jean peeked around the front seat where she and Rachel were the ones most noticeable in the GMC as per Nick's direction. "So, where are all the bodies buried?"

"If you want me to ride the water park slides with you today, I advise caution on your choice of topics. I see what you mean about the Bump and Dagger show, Gus. Good description."

Jean giggled. "The Bump and Dagger show. I like that, Uncle Gus."

"You would," Rachel said. "Does this end our Muerto hijinks for this vacation?"

Silence.

"Gus?"

"We haven't discussed the FBI task force woman who told the pimp Calhoun where we were all staying," Gus answered. "I'm sure Muerto is mulling her over in his mind since we still have signings to do in Seattle, and Great Kate will be in the city for a few more days winding down the task force loose ends."

"Muerto! You can't kill an FBI agent."

Silence.

"Muerto!"

"You wouldn't be so forgiving if our visitors had tried to kill you and Jean while Gus and I were in Seattle," Nick muttered finally.

"Let's go with that logic since this is about Jean and I. We'll take votes from the two of most concern to you. The Momster votes no. Jean?"

Silence.

"Jean!"

Jean folded her arms over chest while staring straight ahead. "She's an FBI agent, Mom. She's supposed to protect people. Because she's stupid, and Dad had to get her replaced with Grace and Tim, she told killers where to find us. I'm not voting. Let Dad decide. He knows stuff we don't."

"Jean's right, Rachel," Gus added. "Give Muerto a chance to consider this on his own. He knew to be watching for those cretins in case that FBI broad was as vindictive as he figured she was. He can't help it he's right all the time in the wrong way."

"It's my curse," Nick pouted comically with hands hiding his face while Deke growled and pried under them with his nose. "I am doomed to see the worst in people and have them prove their low character true."

"Cut the comedy act," Rachel directed. "You win. Let's enjoy the rest of our day and night. I feel like I'm about ready to pop. If my intuition is right, Quinn will be arriving pretty quickly after we get home. I'm going in the pool and float around like a beached whale, belly up."

"Oh great... I'll have to go into therapy for a year to get that word picture out of my mind." Jean fended off the Momster's grab for her ear with a yelp. "Hey... no pinching the ear. I'm going to look like Dumbo the Elephant by the time I'm twelve."

* * *

Gus and Nick sipped their drinks in the cabana while Rachel and Tina swam in the pool. Jean had dumped Nick for the company of two girls near her own age.

"You've considered Calhoun and his buddies will be missed, and someone will be around to ask you questions, especially when their vehicles are found outside of Centralia, right?"

"I couldn't do anything about the vehicles' GPS systems, but hopefully law enforcement won't be trying to track their travels as an afterthought. I stripped their phones, and busted them to pieces. I sent scans of their ID's to Paul so he can be kept in the loop. He knows what Great Kate did. I'll probably let him handle her behind the scenes. Without confessing to murdering three thugs in cold blood, I can't very well do anything in the open about Kate. I'll let Grace and Tim know what she did, so they can steer clear of her in the future. We'll leave it to the 'regular federal authorities' for now."

"Good thinking," Gus replied. "You can always tie that loose end later. She doesn't pose a threat, does she?"

"I don't know, Gus," Nick admitted. "Although I suspected her to be that petty, even I was surprised when Calhoun and his boys showed. I made sure it was her that tipped him off before he died. We have a couple hundred grand more to play with too, but I'll have to wait until I can transfer the money from his accounts to a neutral account somewhere. We'll have time, but I'll get it done in the next couple weeks. I doubt they'll find those three any time soon though."

"When we get home, I'm looking forward to the Muerto Matchmaker gig. I thought it was nuts to tangle with the Kaders again, but when I saw John's face after you mentioned hooking him up with Cala, I figure it will be worth it. How many of those assholes do you think we'll have to kill before they stop messing with her?"

"Who knows? Maybe two or three. I plan on staging this so John can be heroic, and maybe scare the crap out of the Kaders that do make trouble. Avoiding dead bodies with those psychos is anyone's guess though. Man, this is nice, Gus. Since Dom came early, we should be able to do the remaining signings without any after action problems."

"You do realize you just doomed us, right?"

"Payaso. You are the most negative creature on earth."

"No, but I'm partnered with him."

Chapter Fifteen

Death and Life

Cassie Sedwick met Nick and Gus's limo. "Hi guys. Ready for another rollicking good time meeting with the public? I see you couldn't talk Rachel, Jean, Tina, or even Deke the dog into coming along for this final chapter of Nick in the North."

"Seattle's a nice place to visit, but I believe we've been away from our home base long enough," Nick replied after waving for the limo driver to go on. "We dropped our humans off for the Seattle tour, including the Argosy harbor tour. That's about the only thing they haven't done. As to my canine pal, he and I jogged miles into the woods early this morning. Deke was snoring with a beef bone next to him when we left, the slacker. You seem happy this morning, Cass."

"That's the trouble with you, Nick. You don't stop to smell the roses. If you had, you'd know Assassin's Folly is the number one book in the nation. The news you consulted on the Ripper case here in Seattle made headlines all over the world. Need I mention what such a bump does for your other novels?"

Heh...heh, Gus and I were a little busy tracking all inquiries made in regard to my three thug manure deposit in the Lodge woods, dear lady. "That is wonderful, Cass. You know me. I'm writing when I'm not running with Deke or entertaining Rachel and Jean while they whine about everything. Dark Interlude is progressing marvelously well with Diego and Jed completing a mission off the coast of Barbados with the lovely Fatima trying to sabotage their every move."

"Don't you dare kill Fatima!"

Nick sighed. "See Gus. This is what happens when you give agents manuscript updates. They begin thinking they're writing the novel."

"Please Nick?" Cassie made comical praying motions with clasped hands to Gus's amusement while Nick turned away with arms folded across chest. "She's made Diego more human than he has ever been. Fatima can join the crew. Make Diego win her over."

"Please restrain yourself, my dear literary agent. These pleas are beneath you. Of course Fatima must die. Are you insane? She's dueling with a cold blooded assassin without conscience. She will be used, abused, and tossed aside in a landfill."

Cassie gasped, stunned for a moment. Then her brow furrowed. "I hate you."

"I've been getting a lot of that lately."

"I'm calling Rachel. She and I talked for an hour. Rachel loves what you've done with Fatima and Diego. It's the first time she's ever been excited about your writing. That means I'm not the only woman enthralled with the addition of Fatima. Women read. Although you have a nice percentage of women readers, the hint of a duplicitous female foil like Fatima, in a love/hate, no holds barred, passionate affair with Diego in Dark Interlude will triple your female fans. When Rachel hears you're killing off Fatima, she'll beat you within an inch of your Stephen King wannabe life. Just because the King kills off every damn character fans become attached to doesn't mean you have to follow his sadistic ways."

By that time in the rant, both Nick and Gus were expressing loud amused appreciation of Cassie's upbraiding of Nick, especially the Rachel threat.

Damn, there goes my agent sparring. "You shouldn't be speaking to my wife anyway. I'll consider your input, but I better not be getting any more wife involvement threats. You know what happened to the wife in 'The Shining' when she messed with King's writer character."

"Okay, but I'm going to be very disappointed if you take the writer coward's way out by using the shock card to stir reader emotions," Cassie stated.

"Writer coward?" Nick put his arm around Cassie's shoulders, guiding her toward the entrance. "I'll think about letting Fatima live. You need to get a life though, Cass. You're getting caught in the web of fantasy. I love this downtown corner store location. Was that why you had us get here so early? It worked out well for dropping the tour attendees off, but usually you want us to hang with the readers out here on the street."

"I am addicted to Diego," Cassie admitted. Hearing Gus snickering behind her, Cassie spun to face him, jabbing her finger in Gus's chest. "Don't be laughin' at me, Gus Nason. I heard you sold your soul to the devil to keep your character Jed alive and straight in a recurring Diego role. You have no room to talk or laugh at all, buster!"

"Damn that Rachel! Can't you shut off communication between the Bump and your professional life?"

"Sorry, Gus, but you already know I have no control over the Bump. Hey, Cass, did Rachel tell you Gus tagged her and Jean as the Bump and Dagger show?"

"Yes. Disgraceful." Cassie tried to maintain a straight face and failed. "Come on. The crowd will be here soon. The early hour had to do with the store manager's request. The weather's in doubt for the day. He wants to begin the moment any line forms if that's okay with you so we can keep the fans out of the rain."

"Fine with us," Nick replied, following Cassie into the store. "After all, this is our final signing date, so we're set to have a good time. We better have coffee to help get this show on the road though."

"Of course there is." Cassie didn't see Gus and Nick smiling at each other while flashing their flasks like two kids sneaking smokes in the school bathroom.

"Nick!"

Turning toward the sound, Nick saw Grace and Tim showing their ID badges to the store employee. "Gus, can you help Cass get everything in place while I talk with Wyatt and Calamity?"

"Sure. If you're talking any longer than five minutes I'll bring you your coffee loaded."

"Thanks, brother. Hi kids. Gee, that's swell of you two attending my book signing. Slow times in the US Marshals Office, huh?"

"Funny boy," Grace said. "Tim and I wanted you to know if we'd heard about that dimwit Kate spewing your location we would have arrested her on the spot. I would have put that bitch in handcuffs and frog marched her ass to the nearest plane for extradition to DC. Mr. Gilbrech explained what happened and why we need to keep quiet about it."

"I know you and Tim would have told me, especially after following orders not to clue me in on Didricson and Sadun."

"I knew you weren't going to let our Didricson screw-up go any time soon, but we hoped you wouldn't think of us in the same light as Great Kate's nearly painting a target on you inside a police station," Tim replied.

"No, I don't which is why what she did will have to be filed away for future reference. How's the law enforcement news on our three missing bad guys?"

"They've located the cars. The authorities suspect foul play," Tim deadpanned for Nick's amusement. "Nothing other than that though. You know how concerned normal people and police get when pimps and thugs disappear. One of his girls was asking about Calhoun named Ellen Santos. She claimed you kicked around Dominic, and she thought you were going to kill him. Since we do have records of Calhoun and his buddy Lansing staying in our care for a few days before being released, her allegations are falling on deaf ears."

"We would have felt better though if Kate had already boarded a plane back to DC with the task force. I don't know what's holding them here. My task force contact said it's procedural, but that makes no sense. The FBI wouldn't want the expense of those suckers staying around this area for the hell of it," Grace added. "I alerted your boss so in case there is something brewing we don't know about, he can get in front of it."

"Thanks. I appreciate that. I can take the heat though. Those three will remain missing for a long time I believe. If you can keep tabs on Great Kate that would help."

"We will," Tim said. "I'm glad you're leaving for California. The pimp deal will drop over the cliff without you here. I hope your last signing is a blast, Nick. We'll stop in and see you when we finally get home."

"Good, because I want people I trust watching out for the woman and her kids in Santa Cruz until I can end that threat."

"Count on it," Grace stated. "Bye, Nick."

Nick shook hands with them, imagining the matchmaking and killings he had ahead of him back home. *Nick, old lad, you are one sick puppy.*

* * *

"Thank God we had some Irish through the day, brother. I think we paced ourselves perfectly." Gus put away his tablet, checking for anything he forgot when they moved to the backroom after the signing ended.

"Agreed. No BK's, and only three grammar Nazis." Nick toasted Gus with his last Irish coffee. "I bet John was bored out of his mind. What time did he check out of the network?"

"Before noon. He was meeting with Dimah Kader for the first time today. The big chicken talked Dan into going with him so Dimah didn't feel threatened. I bet he needed Dan along so someone other than Dimah spoke more than three words."

"That's harsh Payaso. The great Kabong was only being considerate. El Muerto will assist Kabong when Cala meets with him." Nick put away the last of his papers. "Rachel called. They finished the tour and took a limo back to the Lodge so we don't have to rush around. Here comes Cass with the last roundup. She's beaming, so I know we sold a bunch of books today."

"New record, guys," Cassie said. "The manager was grateful you and Gus stayed for an extra few hours. These Sunday signings are the best, but a three hour window is tough to manage. Staying seven hours with only a few short breaks put you guys on the bookstore hero list. Did I miss anything juicy?"

"Not a thing, Cass. Previewing Dark Interlude worked really well. The crowd loved my chapter one reading when Diego meets Fatima. I think your heroine Fatima is a real hit."

"I knew she-"

"McCarty!" FBI Agent Kaitlin Anderson walked into the back with two other agents. "Hit the road, lady. I need to talk with McCarty. You go with her, Nason."

"They're not going anywhere," Nick said. "I figured you'd be around today after I talked with Grace and Tim this morning. My friends you just insulted will be staying."

"It's your funeral. Dominic Calhoun, Rafe Lansing, and Jess Boyer are all missing after their friends said they were coming to talk with you. Where are they?"

Liar. No way did those three goons tell anyone they were meeting with me. "Two of those men I've never heard of, and I had no meeting with them. I don't know what friends of theirs you're referring to; but if they told you those three were meeting with me, they're mistaken. If those guys are missing, file a missing persons report. Since when does a special task force with the FBI work on missing persons cases not crossing state lines? Let the local police handle it."

"You'd like that McCarty," Anderson said. "We found their abandoned vehicles in Centralia. What did you do with the bodies?"

Cassie gasped, covering her mouth with her hand, looking wildly at Nick. "Let me get you a lawyer, Nick."

"It's okay, Cass," Nick assured her, taking out his iPhone slowly and carefully. He spoke only a few words. "Yes Sir, Agent Anderson is with me now. Sure. Wait one."

"Either of you other guys named Burnison?"

The agent on Anderson's left spoke. "I'm Burnison."

Nick handed him his phone, noticing Anderson's color becoming red raged. "This is for you."

"Agent Burnison here." Burnison's demeanor stiffened, and his mouth tightened to a thin slash. "Yes Sir, I understand. I will call you before the plane leaves, Sir."

Burnison handed Nick back his phone. He then held out his hand to Anderson. "Gun and badge, Anderson."

"What the hell? Have you lost your mind?"

"That was the Director on the phone. You're under arrest, and I am to strip you of weapon and badge. If you don't comply I will draw on you."

"This is a mistake!" Anderson complied as Burnison gripped his weapon.

"Restrain her, Dick," Burnison directed. "Put your hands behind your back, Kaitlin. Agent Scone will then handcuff you. Do it now."

The now sullen Anderson did as ordered. "Are you sure about this, Mal?"

"The Director of the FBI just now told me to cuff Kaitlin and take her badge and gun. We're to pack our things and get the hell back to DC on the first flight available. Yeah... I'm sure." Burnison turned to Nick. "I'm very sorry for this inconvenience, Marshal McCarty."

"Thank you for your cooperation, Agent Burnison. I'm sorry it went down like this, but I made some calls when I was told your task force was still in town. Have a nice flight home, Sir."

Burnison nodded and took Anderson's arm. She forced a turn toward Nick. "This isn't over, McCarty!"

For your sake, I hope you're wrong. "You okay, Cass?"

"What the hell was that all about, Nick?"

"Sometimes my consultations with federal task forces don't meet with the approval of all task force members. Then one of them does something stupid and I have to make an adjustment. Often, only a stern warning like today is all that's needed, but in rare cases a more serious statement has to be made."

"That was just the stern warning?"

"Believe me," Gus said, putting his arm around Cassie's shoulders, "that was a stern warning. Is there a bar around here?"

"Sure."

"Let's take Nick to it and make him buy us a couple of drinks, Cass."

"That sounds wonderful, Gus. Doesn't it, Nick?"

"Yep. Indeed it does. We can't overdo it though, because Gus and I have to pack. We're going home tomorrow, and I have to take Deke for a long walk tonight."

"Do you think that Agent Anderson will make trouble for you?"

"Possibly," Nick answered, "but only for a short time."

* * *

"Dante. Chino says be at the Torch Lite Inn at noon." The young man called out from the passenger window of a 1962 midnight blue Buick Electra.

Dante Rivera had turned the moment he heard the street fill with noise behind him as he neared the rundown apartment house on 2nd Street. He relaxed when he saw the familiar car. "What kind of business we into at high noon, Pero."

"Sureño business, Cabrone. Be there."

Rivera watched the Buick roll down the street music making the houses vibrate as it went by. Suddenly, he wasn't alone. Dante knew it a split second before the needle pain in his neck erased pain, thought, and consciousness. He awoke with his head pounding, bound and gagged in the back of an empty delivery van. Three men all in black, one with a full face clown mask and the other two with black silk masks. They sat calmly on small beach chairs.

"He's awake," one of the black masked men said, moving over Dante and removing the gag. "Hey kid. How you feeling?"

"Muer...Muerto!"

The masked man laughed as did his companions. "Ah, you know El Muerto, huh?"

"Yes!" Dante stared at the three men with terrified eyes. "I know El Muerto, Payaso, and El Kabong! Please... kill me quick, Muerto! Don't do it with the bleach."

El Muerto patted Dante's arm with his black gloved hand. "Let's talk about that, Dante. El Muerto is here for another man who you have been working for. If you help El Muerto, I will let you live. I want Chino Salermo."

Dante became excited. "I know him, Muerto. He orders us around like slaves, telling us we will be rich and part of the Lino Verducci family."

"You don't believe him?"

"He will get us all killed or in prison. I can tell. We only exist as a gang if we don't disrupt the tourist trade. Chino wants to run everything. He cares for nothing. I have been in the Sureños since I was a kid. It's just me and my Mom. Sureños will kill us if I quit."

"There's a million stories in the naked city, kid."

"Muerto!"

"Okay...okay... Payaso wants Muerto to help you, Dante. Do you know any places where Chino likes to hang out?"

"There is a bar on Ocean Street called the Jury Room. He goes there late at night with his bodyguards. He made us meet him there a few times. It is where he holds court. Chino thinks it is funny to conduct business in a place called the Jury Room. It's

363

Friday night. He will stay until closing all weekend. His men are killers, Muerto."

"Did you just insult me, kid?"

As Payaso and Kabong laughed, Dante shook his head violently in the negative. "No Muerto! I merely meant to warn you."

"Good info. We're going to take you home. Stay in tonight with your Mom. Is she home?"

"Yes. She cleans motels on the boardwalk during the day, but she will be home tonight. You are really going to let me live, Muerto?"

The masked man reached back and Payaso gave him a small briefcase. Muerto cut Dante free of his restraints and gave a packet of money to the stunned teen. "This is five thousand dollars. Stay home and call no one. Don't answer your door. Don't let your Mom call anyone. Is that clear?"

"Yes, Muerto!"

"Drive us back to Dante's place, OG."

The van began moving. After five minutes driving, the van slowed to a stop. Payaso opened the sliding side door, and Kabong helped Dante to the door and outside. "Don't look around, kid. Go home."

Dante nodded without turning, and walked straight to the apartment he shared with his Mom. He smelled dinner cooking. For the first time in a long while, he thought of his Mom's pleas for Dante to get out of the Sureños. He knew better than to flash the money anywhere, including in front of his Mom. She would not believe his story, but perhaps he could change things now in secret. He went in the kitchen and sat down.

"Mom. We must stay inside tonight and lock the doors. We cannot call anyone. I heard something bad is happening tonight possibly with the Sureños."

Dante's Mom quickly sat down opposite her son, grabbing his hand. "You are not in trouble are you? Please tell me you didn't do something foolish."

"No Ma. I did something right, and now I am here to keep us safe. We must stay in as I have explained. Do you think I could get a job cleaning with you?"

"Yes! We need good workers all the time. Let me get you some dinner."

"Sure, Ma. Thanks."

She returned to her stove preparations. "Who is it that warned you of this danger?"

"Someone named El Muerto."

His Mom spun around. "The dead one?"

"He is not dead, and he showed me the light."

His Mom made the sign of the cross in a quick reverent motion.

* * *

"You were going to kill that kid, Muerto," Gus said as the van drove away from Dante's house.

"Was not," Nick lied. He worked assembling his Barrett sniper rifle. Once finished with the assembly, he used his portable bore scope to check the rifle's accuracy. "Would I have given Dante five grand after we spent the day checking him out on the police blotter if I meant to kill him?"

"Yep," Gus answered.

"Yes," John agreed.

"Ditto, and don't give me any of that 'Et tu, Dan' shit either."

"El Muerto is hurt by these unfounded allegations. The compassionate El Muerto prays every day to be able to help the poor and downtrodden gangbangers of the world."

"Gag."

"Barf."

"Ditto," Dan called out in turn while driving toward the Jury Room bar. "How do you want to handle this?"

"Feel like sipping a few brews in the bar and watching TV while the Unholy Trio find a good spot for a killing?"

"That sounds right down my alley," Dan answered. "Someone else will have to drive home though. "So, you want me to go in this Jury Room bar, make sure Chino is there, and clue you in when he leaves?"

"That's the plan. The three of us will network with each other. Wear your ball cap the whole time in the bar low over your forehead, and keep your windbreaker on. When Chino leaves, you leave, and walk in the opposite direction along Ocean until we swing by to pick you up."

"Got it. Here we are. I'll go around the block so you can check it out."

"This is perfect," Nick said. "The Jury Room has an open parking lot. Check out what's opposite the place."

"Damn," Gus muttered. "A two story Jack in the Box. Who writes this lucky ass script?"

"This is most fortunate," John agreed.

"There is no lucky or fortunate. There is only El Muerto."

"Gag."

"Barf."

"Ditto."

* * *

Dan entered the Jury Room. It was cool, dark, and smelled of smoke. He sat at the bar, and a man with a handle bar mustache took his order of a draft beer. Dan liked the place right away. He hadn't frequented dive bars for over four decades, but this one felt good. He spotted Chino and his two men entertaining two young women at a table near where a small band was performing. Dan texted the sighting, and sipped his beer with calm enjoyment.

Outside, behind the Jack in the Box restaurant, Nick checked the building. "I can be in position in seconds. We'll wait until Jack closes. I'll go from the van roof to the second tier of the building. John throws my bag to me and then on the roof I go. You two take off until I need picked up, or Dan gets into trouble. Let's go wait for closing."

Two hours later, the van drove next to the Jack in the Box with Nick lying flat on the top. He jumped quickly over to the second tier. John threw his bag into his arms and Gus drove away. Nick vaulted to the roof after throwing his bag over the top first. Minutes later, Nick was in place with his Barrett, a black tarp over him as he sighted in the Jury Room parking lot.

* * *

"I want that bitch found!" Chino Salermo turned away from the Sureño gang member reporting to him. "Get the fuck out of my sight!"

The gangbanger hurried out of the bar, and Chino turned to his men. "We know the bitch works at one of the hotels. No more game playing. I want the Sureños on the street with her picture going to every fucking hotel in Santa Cruz! Lino called twice today. He wants this shit done. It's past midnight. Let's get the hell out of here. The band sucks anyhow."

As they were walking out, Chino bumped into an old man moving off his stool. He gave the old guy a push into the bar. "Watch where you're goin' Gramps."

"Sorry Sir. It won't happen again... ever."

Chino glared at the grinning old man leaning against the bar. "You're lucky I don't have time to wipe that fuckin' grin off your face."

"Yep. That's me, Sir. Mr. Lucky."

Chino led his men outside toward his gray BMW at the far end of the parking lot. He beeped it open. Then to his men, it seemed as if Salermo's head exploded. While they stood staring at their boss, they died the same way, the silent fifty caliber rounds pulping their heads.

* * *

The van drove alongside Dan, who was weaving slightly. The sliding side door opened. "Get in here while you can still walk, Dan."

"I can't help it, Gus. I haven't had a drink in a while and those three beers did me in. I'm a lightweight."

"How'd it go?" Dan sat on one of the beach chairs while massaging his knees.

"Messy," John answered. "Very effective, but messy."

"You're not going to believe this, Dan. While we were waiting for Chino, we've been hacking around in Lino's business, and spots where he's likely to be in New York," Gus said over his shoulder as he drove. "It even freaked Muerto a little."

"Did not," Nick lied. He finished disassembling the Barrett and putting it away. *Damn spooky is more like it.*

"I ain't going to live forever. Are you going to tell me or not?"

Nick chuckled. "Lino Verducci has the same office as Hayden Tanus did."

"Hayden Tanus? Who... oh shit! He's the guy that put a hit out on Rachel and Jean, and this Verducci guy's in the same office? No wonder you're creeped out, Muerto."

"El Muerto does not get creeped out."

"Bullshit," Dan retorted. "That's dangerous mind altering Karma. You put a hole in Tanus's head through his picture window from a mile away. If you do Lino's head the same way through the same window don't you turn into a werewolf or something?"

Gus had to drive off the road. Luckily, they hadn't reached the freeway. It was only after minutes of pounding the steering wheel while trying to regain control enough to drive that Gus was able to continue the journey home. He listened contentedly to the continued hilarity in the back over Dan's werewolf comment.

* * *

John chuckled once again. Dan glanced over at him from the passenger seat of the van. "I must be getting good at the one liners to keep you entertained this long."

"That werewolf comment was very good. You almost caused a crash, and Muerto nearly went into a coma laughing."

369

"Hey… how did you get stuck with van disposal?"

"There's no hurry to get it back to Jerry. We covered the license plate when needed, so I will drive it to the valley for the night. You haven't met Jerry yet. Would you like to ride over with me tomorrow morning? I will not be taking it to him until ten."

"That sounds good to me," Dan replied as John slowed alongside his house to a stop. "I'll go with you when you meet Cala too. I enjoyed meeting Dimah. I thought the meeting went very well too. She liked you. I could tell. When do you plan to spring the suggestion Cala stay with you in the Valley to keep her safe?"

"When I meet her and see if she likes me. Muerto is going with me that day as a reference. I think it would be good to have a Geezer along too. People trust old guys."

"Thanks, Kabong. I'll enjoy going with you and Muerto. We'll have you married in no time. Believe me, John, there's nothing like having a life's partner. It's sometimes a rough road, but worth every mile traveled. Goodnight."

"See you tomorrow morning, Dan." John drove off after Dan closed the passenger side door.

Dan looked around at his neighborhood and the sky above, thinking about going for a late night walk rather than face the inside of his empty house. He took a deep breath. *C'mon old man, you need some sleep. It ain't getting any easier after you walk around the block.*

He walked to his door, appreciating the clear view of sky and stars. *It's nice not having fog once in a while.* Dan unlocked the door and walked inside the dark entryway, closing the door behind him, but didn't get a chance to lock it. The knife blade went in his left side but glanced off his ribcage. Dan grunted in pain but spun into his attacker, driving him against the wall. He clutched his attacker's throat with both hands. A smile formed in spite of the pain as the knife sliced into his side again. Dan hip tossed the hooded figure to the floor, digging his fingers into the man's throat with every ounce of fading strength he had left. The attacker panicked without air, letting the knife drop and grabbing Dan's hands weakly. *Too late for that, kid.*

With grainy blackness filling his senses, Dan choked the life out of his attacker. He didn't let go until beginning to lose consciousness. By then Dan held only a limp, dead form. Falling away from the body, Dan rolled to his back, grinning into the descending darkness. *Hey, baby... long time, no see.*

     * * *

Nick woke, feeling the sudden cold wetness. He rolled toward Rachel, pulling away the covers. *Uh oh.* "Rach, your water broke."

"Huh... oh shit!" Rachel started to jump out of bed, but Nick stopped her.

"Calm down, Hon. I'll get you cleaned real fast, and then we'll load you in the car. You call Payaso while I get wet towels and wipes."

"Yes! It's finally happening," Rachel replied happily while reaching for the phone. "Hurry up, Muerto. When the contractions start I want to be at the hospital away from your 'Pressure Point' birth technique."

"Damn big mouth, Payaso." Nick helped Rachel strip out of her nighty while she told Gus what had happened. He wiped her off thoroughly before helping her over to the dresser where Rachel had what she wanted to wear to the hospital already set out.

"Gus will be over in a couple minutes to stay with Jean." Rachel let Nick help her put on the elastic waist adult diaper and a clean flannel nighty. "I'll take my cotton robe. I'm fine. Get dressed, Muerto. You already have the hospital bag in the trunk. Unless you left one of your dead bodies in it, we'll be able to leave the moment Gus arrives."

"The dead body comment is not appreciated by El Muerto."

"Boo hoo."

* * *

John knocked on Dan's door. When no one answered, he pounded on the door with a big grin. "Answer the door old man. I am here early. The heir to the great Muerto has arrived. We will go to the hospital together."

John looked around. He didn't want the police called because of his noisy attempt to awaken his friend. He tried ringing the doorbell a few times. "I thought you old guys leaped out of bed at dawn," John muttered. He tried the door knob. It turned.

He drew his 9mm Smith and Wesson automatic. The door opened partially under his pressure but was blocked by something against it on the other side. Enough light shone in, John could see two bodies lying next to each other. He forced the door open carefully until able to slide in the opening. Knowing he could no longer help his friend, John searched the house with weapon at the ready. He found a canvas bag filled with jewelry, Dan's laptop, and other items that looked as if they were made of silver or gold. John left it and finished his search. When certain there were no others in the house, he returned to his friend, crouching next to him while avoiding the pool of blood. John bowed his head, grasping Dan's cold hand for a moment. He then walked around to the dead burglar.

"It is good you died so quickly by my friend's hand. If you were still alive, it would be many days before death found you. By then, you would have cried out joyously as if to a loved one."

John hesitated, but then called Nick. He knew Gus was with Jean.

* * *

A grim faced Nick slid in Dan's door in the same manner as John had before him. He nodded at John who stood silently near Dan's body. In a moment of seeing the discarded knife, bloody handed assailant with bulging eyes, and Dan's wounds, Nick knew immediately what had happened. He knelt down next to his friend, noticing the slight smile on the old man's mouth. Nick closed Dan's sightless eyes gently, grinning down at him.

"You died with your boots on, Geezer. I pray it be so for me one day."

"And I," John added solemnly."

* * *

A nearly full moon with star filled sky provided some light for the group congregated around a small tidal pool. Neil Dickerson stood near his squad car in dress uniform, making certain there would be no interruption to the small ceremony on the beach. Rachel held the newborn Quinn in her arms tightly as Jean tried not to cry next to her with arms around Rachel's waist. Gus, John, and Tina stood near Rachel on the other side with Deke sitting silently in front of them. Nick stood with Dan's children next to the tidal pool where he had watched Dan stir in his wife Carol's ashes. Dan Jr. held out the bag with Dan's ashes to Nick.

"Would...would you do it for us, Nick, and... and the Psalm and movie line?"

Nick accepted the bag. "I'd be honored."

He knelt next to the pool with constant movement of ocean water swirling in over the rocks and back out. Nick poured his friend's ashes into the pool slowly, stirring them in with his hand while reciting the Twenty-Third Psalm, his companions joining in. When the bag was empty, Nick stood for the last part.

"He was born in the time of blood and dyin', and never questioned a bit of it. He never went back on his folks or his kind. I rode with him. I've got no complaints."

After a pause, Nick went on. "Jesus said, 'I am the resurrection, and the life: he that believeth in me, though he were dead, yet shall he live'. Amen."

A chorus of amens drifted out into the night air.

* * *

Lino Verducci smiled out at the clear morning below him, the Upper East Side vista a magnificent sight. He sighed, knowing his morning would be spent deciding on another contingent of his men to solve his Santa Cruz problem. *For now*, he thought, *I will enjoy this incredible view. Just because some shipping clown got popped here in this beautiful office I got it for a steal.*

The .50 caliber round left little of Verducci's head or smile left on its way through.

* * *

Nick stopped for gas near Bloomsburg, PA. As he pumped gas, a Toyota Corolla rolled into a spot on the other side of the pump opposite Nick. A young woman in her early twenties with a bright smile waved at him as she exited the vehicle. He grinned and waved back. She began pumping gas.

"It's a nice day to travel," the woman commented to Nick.

He nodded. "Yes, it is."

"Where are you headed?"

"Full circle."

The End

Future Nick and Jean Bonus Story II

The Salvatores

"We'll need your boyfriend in on this."

"No way, Dad! And he's not my boyfriend!" Jean launched a fake roundhouse kick, dropped the leg down, and tried to leg whip her Dad with the opposite leg.

Nick didn't take the bait. Instead, he dived atop the assaulting appendage, rolling and locking Jean's leg in a hold she fought to the last second trying to prevent. Failing, she had no recourse but to tap out.

"Damn it!" Jean pounded the mat while their audience hooted with catcalls and whistles. "How did you know the roundhouse was a feint?"

"I'm older and wiser." Nick held out a helping hand, only to have it slapped away. "Didn't I ever teach you anything about sportsmanship?"

"Yeah. Direct from Vince Lombardi, that old Green Bay Packers coach. It was 'Winning isn't everything, it's the only thing'."

"Did not. You've never heard me say that, have you, Quinn?"

Jean jabbed a warning finger in Quinn's direction. "Don't even think about answering that, Daddy's little sock puppet."

"Mom, Jean's calling me names again," Quinn complained in his deep base voice.

"Jean! How many times have I told you not to pick on your younger brother? He can't help it because he's Daddy's little sock puppet."

Quinn sighed as Jean enjoyed Rachel's dig at Quinn. "This is about my missing Easter Sunday dinner, isn't it? It was my weekend on duty. I can't say I'm sorry, but my Mommy wants me home for an Easter Egg Hunt."

"We didn't have an Easter Egg Hunt," Rachel corrected him. "We had a nice dinner together with our actual family. I told you not to join the Marine Reserves. We have plenty of money to send you to college without scholarships from military branches of the service. Now, whenever the crazies start killing each other overseas, I have to worry about you getting sent at a moment's notice."

"He's serving his country, Rach," Nick pointed out. "Be proud of Quinn, and quit nagging the crap out of him."

"Oh...oh hell no, you did not tell me to stay out of my own son's business, Nick McCarty! That would mean war has been declared." Rachel tied her hair back, popped open a couple of the top buttons on her blouse, and pulled the blouse out of her jeans with fists up. "Mamma goin' ta' kick your ass!"

By this time, coupled with her aggressive movements toward Nick, and wardrobe adjustment, Nick was not the only one enjoying the show. He backed away as Rachel made feinting moves with her fists. "May I remind you, you're still working the diner even though we have more money than you can spend? You were proud of Jean for doing a stint in the Marines."

Rachel straightened from her fighting stance. "That was because Jean was too dumb for college, and they didn't have knife throwing scholarships."

"What?!"

Rachel went into her fighting stance. "C'mon, sissy-girl, Momma got your bad attitude right here."

"Dad? What the hell is this?" Jean gestured at her posing Mom. "Is she on drugs?"

"She's been watching that new reality show 'Trailer Trash Mamma'," Nick explained. "Now, every time she wants to act out, we get 'Trailer Trash Momma'. If I don't have her tea by the bedside in time, I get a dose of Momma interspersed throughout my day."

"Oh no you didn't," Rachel spun on Nick again, hands on hips this time. "Did you just disrespect Momma in front of her troglodyte children? I don't think so. I'll open up a can of kick your balls into yo' nose, Nicky Pooh."

"Troglodytes? Really?" Jean also turned on her Dad. "Do something, Nicky Pooh. Can't you do anything with her?"

Nick shrugged. "You bunch are lucky. At home, she'll do it naked if I cross her before her shower."

"Ewww…ewww…ewww…ewww!" Jean danced around with a disgusted look on her face. "Too much information, Nicky Pooh! Quinn… you baby blue Marine… say something!"

"Don't look at me. I'm just Dad's little sock puppet. Besides, she may be mental, and start stripping into Big Momma."

That dig jolted Rachel out of her humorous acting out. "Did you just say Big Momma? What the hell is that supposed to mean? Did you call me fat?"

"Uh oh," Quinn said, walking over to put an arm around Rachel's shoulders. She tried to attack him, but he simply picked her up, and began walking from their workout room to the stairs. "Uncle Gus and Uncle John are bored to tears, Mom. The match is over. Let's go to the deck. It's clear and there's a full moon. I want to hear about this new job Jean wants to take on for Phil Salvatore. That she doesn't want to collaborate with the love of her life is very curious."

"What?!" Jean ran at Quinn from the rear as he climbed the stairs with Rachel. Nick caught her in mid leap with Gus and John enjoying the McCarty show as they followed along. "Let me go, Dad! I'm helping Big Momma kick the Baby Blue Marine's ass!"

"Not happening, Viper. Settle down. We need to discuss this Salvatore case. You have my attention now, and you didn't need to challenge me to a duel to get it. I believe you figured on making me tap out tonight. Is that why Payaso and Kabong were invited early?"

Jean went limp. Nick released her. "Maybe. Quinn hasn't made you tap out yet, and he's three times as strong as you are. I wanted to be the first. I thought tonight was the night."

"It was a good show," Gus said. "I thought you had Muerto on the ropes, and the Big Momma show was worth the price of admission by itself."

"Very amusing," John added. "It must be very entertaining watching that TV show with Big Momma. You've been keeping that gem under wraps, Muerto."

"My ears are buzzing," Rachel called over her shoulder. "If I hear any more Big Momma jokes, Momma gonna' punish!"

"I thought it was just a phase she was going through," Nick admitted. "I didn't know she planned to adopt it as a life style change. It has made life interesting lately. The only problem about the entertainment is once she gets in character, it's hard as hell to get her out. Are you done yet, Momma?"

"Maybe. Make this big ape put me down."

Quinn laughed and released Rachel. "Sorry, Mom. You were getting scary. Have you really been torturing Dad with Trailer Trash Momma?"

"Maybe." Rachel glanced back at Nick as they reached the second floor. "I had to get a rise out of him somehow. He's so laid back lately writing those damn novels, I have to poke him with a stick sometimes to see if he's still breathing."

"He brings you tea every morning, cooks your breakfast, cleans the house, and he's been your damn sex slave forever, Trailer Trash," Jean went on the attack. "If Dad sits down for ten minutes you want to shove a broom up his ass, and make him mop the floor on his way out to get you chocolate bon-bons."

Rachel tried a gasp of outrage, but it turned into a laughing fit as they entered the balcony area. "Okay... good one... snot. Now, what's this shit with you playing hard to get with Sonny, you scarred up little turd? You're lucky he gives you a second look."

"Scarred up... why you... if you weren't my Mom, I'd put a hurtin' on you." Jean pointed at Rachel threateningly while taking the shot glass Quinn poured her with the other. "You need to go on a retreat... to Alaska, for about five years. That should give you some perspective."

Nick moved behind Rachel, and began massaging her shoulders. "Momma's not going anywhere. Fill us in on Phil. I thought because he forbid Sonny to have anything to do with you, and Sonny ignored him, that Phil didn't speak to you anymore."

Jean sat down, sipping her shot while Quinn filled everyone else's drink order. "Ever since he got into real estate a while back, he's been moving in some weird circles. Phil tapped into his contacts when he decided to run for congress. He's been walking a tightrope ever since he won the congressional seat, because money drives everything in the political world. Phil didn't do anything wrong, but anything that happens on a personal basis shuts off the campaign funds. I'm only telling you all this because I told Clarice I wouldn't help her at all if I didn't do full disclosure with all of you."

"Clarice must be desperate. She hates you and me," Rachel said. "What the hell did she... oh...my...God... no... say it isn't so. Saint Clarice had an affair? At her age?"

"She's only in her forties, Ma. Don't be hatin'. Yes, she had an affair. She doesn't hate us. Clarice would rather not be anywhere around us. To her, we are 'Trailer Trash Momma' and her crew. Plus, she knows about Dad. They're flying high in the Washington DC circles again."

"The only reason they're anywhere near DC is because your Dad paid their way into the country club here, the ungrateful bastards! I don't know how those two phonies ever raised a stand-up guy like Sonny."

"I do," Jean said. "He's been hangin' out with us since he was nine. Then he joined the Marines. Done deal."

"You're sweet on him, you little honey bun," Rachel said. "You two were wild for each other, then bang, you get schooled and scarred, and suddenly you're a damn martyr loner bitch from hell."

Nick caught Jean in midair, kicking and arms swimming with clawed fingers at a laughing Rachel. "I...I'll get you for that! Let me go, Dad! She's toast. She can't come back from that one!"

"I always figured in my old age, I'd be able to quit refereeing these matches, Gus."

"I told you, John and I could convert the old interrogation horror room into cells where we could house these two when they start going for each other's throat. Cala wouldn't mind, would she, John?"

"No. She laughs her ass off when I tell her about the latest McCarty girls' fight night. Our kids love them. When I've been over here with everyone, they sit there with their mouths open and eyes big while these two go at it. Cala would agree to be the jailer."

381

"No cells for Momma and the Daughter of Darkness," Nick said, giving Jean a shake. "Calm down. We have to hear the rest of this affair business. What kind of downside would her having an affair cause? I can understand you not wanting Sonny to know about his Mom's affair."

Jean relaxed and Nick let her go. "He suspects something's wrong. I know that much. Mom's right. I can't be around him. We had a falling out after I nearly had my face cut off. He wanted me to quit. I told him there was no way. Things changed. I know we've been on the outs with the Salvatores. After your friend let them join the Corral de Tierra Country Club, they waited exactly six months to try and get you and Mom booted out of the membership, even though you only went there to have a meal once in a while with Julius Danvers."

"Didn't you have to intercede with Julius because he was going to kick their asses out instead, Nick?"

"No use dredging those bottom feeding times out now, Gus," Nick replied. "Okay, so Clarice had an affair. Tell us why we should care, or for that matter why anyone should care. An older woman has an affair, and her husband is a congressman. All Phil has to do is have an affair, and they'll probably be selected as role models of the year in DC."

Jean grinned at Nick while pulling out her cell-phone. "Because she was drugged, and screwed. Check these out."

Nick took the phone with some hesitation. They were compromising pictures of a naked Clarice with a boy, who looked about fourteen. He handed the phone to Rachel, with Gus and John moving behind her for a look. "Who did Clarice think she was having an affair with when they drugged her, and made the movie and pictures?"

"That's where things get really interesting," Jean replied. "Douglas Cameron. They were at a party in DC. Phil did his usual disappearing act, making all night deals in the backroom with the other crooks and thieves. He called and told her he had slipped out with one of his cohorts. Apparently, Phil does it all the time. Then he calls, and tells her to take a cab home. Phil's the head of the House Ways and Means Committee. The golden boy Senator from Maine with the Mommy who was also a Senator, chatted with the lovely Clarice, and took her to a nearby hotel. He made them drinks in the room. She woke up with those pictures on her phone."

"I can't stand the sight of that bitch, but I know she would never do something like this," Rachel said. "I feel bad for Sonny though. What the heck would this Cameron guy want? Those two high society parasites are hocked up to their eyeballs. Your Dad still pays for their country club membership."

"You do?" Jean looked at Nick as if he had a third eye. "What the hell's wrong with you Nicky pooh? Those tarantulas have always treated you and Mom like shit."

"Because Dad's not like them, and he likes Sonny," Quinn said. "Besides, Dad, Uncle Gus, and Uncle John have enough money to buy a small country, and yet they live like paupers, so he might as well do good deeds."

"That's enough bad mouthin' the Unholy Trio, kid," Gus replied. "We've went all over the world and this country, into one adventure or another, always with first class accommodations. Isn't that right, Brother Kabong?"

"Yes, Brother Payaso," John agreed. "This disrespect of our conservative ways is most unappreciated."

"Sonny made peace with his folks a long time ago. He can deal with anything we do to help them out," Nick said. "Although we live conservatively as John states, we've done plenty, and raised you two ingrates pretty well. Your Mom's right. Although I'm paying their way in a couple of things, I don't like Phil and Clarice, but it made things easier on Sonny, and I'm not the only one who likes him. We all do. As you pointed out, Jean, the kid practically lived here. The Unholy Trio coached everyone's sports choices growing up too, including some like lacrosse none of us knew anything about. Let's keep focused on bringing life here in our home base back to normal. You're on again, Jean. What is it Cameron wants from Clarice?"

"That's the tricky part, Dad. He wants their enemies list database."

Nick poured another drink and sipped it. "Damn. That answers a lot of questions I've had over the years. I guess what goes around actually does come around. They've been blackmailing people with secret files Phil accumulated from what source?"

"Clarice admitted they've bugged many parties in DC, and they're really good at it. Other sources include Phil's having access to all travel plans through his work in the passport bureau for all those years before he was elected to Congress. He paid to have any suspected trips made by potential congressional leaders monitored. She says they have a larger database than Hillary Clinton's nine hundred FBI files."

"We need to all be in agreement on this. I want the database, and I want those two knowing I'll have the 'Sword of Damocles' hanging over their heads if I even suspect they're using a copy on someone."

"That's the only way I told Clarice I would even take this to you," Jean said. "She hated that, because it would mean letting Phil know what happened. Plus, of course, she probably saw a few of their plans go out the window. I see it in your eyes, Mom. You want to know if she played the outrage card, right?"

"Yep. I know that bitch. Tell Momma what she said."

Jean cleared her throat comically, and launched into her incredibly good Clarice imitation she had perfected over the years with the slight Boston high class drawl. Coupled with her perfect mimic of Clarice's facial tics, it was an entertaining delivery. "Really, Jean? You're speaking of blackmailing me to obtain your help, dear? I…I'm the victim here. Can we not work together to fix this despicable crime against me without a hidden agenda on your part? You've been like a daughter to Phil and I."

Momma went off again while the others were enjoying Jean's show. Back went the hair, buttons undone, and shirttail out once again. "Oh…oh no she didn't! She did not play the 'like a daughter' card! Momma gonna' fry her grits for that one. Momma gonna' bitch slap her so hard, it'll kill Snow White and all seven of her dwarfs. War has been declared!"

Nick fronted Rachel with calming motions as the outburst amused everyone else. "Easy Momma. Jean hasn't told us what she said in answer to Clarice. We need the rest of the story. We'll get to the retribution part after we solve this dilemma."

Rachel took a deep breath and pointed at Nick. "Listen to me closely, Nicky Pooh. If you ever pay another country club fee for those two dead beat hustlers, you'd best learn to sleep with one eye open cause Momma gonna' tuck you in without some of your parts."

Nick hugged her to him. "Done deal. That damn 'like a daughter' shot killed the country club golden goose. Now sit down with me, and let's hear the rest of the story."

Nick refreshed their drinks. Although he enjoyed the hell out of the interaction between Rachel and Jean, he would not touch the case without Jean's assurance they would be relieving the Salvatores of their enemies database. "Go on, Jean."

Jean patted her Mom's shoulder. "I told Clarice if Sonny wasn't her son, I would break every bone in her face for saying that. Then I told her we would have the database and all copies or she could kiss my ass. Then I walked out, telling her to call me if she decides to abide by my terms in writing, including a confession to creating the enemies database in the first place as my insurance."

Jean grinned as Rachel pumped her fist. "That's not all. She has to read the statement and sign it while on a digital recording. I thought Clarice was going to have a stroke. She was still gasping for air when I left. Phil called me today. He told me they agree to the terms, but he was disappointed in me. I told Phil he could shove his disappointment up his ass, and one more phrase like that and I'd help Cameron bury him."

Jean was soaking up the laughs she garnered from her audience until she saw her Dad's eyes. The killing beast she knew to be lurking only slightly below the surface still warred for control of her affable Father. She knew in an instant what solution crossed his mind about ending an enemies database and the people who created it. The solution would have nothing to do with extricating Phil and Clarice from anything other than life. "Don't think about it, Dad! I'm serious. This is just business. You know how Phil is."

"Yeah… I know how Phil is." The silence after the statement ended the light hearted moment.

"They're Sonny's Dad and Mom, Muerto," Gus said quietly.

"He's a great kid," John added.

Nick breathed in deeply as Rachel gripped his hand with a smile. "I know. If we're doing this we have to have Sonny on board even if it's for no other reason than to keep me from slitting his parents' throats. We need him on the inside of the Salvatore home. Otherwise those flakes will find some way to screw us. If that's a problem Jean, then we need to bail on this now."

"Okay, Dad. I'll call him tomorrow. Do you have some thoughts on how we proceed?"

"Yep. We find the boy in the movie first. Once we have the kid safely in our custody, we go after the film crew. We're going to make it so Douglas Cameron couldn't run for dog catcher even with the enemies database. We'll start fresh in the morning after we talk to Sonny. Then we find that boy."

"I'll go over the film tonight," Quinn said. "I may be able to get a line on the crew that did the filming by comparing their work on a broad scale spectrum.

Just then, a little white ball of fur with a huge head peeked into the room with a curious bark. Nick patted his leg. "C'mon, Sam, you can come in now."

The puppy ran full speed and leaped into Nick's lap, standing on his hind legs with forepaws on the table, looking around at the others as if he were calling a meeting into session.

"It's time for the chairman of the board to walk down to the beach. Want to accompany us, Momma?"

Rachel patted the dog's head. "Sure. You know if Sam's body ever grows into proportion to his head, he's going to be about twice Deke's size."

"Yep, I know. I couldn't leave the bugger wandering around on the street though."

"Well let's get walkin'. Momma gonna need her sex slave tonight."

"Eeeeeeuuuuuhhhhh..." Jean was up dancing around making gagging noises while the others laughed. "I swear, Mom. Damn it! You say stuff like that just to see if you can make my head explode."

"Yeah… so what's your point?"

* * *

Sonny Salvatore stared out the window on the McCarty deck. He spent many times visiting on the deck doing homework with Jean while her Dad wrote on his laptop, and her Mom played with Quinn. He knew Nick was a killer on a level unmeasurable by normal or combat standards. Early on, Sonny recognized this was no normal household with parents, kids, and dog. He visited the McCartys every chance he got. Sonny knew parents weren't perfect. His folks were the poster people for that phrase, but on top of the lies Sonny knew down deep he was simply a prop for whatever new scheme his parents cooked up. When he was with Jean and her family, they treated him like one of the family. He wasn't the only one either. Many people without blood connection were members of the McCarty family. Over the years, Sonny became Quinn's older brother, but never a brother to Jean. He loved Jean with an intensity that still made him ache. They fought, broke up, and made up so many times he had lost track. They were like oil and water. That she thought he would care about her facial scars still pissed him off. He glanced back at her as she sat next to Nick and Quinn, noticing for the first time the other members of their motley crew were watching him with smiling faces.

"We can't pick our parents, Sonny," Gus said.

"I was raised by wolves," Sonny declared, drawing laughter from everyone at his line from a McCarty favorite movie: the old Val Kilmer movie titled 'Spartan'.

"Did you think of anything useful?" Jean dug right in.

"I did. These political action committees have video companies they rely on all the time. My folks have one they trust as does every politician. When they need an event filmed for their own propaganda, they must trust the company not to leak embarrassing footage, stills, or scenes that put them in a bad light with the public. If their video people can be bought, they're screwed. If Cameron is behind this, the film crew he uses is the only one he would ever trust with something containing a young kid. Cameron would never figure my Mom would call you bunch of pirates. Big error. My Mom would call the Devil himself if she had his number."

"She did, and she does," John joked.

"Ha… ha… thanks, Kabong." Nick smiled at the humorous appreciation John's remark garnered. It wasn't the first time he'd been called the Devil. "Good input, Sonny. We'll go at it your way because I'm having no luck with recognition software, or even overseas databases, for getting a line on the boy. I'm hoping he's still alive."

"One problem is these people make their money keeping secrets. They won't give up Cameron or help in any way," Sonny added.

"Sure they will," Nick replied.

* * *

Sonny and Jean walked Sam down to the beach together. "I'm glad you called me."

"Dad made me. He wouldn't agree to help without what you could find out when you visit your folks. I know you don't live with them, but you can visit and feel them out so we don't get blindsided. You've been able to tell when they're lyin' since we were kids."

Sonny kept silent, and Jean knew she'd hurt him. He was nearly as tall as Quinn's six foot, four inch height, but leaner. When his jaw tightened, she could see it even with only moonlight. She changed Sam's leash over to her other hand, and grasped Sonny's.

"Sorry, Tyson. I didn't mean it to come out like that. I wanted to call you."

Sonny nodded. "We're always like that now, poking each other the wrong way every time we speak."

Jean stopped. She grabbed his jacket front, looking up into his face. "Maybe we shouldn't speak then."

The next few moments were a torrid reuniting of a man and woman who ached to be with each other, but let conflicting personalities blind them. Sam let out a squeak bark to let them know he was there. Jean broke away with a gasp.

"Damn… I've missed you. My Mom called me a scarred up little turd, and I should be thankful you give me a second look. She's right in a way. I screwed up, and went against my Dad's orders. I paid the price and got cut. Since then I've been a bitch just like Mom said."

Sonny hugged her tightly. "I love you more than anything in the world you scarred up little turd."

It took Sam wrapping the two in his leash and growling to break up the two humans a second time. They resumed the walk.

"I know I shouldn't ask, but what did your Dad mean when he said 'Sure they will'?"

Jean giggled, clutching Sonny's arm, and leaning into him. "It means when he researches the film company you suggested he find tied to Cameron, he'll find the most likely tool, and question him or her. They'll tell him where he can find the boy."

"I'm beginning to see a cold dark picture forming of that explanation."

Jean shrugged. "We're Marines, and we're both killers. Compared to Dad though, we're what they call Snow Whites.

Don't worry about that part. The Unholy Trio doesn't have any Snow Whites amongst them. Tyson... where are you staying tonight?"

"At my apartment... with you I pray to God."

"I believe I can answer that prayer for him."

* * *

The two men walked out of their studio, arguing about the lateness of the hour, their project timetable, and how they could blame someone else for it. When they reached their vehicle in the underground parking garage, they continued the rant until the sliding door opened on the van next to them. Three masked figures surrounded them, one with a hideous clown mask. One with a black mask aimed a large barreled automatic at them before addressing them in a synthesized voice.

"Get in the van, or I shoot your dicks off. Want a demo?"

The two men scrambled into the van. A driver separated from them by a black curtain drove away while they were restrained with plastic ties and duct tape over their mouths until they exited the parking garage. The van stayed in motion for fifteen minutes before slowing to a stop, and its hybrid engine shut off. The men's duct tape gags were removed.

"You...you're the Unholy Trio! We...we're just movie guys, El Muerto!"

"I'm glad you know of us. Then you also know what we're capable of when we don't get what we want," Nick said. "I know you did an extortion movie for Douglas Cameron with Clarice Salvatore drugged with a young teenage boy. I want to know where that boy is. My associate, Payaso, will then film you two weasels taking us through the whole operation from when Cameron asked for it to be done, all the way through to its blackmailing end."

Silence. Terrified silence, but silence.

"Uh oh. What we have here is a failure to communicate. El Kabong, my brother, flip a coin to see which one of these gentlemen gets to have his intestines washed in bleach so his friend can be motivated." By the time Nick got his scalpel out, and John flipped the coin, the two men were screaming to talk.

"Silence! Usually I go ahead with the demo once I get stone-walled. I'll give you two one more chance. Payaso will film you two. Leave nothing out. If you make us happy I will take you both back to the parking garage. If my brother, El Kabong, doesn't receive confirmation of the boy's whereabouts, the coin flip will be for real and unstoppable. I have minions ready to do my bidding. We know the boy is being held locally in DC if he is still alive. I hope for your sakes he is alive."

"He is, Muerto! He is!"

"Good. Begin. As I stated, leave out nothing."

* * *

Two huge black masked figures, and a smaller slender one entered the DC crack-house with silent care. They looked around the inside pit of hell, filled with the lost, the desperate, and the damned. The two guards who had been sleeping on chairs at the entrance woke and reached for their weapons. In seconds, they were thrown to the floor, gagged and restrained by the two larger figures. Jean kept watch with weapon at the ready.

"What now, Viper?"

"Dad would close his eyes, pretend he was the old 'Mentalist', and lead us straight to the kid. This place is activating my barf reflex. When I get queasy, I get violent. I say turn on all the lights, and start beating our way to the kid and shoot anything with a weapon. That would get me yelled at when we got back.

Watch our six, Cracker, while Kong and I question one of the guards."

"How did I get a tag like Cracker exactly," Sonny asked while guarding their front.

"You were born into it. Kong here got his name from a childhood memory of my Mom's making. Now shut up and watch our six or I'll change your tag to Snow White."

Quinn chuckled, gripped one of the guards, and lifted him to a chair as if he were a bag of potato chips. Jean did knife tricks in front of the man's eyes while Quinn removed the duct tape over his mouth. He then held up his phone with a still of the boy in front of the guard. Jean jabbed the point of her blade a quarter inch deep in the man's neck.

"Where's the boy in the picture?" Jean removed the tip from his neck.

"Second...second door on the right... upstairs."

Quinn covered his mouth again.

"Stay here, Kong while Cracker and I check on the boy."

"Yell if you need me."

"I will. You watch your back down here, kid. If something happens to you, the Momster will slice and dice me."

"I'll be here when you return, Sis."

Sonny followed Jean's lead. As they passed the first room on the right, a dark figure stumbled out with a garbled yell. Jean pistol whipped him to his knees and kicked him in the face. Sonny side kicked the next one at the doorway, sending him crashing all the way to the far wall. Sonny slammed the door shut, and Jean went on to the second room. She and Sonny positioned themselves on each side of the door. Jean then twisted the knob and pushed on the door. A shotgun blast tore a huge hole in the wall opposite the room. Sonny went in left and Jean right. The man with the shotgun hesitated. He was double tapped from both sides, his head a bloody mess as he dropped, shotgun clattering to the floor. A boy sat on two piled mattresses on the floor. He looked up at Jean with only mild interest.

"This is him, Cracker. Hi kid. I think I have a nicer place for you to stay. It doesn't look like you have much to lose."

"Okay," the boy said simply. He slipped on tennis shoes without laces, and a ragged black hoodie. "I don't think they'll let you take me."

"Probably not," Jean said, putting her arm around the boy's shoulders. "We won't be asking permission."

The boy smiled. "They have a silent alarm when anything happens here. Then guys arrive with bad ass weapons. I like you. Maybe you should leave me and go out the window. I'll be okay."

"I'm Viper, and this guy is Cracker. We're going to get you out of here just fine. Come on. I want you to meet my brother Kong."

The boy let Jean guide him. "You have cool names. Mine's Benny."

Near the door, Quinn signaled them to wait. "We have company."

Three men exited an SUV across the street, and jogged toward the house.

"I told you," the boy said with sadness.

Before the men reached the sidewalk, silent death rained down on them in short bursts, pulping their heads like overripe melons.

Benny's eyes widened. "Wow."

"That's the Terminator, Benny," Jean explained. "Come on. We have a little dog named Sam in California. I bet he'd like to meet you. We've decided to take you home with us. It's too hard to explain stuff here in DC."

"Okay… sure. I'd like that."

* * *

On board the private jet, Nick shook hands with Clyde Bacall, who met Nick and his group at the plane's entrance. "Hey, Clyde. How's Terry and the kids?"

"Doing real good, Nick. Paul didn't say what you were up to this trip. Is there anything you want done?"

"Nope. I think we have everything we need. Here." Nick handed him a briefcase, while keeping an arm around Benny.

"What's this?"

"You know. A little something for the kids."

"Thanks, Nick. You know it's not necessary. I wouldn't have shit if not for you."

"It's a small thing, brother. Tell Paul I said hi, and I expect him and Ginny out at my place in two weeks."

"I'll tell him. Will there be a follow up to this?"

"Possibly, but I'm hoping it ends with tonight's work. Take care, Clyde."

"I will." Clyde walked down the steps, embracing Rachel and Jean, and shaking hands with Quinn, Gus, John, and Sonny.

Fifteen minutes later, they were on their way to California.

* * *

Phil met with Nick and company on Dan and Carol's beach. He walked distastefully in the sand toward the beach chairs. Nick, Rachel, Tina, Gus, John, and Cala sat on the chairs sharing a beverage, some Irish, some not. Jean, Sonny, Quinn, Benny, and Sam the dog were entertaining John and Cala's three kids. They took turns playing keep away from Sam, and feeding the birds swooping down for crumbs.

"Really, Nick… was this necessary?"

"It was, Phil. I'm not much on doing things behind people's backs. Doug Cameron resigned yesterday as I'm sure you heard because we sent him a movie implicating him in at least a half dozen felonies. That ends your problem. I have the database, and the digital confession you and Clarice did for our safekeeping. That means in case even one of those database items gets leaked to the press, you and Clarice will be in the middle of a shit storm. That ends my problem with you. Sonny told me you wished to speak with me and my team. This is where we meet. What can I do for you?"

"Julius is kicking us off the board and out of the country club. He says you removed your support."

"No. I stopped paying your fees. I have nothing to do with the country club board, and I didn't blackball you. Did you ask Julius why you can't keep your membership on your own dime?"

"Yes… he said the only reason we were ever allowed to have a membership was because of you. That's all he would say. Clarice is very unhappy about this."

Nick stayed silent as if waiting for Phil to go on, only to take a slap to the back of the head from Rachel.

"Someone better get their yap workin' or Momma gonna take over this meetin'."

Nick sighed as stifled laughter erupted amongst the seated company. Nick stood, took Phil by the arm, and led him away, speaking in muffled tones to him. Phil stopped abruptly, looking at Nick in horror, his mouth working, but no words coming out. Nick said something else, and Phil ran for his car. Nick returned to his seat.

Rachel handed Nick a fresh Irish coffee. "Very good, Nicky Pooh. Now, Momma wants to know what you said to the bad man."

Nick sipped his Irish. "Well, I may have told him that unless he and the lovely Clarice wanted to wake up one night strapped to their bed with their intestines hanging out, and me pouring Clorox slowly on them, he'd better forget he ever knew me until our kids' wedding. When he didn't move right away I told him he had five seconds to get off the beach or I'd start the fun tonight."

"I think I love you, Nicky Pooh."

"Does that mean no more Trailer Trash Momma?"

"In your dreams, Nicky Pooh."

The End... for now.

Thank you for purchasing and reading Cold Blooded Book IV: Bloody Shadows. If you enjoyed the novel, and the bonus future Nick and Jean story, please take a moment and leave a review. Your consideration would be much appreciated. Please visit my Amazon Author's Page if you would like to preview any of my other novels. Thanks again for your support.

Bernard Lee DeLeo

Please do not be hesitant asking questions concerning any subject about writing, publishing, or characterization. My publisher, RJ Parker and I answer questions all the time on the Facebook page. Previews and release dates are updated on the fan page constantly. Thank you.

Author's Face Book Page -
https://www.facebook.com/groups/BernardLeeDeLeo/

Author's Contact Links -
http://rjparkerpublishing.com/bernard-lee-deleo.html

Made in the USA
Middletown, DE
28 May 2015